THREE SUS

SHADOWS

OF

TRUST

From Best-Selling Author

TRACI HUNTER ABRAMSON

All statements of fact, opinion, or analysis expressed are those of the author and do not reflect the official positions or views of the US Government. Nothing in the contents should be construed as asserting or implying US Government authentication of information or endorsement of the author's views.

Cover image: *Burglar standing outside front door* © Zainab, generated with AI, stock.adobe.com
Cover design by Kevin Jorgensen

Cover design copyright © 2025 by Covenant Communications, Inc.

Published by Covenant Communications, Inc.
American Fork, Utah

Copyright © 2025 by Traci Hunter Abramson
All rights reserved. No part of this book may be reproduced in any format or in any medium without the written permission of the publisher, Covenant Communications, Inc., PO Box 416, American Fork, UT 84003. The views expressed within this work are the sole responsibility of the author and do not necessarily reflect the position of Covenant Communications, Inc., or any other entity.

This is a work of fiction. The characters, names, incidents, places, and dialogue are either products of the author's imagination, and are not to be construed as real, or are used fictitiously.

Library of Congress Cataloging-in-Publication Data

Name: Traci Hunter Abramson
Title: Shadows of Trust / Traci Hunter Abramson
Description: American Fork, UT : Covenant Communications, Inc. [2025]
Identifiers: Library of Congress Control Number 2024945044 | 978-1-52442-837-2
LC record available at https://lccn.loc.gov/2024945044

Printed in the United States of America
First Printing: August 2025

34 33 32 31 30 29 28 27 26 25   10 9 8 7 6 5 4 3 2 1

CONTENTS

Hunted 1

Secrets of St. Augustine 95

Shadows of Trust 201

for all the parents
who have loved your children through life's challenges

ACKNOWLEDGMENTS

So many people have helped with these three novellas, but I want to especially thank my two fabulous editors, Ashley Gebert and Samantha Millburn for helping me through every step from the creation process through the final product. Thanks as well to my beta readers, Lara Abramson, Scott Abramson, Mandy Biesinger, Susan Karl, and Ellie Whitney.

I also want to thank the various critique partners who have helped me over the years as these novellas were drafted: Ashley Gebert, Daniel Quilter, Eliza Sanders, Ellie Whitney, Paige Edwards, Kyla Beecroft, Jen Leigh, and Kathryn Brown.

My appreciation goes out to Parker Richards for sharing his insight and experiences as I created this final novella. It truly helped give the story so much more authenticity.

As always, thank you to the CIA's Publication Classification Review Board for all you do and for your continued support.

Finally, thank you to my family for sharing me with my fictional worlds and to my readers who continue to allow me to do what I love.

HUNTED

CHAPTER 1

S<small>HE WAS GOING TO DIE</small> this time. She was sure of it. Reagan pressed back into the corner of the living room, wishing she could make herself invisible, clasping her arms tightly around her legs.

Her dark hair was matted from sweat and tears, and she could taste the blood from the last time the back of Laith's hand had connected with her cheek. A slight breeze carried the scent of fall through the open window and into the dingy three-room cabin, but the fresh air couldn't hide the underlying smell of dust and despair.

Her mother had promised this time would be different. Her mom had been so convinced that this latest in her string of loser husbands was going to make their lives better. If only she had known how bad things were really going to get.

The colonel looked over the paper he held in his hand, his dark hair cut short, his military uniform perfectly pressed. He looked like he should be in an office somewhere instead of in the middle of the woods. Reagan recognized the sergeant stripes on his sleeve but had never dared question why Laith always called him Colonel. He motioned toward Reagan, causing her to shrink farther into the corner. "What about the girl?"

"I'll take care of her." Laith didn't even look at her, dismissing her with a vague gesture, like she was some piece of trash that needed to be taken out to the curb.

"Make sure you do. She's seen too much." The colonel turned and gave her a hard stare. "She knows too much."

Laith's voice took on an edge. "I told you I'd take care of it."

Reagan bit back a sob. The heavy crate of automatic weapons in the middle of the sparsely furnished living room was proof that she wasn't the only one about to die.

How could her mother have missed this? She could understand not knowing that the colonel was a criminal in the making. After all, who would expect a marine sergeant to be involved in a plan to hurt his own countrymen? Laith, on the other hand, was always talking about guns when he wasn't complaining about everything and everyone.

"Help me load this into my truck." The colonel motioned to the guns.

The two men circled the crate so they could heft it together, then maneuvered it out the front door of the secluded cabin. Reagan looked up to find herself alone. She thought of what these men were planning, what they were capable of. Something bubbled up inside of her, something resembling anger.

She had a choice. Cower in a corner knowing that the next few minutes would be her last or fight to stay alive.

A surge of resentment and adrenaline made the decision for her. She wasn't going to let Laith decide her future for her. She wasn't going to die like her mother. Afraid to reconsider her choices, she forced herself to stand. Despite the throbbing in her ribs, she limped across the room to the back door.

Footsteps sounded on the gravel driveway, followed by a shout. A sudden sense of urgency overwhelmed her. Without looking back, she burst through the door, refusing to let the pain stop her.

As she stumbled across the yard, she let a yelp of surprise escape her when a gunshot rang out and sent bits of bark flying. She ducked behind a tree and gasped for breath. Whatever emotions had been swirling inside her were quickly replaced by terror.

Footsteps crunching through the fallen leaves grew closer, and Reagan's will to survive eclipsed everything else. Her heart beating wildly, she pushed away from the tree and ran.

* * *

Jill Valdez stood on the back deck of the rented cabin and stared at the wild clash of colors. Fall made the Virginia countryside look like God had painted a glorious masterpiece for everyone to see. If only she didn't feel like God had turned His back on her.

Five years of trying to have children and more medical tests than she could count had brought her to this point. She had tried everything: prayers, trips to the temple, blessings. Nothing had worked. Nothing had given her the answers she had so desperately wanted. Now she had to face reality, the one she had been avoiding for so long. She would never be a mother.

The doctors had presented the finality of that fact more than two months ago, but she still struggled with the news. Only days after that last doctor's appointment, she had returned to work as a second grade teacher, and three of her coworkers had announced the exciting news that they were pregnant. A number of others had discussed their latest challenges of daycare and giving up their summer freedoms with their children to come back to work.

Jill had remained silent, feeling more and more alone. She tried hard not to be resentful. After all, it wasn't that she begrudged these women their chance to have families. She just wanted to join their ranks.

Her husband, Doug, didn't say much, but she knew he was equally disappointed. He seemed to have gotten over the initial shock more quickly, almost as though he was determined to readjust their life plans so they could leave this chapter of disappointment behind them. She suspected he had already resigned himself to the likelihood that they would remain childless long before the doctor had given them the final test results.

Jill, on the other hand, had stubbornly clung to every shred of faith that something could change their circumstances, right up until the doctor had told them all hope was lost. Of course, hope wouldn't have been lost if surrogacy or adoption was a possibility, but Doug refused to consider either alternative.

Paid surrogacy was illegal in Virginia, so that route was highly unlikely, and every time she tried to broach the subject of adoption, Doug would shut down the conversation. For the first time in her marriage, she felt like there was a huge chasm between them, and neither of them could find the bridge to cross it.

This weekend away had been Doug's idea, a chance to recapture some shred of the relationship they had once shared before doctor visits and fertility treatments had consumed their lives. The foundation was still there. She knew it was. In those rare moments when she could forget about their lack of children, her marriage was wonderful. She simply couldn't quite bring herself to envision a life with only the two of them for the next fifty years.

She had seen Doug with his nieces and nephews and had always appreciated how he could get down on their level to play ball or a board game. She had spent the past seven years teaching other people's children and now she had no hope of ever teaching her own.

The door behind her opened, and she turned to see Doug step outside. He wasn't smiling; his face looked almost dangerous with his mouth firm and his dark eyes brooding.

"Are you okay?" Jill asked.

Doug answered her question with one of his own. "Are you still mad?"

Her stomach clenched as she prepared for what would likely be a repeat of the adoption argument. She had promised herself she wouldn't bring it up this weekend, but how could she hold all of these tumultuous emotions inside? Why should she have to?

"I'm not mad. I just don't understand you right now." Jill folded her arms across her chest. "I know you have so much love to give. I don't know why you're so unwilling to consider adoption."

His jaw clenched. For a moment he didn't answer her, but finally he said wearily, "You aren't going to let this go, are you?"

"I've tried, Doug. I have. I just don't know how to take a dream that's been a part of me since I was a little girl and set it aside. It's bad enough that we can't have our own kids, but it's hard to accept that you're choosing to keep us childless."

He shook his head in obvious frustration and turned his attention toward the trees.

***

Doug tried to understand where Jill was coming from. He wasn't blind to the turmoil this ordeal had put her through, but he kept wondering when she was going to come to terms with reality. He imagined for a moment what it would be like to add another person to their family, someone who would come to them through circumstance rather than genetics.

He struggled against the idea of adoption, but not because of the reasons Jill thought. He had no doubt that they could make room in their hearts and their lives for someone else, even if it wasn't their own biological child. He just worried about whether they could handle the baggage that might come with a child who had been unwanted, abandoned, or even neglected and abused.

As an FBI agent, he had seen all too often the emotional scars imposed on children born to parents who didn't want them or who weren't in a position to care for them properly. For weeks he had wrestled with the idea that maybe he and Jill could make a difference in a child's life, but his prayers continually left him searching for an answer that wouldn't come.

He heard a rustle in the leaves that sounded oddly out of place, and he scanned the surrounding woods. "Did you hear that?"

"What?"

Doug heard it again. A crunch of leaves the wind hadn't caused. His hand shifted instinctively to rest on the gun holstered in the front of his waistband. As an FBI agent, he was required to be armed at all times, even when on vacation. The sound grew louder. "Something's out there."

"It's probably just . . ."

Doug held up a hand, signaling for her to be quiet. He listened closely, trying to determine if the footsteps were human or animal. Then he heard it. The unmistakable sound of a gunshot. "Go inside," Doug said urgently, drawing his gun. "And stay down."

Jill didn't argue. She quickly hurried inside as Doug rushed down the stairs to take cover behind the nearest tree. That was when he saw her.

The girl couldn't have been more than twelve or thirteen, her dark hair tangled, her eyes wild with fear. One of her arms was wrapped tightly around her ribs as though she was trying to control the pain centered there.

She stumbled forward. Another shot sounded, and bark flew off the tree beside her and leaves rained down to the ground.

Doug's training kicked in, the instinct to protect dominating. He shifted so the girl could see him and motioned for her to continue toward him. "Hurry. It's safe here."

The girl stopped, clearly caught between whatever was chasing her and the unknown now standing before her. She looked back, terror still shining in her eyes. Then, after only a brief hesitation, she altered her course toward Doug, running as fast as she could manage.

She was nearly to him when he noticed a flash of color through the trees. Taking preventative measures, Doug shifted and fired once at a nearby tree in the hope of scaring off the girl's pursuer.

The figure in the woods quickly ducked for cover. Doug motioned for the girl to go inside. He waited until she was nearly to the door before shooting once more high into the trees. Then he pounded up the steps and dashed into the cabin.

The girl was on the floor, pressed against the wall below the window. Jill was crouched down a short distance from her, her cell phone pressed to her ear.

"Stay down," Doug said, listening for any other signs that the girl's pursuer was approaching. "Jill, are you okay?"

She nodded. "I called 911. The police should be here any minute."

The words were barely out of her mouth when Doug heard the distant sirens. Cautiously, he moved to the window and peered out. Whoever had been chasing the girl wasn't visible now. He ducked back down and turned to look at the girl.

"Are you okay?"

She looked up at him with the oddest expression. For a moment, Doug wondered if she spoke English. Then somehow, he understood. It wasn't the words that were foreign to her. It was the question itself. She was one of the broken children, unfamiliar with the concept that someone would take the time to see her, that someone might actually care.

CHAPTER 2

Jill waited until after Doug went outside to meet with the local police before she turned to the girl. Her own heart was still pounding with adrenaline, but she managed to keep her voice calm as she spoke. "Everything is going to be okay."

The girl's eyes were bright green and wild with fear, her lip bleeding and swollen from what appeared to be a blow to the face. Her narrow frame shook with each breath, and Jill suspected she was in a state of shock. "What's your name, honey?"

She didn't answer, but her eyes darted to the window above her.

"Don't worry. My husband will make sure that whoever was out there won't hurt you." Jill stood and closed the distance between them, crouching down in front of the girl. "My name is Jill," she offered. "That's my husband, Doug, out there. He's with the FBI. You can trust him." She hesitated, waiting until the girl looked at her once more. "You can trust me."

"Reagan." She shifted slightly and winced. "My name is Reagan Bower."

"Where does it hurt?"

Her shoulder lifted slightly.

"Can you tell me who was chasing you?" Jill asked gently.

Tears filled Reagan's eyes. "Laith and the colonel. They were going to kill me."

"Why?" The question popped out of Jill's mouth before she could censor it. She tried to keep her voice calm when she continued. "Why would anyone want to kill you?"

"Because I know too much." Warily, she looked at Jill, multiple emotions visible on her face. "They're going to shoot people. Lots of people." Reagan drew a deep breath and winced again in pain.

"I think we need to take you to the hospital and make sure you're okay."

"No! They'll find me. I can't let them find me," Reagan insisted with absolute certainty as her face paled with another rush of pain.

"It'll be okay. We'll keep you safe."

Reagan leaned weakly back against the wall. "Please don't let them find me." Her voice faded to a whisper.

Jill continued to offer assurance, but less than a minute later, Reagan's eyes glazed over and then fluttered closed.

* * *

Doug stood a few yards away from the emergency room so he could talk on the phone without being overheard but still keep an eye on the entrance.

He dialed the number for Hector Flores, one of his fellow FBI agents. "Hector, I need a favor."

"I thought you were taking a few days off," Hector said in his easygoing tone.

"Not anymore. I had an incident at the cabin, and I was hoping you could do some background for me."

"What kind of incident?"

"The kind that involved a young girl being chased by someone who wanted her dead."

"A young girl? Who is she?"

"Her name is Reagan Bower. Can you see what you can find out about her? She said one of the men after her is named Laith."

"I'll see what I can dig up."

"Thanks." Remembering Reagan's panic about someone finding her, he added, "The girl is worried about being found, so we need to keep this need-to-know."

"You got it," Hector said. "I'll see what I can dig up. Give me the name of the hospital, and I'll head down there. It sounds like you could use some backup."

"I'd appreciate it." Doug gave Hector his location and headed for the entrance. If he was lucky, maybe the girl would be awake by now and could tell him what was really going on.

* * *

Reagan sat silently on the edge of the hospital bed. Everyone kept asking her questions, but she didn't trust these people. How could she be sure they wouldn't send her back? Then she saw Jill, the blonde woman who had tended to her when she had first arrived at the cabin. She remembered the way Jill had promised to keep her safe, and she wanted desperately to believe her.

"How are you feeling?" Jill asked, her voice sounding genuinely concerned.

Reagan wasn't sure what to say. Her ribs still hurt from her latest beating, but she was used to the beatings. Laith often used his fists or the back of his hand to remind her who was in charge. The nurse had offered her painkillers, but Reagan had refused them. She didn't take pills, and she wasn't about to start.

Fresh, white bandages covered most of her arms. Her race through the woods had resulted in an array of shallow cuts and scratches. Those were minor in comparison to what would have happened had she not run away. She still could barely believe the colonel had told Laith to kill her.

She pushed that memory aside, not able to face it. Mustering up her courage, she forced herself to ask about her future. Her voice wavered. "What happens now?"

"Where is your family?"

"I don't have a family."

Jill stepped forward. "Can you tell me what happened to them?"

"The doctors said my mom overdosed." Reagan said the words, but still wasn't quite able to believe them. She knew her mom had always taken lots of pills for her depression, and she'd always known when to stop. But three months ago, she hadn't stopped in time. Reagan had come home from school and found her passed out on the couch. Only that time, her mother never woke up.

"What about your father?"

"I never knew my father."

"Who's been taking care of you?"

"I was living with my stepfather, if that's what you mean." Reagan's eyes hardened. "But he never took care of me. He's the one who wants me dead."

"Laith is your stepfather?"

Slowly, she nodded.

Before Jill could ask any more questions, Doug appeared in the doorway, his expression serious. The way he looked at her, Reagan guessed he had been listening to her talk to Jill, that he had been spying on them.

"Is everything okay?" Jill asked him.

"I just talked to the doctor. He said that child protective services has been called." He looked right at Reagan, and she shifted uncomfortably. She wasn't used to people looking at her and acting like they could really see her. He continued. "Since you don't have any family to speak of, you'll be put into foster care for now."

"No." Reagan shook her head vehemently, panic welling up inside her. "Please don't let them take me. He'll find me." She pressed her lips together and forced herself to draw a breath. "And if he finds me, he'll kill me."

Doug looked at Jill now, and Reagan thought she saw something pass between them, like they were talking without actually saying any words. Jill nodded, and then Doug stepped forward. "I might be able to work something out so you can come home with us. Would that be okay with you?"

Reagan didn't know what she'd been hoping for, but she definitely hadn't expected this. She stared at Doug, not sure what to think of him. His eyes were dark and direct, the hard planes and angles of his face making him look dangerous. At least he didn't have that evil vibe like the colonel.

She shifted her gaze to Jill, a little surprised to see the hopeful expression on her face. Not able to figure their angle, she drew a breath and forced herself to ask, "Why would you want to help me?"

Jill's voice was direct and sincere. "Because we can."

Doug's expression remained serious. "There is one catch. When we get home, I want you to talk to me. I want you to tell me everything you can remember."

She considered the alternative and slowly nodded her head. "Okay."

* * *

Doug waited in the hospital lobby, already second-guessing his decision. What was he thinking, taking in a thirteen-year-old girl? He lifted his eyes heavenward. This was exactly the reason that he didn't want to consider adoption—a child who clearly had a ton or two of emotional baggage.

Her mistrust of men in general was obvious, though Doug had to admit he felt a small sense of satisfaction that he appeared exempt. She wasn't as comfortable with him as she was with Jill, but from what the police had told him, so far, she had refused to talk to anyone besides them.

A middle-aged man wearing a dull brown suit and holding a well-worn briefcase approached. "Mr. Valdez?"

"That's right." Doug stood, accepting the hand the man offered.

"I'm Brian Wendall with child protective services. I'm here to take over Reagan Bower's case. The nurse said I needed to talk to you before they could release her into foster care."

"There's been a misunderstanding," Doug told him. "She'll be staying with me and my wife for the time being."

"This is highly unusual." He frowned and drew a file out of his bag. He looked over the thin file. "According to our records, her stepfather was granted guardianship after her mother died." He looked up at him now. "Has anyone made any effort to contact the stepfather?"

"Oh, I've definitely made an effort to contact him."

Brian looked up at Doug, confused. "Am I missing something?"

"If you haven't been told that she's in the hospital because of injuries sustained from her stepfather's abuse, then yes, you're missing something." Doug tried to keep his frustration out of his voice but knew he wasn't succeeding.

Brian's brow furrowed. "I thought the minor was in an accident."

"It was no accident." Doug drew out his identification and flashed his badge. "Maybe it will help smooth out the process if you check the little box that says the minor is in protective custody."

"I understand you want to help," Brian said, his tone placating. "But my job is to make sure the minor is in a safe environment. Just because you have a badge doesn't mean you're the best choice."

Doug bristled at his words. He couldn't say why he was so determined to fight for this girl, but something deep in his gut, something he couldn't explain, pushed him to dig in his heels. "She trusts us. That makes my wife and me the best choice."

Brian gave Doug a haughty look. "Are you approved foster parents?"

"No," Doug said, his eyes meeting Brian's. "But we're keeping her."

"Mr. Valdez, you can't just decide to take over guardianship of a minor child."

"Actually, this badge says I can," Doug said, even though he knew he was severely stretching the truth.

"It doesn't work that way." Brian held up the file in his hand. "If you want to apply to be her temporary guardian, I'm sure you can petition the court. In the meantime, she needs to come with me."

"You're not taking her." Doug's resolve strengthened. He drew a breath, reminding himself that he needed this man on his side. "Look, we both want the same thing. We want Reagan safe. Until we know more about her stepfather and his whereabouts, she needs to stay in protective custody. I would really appreciate it if you could give me a few days to find out what really happened today. After that, we can reevaluate the situation."

The man frowned again, clearly considering. "Even if the FBI wants to maintain custody for now, I'll still need your contact information, and we'll have to schedule a home visit."

Doug nodded, but Reagan's earlier concern that her stepfather would be able to find her if she went into foster care also resonated through his brain. He took the paper the social worker handed him.

The thought popped into his head that this man didn't really need his personal information since Reagan was technically in protective custody. Rather than filling out his own phone number and address, he wrote down the information for FBI headquarters.

He supposed he should at least give the man his direct line at the Washington Field Office, but someone at headquarters could patch through any calls from him. Besides, this would ensure that no one would know which FBI office he worked at. If anyone did try to search for Reagan, the only thing they would find would be a web of misdirection and secrecy.

"I'll give you a call on Monday," Brian said as he took the paper back from him. "Here's my card if you need anything before then."

"Thanks."

"Good luck." Brian gave him a skeptical look. "I have a feeling you're going to need it."

* * *

"What was I thinking?" Doug muttered as he climbed into bed beside his wife. Jill had already settled their new charge into their guest bedroom and seemed fine with this unexpected situation. Personally, he felt that rather than go to sleep, he should be standing guard outside of the girl's room to make sure nothing else happened to her. He kept his voice low when he added, "We're not equipped to look after a teenager."

Jill rolled onto her side and propped herself up on her elbow so she was facing him. "Doug, we were just talking about adopting. Then, not an hour later, Reagan showed up. Maybe it's fate."

"We were arguing about adoption. I certainly wasn't agreeing to it, especially not to adopting a teenager who has been living with some kind of criminal."

"She's not a criminal," Jill stated simply, "and it sounds like she doesn't have anyone. Maybe she's supposed to be here."

"Jill, I can't do this with you right now," Doug said wearily. "This situation is stressful enough without having you badgering me about the size of our family while we're trying to care for Reagan."

Jill's voice grew defensive. "I only want to help her."

Doug put his hand on hers, and his voice gentled. "I know you want to help, but promise me you won't get too attached. We have no idea what we're dealing with."

Jill was quiet for a moment. "Did you notice how she wouldn't talk to anyone but us?"

"Yeah." Doug reached over and turned out the light on his night table. "I noticed."

CHAPTER 3

"Don't you answer your phone?" Hector said by way of greeting when Doug opened his front door to find his partner on the other side.

"Sorry. I turned it off last night when I was at the hospital, and I don't think I remembered to turn it back on." Doug motioned him inside. He pointed at the thick file in his hand. "What's that?"

"The file on the girl." Hector handed it to Doug. "Apparently, social services has been monitoring her for a while, but they've never had cause to remove her from her home."

"How did you get this?"

"After I called to let child protective services know we were keeping her in protective custody, they put me in touch with her caseworker," Hector said.

"Then why did he give me such a hard time last night about us releasing Reagan over to CPS?"

"Who?"

"Brian Wendall. He caught up with me in the waiting room last night when I was waiting for Reagan to be released."

"Something's not right here." Hector shook his head. "Reagan's caseworker is a woman named Marla Duncan. She's the only person from CPS who was at the hospital last night."

"Then who is Brian Wendall?"

"Let's see if we can find out." Hector retrieved his phone from his pocket and dialed the number listed inside Reagan's file. Doug listened to the one-sided conversation, unable to decipher anything from Hector's one-word answers. As soon as Hector hung up, he shook his head. "Social services hasn't ever heard of Brian Wendall."

"Let's assume for a minute that it was Reagan's stepfather or this colonel she was talking about who came looking for her. How did he know she was there?"

"He might have just played a hunch. You were in a rural area, and that was the only hospital around."

"Or someone could have followed us there. The road to our cabin was the only way out." Doug shook his head. "I'm not sure what this girl is involved with, but it sounds like someone is pretty intent on getting to her."

"Did you give this Wendall guy any information that would help him find her? Or you?"

"He has my name, but I put down the address and phone number for FBI headquarters."

Hector's eyebrows lifted. "He might be able track you down through DMV or property records."

"No, he won't," Doug said. "I haven't changed over my driver's license since I moved here from Florida, and we're renting our house."

"That's lucky."

"It's not luck. It's habit. After working for so many years with witness protection, I make it a point to separate work and home."

"That explains why the higher-ups signed off on Reagan staying here." Hector glanced toward the kitchen, where Jill was busily making pancakes. "What about Jill?"

"I didn't give him Jill's name, and she hasn't changed her driver's license either. Something about the guy rubbed me the wrong way. I guess now I know why."

Hector nodded. "Look, I know the girl has been through a lot, but we really need to know what she knows."

"She promised to talk to us this morning. I'll let you know as soon as I find out anything. In the meantime, can you run a check on Brian Wendall?" Doug retrieved from his wallet the business card the fake caseworker had given him. "Here's the information Wendall gave me. Maybe we can track him down through his phone number."

"I'll see what I can do."

"Thanks, Hector. I appreciate it."

"Talk to you later."

* * *

Reagan sat at the kitchen table, her hair still damp from her shower, the thick terrycloth robe Jill had given her wrapped tightly around her. She had read about places like this in books, seen them on TV, but she hadn't really believed people lived like this until now.

It wasn't the house itself, although the townhouse was definitely a lot nicer than the various apartments and trailers she'd lived in over the years. There was something else about it, almost like there was some warm feeling in the air. She couldn't quite put it into words, but it wasn't something she had ever felt before.

Not a single pill bottle was visible anywhere, nor could she see any empty beer cans or liquor bottles littering the tables or countertops. She didn't even see a single ashtray.

Her eyes swept the room, and she noticed a couple of tennis rackets leaning against the wall next to a wire bucket filled with tennis balls. A pair of shoes lay haphazardly beside it, thick white socks tucked inside them. The kitchen was clean and tidy, except for several books stacked on the corner of the counter, a notebook and pen lying beside them. She also noticed the green ceramic frog cookie jar. She knew it was a cookie jar because Jill had pulled the top off when she had given her a snack last night before she went to bed.

A bedtime snack. That was another thing she had heard about but had never before experienced.

Everything about these people was foreign to her. She had expected Doug to question her when they arrived at their home last night, but Jill had given her something to eat, shown her to her room, given her clean oversized pajamas to sleep in, and told her to get some rest. She had promised Reagan she would be safe and insisted they could wait until the next day to talk.

Reagan had stood just inside the bedroom door for several minutes, trying to listen to Jill and Doug talk, but all she had heard was someone playing the answering machine and some bishop asking to meet with them. She couldn't recall ever meeting a bishop and wasn't quite sure if she could picture what one would even look like.

When she had awoken, she'd ignored her hunger pains that had resulted from sleeping so long. Instead, she opted for a shower in an effort to erase any lingering traces of her life with Laith. Now she was sitting here in the sunny yellow kitchen, her stomach full and the scent of pancakes lingering in the air.

"Do you think you can answer some questions for me now?" Doug asked from his seat across from her.

Reagan instantly stiffened. She didn't like thinking about her yesterdays, about the years of taking care of her mom while trying to avoid whatever man was currently hanging around the house. She didn't want to remember those last three months in the dusty cabin while Laith saw her only as someone who could put a meal on the table for him while he plotted and planned to hurt people. She especially didn't want to think about how she had dashed out the back door when Laith and the colonel had hauled a crate of weapons outside to the colonel's truck.

She forced herself to look at Doug. He had a way of looking at her that made her want to squirm in her seat, but she had promised she would try to tell him what he wanted to know. Her mom had taught her to always keep her promises. "I can try."

"You said yesterday that Laith was going to shoot lots of people."

Reagan nodded.

"Do you know any details? Can you tell me about it?"

She drew a deep breath and let it out. "The colonel was helping him plan it."

"Plan what, exactly?"

"There are other people who think like they do. They have guns." Her eyes darkened. "Lots of guns."

"Have you seen the other people who think like them?" Doug asked.

"Yeah. They come to the cabin to practice shooting."

"How many were there?"

"I saw three besides Laith and the colonel. One of them is named Wendall or something like that. I don't know about the other two."

"Brian Wendall?"

"That might be it." Reagan wasn't sure if it was a good thing Doug knew Wendall's full name or if it was a sign that something bad was going to happen. "How did you know about him?"

"Just tracking down some leads." Doug shifted gears and asked, "Where are they planning on using these guns?"

"Some party." Reagan struggled against the memories, wanting to help Doug but not wanting to relive those moments when Laith and the colonel had tried to enlist her in their plans. "I saw a picture of the hotel the party is supposed to be at. I could see the Washington Monument in the background."

"Do you think you would recognize the hotel if you saw it again?"

Her shoulders lifted. "Maybe."

Jill slid into the seat next to her. "Did Laith or the colonel say when they were planning this attack?"

"I know it's soon, and it's supposed to be on a Saturday night."

"Is there anything else you can remember?" Doug prompted.

Reagan nodded. "They said something about being in costume."

"Did they say why?"

"Something about blending in. They said no one would know their guns were real if they were all in costume."

Jill looked up at Doug. "Halloween is in a few weeks."

"I'll have Hector run a list for me of costume parties in the DC metro area." Doug picked up the cordless phone on the counter and dialed a number. "I'll be right back."

Reagan watched him walk out of the room. Jill stood up and moved over to the sink, where she began loading their dirty dishes into the dishwasher. Reagan stayed where she was, not sure what she was supposed to do. Before her mom had died, she'd spent most of her time hiding in her room with the handful of books she had managed to collect from the used bookstore in her old town.

Sometimes, if Laith wasn't home, she could watch television, but usually, her mom said it was too loud. When Laith was around, the last thing she wanted was to be anywhere that he could see her.

Reagan eyed the books on the counter, a tattered version of Little Women topping the pile.

"I washed your clothes last night. They're in the dryer." Jill pointed at the stacked washer and dryer in the far corner of the kitchen. "Go ahead and get dressed, and we can go run some errands."

Apprehensively, Reagan stood and did as she was told. When she returned a minute later, dressed in her old jeans and T-shirt, her battered tennis shoes in her hand, she asked timidly, "Where are we going?"

Amusement and humor sparked in Jill's eyes. "Shopping."

"Shopping for what?"

"Clothes. Shoes. Whatever we need so you can feel at home here."

Reagan goggled at her. "You're buying me new clothes?"

Before Jill could respond, Doug came in and sat down in a chair, leaning over to retrieve the tennis shoes in the corner. "I'll come with you."

"You? Shopping?" Jill laughed. "This should be good."

Reagan stared at her, not sure what to think of the playful tone or the spontaneous laughter. Bracing, she shifted her eyes to look over at Doug, waiting for him to scold Jill for talking to him that way, or worse, for his eyes to go dark and mean when his hand lifted. But Doug just tied up his laces like it was no big deal.

She looked back at Jill, daring to ask the question, "Doesn't he like to go shopping?"

"Oh, no. He doesn't go to the mall." Jill shook her head. She leaned closer to Reagan and whispered, "Of course, we do have his handcuffs around here if we need them."

Jill's humor was contagious, and Reagan barely resisted letting out a giggle of her own. She sat down to put her shoes on. Then logic made her ask the simple question, "If you hate shopping, how come you're coming with us?"

"I just want you to be safe. We haven't found Laith yet, and I don't want to take any chances."

Her stomach clenched at the straightforward admission. "Oh."

"I'm sure it will be fine," Doug assured her. "The hospital where you were treated is three hours away from here. It's just my job to make sure you stay safe. Besides, Jill loves to torture me with this kind of stuff."

"Come on," Jill said lightly as she motioned toward the door. "It will be an adventure."

CHAPTER 4

Jill led Reagan through the mall, Reagan's eyes focused on the floor rather than on the window displays. The few times Jill had asked her opinion on a piece of clothing, Reagan had simply shrugged as though she was afraid of expressing her opinion. She couldn't tell if Reagan really didn't care what she wore or if she was afraid of asking for too much. Either way, Jill was determined to make sure the poor kid had something to wear besides the raggedy pair of jeans and the T-shirt she showed up in.

After two hours of unsuccessful shopping, they followed the scents of grilled meat, Chinese food, and french fries to the food court, where they grabbed a quick lunch. While they ate, Doug pulled out his cell phone, undoubtedly to see if Hector had called with any new information. Jill suppressed a smile when Doug grumbled to himself about forgetting to turn the phone back on after they'd left the hospital the night before. He turned it on and listened to a handful of messages, but from his expression, she guessed that none of them gave him the updates he'd been hoping for.

After they finished eating, they headed back toward the stores. Now refueled, Jill was ready to make some progress whether Reagan was ready for it or not.

"Let's go in here." Jill pointed at a large department store. She could almost hear her husband's groan. She hadn't been exaggerating when she told Reagan that Doug hated shopping. Anything he couldn't buy online, he figured he could do without.

Jill led the way to a rack of jeans. "How about these?"

When Reagan responded with her typical shrug, Jill started selecting several pairs that looked like they would fit. She then moved over to a rack of plain T-shirts.

"What's your favorite color?"

Another shrug.

Jill picked up another assortment and handed a stack to Reagan. "Let's have you try these on so we can figure out your size."

She led the way to the dressing room, Doug taking up a guard-like post a short distance from the entrance.

For the next hour, Jill collected samples of clothes from the racks in the juniors department and kept up a constant parade of shirts, pants, skirts, and dresses to the dressing room. As she might with her second graders, she gave Reagan choices between two or three alternatives, gradually coaxing her into giving her timid opinion. When Jill was finally satisfied that Reagan had the basics, she led the way to the shoe department.

Doug followed along silently, carting their purchases as they moved from shoes to accessories to pajamas. When Jill started ushering Reagan toward socks and underwear, both Doug's and Reagan's cheeks colored.

Fully aware that Doug's presence would continue to make Reagan uncomfortable, Jill turned to him and said, "Doug, why don't you take all of that stuff out to the car. I'm sure we'll be fine for a few minutes by ourselves."

Clearly eager for an escape route, Doug agreed. "Okay. Where do you want me to meet you?"

"How about the bookstore?" Jill nodded toward Reagan. "I'm sure Reagan could use some books or magazines to keep her occupied."

"Okay." He made sure his cell phone was still on. "Call me if you need me. Otherwise, I'll see you there in fifteen minutes."

* * *

Doug loaded shopping bags into the trunk, shifting them so the shoe boxes wouldn't get crushed when he closed it. The large boot box clunked with Reagan's muddy tennis shoes that she had put in it, the new boots now on Reagan's size-eight feet.

Doug was just walking back into the mall when his phone rang. He saw Hector's name on caller ID.

"Hey, Hector. What's up?"

"We have a problem," Hector said, tension in his voice. "I set up a couple of alerts to make sure no one tried to track you down since you gave that fake CPS guy your name."

"Yeah. And?"

"One of them just popped. Someone ran a background check on you last night."

Doug thought over his personal information in an effort to identify any vulnerabilities. When they had first met, Jill had been rooming with a witness he was assigned to protect. Because of their association and his determination to keep both his witness and then-girlfriend safe, he had set up a trust to pay his expenses. His lease and his utilities went through the trust, in essence making his home a safe house. He drove a government car so there was nothing to trace back to him there. Besides, if someone had figured out what car he drove, they could have traced the GPS and found him last night.

Then he thought of his cell phone, the only item that was listed in his own name. He hadn't remembered to turn it on until he'd checked for messages when he was eating lunch with Jill and Reagan.

"Do me a favor and run a GPS trace on my phone. See what you can find."

"I already did," Hector told him. "I can clearly see that you are in Tysons Corner right now."

"Great," Doug muttered, instantly looking around for any perceivable threats. "Can you back trace my history to my house?"

"No. When I set the alerts for you, I had the cell phone company clear your history. Since you didn't have your phone on last night, I don't think anyone could tie you back to your house. At least, not unless you take your cell phone home with you while it's on."

"Where are you right now?"

"I'm heading your way. I'll be there in five to ten minutes. I thought you might need some backup."

"I appreciate it." Doug caught a glimpse of a familiar face. Striding toward the department store, where he had left Jill and Reagan, was the man who had claimed to be Reagan's social worker. "Hector, hurry. We have a problem."

* * *

Jill rolled her eyes when she pulled her ringing cell phone from her purse to see her husband's phone number displayed on the touch screen. "Two minutes late, and he's already wondering where we are."

As soon as she said hello, Doug responded with a tense, "Where are you?"

"Sorry. There was a line in the lingerie department. We're just leaving now."

"No, don't." Doug's tone made Jill stiffen.

"What's wrong?"

"I think someone is here looking for Reagan. I want you to take her back into the dressing rooms."

Jill listened to Doug outline his plan as she steered a bewildered Reagan toward the closest dressing room in the women's department.

"What's wrong?" Reagan asked the moment Jill hung up.

Jill considered censoring her answer. After all, she didn't want to traumatize the girl any further. The wariness in Reagan's eyes swayed Jill to trust her with the truth. "Doug saw someone here who was asking about you at the hospital."

Terror flashed in her eyes. "They found me."

Jill reached out and put her hands on Reagan's shoulders, partially as a gesture of comfort and partially to hold her in place so she couldn't dart back out of the dressing rooms. "Doug has a plan. I need you to trust him," Jill said firmly. Her voice softened when Reagan's terrified eyes shifted to look directly at her once more. "I need you to trust me."

Reagan sucked in a deep breath and let it out with a shudder. "What do I have to do?"

"You can start by going into one of these dressing rooms so you're out of sight. I'm going to go out and get some clothes for you to change into."

"But we already bought a bunch of clothes."

"Yes, but they're all in the car. Doug doesn't want you wearing your old clothes out in the mall in case someone might recognize you," Jill explained. "And I think I can find an outfit that will help you look older. I want you to look like you're someone else."

"Okay." Reagan looked at her doubtfully, but she stepped into one of the open dressing rooms.

"Just stay in there. I'll be right back." Jill walked to the edge of the dressing room, hating that she had to leave Reagan alone even for a minute. She looked around, noticing a mannequin dressed in an oversized cream-colored sweater and trendy pants the color of dark chocolate. Accenting the outfit was an earth-toned scarf and a cute little cap.

Jill noticed a saleswoman and motioned to her. "Excuse me. My sister loved that outfit on the mannequin over there. Could you help me find everything for it?"

The woman's eyes lit up with the prospect of the sale. "Absolutely. What sizes do you need?"

"Let's go with a medium for the sweater. Probably a size four or six for the pants."

"Did you want the accessories too?"

"That would be great. Thanks."

The woman nodded. "I'll be right back with those."

Jill stayed where she was near the dressing room entrance, a little afraid that Reagan's obvious fear might prompt her to try to sneak out and take her chances on her own.

Sure enough, when Jill poked her head into the dressing room, Reagan was stepping out of the changing stall.

"The saleswoman is getting an outfit for you to try on. She'll be right back with it." Jill motioned her back into the stall. "Just hang out here for a couple more minutes."

"Okay."

Jill stepped back out as the woman arrived with the selections. "Thank you so much. This is perfect."

"Absolutely. Please let me know if I can get anything else for you or if you need different sizes."

"I will. Thanks." Jill turned and moved back into the dressing room, where Reagan was standing outside a changing stall. "Reagan, here. Try these on."

Without a word, Reagan accepted the offerings and ducked back into the stall to change. When she opened the door again, Jill studied her. The pants were tucked into the new boots she had decided to wear after trying them on in the shoe department, and the sweater hung past her hips. Jill stepped forward and arranged the scarf artistically around Reagan's neck and then opened up her purse and dug out some mascara and lipstick.

"Here. Let's see if we can make you look a little older." Jill carefully helped Reagan apply the makeup. When Jill stepped back, she smiled. With the light makeup and dressed in the latest fashions, Reagan no longer looked like a teenager. Unless someone really looked closely, they would guess her to be in her early twenties.

"This is great. You look ten years older." Jill took the cap off of Reagan's head. "Try to tuck your hair up into the hat."

Reagan took her long brown hair and twisted it up so it was no longer visible beneath the cap.

"Perfect." Jill stepped closer and started removing the price tags.

"What are you doing?" Reagan lowered her voice. "You aren't planning on us stealing these clothes, are you? I thought your husband was a cop."

"Don't worry. We're going to pay for this. We're just being creative about it."

Though she was obviously skeptical, Reagan pulled the tags from the hat and scarf and handed them over to Jill.

When Jill had all of the tags in her hand, she said, "Wait here for another minute. I'll be right back."

"How did those work out?" The saleslady asked her when Jill reemerged from the dressing room.

"Great." She glanced over at a trio of women walking by, all three of them carrying purses. "I think if I can find her a purse to go with it, we'll be all set."

"We have a few over here." She motioned to the display beside the checkout counter. "Otherwise, we'll need to go over to accessories."

Jill studied the half dozen styles available in the women's department, selecting one with a long strap in the same chocolate brown as the pants Reagan was now wearing. "This should work." She pulled the tag off and handed it, along with the others, to the saleswoman. "I hope it's okay, but she wants to wear the outfit out of here. Can I get a shopping bag for her old clothes?"

"Absolutely." The saleswoman handed her a bag, exchanging it for Jill's credit card.

"Go ahead and ring me up. I'll be right back to sign." Jill went back to where Reagan was waiting nervously and handed her the new purse. "Take this and come wait just inside the door here. When I tell you, we're going outside. One of Doug's friends will be waiting for us with a car."

"Are you sure this is going to work?" Reagan whispered. "What if someone recognizes me? What if Laith is here?"

"He'd probably walk right past you and never even know it," Jill said with feigned confidence. She straightened her shoulders and uttered a silent prayer, then pulled her cell phone from her purse and called Doug. "We're ready. We're in the women's department on the second floor and just need to pay."

"The minute you sign the credit card receipt, head for the elevator and go down to the first floor. Hector is waiting outside with a car. He'll hand you the keys, and then I want you to drive over to the Whitmores' house."

"The Whitmores? Why there?"

"Because they're close by, and they've got a great security system."

"Okay." Jill tried to keep her voice casual despite the worry pulsing through her. "Be careful."

"I will. You too."

CHAPTER 5

Doug stayed on the move, weaving his way through the food court, ducking in and out of stores. As soon as Hector called and said Jill and Reagan were safely on their way to the Whitmores' house, Doug searched for the right spot to carry out his plan.

As usual, the mall was bustling with activity both in the shops and in the parking lot. He glanced down at his watch—3:15 p.m. He slowed slightly as he passed by a directory. Then he continued strolling toward one of the many sit-down restaurants, choosing one on the opposite side of the mall from where he had left Jill and Reagan.

He walked to the entrance, pleased to see it nearly empty. Besides a couple of men sitting at the bar, discussing the upcoming football game, only three tables were occupied. Realizing that he wasn't going to find any place in the mall less populated on a Saturday afternoon, Doug texted his location to Hector and headed inside.

A woman stood by the entrance and offered him a smile. "Sir, would you like a table?"

Doug nodded. "I have a business associate who is meeting me here. Do you have one that is out of the way? Maybe somewhere in the back?"

"How about over here?" The hostess drew out two menus and led the way past several tables and then turned to the left and motioned to a corner booth.

"This is perfect." Doug slid into the booth and accepted the menu. Then he glanced up at her. "Can you tell me where your restroom is?"

"Right over there." She pointed at the little hallway directly across from his table.

"Thanks." Doug waited for her to leave him and then slipped his phone from his pocket. He leaned down and placed it on the floor beneath the table.

He heard Hector come in and sit at a table near the entrance. Knowing that his backup was now in place, Doug crossed to the restroom and waited.

He didn't have to wait long. Not ten minutes after he had taken up his position outside of the men's room, he heard the fake social worker's voice when he greeted the hostess and asked if he could look inside for a friend he was supposed to meet there.

Doug pulled his weapon free of its holster, trying to hear the footsteps over the light music playing through the overhead speakers. Seconds ticked by, and Doug could only imagine that Brian was taking his time to search for him at the handful of tables that currently had customers.

Finally, the familiar figure stepped into view, turning the corner to the secluded section where the waitress had seated Doug several minutes earlier. Then Brian Wendall turned and froze when he saw Doug standing a few yards behind him, his gun already drawn and aimed at Brian's heart.

"Hello again," Doug said dryly. "I think you have some explaining to do."

"What's going on?" The man stood frozen, his face pale. "Why are you pointing that thing at me?"

Out of the corner of his eye, Doug saw Hector moving forward, his own gun drawn. A ten-year-old boy stood up in the booth and pointed while the two men at the bar ducked for cover. At least no one was screaming. Doug hated when that happened.

He kept his gun steady, his eyes searching for the truth in the other man's face. "Why are you following me?"

"I'm not. I just came in here for lunch."

"Lunch will have to wait." Doug kept his gun trained on the man who had claimed to be Reagan's social worker. When Hector moved into position beside him, Doug holstered his weapon and pushed Wendall up against the wall to search him for weapons. Immediately, he found the handgun holstered at the man's shoulder. "What do we have here?"

The man's jaw clenched, but he said nothing.

Doug finished searching him for weapons and then pulled his handcuffs from his pocket and secured the man's hands. After he handed the man over to Hector, he retrieved his phone and turned it off so it could no longer be traced. With a nod to Hector, he said, "Let's go. Maybe once we get to FBI headquarters, you can tell us why you're following me."

* * *

Reagan stared out the window, her hands gripped tightly in her lap. She and Jill had made it out of the mall safely enough, but she knew now that Laith was going to find her. Eventually, a time would come when Jill and Doug wouldn't be able to hide her from him. And when that happened, her life would be over.

She squeezed her eyes shut against the tears that threatened.

"Are you okay?" Jill asked, her tone soft and understanding.

Reagan didn't trust her voice, so she didn't say anything at all.

"I know this must have been frightening for you, but I promise Doug will figure out how someone was able to track us down, and he'll fix the problem to make sure it doesn't happen again." Jill turned into a neighborhood with ridiculously large houses. After making a couple of turns, she pulled into a long driveway that led up to what Reagan could only describe as a mansion.

"What are we doing here?"

"Hopefully visiting some friends," Jill told her. "If they aren't here, we'll just have to wait in the car until we hear from Doug."

Jill led the way up the front walk and rang the bell. Reluctantly, Reagan followed behind her.

Footsteps sounded inside, and then the front door swung open to reveal a tall, dark-haired woman. She was older than Jill, probably old enough to be a grandma, and her smile was instant and friendly.

"Jill. It's so good to see you." The woman stepped forward, her arms outstretched for a hug. "I didn't know you were going to be in our neighborhood today."

"I hadn't planned on it," Jill admitted. She returned the woman's hug, then pulled back, her tone apologetic. "I'm sorry to drop in unannounced, but would you mind some company for a little while?"

"Not at all." She waved them in. "Who's your friend?"

"Katherine Whitmore, this is my foster daughter, Reagan Bower," Jill said, leading the way into the house. "Reagan, Mrs. Whitmore is a good friend of mine and Doug's."

Reagan stared at Jill, shocked by her casual reference to her as a foster child.

"I didn't know you were a foster parent," Katherine said excitedly. "That's wonderful. When did this happen?"

"Just yesterday." Jill glanced at Reagan. "We were kind of thrown together through unexpected circumstances, but it's been nice having her in the house."

"Well, come in and sit down. I want to hear everything that has been going on with you lately. We haven't talked in weeks." Katherine led them into an enormous living room, one that had to be as large as the entire apartment Reagan used to live in with her mother.

Reagan's eyes were drawn to the tall, built-in bookshelves on the far wall—shelves and shelves of books. She stood at the edge of the room, unaware that she was staring until Jill nudged her forward and led her to a chair beside the sofa. On the coffee table in front of her, she saw several more books fanned out so the covers were easy to see.

A car engine sounded in the driveway, and Reagan tensed. A moment later, she heard the rumble she guessed was a garage door opening and then closing, followed by a door slamming somewhere deep in the house. Then a tall, silver-haired man walked in.

"Hi there." The man's smile encompassed all of them, and he leaned down to give Katherine a kiss before crossing to where Jill was sitting.

Jill stood and shook the man's hand. "Hello, Senator. How are you?"

"Wonderful." His eyes swept down to look at Reagan, and she could feel herself shrink back against the chair cushion.

"This is Reagan. She's going to be staying with Doug and me for a while."

"Good to meet you," the senator said, but he didn't move any closer.

Reagan remained silent, wondering absently if he was really a senator or if he was like the colonel, someone who liked to pretend to have more power than he really did.

"Where's Doug?" the senator asked.

"He had a little problem with work he needed to take care of, but we were in the area, so he suggested that he meet us here. I hope that's okay."

"Of course." He nodded. "I was thinking about throwing some steaks on the grill for dinner. Can we talk you into joining us?"

Jill hesitated briefly. "Actually, that would be great, if you don't mind."

Katherine stood. "In that case, why don't we move into the kitchen, and I can get started on a salad."

"Sure. What can I do to help?" Jill stood as well.

"Just come in and keep me company." Katherine looked down at Reagan. She must have noticed the way Reagan was staring at the books in front of her. "Reagan, do you like to read?"

"Yeah, I guess," she said noncommittally. In truth, reading was one of the few things she truly enjoyed.

"Those books on the table are ones I have doubles of. If you want, go ahead and look through them. You're welcome to take any that you want."

"Really?" Reagan heard the wonder in her voice, but she didn't care.

"Absolutely. I've read a few of them already, and they were excellent." Katherine took a step toward the doorway that Reagan assumed led to the kitchen. "And when you're done looking at those, come on into the kitchen. After Jill and I finish making the salad, you can walk with us to feed the horses."

Reagan nodded numbly. New clothes, free books, real horses. She supposed everyone should get a glimpse of a fairy tale at some point in their life. Then she swallowed hard. Maybe today was someone's idea of a bad joke. She would get to see what life could be like for lucky people. Then she would die.

She picked up the book closest to her. If she was going to die, she might as well die happy. Flipping open the cover, she started to read.

CHAPTER 6

Questioning Brian Wendall took all of ten minutes. The man wasn't talking, and Doug was convinced that no amount of threats or cajoling would get this man to betray whomever he was in league with. Doug had run his fingerprints but found he wasn't in any of the criminal databases. According to the background check that followed, Doug learned little more than the man's name and address and that he owned a private security firm.

His story about freelancing with child protective services certainly hadn't checked out, but other than that, he appeared to be a model citizen. At least, he had been a model citizen right up until they had arrested him for attempted kidnapping. Doug hadn't found any known associations between Brian Wendall and Laith Mansour other than Reagan's mention of seeing them together, but Wendall was tucked away safely in jail just in case. Doug had no doubt Laith had sent this man to find Reagan, but how had he been able to trace Doug's cell phone?

Questions continued to roll through Doug's mind on the drive to the Whitmores' home. Where was Laith Mansour hiding? Who was the colonel? And most importantly, why would anyone want Reagan dead?

Hector had offered to run a security check for Doug and make sure these guys, whoever they were, hadn't managed to trace him back to his house. Doug expected that by the time he was ready to take Jill and Reagan home, he would know whether it was safe to do so.

He arrived at the senator's oak-lined property, appreciating the elegant home with its circular driveway, and knocked on the front door, concerned when no one answered. On impulse, he followed the scent of grilled meat to the back patio, where he found Jim Whitmore dressed casually in jeans and a crewneck sweatshirt, a pair of barbecue tongs in his hand.

"Hey, Senator."

"Hi, Doug. We've been expecting you." He flipped one of the steaks. "The girls are at the stables, feeding the horses."

"How's Reagan doing?"

"She hasn't said much, but she seems okay." His eyebrows lifted quizzically. "Why?"

"We had a little scare with her at the mall today. I was just wondering how she's handling it."

"What kind of scare?" Jim asked. "And how did you end up with a teenager living with you?"

"It wasn't planned. Believe me." Feeling overwhelmed both by the run-in at the mall and the shopping marathon that preceded it, Doug wearily ran his fingers through his hair. "This has been a crazy couple of days. I don't even know where to start."

"Why don't you start at the beginning."

Doug had already planned on talking to Jim about the possibility of a target on or around Halloween. He couldn't see any reason not to tell him the rest, so he did what Jim suggested and started at the beginning.

* * *

She must be in shock. Reagan couldn't think of any other reason she would be hallucinating like this. Or maybe she was already dead, and she didn't know it yet.

She looked across the round kitchen table at the man she now knew was a US senator from Virginia, exactly the kind of man Laith and his friends would have loved to take a shot at, and this man was talking to her like she mattered. No one was treating her like some kid who didn't have an opinion or acting like she was some second-class citizen because she was a girl.

These four people were talking to her . . . and listening.

The food was yet another oddity. Steak and salad and mashed potatoes and glazed carrots. And none of it had come from one of those little plastic trays made for the microwave. And the taste. She hadn't known food was supposed to taste this good.

"What do you think, Reagan? Do you have any idea what kind of people Laith would go after?"

Reagan looked over at the senator sheepishly. She didn't want to tell him the truth, but she was afraid not to. Besides, if this wasn't real, it wouldn't hurt for her to be honest. "People like you." She felt her cheeks color at her own words. "He hates anyone in charge of anything, but he especially hates the government."

"I can't think of any kind of costume parties that would have to do with government officials," the senator said. "You're sure these guys are going to be wearing costumes?"

Reagan nodded. "They were talking about dressing up like ninjas, Star Wars characters, stuff like that."

"It's certainly clever," Katherine put in. "Halloween would be a tough time for the authorities to check everyone carrying a weapon since so many costumes use them for props."

"We'll keep checking into possible parties in the DC area. That will be our focus on Monday." Doug pushed back from the table. "For now, we should be getting home."

Jill stood as well. "Thank you so much for dinner and for letting us drop in on you like this."

"We enjoyed having you," Katherine said. Then she turned to Reagan. "And, Reagan, it was so nice meeting you. I hope you enjoy the books. And if you need more, come on back. You're welcome to borrow any of the ones I have whenever you want."

Stunned by the casual offer, Reagan struggled to speak. "Thanks."

They said their good-byes, and Reagan walked outside, hesitating when she looked at the two cars in the driveway, not sure which one she should get into: Doug's or the one she and Jill had come in.

"We'll take my car," Doug told her, clicking his key to unlock the door. "Hector will send someone to pick up the other one later tonight."

As soon as they were settled in Doug's car, Jill voiced Reagan's fear, the one Reagan had been too afraid to speak aloud. "Are you sure it's safe at our house?"

"Yeah," Doug said, his voice surprisingly certain. "Hector went by to make sure everything was okay, and he did a deep background check to make sure nothing could be traced to us. He's confident that our house is still safe."

"I thought you were being overprotective when you took so many precautions when we moved here. Now I'm glad you did."

"How did they find us?" Reagan asked.

"My cell phone." Doug looked back at Reagan, and she could have sworn he looked apologetic. "I didn't realize the social worker last night was a phony. He had my name and tracked me down through the GPS on my phone. Since

I didn't turn it on until we were at the mall, we're sure it couldn't have given away our home location."

"We've sure been blessed through all of this," Jill said and glanced back at Reagan. "The Lord must really be watching out for you."

Reagan could only stare. Why would God care about her? He certainly hadn't cared about her before. As they made their way back to her current home, she stared out the window and wondered how long it would last. That wonder slowly turned to hope, and without her even realizing it, hope shifted into a silent prayer to the God Jill said cared about her.

* * *

"We're going where?" Reagan asked, surprise and a touch of defiance evident in her voice.

"Church," Jill told her again, clearing the last of their breakfast dishes from the table. "You can either wear that dress we bought yesterday or the skirt and one of your new tops."

"Why are we going to church?"

"We go every week." Jill knew a couple of her friends struggled with getting their teenagers to church each week, and she knew it was a stage a lot of kids went through. Of course, her friends' kids had been brought up in the gospel. She suspected Reagan had little if any experience with religion. In fact, she doubted Reagan even knew what it was like to be around people who were generally supportive and friendly. Her background clearly had been something very different from what Jill was used to. "We're leaving in thirty minutes, so you need to get moving."

To Jill's relief, Reagan didn't argue. She disappeared into her room and returned fifteen minutes later dressed and ready to go.

The moment they walked into the chapel, Jill could feel Reagan's reserve settling in. When the bishop approached them, Reagan shrank back farther, positioning herself so she was behind her and Doug, as though using them as a shield.

"Good morning," Bishop Chandler greeted them in general before zeroing in on Jill. "Sister Valdez, I don't know if you got my message, but I was hoping you might have a minute today to meet with me." Then he glanced over at Doug. "I'd like for you to be there too."

Jill glanced back at Reagan, unable to imagine leaving her alone in the foyer at church. "Today might be a little tough. We may need to leave after sacrament meeting. Could we make it another time?"

The bishop hesitated briefly. Then he said, "Of course. I'll have Brother Hawkins give you a call to set up a time." He looked at Reagan. "Who's this?"

"This is Reagan. She's staying with us for a while."

"Good to meet you." The bishop extended his hand. Reagan looked up at Jill as though silently asking if this man was safe. Jill gave her a little nod, and Reagan reluctantly shook his hand.

As soon as the bishop moved on to greet someone else, Jill led the way to the padded pew on the left side, where they normally sat, and then motioned for Reagan to slide in first, leaving Jill between her and Doug. As soon as Jill settled into her seat, she reached out and took a hymn book from the holder in front of her. As an afterthought, she drew out a second book and handed it to Reagan.

The prelude music continued as other ward members filtered into the chapel and took their seats. Jill noticed a family with several teenage girls sit in the long pew in the center, each of the girls carrying that light with them that showed they knew their family and those around them loved and accepted them. Jill glanced over at Reagan, immediately wondering how different her life might have been if she had been given this gift for her whole life.

In Reagan's lap, the hymnal lay open to the first hymn, and her head was bent as she read the words.

Warmth spread through Jill as a simple thought popped into her mind. Reagan had the gospel now. She might not know it, but the simple act of reading that hymn was giving her a glimpse into the truth that the Lord knew who she was. She was safe and protected for the first time in her life. For as long as this lasted, Jill prayed that she could make Reagan feel loved.

CHAPTER 7

Doug sat on his couch early Monday morning and listened to Hector give him the latest details on this case that had been dropped into his lap. Brian Wendall, the man who had been following him at the mall, still wasn't talking, and no one had made any progress with anything that might help them find Reagan's stepfather. The search of the nearby cabin where Laith Mansour had been staying with the girl had given them few answers and had created a lot more questions.

Doug had been relieved that the forensics team hadn't found any sign of bomb residue, but they had found a number of spent shell casings. Further analysis revealed the casings had been from several different guns, all of which were M16 assault rifles.

"The signs definitely suggest this could be some sort of militia group," Hector said with a shrug. "Or it could be a bunch of guys who like guns and have a distorted view of reality."

"Either way, someone was shooting at Reagan the other day."

"That's another thing," Hector said. "The slug we pulled out of the tree near the cabin you were staying at wasn't from an automatic weapon."

"I could have told you that," Doug said. "It was some kind of handgun."

"Yeah. Ballistics said it was a 9 mil, probably fired from a Beretta."

"You know, there's one thing I don't understand."

"What's that?"

"After Reagan's mom died, why did Laith want to keep her around?" Doug asked, considering. "He doesn't have any blood relation to her. It would have been easy enough to hand her over to social services and walk away."

"That's a good question. Maybe he was worried she already knew too much and would talk," Hector said. "After all, he did try to kill her."

"Again, why wait? If Laith had wanted her dead, he could have gone after her weeks ago. Why now?" Doug heard the slight movement in the hallway and turned in time to see Reagan jump back out of sight. "Reagan?"

Doug didn't hear anything, but he suspected she was still standing just out of sight. "Reagan, I know you're there. Come in here, please."

She peeked around the corner, eying Hector as though trying to overcome some unspoken fear.

"It's okay, Reagan. This is Hector Flores. He works with me at the FBI. He only wants to help."

Apparently his words swayed her, and Reagan slowly came into the room, stopping several feet from them.

"You heard us talking?" Doug asked. He could tell by the look in her eyes that she had likely been eavesdropping for several minutes. "Maybe you can help us understand why Laith picked the other day to come after you."

She pressed her lips together. "It was because of the colonel."

"I don't understand."

"Laith wanted me to go to some hotel with them. He wanted me to deliver a package." She drew a breath as though trying to clamp down on her emotions. "When I found out the package was a bomb, I said I didn't want to go."

"Is that when you ran away?"

"Laith told me I had to do what they said, but I said I didn't want to. He hit me, but he knew I wasn't going to change my mind." She shrugged as though the physical abuse was nothing new. "Then the colonel said that I knew too much. The way he was looking at me scared me, so when they were loading up the guns in the colonel's truck, I ran."

"You said the colonel was wearing a military uniform. Do you know which branch he was with?"

"He's a marine," Reagan said with certainty. "And he isn't really a colonel. He had those stripes on the sleeve of his uniform. Colonels don't have those."

"How did you know that?"

She rolled her eyes, and for the first time, Doug caught a glimpse of the girl behind the seemingly reserved exterior. "I watch TV."

Doug tapped a few keys on his computer and pulled up the images of the various rank insignias. "Can you tell me which one of these was on the colonel's uniform?"

Reagan looked at the screen without moving closer. She studied the images for a moment, then pointed. "I'm pretty sure it was the second one."

"So we're looking for a marine staff sergeant with brown hair and brown eyes." Doug considered for a moment. "Any idea what kind of car he drives?"

She nodded. "A black pickup truck. A big one."

"New? Old?"

"It was pretty shiny. I guess that means it's new."

"Any idea what state the license plate was from?"

She shook her head.

"That's okay. This will help," Doug told her. "I'm going to try to access the Marine Corps' personnel database to see if I can run vehicle registrations against rank. A sketch artist is going to come over later to see if you can help us identify the men who were at the cabin. In the meantime, I'd like for you to look at some pictures of hotels. Can you do that for me?"

She nodded obediently. "Okay."

"Great." Doug grabbed one of two rolling chairs beside a long desk in the corner. "Let's get started."

* * *

Jill walked into the living room and found Doug sitting in front of the computer at the desk in the corner and Reagan sitting in a chair beside him, where she could see what he was displaying on the screen.

Since Reagan was the key to a possible threat to national security, Doug's boss had given him permission to work from home so he could fulfill the dual role of making sure she stayed safe and trying to uncover new leads. Hector would work from the office and give Doug any support he needed, as well as provide Doug with the latest updates.

Her heart warmed as she listened to Doug patiently guiding Reagan through photos, his voice gentle and filled with quiet understanding. Jill shifted the tote bag on her shoulder. It was filled with work she had brought home from school with her the previous Thursday, the last day she had worked before she and Doug had taken their short vacation together. It was hard to believe it had been only three days since Reagan had entered their lives.

She knew more about her now, even though Reagan still didn't offer more than basic facts. Reagan had turned thirteen two weeks after her mother died, just days after her stepfather had moved them to the secluded cabin in the woods.

From what Jill had gathered, either Reagan's mother or stepfather had decided to home-school her the previous year. Jill suspected that someone at her middle school had noticed the early signs of abuse or had at least realized that something wasn't right at home, which likely caused the adults in her life to hide her away from any possible prying eyes.

Jill set her bag on the couch. "Good morning."

"Hi, honey." Doug shifted and waited for his usual good morning kiss. "Hey, I forgot to tell you the bishop called last night."

"Oh, I forgot to call Brother Hawkins back to let him know when we could meet with the bishop. He called earlier, but I was hesitant to set up a time since things are so crazy right now."

"Should we be worried that Bishop is calling us himself?" Doug asked.

"Probably. Sounds like one of us is getting a new calling." She thought about the possibilities and the fact that she'd been teaching Relief Society for only a few months. "It must be you." Then she grinned mischievously. "Maybe you're going to be the new early morning seminary teacher."

"You're the teacher in this relationship, not me. I don't think the bishop would trust me to teach anyone over the age of ten." Doug smirked back at her. "Besides, he said you were the one he wants to meet with."

"I guess we'll find out as soon as we talk to him."

"I guess so." Doug dismissed the topic and motioned to the kitchen. "There are some doughnuts in the kitchen if you want one."

"Doughnuts?" Jill looked over at Reagan. "That doesn't sound like a very healthy breakfast."

"Hey, beggars can't be choosers. I asked Hector to pick something up for me on his way over this morning. That's what he showed up with."

"Hector was here? Before eight in the morning?"

"Yeah, he left a few minutes ago." Doug motioned at the computer screen. "Reagan and I are going to figure out which hotel she saw a picture of so we can narrow our search of Halloween activities."

"Are you sure you don't want me to take work off today?" Jill asked hesitantly. She was already worried that if she turned her back on Reagan for too long, Reagan would disappear. She wasn't sure how she felt about leaving the girl's care entirely up to Doug so soon.

"We'll be fine," Doug assured her.

"Okay." Jill hefted her bag again and settled it on her shoulder. "I'm going to grab some breakfast and head out. Call me, though, if you have any problems."

"We will," Doug promised. Then he gave her a wicked grin. "And I saved you a Bavarian-cream-filled."

Jill grinned. "It's times like these I really love you."

"Yeah." Doug gave her a smug look. "I know."

***

Reagan didn't know how she felt about being left alone with a man, even if it was a man who carried a badge. She knew he also carried a gun, and her experience with men and guns hadn't given her any positive memories. Still, Doug seemed okay so far. He kept showing her one photo after another of hotel buildings, usually several pictures of the same one to make sure they didn't miss something.

They spent the morning looking through nearly all of the hotels in DC. Then they took a break and made sandwiches for lunch. Now they were back at it.

Once they'd exhausted the list of DC hotels, Doug started showing her hotels in Virginia that might also have a view of the Washington Monument.

Reagan sat up straighter in her seat when a new photo loaded. "That's it. That's the picture I saw."

"You're sure?"

She nodded. "It was this same picture. It was hanging up on the big project board in the living room for at least a month."

Doug shifted, and his dark eyes pinned her. "What else was on the project board?"

"A bunch of stuff."

"Like what?"

"Pictures of guns. Little boxes with words in them."

"Could you draw what it looked like for me?"

"Maybe." Reagan rolled her shoulders restlessly.

Doug was quiet for a moment. "We've been at this all day. What do you say we get out of here for a little while?"

Reagan didn't know what to say or even what he was offering.

"Have you ever shot a gun?" Doug asked.

Her eyes widened, and she shook her head.

"Do you want to learn?"

"Laith said girls aren't supposed to use guns."

"I think we've already established that Laith is an idiot," Doug said without any heat. "Go put some shoes on. There's a shooting range not far from here, and it's pretty empty this time of day."

Afraid to argue, Reagan did as she was told. Twenty minutes later, she found herself standing at the edge of a wide field while Doug instructed her on the basic safety of firearms.

He demonstrated each aspect of using a handgun until, finally, he told her to put on the funny ear coverings that he said would protect her hearing. Then he showed her where to line up, and he handed her a loaded weapon.

Her first thought was that it was heavier than she had expected it to be. Then she lined up with the target and squeezed the trigger the way Doug had told her. She felt the jolt from the kick of the weapon and a terrifying rush of power.

Wide-eyed, she looked over at Doug, and a look of understanding passed between them.

"Scary, huh?"

She nodded.

"It's okay," Doug assured her. He put a hand on her arm to make sure the gun was pointed toward the target. "Just make sure you remember what I told you. Square up with your target, keep your arms steady, and don't forget to breathe."

Her heart beating rapidly, Reagan followed his instructions. She drew a deep breath, fired again, and, for the first time in her life, found a glimmer of what it was like to feel in control.

CHAPTER 8

Doug was sure he was going to go cross-eyed any minute. He had been staring at photographs, background reports, and traffic video feed for more than a week. Reagan had spent countless hours with him, examining pictures of marine staff sergeants assigned to Virginia as well as the DC area. So far, all they had managed to do was eliminate a lot of possibilities in their search for the colonel.

Reagan had literally looked at the photos of every marine staff sergeant currently assigned to DC, Maryland, and Virginia twice. They had expanded their search to include other sergeant ranks in case she had been mistaken about the exact insignia on the colonel's sleeve, but that was unsuccessful too. Now they were going to widen their search even further to include North and South Carolina.

Doug sighed. It was going to be another long day.

He thought of how many hours Reagan had already spent helping him. She was a trooper. He had to give her that. She hadn't complained once about anything he'd asked her to do, not even the detailed sketch he'd had her draw of Laith's project board or working with the sketch artist to try to identify the men she'd seen at the cabin. In fact, he found her to be helpful in general. She had been good about assisting Jill with basic household chores and had seemed to enjoy helping Jill grade papers for school.

The idea that Reagan should be in school had crossed his mind, but he wasn't willing to take the chance that Laith might be able to find her through the transfer of school records. Reagan also wasn't a candidate for the Witness Protection Program at this point since it appeared that once Laith was captured, she would be safe.

Jill had offered to take some time off to spend it with Reagan, but Doug insisted she save her leave. He knew the day would come eventually when he would have to work somewhere that he couldn't take Reagan with him. He definitely wasn't about to leave Reagan home alone.

Admittedly, it was odd watching his wife leave for work each morning while he remained behind with a timid thirteen-year-old who was more than a little wary of men. Still, he thought they were making progress. She no longer waited for him to tell her she could eat breakfast or lunch; she now recognized that if she was hungry, she could find something to eat for herself.

She also seemed more capable of entertaining herself than when she'd first arrived; she was content to read books or watch television, and she even seemed to enjoy raking leaves and doing simple yard work. He couldn't be sure if she was getting more settled or if he was getting more used to having her around now.

They had been to the shooting range together a half dozen times now, and he took some pride in knowing she was turning into a pretty good shot. She still didn't express her opinion or talk about her feelings, but he supposed that was normal for a kid who was trying to find out where she belonged. Doug could admit that he had wondered what would come next for her. It would be odd when this case ended and she could be placed in a foster home.

A knock sounded at the door. Relieved to have a reason to step away from the computer, he pushed back from his desk and crossed the room. He leaned forward and looked through the peephole before opening the door to Hector.

"Come on in." Doug waved him inside. "Anything new going on?"

"Actually, yes." Hector handed him two files and then sat down on the couch. "We finally found a link between Laith Mansour and the military."

"What's that?" Doug sat in the chair across from him.

"Apparently, Laith was a wannabe Navy SEAL. His aptitude scores were high enough that he was given an out-clause. If he washed out of the SEALs, his recruitment would be nullified."

"I gather he washed out?"

"Oh yeah." Hector nodded. "He didn't even make it through the first day of hell week."

"That gives us a tie to the military but not to the marines."

"It's possible that the sergeant we're looking for is with one of the recon units out of Camp Lejeune in North Carolina. That's the marines' version of a Navy SEAL. From what I understand, the two units could cross paths in some of the specialty schools."

"It's a long shot, but we might as well check it out. Can you dig up the personnel photos for Camp Lejeune? Let's not limit ourselves to recon though."

"I already did. I e-mailed you a link, but that blue file has the printouts of the staff sergeants. I thought it might make it easier for you if Reagan could look at those without tying up your computer."

"Thanks. I appreciate that," Doug said. He set the file down on the arm of the chair and then leaned forward and rested his elbows on his knees. "Anything new on the hotel?"

Hector shook his head. "The hotel manager said they don't have any events scheduled for Halloween, and they don't have any kind of costume parties planned for the weekend before Halloween."

"Reagan said the colonel wanted her to take a package into the hotel. There has to be a specific reason for these guys to pick that location to plant a bomb." Doug hesitated a moment, and Hector's words caught up with him. "Wait a minute. You said the hotel manager told you that there isn't a costume party this weekend. Do they have any other events scheduled?"

"I don't know. He didn't say."

"Find out."

Hector nodded, pulling his phone from his pocket. He scrolled through phone numbers and made the call. Doug listened to the one-sided conversation, seeing by the light in his partner's eyes that something indeed had been missed.

"Well?" Doug asked as soon as Hector hung up.

"You were right. The hotel manager doesn't know specifically what the event is that's planned, but the banquet facilities have been reserved for Saturday night."

"Who reserved it?"

"The Department of Defense."

"Any chance the manager gave you a contact name?"

"He's looking it up and said he'd get back to me, but get this"—excitement laced his voice—"the manager mentioned that the convention center across the street has a huge anime convention the same weekend. That will be going on the Friday and Saturday before Halloween."

"Anime convention?"

"Yeah, you know, those Japanese cartoons?"

"Like Pokémon?"

Hector nodded. "A good number of the participants dress up like their favorite characters, and they flood that part of the city."

"Which means anyone in costume would blend right in, and no one would look at them twice."

"Exactly."

"Let me know when you get that contact info for the event at the hotel. Let's see if we can figure out if these guys have a specific target in mind or if they're just trying to strike out at the DoD in general."

"You got it."

* * *

Jill debated whether she should call the Young Women president and cancel. Several weeks ago, she had agreed to help out with their Wednesday night activity this week when she found out the bishop was going to be out of town for business and several of the Young Women leaders had conflicts.

Selfishly, she wanted to stay home to spend time with Reagan. She felt like she'd had far too little time with the girl so far, and she found herself envying Doug and the bond he seemed to be forging with Reagan. Realizing that Reagan would probably benefit from being around some kids her own age, Jill walked into the living room, where Reagan was watching television. "Hey, why don't you go get some shoes on and come with me."

Reagan looked at her skeptically. "Come with you where?"

"The youth in our church are having an activity tonight. It'll be a lot of fun."

Reagan immediately shook her head. "I don't want to go. I want to stay here."

Jill hesitated, not sure if she should press or let Reagan get her way. She had hoped to introduce Reagan to some of the girls from church the previous Sunday, but Reagan had been just as wary at church her second time attending as she had been during her first. When Doug had whispered in Jill's ear, suggesting that they not push her to stay, Jill had reluctantly agreed.

She could understand Reagan's resistance, but she also knew it would be easier on her to meet some of the youth in a social setting where Jill could stay right by her side rather than in church, where she would have to go into a class by herself.

"Just come with me," Jill urged her. "It will be fun. I promise."

"I don't want to go," she repeated with a slight whine.

Jill took the whine as a good sign. Finally, Reagan was starting to sound like a typical thirteen-year-old, right down to balking at going to an event with a bunch of strangers. "Don't you think it's about time you meet some kids your age?" Jill asked.

A pained expression crossed Reagan's face. "I wouldn't know what to say."

"Saying hello is always a good place to start." Realizing that social settings were probably foreign to Reagan, Jill gentled her voice. "Reagan, you can stay with me the whole time if you want. I just really want the chance to spend time with you. It's hard going to work every day when I'd much rather be here at home with you and Doug."

"I thought you liked your work."

"I do," she said. "But I like you and Doug better."

Surprise reflected in Reagan's eyes before her lips curved up slightly. "I guess I can go with you."

"Thanks. I promise it'll be fun."

* * *

Reagan decided that Jill needed to seriously rethink her definition of fun. Two dozen teenagers were gathered along the curb in the quiet neighborhood, several of them with rakes in hand.

She looked over at Jill suspiciously. She had neglected to mention that the activity she was dragging her to was a service project at some older couple's house. "What exactly are we supposed to do here?"

"Nothing too strenuous. We'll rake up the leaves in the yard, harvest the last of their pumpkins, and then turn their garden so it's ready for spring."

"Why don't they just do this stuff themselves? Or hire someone?"

"They used to have their kids help, but they've all grown up and moved out of the area. And they don't need to hire someone, because we can do the work for them." Jill climbed out of the car. "Come on."

Reluctantly, Reagan followed. They were halfway across the leaf-covered lawn when two girls about Reagan's age crossed toward them.

"Sister Valdez!" The tall blonde girl bounded toward them, reaching her arms out for a hug as soon as she was in reach.

To Reagan's surprise, Jill hugged her back and then turned to give the other girl a hug too. "How are you girls doing?"

"Good," the shorter brunette replied.

Then the energetic blonde spoke again. "I'm so glad you're here."

"Me too." Jill stepped back and put a hand on Reagan's shoulder. "Reagan, this is Amber and Jasmine."

The two girls greeted her just as some lady across the yard motioned for everyone to gather around. Jill nudged Reagan forward, and Reagan was surprised when all of the chatter ceased and everyone folded their arms for a prayer.

As soon as the prayer concluded, Amber turned to her. "We're supposed to be picking pumpkins. Want to come with us?"

Surprised by the invitation, Reagan looked back at Jill. As though she knew Reagan wasn't sure what to do, Jill stepped forward and said, "That sounds fun. I'll come too."

Amber led the way to the field in back of the house. Reagan's eyes widened when she saw the rows and rows of tangled vines, pumpkins in various sizes visible at random intervals. Two wheelbarrows were parked on the side of the garden next to an older man who was holding several pairs of scissors and some kind of clippers.

The man handed out the various cutting utensils and then showed them how to harvest the pumpkins. Reagan followed Amber and Jasmine's lead, cutting pumpkins from the vine and loading them into the wheelbarrows. Jill helped for a few minutes, but then one of the other grown-ups pulled her aside.

At first, Reagan worked in silence a few yards from the other girls. Then Jasmine started working in the row beside her. "So do you live here now?"

Reagan didn't quite know how to answer, nor did she want to explain that she didn't really live anywhere. Keeping it simple, she said, "Yeah. For now."

"Where did you move from?"

"I moved around a lot."

Jasmine tried to lift an enormous pumpkin but couldn't quite manage it. "Hey, Reagan, can you help me with this one? It's seriously heavy."

"Sure." Reagan shifted and grabbed one side of the pumpkin. Together, they carried it to the wheelbarrow.

"Are you coming to our ward's trunk or treat? It's a week from Saturday."

Reagan thought of what was supposed to be happening on that particular Saturday, what Laith and his friends had planned. "I don't think so. I think I have to help Doug with something."

"Bummer." Jasmine considered for a minute. "Maybe you can come out trick-or-treating with us on Halloween."

"You go trick-or-treating? I thought that was just for little kids."

"Not around here." Jasmine shook her head. "Halloween is pretty much a big party in our neighborhood. All of the adults hang out in their cul de sacs to give out candy, and everyone from babies to teenagers dress-up and trick-or-treat. It's a lot of fun. You should come."

Reagan let herself wonder for a moment where she would be two weeks from now, desperately hoping she would still be here, that she could make plans for something as silly as trick-or-treating. Not that she had a costume, but it might be fun to walk around with Jasmine and see what everyone else did for the holiday.

When Reagan didn't answer right away, Jasmine continued. "Jill has my number. I'm sure she would be cool with it."

"I'll talk to her about it."

"Great."

CHAPTER 9

Doug's eyebrows lifted when he heard the door open and laughter ring out. Reagan's laughter.

"I've never heard anyone scream so loud," Reagan said with a giggle as she walked into the room.

"Well, she did have the head of a scarecrow land right on top of her." Jill grinned back at her.

Doug looked at them and found himself grinning. "Can I assume you had fun?"

"I think so." Jill looked over at Reagan as though looking for confirmation. Reagan nodded, but her smile faded slightly.

"Reagan hung out with Jasmine and Amber tonight," Jill told him.

"Those two will talk your ear off," Doug commented humorously.

Reagan seemed to muster her courage and then blurted out, "Jasmine wants me to go trick-or-treating with her."

"That sounds like fun," Jill said without missing a beat. Then she turned and gave Doug that look, the one that silently pleaded for him to back her up.

Doug was quick enough to understand there was a lot more going on here than a simple request. Halloween was two weeks away, but it was also after the threat Laith posed. Reagan wanted to know if she was staying with them that long, and Jill was asking for him to let her.

He wasn't sure exactly how he felt about extending Reagan's stay, but he had to admit he was kind of getting used to having her around. He considered for a moment. "I don't see why you can't go out. I'm sure Jill can help you figure something out for a costume."

"Really?" Hope lit Reagan's eyes.

"You can call Jasmine tomorrow afternoon and let her know," Jill suggested. "For now, you need to get to bed and get some sleep."

Obediently, Reagan started toward the hall and then turned back. After a brief hesitation, she moved toward Jill and gave her a hug. Jill looked up at Doug, a look of surprise and wonder in her eyes. Then she pulled Reagan closer and pressed a kiss on the top of her head.

"Good night, sweetie," Jill said softly.

"Good night." Reagan pulled away and took an awkward step back. Then she looked at Doug and repeated, "Good night."

"What was that all about?" Doug asked as soon as Reagan had left the room.

"I don't know." Jill smiled, and she closed the distance between them to wrap her arms around his waist. "But I like it."

* * *

Reagan spread the stack of photos out on the kitchen table again. She had been staring at pictures of marine sergeants for so long that she was beginning to think that she could pick one out of a crowd from fifty yards away. Unfortunately, she had yet to find a picture of the colonel.

A sigh escaped her when once again she failed to find anyone who resembled the man she had seen so often at Laith's cabin. None of these men had that cold look in his eyes or that heavy brow that made him look like he was always concentrating.

She picked up the pictures and carried them into the front living room, where Doug was sitting at the desk doing something on the computer. He was muttering to himself, but that wasn't anything new. He always seemed to do that when he was concentrating. And worrying.

Doug didn't have to tell her how worried he was. She might not know him that well, but it didn't take a genius to realize he was stressing out. So were the guys who came by the house to talk to him about Laith and the colonel. They were running out of time, and everyone knew it. Whatever Laith was planning was supposed to happen a week from Saturday.

She waited for the muttering to stop before she stepped forward and handed him the latest pictures.

"You didn't find him?"

Reagan shook her head. "Do you have any more for me to look at?"

"That was the last of the sergeants who are stationed around here." Doug took them from her, and his brow furrowed. "What are the chances that this guy is a former marine?"

"I don't know. When he came over, I always tried to get out of his way."

Sympathy or something like it flashed on Doug's face. He was silent for a moment. Then he asked, "Was he always in uniform when you saw him?"

"Yeah." Reagan nodded. "Always."

"That's odd." Doug turned to his computer and started punching keys. "Most military guys I know are more than happy to put on regular clothes when they're away from work."

"I'm pretty sure he was still working somewhere because he kept bringing these files with him to the cabin."

"What kind of files?"

"I don't know, but they all said 'top secret' on them."

"Are you sure?"

She nodded.

"Did they say anything else? A file name or something like that?"

"Yeah." Reagan struggled to bring the image forward, the manila folder with red stripes across it. "Bluebird. That's what it said on the top."

"Do you know what Bluebird stood for?"

She shook her head.

Doug picked his phone up off of the desk. "I'll call Hector and see if he can dig anything up. Why don't you go put some shoes on, and we'll go out to the shooting range."

"Okay." Reagan walked out of the room, but she stopped as soon as she was out of sight so she could listen to Doug's phone call.

She heard him greet his partner and tell him about the Bluebird file. Then she heard her name mentioned. "Reagan finished going through the rest of those pictures you brought over. We still haven't found the guy."

Doug paused, obviously listening to Hector say something. "She's already looked through the pictures twice. That kid is a trooper, and she's obviously really bright. Considering what she's been through, I'm surprised she's been able to remember as much as she has."

Reagan stood in the hall, frozen in place. Doug and Jill had been nice to her over the past week and a half, but Doug's words surprised her, especially since they were offered in such an offhanded way when he didn't even know she was listening.

After another moment of silence, Doug continued his side of the conversation. "I asked her about that. It sounds like he's still active duty. I think we need to stop limiting our search. Ask Max if he can send over one of our office laptops for me. I want to have her start searching the military database.

We've got to figure out who this guy is, especially since we didn't get any hits on facial recognition for him or the other two guys Reagan told us about."

Reagan waited another second until she heard Doug saying his good-byes. Then she hurried to her room to retrieve her shoes.

"Are you ready?" Doug asked as soon as she reappeared.

"Yeah." Reagan zipped up her jacket.

Doug glanced down at his watch. "Tell you what. Let's swing by and pick up some sandwiches at the deli. We can take lunch to Jill at the school before we go to the range."

"I get to see where Jill works?"

"Sure." Doug glanced at the computer and the stacks of photos and papers beside it. "We both deserve a little downtime before we dive back into this case."

* * *

Reagan carried the white paper bag from the deli in one hand and a soda in the other as she followed Doug through the elementary school hallway, her shoes squeaking on the white vinyl floor. Various art projects decorated the walls, the personalities of both the students and the teachers evident outside each door.

Doug slowed near a doorway, and Reagan could hear Jill's voice coming from inside. "Everyone, it's time to line up for lunch."

Doug moved through the doorway, sidestepping the rush of kids who were now crowding the entrance to the classroom. He looked back at Reagan and motioned for her to follow. Reagan followed him inside, instantly feeling the curious stares of the seven-year-olds who filled the room.

"Hi there," Jill greeted them, excitement and surprise in her voice. "What are you doing here?"

"We brought you lunch," Doug told her.

"Thank you." Jill waved toward the table in the corner. "Go ahead and sit down. I'll be back after I walk them down to the cafeteria."

"Okay." Doug set the two drinks he was holding on the table as Jill ushered her students out into the hall.

Reagan heard one of the little girls ask, "Who's that?"

"That's my husband and my foster daughter," Jill told the girl. Then without breaking stride, she spoke to the boys at the back of the line. "Peter and Jalen, keep your hands to yourselves."

Reagan absorbed the little jolt she felt at hearing herself referred to as Jill's daughter, even knowing that the word foster meant it wouldn't last. Jill had called her their foster daughter before, and Reagan could only wonder if she would ever be more than that to anyone again. Until she'd met Jill and Doug, she hadn't really thought about her lack of family or that her life wasn't quite normal. Now she thought about it all the time.

She put the sandwiches down on the table and turned to look around the room. Colorful posters hung on the walls, along with charts partially filled with colorful stickers. The class rules were prominently displayed by the door. Reagan read the first one. Be Kind. She wondered what life would have been like if the adults in her past had lived by that one.

"Does it seem weird to be in an elementary school again?" Doug asked.

"Yeah." Reagan lowered herself onto one of the chairs beside the table. "I was bummed when Laith said I couldn't go to school anymore."

"Once we find Laith, we'll make sure you can go again," Doug said.

Reagan wanted to ask where she would go to school and if Doug was planning on letting her stay with them, but before she could muster up the courage to ask the question, Jill came bustling back into the room.

"So what did you bring me?" Jill asked, taking a seat beside Doug.

"Turkey and avocado."

"That sounds perfect." She dug her sandwich out of the bag. "So much better than the peanut butter and jelly I had packed from home."

"We figured you wouldn't mind if we brought you something."

"Definitely not." Jill started unwrapping her sandwich, and Reagan followed suit. Jill took a bite, chewed, and swallowed before asking, "What else are you two up to today?"

"We're about to head out to the shooting range."

Jill looked over at Reagan. "Do you like going shooting?"

Reagan rolled the question over in her mind. She still wasn't used to people asking how she felt about things, and she took a moment to consider her answer. Did she like shooting? She did like the rush of power that pulsed through her every time she fired a weapon and the sense of freedom that came from being out among the trees. "Yeah. I like being outside and stuff."

"Doug tried to teach me how to shoot when we first started dating."

Doug lowered his voice and leaned closer to Reagan. "Don't let her fool you. She knows how to shoot just fine."

Reagan heard the humor in his voice and found herself pleased that she recognized the dry sarcasm for what it was. Her lips twitched up into the beginnings of a smile.

"I've spent enough time around you that it would be hard not to know the basics," Jill admitted. She took a sip of her drink and picked up her sandwich again. "Any chance you two want to swing by the grocery store on your way back from the shooting range? If you can pick up some chicken, I'll make some stir fry tonight."

"We can do that," Doug agreed easily.

Reagan looked down at the food in front of her and thought of how different things were now. Two weeks ago, she'd been lucky if she could manage a few scraps of food for herself after Laith and whatever friends he had working with him each day had eaten whatever she'd microwaved for them. Now she had real food in front of her with the promise of another meal in a few hours.

She drew a breath, and a plea echoed through her mind—*Please let this last.*

CHAPTER 10

Jill didn't have to ask Doug how the case was going. She could feel by the tension in the air that he and his coworkers hadn't made any progress in the past couple of days. She had arrived home on Friday night to find a sketch artist working with Reagan again in an effort to identify the man Reagan referred to as the colonel as well as the various men she had seen visiting Laith at the cabin.

She hoped a couple hours in church would help Doug find some peace and maybe even the inspiration he needed to break through the challenges he and his coworkers were facing. She also hoped Reagan would be willing to stay for the entirety of their church services rather than just sacrament meeting.

They took their seats in the chapel, and Jill felt a little lift when Jasmine walked by and greeted Reagan. Jill motioned for Jasmine to stop and talk to her, hoping to ease Reagan's transition.

"Jasmine, would you mind taking Reagan to Young Women's with you today? She doesn't know where it is."

"Sure, no problem," Jasmine said enthusiastically. "You can sit with me and Amber."

"Thanks," Reagan said, even though she looked a little overwhelmed.

"Don't worry," Jill assured her. "All of the girls are really nice. They're the same ones who were at the activity on Wednesday night." When Reagan continued to look at her warily, she added, "Besides, I'm sure someone will make sure everyone hears about Melissa and the scarecrow."

Humor lit Reagan's eyes. "That was so funny."

Jill put her arm around Reagan and gave her shoulders a friendly squeeze. "I'm really glad you're here."

Surprise replaced the humor on Reagan's face, and she gave Jill a thoughtful look. "Me too."

* * *

Reagan had never seen anyone work so hard before. Every morning when Reagan woke up, Doug was either on the phone or doing something on the computer. Other FBI agents came by the house every day now, sometimes staying for several hours before leaving them alone again.

She thought of all of the preparations Laith and his friends had made, the conversations she had overheard. Laith's plans were always focused on steering clear of the authorities. Now Reagan knew what the other side of the equation looked like. The authorities were definitely looking for him.

Doug's friends were just as wary about talking in front of her as Laith's had been, but their way of communicating their desire for privacy was so vastly different. While Laith had shouted or used the back of his hand to send her scampering into the other room, Doug and his friends just asked her to give them some time alone. They even said please most of the time.

When Reagan thought of the men who had paraded through her mother's life and, by extension, through her life, she found herself wondering why her mom had never been able to meet anyone like Doug and his friends.

She supposed deep down she knew the answer. It was because of the drugs. She doubted someone like Doug would sit around and watch someone take so many pills that they were passed out more often than not. Reagan didn't know if anything could have changed what happened to her mom, but she did know she didn't want to live like that again.

Reagan finished getting dressed and went into the kitchen in search of breakfast. She smiled a little at the certainty that the refrigerator and pantry were well stocked and that she was allowed to help herself to the contents.

When she turned the corner, she saw Doug buttering a piece of toast and Jill standing behind him, her arms wrapped around his waist.

"If there's anything I can do, just tell me," Jill was saying. "I can take some leave if you want to go into the office."

"No." Doug shook his head and put the butter knife down long enough to pat Jill's hand. "Reagan's been a big help, and some of the guys are coming to meet me here this morning."

"Okay." Jill stepped back and motioned to the refrigerator. "I made some chicken salad last night, and there are still some cookies in the cookie jar."

Her tone changed a little when she added, "Make sure there are some cookies left when I get home."

"I won't let Reagan eat them all," Doug said without missing a beat.

Reagan stepped forward. She thought he might be joking, but she wasn't sure. She saw the humor in Jill's eyes when Jill turned and saw her, and Reagan let herself say what she was thinking. "You do know that Doug's the one who eats all of the cookies, right?"

Jill gave her a knowing look. "Of that I have little doubt."

"The problem with being the only man in the house is that I'm outnumbered," Doug said.

"You love it, and you know it." Jill reached up and kissed him. "I'll see you both tonight."

Reagan felt that familiar warm glow move through her when Jill gave her a quick hug before collecting her things and heading out the door.

"Since you told on me, I guess it's your turn to clean the kitchen."

"It was my turn yesterday," Reagan retorted.

"Yeah, but I'm older." Doug took a step toward the living room and then turned back to give her a wicked grin. "And make sure you don't eat all of the cookies."

Reagan fought back the grin trying to form. Barely.

* * *

"Thanks for meeting me here," Doug said the moment his boss, Max Barnett, walked into Doug's living room, followed by Hector. "I'm still leery of going into the office until Laith Mansour and his buddies are in custody."

"Where's the girl now?"

"In her room," Doug said. "Were you able to convince DoD to cancel or relocate their event?"

Max shook his head. "I don't know exactly what's going on at this thing, but I get the impression that there's more to it than meets the eye."

"What do you mean?"

"The contact name and number were a front. The woman didn't know any details other than that she needed to make some basic arrangements with the hotel," Max told him. "According to the hotel manager, a large block of rooms was reserved, but there wasn't any link established between it and the banquet hall reservation."

"That's odd," Doug agreed. "What do you think is going on?"

"I don't know. Maybe it's really CIA or DIA holding something. Until we figure it out, we can't talk to the people in charge, much less warn them."

"I'll see if I can work on that angle." Doug led them into the kitchen, where the sketch Reagan had helped him create was laid out on the table.

"What's this?"

"Reagan told me Laith kept a project board in his cabin. This is what we've been able to reproduce from what she remembers." The sketch Reagan had originally drawn had been crude, but it had given him enough details for them to create something a little more usable.

"Is this supposed to be the hotel here?"

"Yeah." Doug nodded. "From what I've been able to piece together, Reagan was going to deliver a bomb disguised as a delivery for the conference in the hotel. It would likely have been disguised as a floral arrangement or a box of educational materials."

"What are these four guns supposed to represent?" Max pointed at the sketches of weapons that were located on the paths near the two main entrances into the hotel.

"Shooters."

"You think we have four shooters?"

"We think so now that we have Wendall in custody."

"Then why would they need a whole case of weapons?"

"Reagan said their costumes all had hidden pockets sewn inside of them."

"She thinks they were going to hide extra guns there?"

"There and maybe in and around the hotel." Doug nodded. "With the anime convention starting on Friday, I think they'll probably try to stash several around the grounds. It's possible they might have even planned to rent a room so they could have direct access on the inside."

"Then we could have even more shooters than the ones shown here on the outside."

"I asked Reagan how many people she could remember coming in and out of Laith's cabin. She recognized Wendall, the guy who was looking for her at the mall. Then there was Laith, the colonel, and two others."

"That gives us four who still aren't in custody," Hector commented. "Even knowing where they're planning on positioning themselves, this isn't going to be easy."

"Reagan has been working with a sketch artist. We're trying to use the composite sketches to help us ID the man she calls the colonel, along with the other two men."

"We're running out of time. The anime convention starts in two days," Hector said. "And the vendors will start setting up tomorrow."

"I've got some undercover agents working at the convention center, hoping to find these guys before Saturday," Max told him.

"I don't know how we're going to find them, especially since they'll be in costume."

"I can find them." The voice came from the doorway.

"Reagan." Doug looked at Max apologetically before speaking to her. "I told you to stay in your room while I was in my meeting."

"I can find them," she repeated. Her eyes were dark and determined. "I can help you stop Laith and his friends before they shoot people."

Max looked over at Doug, clearly considering the possibilities. "You know, she is the only one who has seen the costumes, and she's more likely than any of us to recognize these guys from a distance since she's seen them before."

Doug shook his head. "It's too dangerous."

"Doug, if we don't find these guys before Saturday, we may not have a choice. We can't sit by and watch a mass shooting take place, not without using every available resource to stop it."

Doug knew Max's words were true. Hadn't he agreed to take Reagan into his home as much to gain information as to protect her? He looked over at her now. She was no longer the terrified stranger who had appeared at their cabin, nor was she simply an informant who needed to be kept safe. Something had changed over the past few weeks, something that left worry churning through him at the thought of putting her in harm's way.

A sense of panic rippled through him, but he nodded. "Just understand, having Reagan there is our last resort."

Max's eyes met his. "Agreed."

CHAPTER 11

Doug didn't waste any time following their few remaining leads. Max and Hector were barely out the door before Doug made a quick phone call. Call waiting beeped, and he saw that the bishop was calling again. This was at least the fourth time in the past couple of weeks that he had called their house. Not able to deal with whatever he might want at the moment, Doug finished up on the phone and ushered Reagan out to the car.

"Where are we going?" Reagan asked, pulling on the hooded sweatshirt Doug had insisted she take with her to ward off the cool weather.

"The Whitmores' house."

Reagan's eyebrows drew together. "How come?"

"Because I think the senator can help me piece together some of the information we're still missing."

"Why would the senator know anything about Laith?"

"He wouldn't, but he might know about Bluebird. Or he might know how we can find out about it." Doug climbed into the car and waited for Reagan to take her seat beside him. After reminding her to fasten her seat belt, something he still hadn't managed to drum into her head, he put the car into gear and started toward Great Falls.

When they knocked on the Whitmores' front door, it was Katherine rather than the senator who answered.

"What perfect timing," Katherine said with a smile. "I was just going to go out for a little ride. Any chance Reagan has time to come with me?"

Reagan's eyes lit up with both wonder and a hint of trepidation. "Me? Ride a horse?"

"Absolutely. My daughter's horse would love to get out of the pasture for a while." Katherine shifted her attention to Doug. "Is that okay with you? Jim seemed to think that the two of you might need a while to talk."

Doug could tell by the expression on Reagan's face that this would be a new experience for her. "Reagan, do you want to learn how to ride?"

She hesitated for only a moment. Then she nodded.

"Okay, then. Just be careful."

"I'll take good care of her," Katherine promised, motioning for both of them to come inside. She waved toward the study to their right. "Jim is in his office. You can go on in."

"Thanks." Doug watched Katherine lead Reagan toward the back door before he crossed to Jim's office and knocked.

Jim looked up from the papers spread out on his desk. "Come in."

"Thanks for seeing me on such short notice."

"It sounded important."

"I think it is." Doug nodded. "I'm hoping you can shake loose some information. This thing with Reagan has led us to a roadblock of red tape, and we don't have a lot of time to untangle it."

"In that case, tell me what you know, and we'll see what I can do."

* * *

Reagan fetched pads and saddles and bridles, carrying whatever gear Katherine needed but not daring to get too close to the horses. Once Katherine had both of their horses saddled, Reagan followed Katherine's directions, standing on the left side of the horse and placing her foot in the stirrup. Awkwardly, she swung herself up into the saddle, grabbing on to the saddle horn for balance when the animal beneath her sidestepped.

"It's okay." Katherine's voice was soothing, and she patted the horse on the neck. "Here you go. Sit up straight in the saddle, and hold on to the reins."

Reagan took the leather straps Katherine handed her, not sure she was ready to try this without someone right by her side. But before she could protest, Katherine swung herself into her saddle and nudged her horse so she was right beside Reagan's mount.

Very patiently, Katherine instructed her, slowly walking with her around the pasture, teaching her the basics of riding and how to steer and stop her horse.

She was just starting to get the hang of it when Doug and the senator appeared. The senator waved at his wife, and she guided her horse to the fence, where he was waiting for her.

"Doug and I have to go to a meeting. Is it okay if Reagan stays here with you?"

"Absolutely. I think she's about ready to hit the trail."

"Okay." The senator stepped back. "Have fun."

Doug offered Reagan a wave before disappearing back down the path toward the house.

"What do you mean 'hit the trail'?"

"I mean you know enough that you're ready to leave the pasture and go out for a trail ride." Katherine gave her a look of confidence and challenge. "Are you ready?"

Reagan's heartbeat quickened. "Do you really think I can do this?"

"Absolutely." Katherine gave her a definite nod. "And I'll be right there with you."

Anxiety and anticipation twined together and spurted through Reagan as one emotion. She took a deep breath. "Okay. Let's go."

* * *

Doug followed the senator and their escort through CIA security. He was both relieved and concerned that Jim had identified the agency overseeing Bluebird—relieved because he now knew who had the answers he was looking for and concerned that the CIA project manager might resist giving him those answers.

The fact that they had to come to CIA headquarters instead of talking over a secure line cemented the fact that this was a highly classified project, one the CIA had clearly gone to great lengths to protect.

They were shown to an elevator and then taken to a reception area in the original headquarters building. After a couple of minutes, the secretary showed them into a private office.

A man who looked to be around fifty stood and circled his desk to offer his hand to the senator. "Senator Whitmore, I'm Simon Keaton. I appreciate your coming in to meet with me."

"Thanks for fitting us into your schedule," Jim said and motioned to Doug. "This is Doug Valdez from the FBI."

"Please, sit down." Simon moved back to take his seat behind his desk while Jim and Doug lowered themselves into the chairs across from him. "I understand you were inquiring about Bluebird."

"That's right." Doug nodded. "We have reason to believe this project may be the target of a potential terrorist attack."

"There must be some mistake." Simon shook his head. "Besides being highly classified, this project isn't likely to be of high value for a potential terrorist."

"The fact that we're aware of the project proves that the secret is already out," Jim said before Doug could demand that they share information.

Simon acknowledged that with a nod. "Just understand that what I tell you here can't be shared with anyone unless they are cleared by this agency."

"I understand," Doug said.

"For some time, the military has become increasingly concerned with individuals within their ranks trying to breed dissidence in the name of religion."

"You're talking about Jihadist extremists."

"Yes. The Fort Hood shooting proved that the military's concerns were warranted," he said. "This agency has been involved in a joint operation to try to identify any individuals who are communicating with terrorists overseas."

"What does Bluebird stand for?"

"Bluebird is an undercover operative the military planted within those ranks. He is a practicing Muslim, one who has served this country diligently. Three years ago, he informed his superiors that a member of his unit tried to recruit him in helping with their movement, one that encourages violence against anyone who doesn't share their beliefs."

"Bluebird is the code name for him?"

"That's right."

Doug turned this latest piece of information over in his mind, trying to fit this piece of the puzzle in with everything Reagan had told him. "By any chance, is he involved in some meeting this Saturday night in Arlington?"

Simon's face paled. "How could you know that?"

"Because I have been working on the threat assessment of a suspected attack, likely a mass shooting on Saturday at a hotel in Crystal City," Doug told him. "We believe that the shooters are going to use an anime convention as cover so they won't be noticed carrying around weapons."

"The convention is exactly the reason we chose this location. We knew it would be an easy way to put our people in disguise without anyone being suspicious." Simon shook his head. "What else do you know?"

"Our information suggests that one of the men involved is a marine sergeant, and at least one other is a civilian."

Simon stood and moved to where a heavy black filing cabinet was located in the corner of the room. He pulled open the second drawer and retrieved a file. He then flipped it open, perused the contents for a moment, and plucked out three photographs.

"Do any of these match the description of the sergeant you're looking for?"

Doug took the photographs from him and studied the top one. He shook his head and then flipped it over. Although he hadn't ever seen the man, the face staring back at him fit the composite the sketch artist had done from Reagan's description.

"This could be him. I'd have to show it to my witness to be sure." Doug checked the third photo, now convinced that the second one was likely their man. "Who is he?"

"Rafi Abba. He's assigned to a unit out of Camp Pendleton, but he's been working here in the DC area for the past three years. He's the man who tried to recruit Bluebird."

"Somehow, he knows Bluebird is feeding you information."

"How did you find out about Bluebird? Who is your witness?"

"A thirteen-year-old girl named Reagan. Her stepfather is Laith Mansour. From what Reagan has told us, it sounds like Mansour is not only Abba's accomplice but is likely one of the masterminds behind the attack."

"Are you sure you can trust her?" Simon asked skeptically.

"She doesn't have any reason to lie," Doug said, instantly defensive. "They were planning on using her to deliver a bomb to the hotel. When she refused, they tried to kill her."

"Where is she now?"

"I have her in protective custody." Doug held up the photo again. "Can I get a copy to show her? If you want, you can even do a lineup sheet."

"That won't be necessary. I don't think any of us doubt that this is the man behind the planned attack." He shook his head. "The question is how do we proceed? Since we're talking about a threat on US soil, obviously, the FBI will take the lead, but I do want my people involved."

"With this happening in three days, we can use the help," Doug said.

"In that case, let's compare notes and figure out how we can stop this thing."

CHAPTER 12

Jill walked into her bedroom and found Doug sitting up in bed, a notepad in one hand, a pen in the other, and a scatter of notes on his lap and bedside table. "I thought you said you weren't going to bring your work to bed with you anymore."

"I'm not." Doug glanced up at her. "As soon as this case is over."

"Do you want to talk about it?"

Rather than answer her, he asked, "How was Young Women's? Did Reagan have fun?"

"She did." Jill kicked her shoes off. "Jasmine has been really sweet to make sure Reagan is included, and the other girls seem to be pretty accepting of her. It's nice to see."

Doug looked at her suspiciously. "You sound like you're getting pretty attached."

Jill turned to face him, her eyebrows lifting. "Aren't you?"

"What do you mean?"

"I mean, you take her out shooting nearly every day, and you spend all day with her."

"Yeah, because she's our main source of information on the people trying to create terror two days from now," Doug said edgily.

Jill ignored his defensive tone. "It may have started out that way, but you can't fool me. You care about Reagan, and not just because of what she knows about your case."

"Of course I care. She's a good kid." His shoulder jerked up. "But that doesn't mean I'm ready to parent a teenage girl."

"I think you already are," Jill said. She dressed for bed and climbed in next to him. "What's going on with this case? Can you talk to me about it?"

"I can't tell you much. This case took a turn I hadn't expected." He seemed to consider for a moment. Then he laid his notebook down and sighed. "It looks like the whole bombing and mass shooting is really a front. We think Laith and the colonel are going after a specific target. We know who the target is now, and we can keep him safe without these guys knowing we're onto them. We fully expect they'll go forward with their plans."

"You still haven't found Laith?"

Doug shook his head. "He hasn't been seen since the day Reagan ran away from him."

Jill put a hand on Doug's arm and said sympathetically, "You're worried."

"If we can't find these guys before Saturday, Max wants me to bring Reagan up to our temporary control center so she can help us try to identify the players."

"You can't let them take Reagan up there." Jill sat up in bed and shifted to face him more fully. "If Laith or the colonel finds her, they'll try to kill her."

"I know." Doug let out a frustrated sigh. "We'll take every precaution, but Max is right. She may be the only person who can help us find the men we haven't yet identified."

"I don't like it." Jill shook her head. "She's finally starting to feel safe. I don't know if she can handle facing these men again, even if she only has to see them on video."

"I agree, but she volunteered."

Jill's jaw dropped. "What?"

"She's determined to stop them." His statement held pride. "Like I said, she's a good kid. We just have to pray we can find these guys before they have a chance to strike. That way she won't have to face all of these demons from her past."

"I've definitely got the praying part covered."

"I figured you did." Doug leaned forward and pressed his lips to Jill's. "I love you, you know."

"Yeah, I know." Jill reached for his hand and gave it a squeeze. "And I think you love your new daughter too."

Doug shook his head. "Jill, don't do that. I'm not ready to think about what happens next, not until we get through this weekend."

"Just promise me you'll consider letting Reagan stay," Jill said, a flutter of excitement rippling through her. "I'm starting to think that maybe she's one of the answers to our prayers."

"You seem to have forgotten that we weren't exactly praying for the same things before Reagan showed up."

"We're praying for the same things now," Jill said softly. "Please at least promise you'll think about it."

"I'll think about it." Doug's eyes met hers. "Later."

* * *

Reagan heard the doorbell, followed by Doug's footsteps heading for the entryway. Quietly, she slipped out of her bedroom and made her way to her usual spot in the hall so she could hear what was going on. She hated not knowing what was happening, and she suspected something had changed yesterday when she hadn't been around.

Doug's stress level had been steadily rising for the past week, but his meeting with the senator yesterday afternoon seemed to have left him even more on edge. She had been so focused on her ride with Katherine and the new books Katherine had sent home with her that she hadn't noticed the extra tension until they'd started their drive home. Then the silence had been nearly unbearable.

Reagan had even dared to ask Doug if something was wrong, but he had just said he had a lot on his mind. That had ended the conversation.

She had to admit that she had been relieved to get out of the house with Jill last night for the Church activity. It was nice spending that hour or two pretending her life was normal, pretending she didn't know what was about to happen.

Before she had gone with Jill the first time, Doug had made her promise that she wouldn't talk about what she knew with anyone. Not that she would anyway. After all, who would believe her? She was still amazed that Doug and Jill believed everything she had told them, that they trusted her to tell the truth.

She recognized the lowered voices now, both Doug's and Hector's. She edged closer to the doorway.

She had a feeling Doug knew she was always listening, but he hadn't ever told her to stop. Besides, she wanted to make sure she didn't miss anything.

"We're all set," Hector told Doug. "We have two rooms in the hotel where the shooting is expected to take place. One is on the second floor just up the stairs from the banquet hall. It's one of the rooms the CIA had reserved for Bluebird. If anyone comes looking for him there, our agents will be ready."

"And the second room?"

"Because of the anime convention, the only other room we could get was the presidential suite. That's where we'll be setting up our taskforce headquarters."

"Are the surveillance vans in place?" Doug asked.

"Yeah. We have one disguised as a maid service van inside the parking garage near the elevator. Then we have two more at opposite corners of the building. The imagery is feeding up to the equipment in the presidential suite," Hector told him. "We also have agents interspersed throughout a two-block radius to keep an eye out for any of our suspects."

"What about Bluebird?"

"The CIA wanted to put him in a safe house, but he refused. He said he wants to be there to help identify these guys. He's already moved into our hotel suite, and he'll stay there until we get through this."

"That's gutsy," Doug commented. "I would have thought he'd want to stay out of the line of fire, especially since we think he's the real target."

"I thought so too, but this guy is determined to help us stop this attack before anyone gets hurt. Besides, no one will know he's there. If anyone looks for him, they'll go to the room on the second floor, where we have people waiting for them."

"Still no sign of any of our suspects?"

"Not yet. If we're right, they'll show up sometime today. The vendors have already started setting up, but so far, we haven't seen anyone in costume," Hector told him. "According to the event coordinator, attendees can start picking up their passes at seven o'clock tonight. The lines for the actual event usually start up around four in the morning."

"Great," Doug muttered. Reagan could hear him shuffling papers before he continued. "According to the CIA, the Bluebird meeting was scheduled for seven o'clock on Saturday night, and it was expected to last for several hours." He paused for a moment again, and Reagan strained to hear to make sure she wasn't missing something. Then she heard Doug's voice again. "Logically, these guys would make their move a little after the meeting is scheduled to start. That way they'd be sure Bluebird is already there."

"I agree. They would also have an easy time blending in around then since that's dinnertime and plenty of the convention goers will be walking around town, going out for something to eat," Hector said. "We have our undercover guys in place with the hotel staff. No one besides our agents and the hotel manager will have access to the conference room, so we'll know if they try to plant any kind of explosives."

"Have our guys already done an initial sweep to make sure something isn't already planted there?"

"They should be finishing that up now," Hector told him. "Are you ready to head up there? Max wants you on scene."

"Let me call Jill. I'll see if she can get a substitute teacher so she can take off the rest of today. I don't want to leave Reagan here alone."

"Okay. Let me know if you have a problem. Otherwise, I'll see you over there in an hour or so."

Reagan heard the two men walk to the front door. Then she heard Doug walking back toward the kitchen.

"Reagan, you can come out now."

She froze, not prepared to go out and face Doug and the truth that she had been spying on him. Mustering her courage, she emerged from the hall and gave him a sheepish look.

Doug just stared at her, his eyebrows lifted in that cocky look of his. "I'm assuming you heard all of that so I don't need to tell you what's going on."

"Why can't I come with you today?" she asked. "I might be able to help."

"Honestly, I'm hoping we can find these guys before Saturday so you won't have to go to the hotel at all." Doug picked the house phone up off of the kitchen counter. "This isn't fun and games. It can be dangerous."

"I know that," Reagan said, even though she didn't want to think about that part. She just wanted to stay with Doug, where she felt safe. "But I want to help."

"You can help by staying where I know you're safe." Before she could object further, Doug said, "One of the reasons I'm going to Crystal City today is to check out the layout of the hotel to make sure we can get you inside without putting you in danger."

Resigned, she watched Doug call Jill and listened to him work out the logistics of how soon Jill could come home. As soon as he hung up, Reagan said, "You're going to be careful, right?"

He reached over and gave her arm a squeeze. "Kiddo, I'm always careful."

She took a deep breath and let it out. "I was just checking."

CHAPTER 13

"Zoom in on that guy." Doug pointed at the computer screen, where the surveillance video was visible. The man known only as Bluebird stood beside him, watching the screen as well.

Aaron Lithcombe, the computer tech, did as he was asked, zooming in on the image Doug indicated. Before Doug could comment, Bluebird shook his head. "That's not one of them. He's too short."

Doug shifted his attention to the bulletin board situated on an easel in the corner of the room. On it were four sets of images. Using the composite sketches that had been created with Reagan's help, the CIA and Bluebird had identified the remaining suspects.

Except for Laith, all three of the other suspects were currently serving in the military. One of them, Ferran Sarabi, was naval intelligence and had been involved in supporting Bluebird in his intelligence gathering efforts. No one was quite sure if he had already been involved with Jihadist extremists when he'd started with the operation or if he had been converted sometime in the past couple of years and then had started feeding information to Laith and his co-conspirators. Regardless, they were quite certain he was the source of the leak.

"Wait. Back that one up," Bluebird said, his voice taking on a sense of urgency.

Doug turned and looked at the screen. The tall man walking along the sidewalk was dressed in some sort of dark-colored robe, making him look like a cross between the grim reaper and cartoon royalty. Doug's focus narrowed when he saw the thick staff gripped in his right hand. "That prop is long enough and thick enough to hide a weapon, but with his mask on, there's no way to be sure who he is."

Bluebird nodded. "Look at the way he's walking though. Everyone else is checking out the other costumes, and most of them have those badges for the anime convention hanging around their necks."

"Our guy doesn't have one." A sense of anticipation hummed through him.

Aaron zoomed in on the man's staff. "He could just be going to the costume party down the street. We know there's one at the Hyatt tonight."

Doug shook his head. "He looks like he's checking out the area rather than the people."

Aaron shifted in his seat to look at Doug. "Do you want me to have one of our units pick him up?"

Bluebird shook his head before Doug could respond. "If we pick him up and the others notice, there's no telling what they might do. We need to bring him in without them realizing we're onto them."

Doug agreed with his logic, but he was also anxious to put this guy in custody, where they could be sure he wasn't a danger to anyone. The last thing he wanted was for this investigation to stretch out another night. If they couldn't identify all of the players tonight, he knew Reagan would end up sitting here with him tomorrow. "Do you have any suggestions?"

"I bet we could come up with something." Bluebird nodded.

Doug noticed someone stop a girl dressed as Pikachu and then point down the street. "I think I have an idea." He looked at Aaron. "Have our guys track him, and tell Hector I need him up here. We'll need a few minutes."

"Okay. You got it."

* * *

"I look ridiculous." Hector gave Doug a pleading look from beneath a wide-brimmed straw hat. "Please tell me I don't have to go out in public like this."

Doug fought back a grin as Alicia, another one of their agents, leaned down to cuff the bright blue pants of the anime costume she had prepared for just such an emergency. The red shirt wouldn't have been so bad, but set against the bright yellow sash tied around Hector's waist, it made him look like he could have stepped out of a pirate cartoon.

Alicia stood. "Stop whining," she said, stepping back to admire her handiwork. She glanced over at Doug. "I think that's as good as it's going to get."

"Why do I have to be in costume?"

"Because." Doug didn't offer any explanation beyond the single word. "Are you ready?"

Hector let out a long-suffering sigh. "Let's get this over with."

"Okay." Doug looked over at Alicia and asked, "You know what to do?"

"I've got this." She nodded and held up her hand to show a miniature tranquilizer dart fastened to the palm of her glove. She moved toward the hotel room door. "Come on, Hector. Let's see how convincing you can be."

Hector followed her but turned and looked at Doug before opening the door. "Just know, you are going to pay for this."

"Have fun, kids," Doug said sarcastically. He watched them leave, ignoring the exasperated look Hector shot his way, and then shifted to stand beside Bluebird to watch the current images. "Do we still have our guy in sight?"

"Yeah. He walked by our hotel, and now it looks like he's circling around again." Aaron looked up at Doug. "Maybe this guy really is just someone who's lost."

"Where's his staff?"

"What?" Aaron zoomed in to reveal that the character in question was no longer carrying any props. "He must have stashed it somewhere."

"He really could be involved. We figured these guys might use today to plant weapons in preparation for tomorrow."

"Hector is asking whether you want them to proceed," Aaron said.

Doug looked over at Bluebird, seeing the same determination in his eyes that he was sure his own mirrored. "Proceed."

Two minutes later, Alicia appeared on the edge of the screen when she took her position several yards behind their suspect. Then Hector stepped into their suspect's path. The robed figure tried to step around him, shaking his head when Hector spoke to him. Even on the screen, Doug could sense the man's nervousness, an emotional overreaction to someone asking for simple directions.

As planned, Hector blocked his path and continued to try to engage him. He succeeded in slowing him down long enough for Alicia to close the distance between them. When she was only a few feet away, she appeared to stumble and slap a hand on their suspect to keep her balance. The tranquilizer dart hidden on her glove did its job, and a few seconds later, the man fell to the ground.

* * *

"You can't let her go with you." Jill crossed her arms and straightened her shoulders. "Doug, it's too dangerous."

"You think I'm happy about this?" Doug's voice took on an edge. "I don't have a choice. We only managed to identify one suspect yesterday, and he's not talking. That leaves three more unaccounted for, three more people who pose a serious threat."

Jill's chest tightened. She understood that Reagan had come to live with them because of the past she had suffered, because she knew things these potential gunmen didn't want her to know. But that logic paled behind Jill's protective instincts and her overwhelming desire to keep Reagan close. "She's just a kid."

"No, Jill. She's not just a kid. She's the girl who might just be able to stop a mass shooting before anyone gets hurt." Doug raked both hands through his short, dark hair. "I don't like this any more than you do. If there were another way, I'd jump at it. Unfortunately, I don't have a choice in the matter. Max said I have to bring her in."

She recognized the weariness of Doug's gesture and realized he was as conflicted as she was. Jill also knew her concerns weren't just for Reagan but for Doug as well. For their entire marriage, she had faced the reality that someday Doug might walk out of their house and never come home again. She tried not to think about it, but today, she couldn't stop the worst-case scenarios from racing through her mind. Today, she had so much more to lose.

Biting back the swirl of emotions, she wrapped her arms around his waist. "I'm scared."

"I know." Doug pulled her close, and Jill suspected his emotions were in as much upheaval as her own. "I'll keep her safe."

"Keep yourself safe too."

"I will." He edged back and looked down at her. "I'll call you as soon as we're on our way home."

Jill clung to his waist, not quite ready to let him go. Doug indulged her, keeping his arms around her while a minute stretched into two. Then she tipped her head back, reached up, and kissed him. The kiss was meant to soothe, but she could feel a tangle of underlying emotions swirling through both of them.

When she pulled back, she reached down and squeezed his hand. "I'll be praying for you tonight."

"I appreciate that," Doug said. "I'll take all the help I can get."

CHAPTER 14

"I don't like this," Doug said, worry curling uncomfortably in his stomach. He had done what his boss had demanded and brought Reagan into FBI headquarters to prepare for the stakeout this afternoon. Reagan had told him Laith was planning to strike on a Saturday night, but he never imagined she would end up personally involved in helping prevent it. Unfortunately, with every minute that passed, he felt more pressed to shield Reagan from anything that might put her in danger.

Max gave him a knowing look. "None of us are thrilled that we weren't able to stop this before now."

"There's got to be a way we can do this without Reagan there. She should be home, where she's safe."

"She doesn't have a home," Max reminded him. "And she isn't going to be safe until Laith and his co-conspirators are in custody."

Doug instantly thought of Reagan's bedroom in his home, of the jacket hanging on her doorknob, the shoes on the floor, and books on her bedside table. For the first few days after she'd arrived, he might have still considered that room a guest room, but somewhere along the line, it had become Reagan's room, and his home had become Reagan's home.

Max must have sensed the turmoil and concern swirling inside him because his tone held understanding when he continued. "Doug, you know as well as I do that we need her. There's no way we're going to be able to identify these guys without her. She's seen all of the players, and she knows what the costumes look like. She's our best chance of stopping this thing before it turns deadly."

"It's possible they changed the costumes after Reagan ran away."

"Which is even more reason that she might be the only one to recognize them."

Even though his protective instincts urged him to protest further, he knew Max's words were true. He gave a resigned nod. "I know you're right." He considered for a minute. "I want her to wear a vest though."

"I doubt she'll need it since we'll keep her in the hotel suite, out of sight, but Alicia is taking care of it. We're taking every precaution we can think of."

"I still don't like it."

"None of us do." Max gestured toward the door.

Doug turned to see Alicia leading Reagan into the room. He wouldn't have recognized her had he not been living with her for the past few weeks. Alicia had outfitted her with a costume to help disguise her in case Laith or his friends caught a glimpse of her. She wore dark pants and a white dress shirt, black tie, and teal blazer. Her hair was tucked up under a short black wig.

He tried to fight the unsettled feeling that wouldn't go away. "Are you all set?"

Reagan nodded. She was good at hiding her emotions, and he could tell she was trying hard to keep everyone from seeing her fear. But he saw it.

"You don't have to do this, you know."

"Yeah, I do." She drew a deep breath and gave him a long, level look. "You said yourself that I'm your best chance of finding these guys."

Doug put a hand on her shoulder and gave her a reassuring squeeze. "This will all be over soon."

"Let's get this show on the road," Max said.

* * *

"We're almost there. Keep an eye out for anyone who looks familiar," Doug said as they passed the Pentagon City mall.

Reagan looked over at him, noting that he was wearing the clothes he normally wore to church. "How come you aren't in costume?"

"I'll be staying up in the command center with you, so I don't really need to blend in with the street scene."

"Yeah, but Laith might recognize you." A flash of concern sounded in her voice. "You did shoot at him."

"I doubt he would be able to pick me out of a crowd. He never got close enough to get a good look at me, just like I barely saw him through the trees."

"I guess." Reagan stared out the window, noticing the Halloween decorations on the various homes and businesses they passed. A fake graveyard had been set up in one yard, complete with creepy figures hanging from the tree behind it. Another yard had jack-o-lanterns lining the sidewalk, the odd-shaped faces flickering with candlelight.

Doug turned another corner, and suddenly, the sidewalks seemed flooded with people in costume.

Six teenagers dressed up like anime characters crowded the sidewalk as they spoke excitedly. A couple in their early twenties dressed as some kind of samurais tried to push past them.

Two more people dressed as Star Wars characters, complete with masks, posed outside a restaurant while someone snapped a picture of them.

"This isn't going to be easy," Doug muttered, but Reagan couldn't tell if he was talking to her or to himself.

"How are we supposed to find them with all of these people around?" Reagan asked.

"We have surveillance vans around the hotel, and we're tapped into the hotel security cameras. You'll have a lot of video feed to look at in the hotel room, but you won't be the only one searching."

"I just want this over with so we can go home," Reagan admitted.

"That makes two of us," Doug agreed. He drove slowly as they passed the parade of pedestrians. He stopped at a red light, and Reagan continued to stare out the window, overwhelmed by the crowds.

"Anything?" Doug asked.

"I don't think so."

Doug's phone rang, and he hit the button to put the call on speaker. "Valdez."

"Doug, we've spotted one of the suspects. Ferran Sarabi is dressed up like a ninja, and he's a half block from the hotel."

"We're only three blocks away."

"Sarabi is near the front entrance. If you drive around the back of the hotel to get to the parking garage, you'll miss the action."

"Got it." Doug turned on his blinker to make a right turn. "Call me back when you have him in custody."

"Will do."

Doug ended the call and gave Reagan a hopeful look. "That's one down. Only two more."

"Laith and the colonel," Reagan said, stating the obvious.

"Yeah." Doug nodded. "Laith and the colonel."

* * *

Doug shook his head in frustration. Dozens of federal agents littered the area, and somehow, their suspect had managed to escape them.

"They're still in pursuit," Max said as Doug pulled into a parking spot three rows away from the elevators leading to the hotel. "Is Alicia with you?"

"She just pulled in behind me."

"Let her know what's going on. I'll get back to you as soon as I know anything."

Doug turned off the engine and climbed out of the car. Reagan followed suit and stood awkwardly while Alicia parked beside them and then approached Doug.

"What's going on?"

"Our guys spotted one of the suspects, and they're in pursuit," Doug told her. "Can you take Reagan upstairs? I'm going to make sure no one followed us here."

"Sure."

Doug nodded at Reagan. "Go with Alicia. I'll be up in a minute."

Wordlessly, Reagan let herself be led through the cars toward the elevators. Doug shifted his attention, alert for any movement. He noticed an older couple heading for their car, the man taking the time to open the door for his wife before circling around to get in.

Doug worked his way along the rows of cars, glancing back when the couple's sedan started toward the exit. That's when he caught a quick blur of movement.

For a second, he thought he'd imagined it, but as he continued staring, he saw it again, along with a flash of color moving toward the elevators, where Alicia and Reagan were now standing.

"Watch out!" Doug shouted just as the man known as the colonel emerged with a gun in his hand.

At the shouted warning, Alicia whirled to face the colonel, but she was still in the motion of drawing her weapon when the colonel struck his hand out and knocked her to the ground.

Reagan screamed, the colonel now turning his gun toward her.

Doug rushed forward, unable to take a shot of his own because of the concrete pillars standing between him and the colonel.

He saw Alicia kick, knocking the colonel to the ground, the colonel's gun skittering across the concrete floor.

Then, to his amazement, Reagan reached down and picked up the weapon, aiming like he'd taught her right at the man who had a moment before been threatening her life.

The elevator doors slid open, and Reagan stumbled back into the open elevator car. Doug couldn't tell if she was trying to escape or just trying to put some distance between her and the man trying to kill her.

Regardless, she continued to aim the gun at the colonel, leaving him frozen in place long enough for Alicia to regain control of her weapon and the suspect.

The elevator doors slid closed before Doug could stop them.

"Go!" Alicia jerked her head toward the stairwell door. "I've got him."

Doug didn't have to be told twice. He pushed the door open and raced up the stairs.

* * *

Reagan would have felt ridiculous standing in the elevator, dressed like a cartoon character, but she was too scared to care at the moment. Every one of her nerves burned inside of her, and she felt like she couldn't even see straight. She didn't realize she was still aiming the gun at the elevator doors until they slid open on the first floor and the two girls dressed like Sailor Moon characters took one look at her and screamed.

Reagan could feel her cheeks flush, and she lowered the gun to her side. The elevator doors started to slide closed, and she instinctively put a hand out to stop them. She didn't know where she should go now, but she was sure she didn't want to go back downstairs to face the colonel.

She looked at the buttons on the elevator, realizing that this one didn't go any higher than the lobby. She could see the bank of elevators just across from her that presumably led upstairs, but she wasn't sure how to get to the suite Doug had told her about, where the FBI was set up.

She could feel tears threatening as emotions bubbled up inside of her—fear, adrenaline, and so many others she couldn't name.

She drew a deep breath and then another. Surely Doug would come find her. He would know that she needed him to keep her safe.

With a great deal of effort, she forced herself to take a step forward and then another. She would wait in the lobby until Doug came. And then everything would be okay.

CHAPTER 15

Doug burst through the stairwell door onto the first floor and raced toward the lobby. Across a wide hallway, he saw Reagan emerge from where he knew the elevators were located. She still clutched a gun in her hand, but her arm was hanging by her side.

His sense of relief lasted only for a heartbeat because as he took in the rest of the scene, he spotted a man in a delivery uniform, a package in one hand. The man would have looked harmless enough if his face hadn't been so familiar. Less than twenty yards away stood the man he had been searching for, the man he had sworn to keep away from Reagan.

Laith Mansour didn't notice him or anyone else in the lobby. He was too busy staring at Reagan, a look of stunned rage on his face.

The next few seconds could have come straight out of Doug's worst nightmare. Laith set the box down on a chair in the lobby, and then his right hand disappeared beneath the jacket he wore.

Doug surged forward when he saw that same hand whip out, a gun now gripped in it. He shouted at the room in general, but his eyes stayed focused on Reagan. "Get down!"

Reagan didn't drop. She simply froze, her eyes wide, the gun gripped in her own hand remaining by her side.

A silent prayer raced through Doug's mind. His hope that the dozen civilians in the lobby would simply drop to the ground and give him a clear shot didn't materialize. Instead, he was faced with a mad chaos as people screamed and scrambled between Laith and him.

Aware that he wouldn't be able to reach Laith in time to prevent a shot, he sprinted toward Reagan. He knew Reagan's vital organs were protected by body armor, but Laith wasn't aiming at her heart. He was aiming at her head.

Laith's shot sounded just as Doug lunged in front of Reagan, one of his arms hooking around her waist so he could pull her to the ground. An instant before they crashed to the floor, his body jerked where a bullet impacted his own bulletproof vest, pain shooting through his chest.

He struggled to lift his weapon to take aim at Laith before he could fire again, but before he could manage it, another shot rang out, and Laith dropped to the ground. Standing a short distance away was a brightly dressed pirate, a straw hat on his head and a gun in his hand.

Hector rushed toward Laith, disarming him and checking for a pulse.

Doug lowered his weapon and let himself lie back on the floor. He turned his head to see Reagan staring at him, her eyes wide, her breathing rapid. Though it pained him to do so, he reached out and grasped her hand. "Are you okay?"

She didn't answer at first, as though her mind was still trying to catch up with what had just happened.

Before Doug could repeat his question, several of his fellow agents rushed into the room. Out of the corner of his eye, Doug noticed the bomb squad enter, their attention solely on the package Laith had been carrying, while other agents began evacuating the civilians. Max was the first to make it through the crowd to where Doug and Reagan were still on the floor. "Where are you hit?"

"I took one in the chest." He winced when he tried to take a deep breath. "It hurts like mad, but I'm okay."

"How about you?" Max asked Reagan. "Are you hurt?"

Reagan looked bewildered now, her eyes shifting from Doug to Max. "He jumped in front of me." The knowledge that Laith had nearly succeeded in killing her was reflected in her eyes. "He got shot for me."

"I'm okay, Reagan." Despite the throbbing in his ribs, Doug forced himself to sit up. "We're both okay now."

Max gave Doug a hand and pulled him up to a stand. He then did the same to Reagan. "The other suspect is in custody. Jerry is taking him in now."

"That's good news," Doug said with relief.

"Is it over?" Reagan asked, her voice teary. "Can we go home now?"

"Yeah." Doug nodded. "We can go home."

* * *

Jill peeked into Reagan's room to see her burrowed in her blankets, her body relaxed in sleep. She still couldn't quite visualize what had happened the night before, not because she hadn't been given the details but rather because the images were so terrifying that she didn't want to let them form.

Doug's boss had insisted he make a stop at the local emergency room before allowing him to come home. Thankfully, he hadn't broken anything, though Jill suspected the bruising and stiffness would bother him for the next week or two.

Reagan whimpered in her sleep and then rolled over, pulling her blanket firmly beneath her chin once more. Jill's heart swelled with love. A mother's love.

She wanted to soothe, to protect. She wanted to help this girl learn how to leave the nightmares behind and find the courage to face the future. Mostly, Jill wanted to be part of that future.

She loved the idea of watching Reagan expand her interests and friendships, of standing on the sidelines of whatever activities she might choose to participate in. Mostly, though, she wanted moments like this one, when she could simply enjoy knowing that she could be part of a child's life.

With a sigh, Jill pulled Reagan's door shut and started down the hall. She hadn't quite figured out how to broach the subject with Doug about adopting Reagan. She knew he wasn't thrilled with the prospect of adoption in general, but surely his feelings had changed over the past few days. She had seen how sensitive he had been to Reagan's needs last night when they'd returned home and the way he'd gotten up every couple hours to make sure she was okay.

Jill walked into the kitchen and started lining up the ingredients she would need to make french toast for breakfast. She was just putting the first pieces on the hot griddle when Doug stumbled into the kitchen, a day's worth of beard shadowing his face, a look of pain in his eyes.

"Did you take any pain meds yet?"

He shook his head. "I wanted to get something in my stomach first."

"This will be ready in a few minutes."

Doug opened the refrigerator and grabbed the orange juice. He poured himself a glass, guzzled it down, and then filled the glass again.

Even though Jill was anxious to talk to Doug about their future with Reagan, she bided her time, waiting until he had a plateful of breakfast in front of him and had downed a couple of his over-the-counter pain pills.

She finished making the french toast, setting some aside for Reagan and fixing herself a plate while waiting for the pain meds to take effect. Then she put her plate on the table and slid into her seat next to Doug. "I want to talk to you about Reagan."

Doug finished chewing the bite in his mouth and gave her a nod. "Yeah, about that."

"Yes?"

"She's been pretty traumatized through this whole ordeal. I don't know that it would be good for her to go into foster care right now."

Hope bloomed inside of Jill. She took a breath and reached over to put her hand on top of Doug's. She waited until his eyes lifted to meet hers before she dared to speak. "Doug, I don't want her to go into foster care. Ever."

He was silent for a moment, his eyes dark and unreadable. Then he drew a deep breath and said, "You want to keep her."

"Yes." Jill squeezed his hand. "I want to keep her."

He stared at Jill for a long moment, but she didn't see resistance in his expression like she had expected. Instead, she saw uncertainty followed by a glimmer of anticipation. The corner of his mouth twitched as though he was trying to keep from smiling, and he tugged on her hand to draw her closer as he stood to face her. "In that case, congratulations, Mrs. Valdez. It's a girl."

"Really?" Her excitement was uncontainable. "You're okay with us adopting Reagan?"

"I am." The smile he had been suppressing broke free, and Jill was amazed to see the elation she felt evident on her husband's face too. "Of course, that's assuming it's what she wants."

Then, to Jill's surprise, Doug turned toward the hallway. "What do you think, Reagan? Are you ready to be an official part of the family?"

Jill looked at him, confused. "She's still sleeping."

"No, she's not." Doug tilted his head toward the hall, a smug look on his face.

To Jill's surprise, Reagan peeked around the corner, her expression caught somewhere between embarrassment and delight.

Jill looked from Reagan to Doug and back again. "You were spying on us?"

"She's pretty good at it," Doug told her before Reagan could respond. "So what do you say? Can we be your new parents?"

"I can be a Valdez?"

"Absolutely." Jill crossed to give her a hug. "Welcome to the family."

The doorbell rang before Reagan could respond, though the delighted wonder on her face said it all. Doug pushed back from the table. "I'll get it."

A moment later, he reappeared with the bishop.

"Bishop Chandler. What brings you by?" Jill asked.

"I wanted a chance to talk to you and Doug before church. I've been wanting to meet with you for the last few weeks, but our schedules haven't lined up."

"Is everything okay?" Jill asked.

"Yes, but I have a calling I want to extend." He looked over at Reagan as though noticing for the first time that she was in the room.

"You remember our daughter, Reagan, right?"

"Your daughter?" The bishop looked from Doug to Jill, confused.

Doug nodded, a hint of a smile evident on his face. "We'll start the official adoption paperwork this week."

"Congratulations." The bishop's shoulders seemed to relax slightly. "In that case, this new calling may work out better with your schedule than I thought." He paused for a moment, focusing on Jill. "Sister Valdez, I would like for you to be our new Young Women president."

"Me?" Jill's eyes widened, and she looked at Doug to gauge his reaction.

Doug held up both hands. "Don't look at me. It's your decision."

She looked back at Bishop Chandler. "Are you sure about this?"

"There are only a few times when I've been absolutely certain about who should be in a calling," the bishop told her. "This is one of those times."

Somewhat bewildered and clearly overwhelmed, she looked at Doug once more. He shrugged and said, "I'll support whatever you decide, but I'm sure you would do a great job."

Then Reagan stepped forward. Her words were tentative, but there was a smile on her face. "Don't worry, Mom. I'll help you out."

Jill blinked back the tears that welled up in her eyes. Her heart bursting with joy, she reached out and pulled Reagan into a hug. Offering the bishop a watery smile, she said simply, "In that case, we accept."

SECRETS OF ST. AUGUSTINE

CHAPTER 1

Layla stood on the terrace of her dorm room as excited chatter carried on the air from the sidewalk and parking lot below. Greetings were exchanged in both French and English. Parents kissed their children's cheeks before enveloping them in hugs. Chauffeurs and valets loaded designer suitcases into the trunks of limousines and other cars designed to show off wealth: Rolls Royce, Ferrari, Bugatti, Porsche, Mercedes, Lamborghini, Aston Martin. The scene could have been used as the backdrop of an ad for luxury automobiles.

Layla scanned the long driveway that skirted the edge of the golf course. The black Bentley her grandmother favored wouldn't be coming today.

It never came.

Anna-Lise bounded into the room, her ponytail swinging behind her. "Are you sure you can't come with me?"

"I wish."

Anna-Lise had invited her to join her and her parents for their trip to Washington, DC, but not once since her grandmother dropped her off at boarding school six years ago had she been allowed to leave France.

"Why did your grand-mère say no? She wouldn't have had to pay for anything."

"I have no idea. Monsieur Auclair didn't say. He only said she told him I couldn't go," Layla said, referring to the headmaster. "It's not like she can't afford it even if your parents didn't offer to pay."

"Did you at least talk to her?"

"I haven't talked to her since last Christmas."

"I can't believe she didn't call you for your birthday." Anna-Lise stuffed her iPad into her newest Chanel bag. "Becoming a teenager is a big deal."

"For all I know, she did call. Monsieur Auclair took my phone right before that." She rolled her eyes. "Happy birthday to me."

"I still don't get why he took it away in the first place."

Layla's offense had been nothing more than using the calculator on her phone during algebra when the battery had died on her school-issued one. The minor infraction had snowballed into a crime she still didn't understand. "You'd think after three weeks he would let me have it back."

"Here. Take this." Anna-Lise fished her cell phone out of her purse. "We're staying in Marseille tonight. Call your grand-mère and see if she'll change her mind. If she says you can go with me, we can pick you up."

"I can't take your phone."

"Sure you can. The internet still isn't fixed in our building, and the computer lab has so many restrictions, you can barely do anything on those computers." Anna-Lise pressed the phone into Layla's hand. "Even if you can't come with me, you don't want to be cut off from everything for all of spring break."

"Monsieur Auclair said the internet is supposed to be fixed any day now."

"He's been saying that for almost a month." Anna-Lise nodded at the phone. "Keep that. Papa can buy me a new one."

Anna-Lise's mom appeared in the doorway. "Honey, it's time to go."

"I'm coming."

Madame Dubois picked up Anna-Lise's suitcase. "I'll take this down to the car."

"Thanks, Mom. I'll be right there." Anna-Lise kissed both of Layla's cheeks. "Call or text my mom's phone if your grand-mère changes her mind."

"I will."

Anna-Lise hurried after her mother, and Layla looked down at the phone in her hand. Might as well call Grand-mère now. If she agreed, maybe Layla could catch Anna-Lise before she left.

Layla dialed her grandmother's villa in Switzerland, the same house her father had grown up in. An irritating beep came over the line, followed by an error message that the number was no longer in service. She dialed the number again with the same results.

Even though she was sure she had the number right, she retrieved the address book that had once belonged to her mother. She looked up her grandmother's number and called a third time. When the irritating beep rang in her ear again, she hung up. What was going on? Why wasn't the number working? Had it been changed without her being told? Surely, her grandmother hadn't sold the family home. Even when she was little, Layla remembered

Grand-mère speaking of the history of their ancestral home and how it had been in the family for generations.

Layla hung up and tried again, this time dialing her grandmother's cell phone, complete with the US country code. A man answered on the third ring.

She hesitated at the unfamiliar voice and the English greeting.

"Hello?" he said again.

"*Bonjour*," Layla said, relying on Madame Poirot's etiquette classes. "*Puis-je parler à Genevieve de Felice?*"

"What?" he asked. "I don't understand."

Had her grandmother hired a new assistant who didn't speak French? "May I speak with Genevieve de Felice?" Layla repeated herself in English.

"I'm sorry. You have the wrong number."

"Are you sure?" Layla recited the number.

"Yeah. I think this used to be Genevieve's phone. You're not the first person to call and ask for her since I changed my number."

"Oh. Sorry."

"No problem."

Layla hung up.

Not ready to give up, she tried again, this time calling the home number for the house in New York. Again, she received a recorded message that the number was no longer in service. Layla's eyebrows drew together. Her grandmother had had the same phone numbers for as long as she could remember.

Why would her grandmother have disconnected her phones? She certainly didn't have money issues.

Grand-mère must have changed her numbers after Layla spoke to her last Christmas, but why hadn't anyone told her?

Layla pulled up the internet on Anna-Lise's phone and searched for her grandmother's name. A string of headlines popped onto the screen.

> *Telecom heiress dies at the age of seventy-three.*

> *Keegan Price named CEO after death of Genevieve de Felice.*

An obituary popped up next.

> *Genevieve Marie de Felice passed away on March 21 after a lengthy illness. Genevieve, the daughter of a Swiss financier, and her late husband, Claude, founded Peaks Communication in*

1977 shortly after moving to New York City. Genevieve is predeceased by both her parents; her husband, Claude; her son, Jean-Yves; and her daughter-in-law, Danielle. She is survived by her granddaughter, Layla de Felice.

Layla's knees wobbled, and she dropped onto her bed. Was this true? Was her grandmother really gone? Was she really alone in the world? And if her grandmother was dead, why hadn't anyone told her? Sure, Layla barely knew the woman, but they were still family.

Her fingers tightened on the cell phone. She should feel something, shouldn't she? Wasn't she supposed to cry when someone died? Her grandfather had died when she was just a baby, but Layla had cried plenty when her parents and her grandparents on her mom's side had died in the plane crash. Maybe that was why Grand-mère had sent her to a French boarding school—so she wouldn't have to deal with the tears and tantrums.

Layla shook those thoughts away. She wasn't seven anymore. She had friends here. She had a life. And as sad as it was, the death of her grandmother simply meant she would get two fewer phone calls each year. Maybe without her grandmother denying her requests to vacation with her friends, she would finally get to do something away from the school for a change.

She probably shouldn't only be thinking about herself right now, but who else was going to care if she didn't? Even with her grandmother not dictating her life, the headmaster could still deny her requests. He did it all the time.

Layla read the date on the obituary again.

Her grandmother had passed away three weeks ago, yet the headmaster had told her only last week that he had called her grandmother about Layla's request to fly to Washington with Anna-Lise.

Suspicion rose within her. Layla pulled out her journal and flipped to the date of her grandmother's death. She only had to turn to the next entry to find the page where she had cried over losing her phone. What was going on? Could the timing be a coincidence? Why didn't they tell her about Grand-mère's death? More importantly, why had the headmaster lied?

* * *

Special Agent Doug Valdez drove his rented BMW XI through the French countryside, diamond-studded cuff links at his wrists and seven-hundred-dollar shoes on his feet. Somehow the price tag didn't make the shoes any more comfortable than his usual twenty-dollar specials, but undercover work required him to look the part. Today's role was that of a wealthy American looking to send his daughter to a boarding school in the south of France. He had the American part down, and he did have a fifteen-year-old daughter. The wealthy part was going to be a stretch.

He navigated through the rolling hills with mansions adorning the grassy peaks. What would it be like to live in a house that big? And how would anyone manage to keep up with the maintenance? He and his wife had talked about trading in their townhouse for something a bit larger, but Doug wasn't crazy about having more lawn to mow. Yet, he couldn't shake the feeling that something was going to change.

Doug turned down a tree-lined drive that skirted the edge of a golf course. According to his directions, the school was nestled in the center of the course. Hardly the place one would expect to find a complex money-laundering operation.

The school came under scrutiny only a few months ago when the FBI discovered tuition was being paid for students who didn't exist. The problem wouldn't have fallen under their jurisdiction except for one significant factor: the money was coming from bank accounts belonging to American children who had passed away, children who were fictionally enrolled at St. Augustine even though they couldn't possibly attend.

In addition to the money coming from such questionable sources, the tuition for those children was significantly higher than expected, sometimes ten times higher. When Doug analyzed the accounts in question, he discovered large cash deposits, always under the reportable limit, flowing in on a regular basis. Everything pointed to someone depositing dirty money as the first step to wash it through inflated payments. What Doug didn't know was how the money was getting back to the people running the operation.

A foursome of golfers stood on the green, one of them holding the flag that identified it as the seventh hole. When Doug rounded a bend in the road, an impressive stone structure came into view. Several smaller buildings were situated on either side. Dorms, maybe?

He drove into a large parking lot and took a spot between a Ferrari and a Porsche. After he climbed out of his car, he appraised his rental. Even though the rented SUV was far more expensive than anything Doug could ever afford, one of these things was most certainly not like the others.

The brisk spring air ruffled his dark hair. Doug straightened his suit jacket and let himself believe he was a wealthy parent interested in sending a child to this school.

A short distance away, two covered golf carts were plugged into a charging station. A carpet of green lawn spanned the space between the parking lot and the dormitories, and manicured hedges lined the walls on either side of the stairs leading to the main entrance.

While the scene was impressive, Doug couldn't imagine sending his daughter away to school. She would undoubtedly love going horseback riding every week, but Doug couldn't stand the idea of her leaving home prematurely. He was already dreading the day she would leave for college. Two and a half more years at home wasn't nearly long enough to suit him.

Doug approached the front doors of the main school building. He didn't know if it was once a French château that had been converted into a school or if the founders had chosen to model it to resemble a stately home, but Doug approved of the look of it. Not enough to spend thirty thousand dollars a year to send his daughter to school here, but for a ritzy private school, he supposed students could do a lot worse.

Doug tried the door only to find it locked. He located the electronic keypad by the entrance and pressed the buzzer. A moment later, a woman in her early forties opened the door.

She said something in French that Doug didn't understand.

"I'm sorry. I don't speak French. Do you speak English?" Doug asked.

"*Oui.*" She nodded and spoke again, this time in heavily accented English. "May I help you?"

"Yes. I'm Doug Smith," Doug said, giving the fake last name assigned to him by the FBI. "I have an appointment to meet with the headmaster."

"Oh, yes. You're interested in enrolling your son for next fall."

"My daughter actually."

"Of course. I'm Veronique Martineau, the admissions director."

"Nice to meet you." Doug shook her hand.

"Please follow me." She led the way into a two-story entryway, sweeping staircases flowing up to open balconies on either side of the room. "The headmaster will meet with you first. After that, I'll be happy to show you around."

"Thank you." Doug followed her past a reception area and down a wide hallway, their footsteps echoing on the hardwood floor. "Is class in session right now?"

"No. Our spring break began today." She glanced over her shoulder. "You're lucky you scheduled for this afternoon. This morning was our pickup time for our boarding students. The parking lots were quite full until an hour ago."

"That must be overwhelming, signing all of your students out at the same time."

"We have a system that works efficiently for all." Veronique didn't elaborate. She knocked on a heavy wooden door. A brass plate on the wall beside it read *Marcel Auclair, Directeur.*

"*Entrez vous,*" a man called from inside.

Veronique pushed open the door. "Monsieur Auclair, this is Doug Smith."

"Oh, yes." The headmaster stood, his light hair perfectly styled and his words spoken with only a slight European accent.

He didn't appear to be much older than Doug, maybe midthirties, and despite his tailored suit and silk tie, the man reminded Doug of a professional poker player with a marked deck.

He rounded his desk and shook Doug's hand. "I am pleased you are considering our school for your daughter."

"Thank you for meeting with me on such short notice," Doug said.

"We are happy to accommodate your schedule." The headmaster motioned for Doug to sit. "Thank you, Madame Martineau."

Veronique nodded. "I will be in the front hall when Mr. Smith is ready for his tour."

As soon as she left and closed the office door, the headmaster said, "I understand you had business in Paris."

"Yes." Doug launched into his cover story. "I'm afraid my business has been taking me away from home far too often the last couple years. My wife and I think a boarding school may be the best situation for our daughter as she prepares for college."

"St. Augustine ranks among the best when it comes to acceptance rates into the top universities in the world."

"Which is why I am here."

"How old is your daughter?"

"Fifteen."

"The perfect age to start at an international school." Mr. Auclair handed Doug a folder customized with the school's logo on the front.

Doug settled back in his seat while the headmaster gave him an overview of the high school–level curriculum, the sporting activities, and the tuition costs. All the while, Doug took in the details of the room. The filing cabinet in the corner, the sleek laptop atop the antique desk, the lack of personal photos, and the Gauguin hanging on the wall. Doug didn't know how much this man made, but he seriously doubted it was enough to purchase a painting worth tens of millions of dollars . . . or more. Was the artwork here to impress people and assure them that the school was financially sound? Or was it an indication of Auclair's personal wealth?

When the headmaster referred to the fee schedule, Doug opened the folder and studied the application form.

"You've given me a lot to think about. Veronique mentioned this is spring break. Will anyone be here if I want to come back and bring my daughter to see the school for herself?"

"We always have staff here to care for any students who choose to stay through the break. We would be delighted to meet your daughter." Auclair stood. "Madame Martineau will be happy to show you around the grounds. If you have any questions she can't answer, please don't hesitate to call me."

"Thank you." After saying his goodbyes, Doug left the headmaster's office and slowly made his way down the hall, reading name plates as he went. Gilles Enard, CEO. Emilie de Grandmaison, primary coordinator.

Veronique appeared at the end of the hall. "Are you ready for your tour?"

"I am."

"Wonderful. Let's get started."

CHAPTER 2

Layla read every article about her grandmother and her family's company from the past three weeks. Several mentioned her grandmother's lengthy illness—another tidbit no one had shared with her—but none of them explained why no one had told her of her grandmother's death. Indignation rose within her. Someone should have said something. And she should have at least been given the chance to attend Grand-mère's funeral.

The memory of her birthday surfaced: the cupcakes Anna-Lise had convinced one of the cooks to bake for them, the match instead of a candle she blew out when she made a wish, the phone call that didn't come. She had thought her grandmother forgot about her or that she had tried to call but couldn't get through. Now she knew better. Of course Grand-mère didn't call. According to the news, she couldn't have. Layla's only remaining living relative was no longer living.

Anna-Lise's cell phone buzzed with an incoming text message. *Did you ask yet?*

Layla texted back. *Not yet.*

What's taking you so long? Go ask.

I will. Layla planned to ask about a lot of things.

She slipped on her Keds, donned her jacket, and stuffed Anna-Lise's phone in her pocket. She stepped into the empty hallway, and her determination faltered. For six years, this school had been her home, with the headmaster ruling her life. Who was she to demand answers?

A little streak of dread shot through her. After all, the last thing she wanted was to be restricted to her room during this next week. It was bad enough that she would be the only student still on campus. If Monsieur Auclair discovered Anna-Lise had given her a new phone, that would likely add to her punishment.

Layla returned to her room, silenced the phone, and hid it beneath her pillow. Summoning her courage, she made her way outside and started down the sidewalk toward the main building.

Layla glanced at the parking lot, confirming Monsieur Auclair's Ferrari was in its usual spot. Her gaze lingered on a gray SUV she hadn't seen before. Who drove that? Maybe one of the cafeteria workers bought a new car.

She reached the main entrance and punched the access code into the security keypad. The doors clicked open. Layla passed by the empty reception desk. Madame Martineau must have left early today.

Nerves fluttered in her stomach, contrasting the heaviness that weighed upon her from being alone in the world. Layla blew out a breath. Needing answers, she forced herself to move forward. She turned the corner into the hall that led to the headmaster's office. Portraits of past headmasters stared down at her from dark paneled walls. The eerie light from the wall sconces didn't quite reach the center of the hall. With all of her classmates gone for the week, the silence made it downright creepy.

She continued forward slowly, her tennis shoes nearly silent on the wooden floor. Maybe she should have changed into her school uniform before speaking with Monsieur Auclair. Surely he wouldn't berate her for wearing jeans and a sweater during break, would he? She stopped outside the headmaster's closed door and lifted her hand to knock.

A man's voice carried from inside the office, but the words were indistinguishable. Her earlier resolve wavering, Layla dropped her hand and leaned closer.

"How do you know this?" Monsieur Auclair asked in English.

"I received an alert that someone was looking at those transactions."

"They won't find anything," Monsieur Auclair insisted. "That money goes into another account."

The other voice rose. "An account with the school's name on it."

"Then we close that account and open a new one."

"No. It's too risky. We don't need these nickels and dimes anymore. You know what you have to do."

Layla leaned even closer, her ear now only an inch from the door.

"I've already tapped into her original trust fund. We are on pace to have it drained by the time she graduates."

"A hundred million dollars is nothing compared to the billions her family is worth," the other man said.

Layla swallowed. The school was stealing from someone? Who?

"The new will and trust documents finalized only last week," Monsieur Auclair said.

"Which was plenty of time to take care of her. How hard is it to get rid of one girl?" the man asked. "A riding accident, an overdose, a suicide. You can run her over with a golf cart for all I care. Just make it happen."

Murder? Layla froze. She couldn't have heard them right.

"It's too risky," Monsieur Auclair said. "If she dies while everyone is away, the authorities are going to suspect me."

The words tumbled through Layla's mind.

"Then take her somewhere else first. You can say she ran away to be with one of her little friends and got hit by a car." The man paused before he added, "The authorities will see it as a tragic accident. With no family to ask questions, we'll be in the clear with all that money to split between us."

"Anna-Lise did invite her to go to Washington, DC, this weekend."

Layla gasped and stumbled a step back. They were talking about her. They wanted *her* dead. Her sneaker squeaked against the floor, and the voices stopped.

Panicked, Layla turned and sprinted toward the exit. The office door opened at the same time.

"That's her!" Irritation filled the headmaster's voice. "She heard us."

"Don't just stand there. Get her!"

Dress shoes pounded against wood.

Layla reached the exit and gasped for air. She fumbled with the door and pushed it open. A quick glance behind her revealed Monsieur Auclair and the other man closing the distance between them. A scream escaped her, and she burst outside.

Her eyes darted both ways. The parking lot? The stables? The dorms? She chose the dorms.

She was halfway to the entrance when the door opened behind her. "Stop!"

Stop? Did they think she was stupid?

Layla increased her speed until she reached her dorm. Fingers trembling, she keyed in her code. She missed a number, and the door remained locked. She glanced behind her. They were almost here. She tried again, this time deliberately hitting each number. The lock clicked open. Relief whooshed through her. She hurried inside and pulled the door closed behind her. Monsieur Auclair grabbed at the door, but it remained firmly shut.

Layla gasped, and her heart pounded. The door rattled. Layla rushed into the common area.

Now what? No one was here. Anna-Lise's phone was upstairs. Did she dare get it? She shook away that thought. Even if she called for help, the police wouldn't get here in time to stop them.

She turned away from the stairs and sprinted to the reception area and the entrance that lay beyond it.

The door behind her creaked open, and Layla ducked behind a plush chair.

"Which way?" the stranger asked.

"Her room is upstairs. I'll check it," Monsieur Auclair said. "Wait here in case she tries to sneak past me."

Footsteps on stairs. Layla pressed her lips together and tried to quiet her breathing. A leather sole against tile followed by silence.

Layla pressed her hand against the plush rug beneath her. Breathing that wasn't her own grew louder. Had the footsteps disappeared because they were muted by the rug or because the man was standing still?

Her heartbeat quickened. Terror clawed up her throat. Could she dare remain hidden here? They were going to find her. She could feel it.

Desperation and urgency surged through her, and she crouched lower. A hand swept over the top of the chair and brushed against her shoulder.

"No!" Layla pushed all of her weight into the chair, knocking the man back a step. She scrambled to her feet and dashed toward the exit.

"Down here!" the man shouted.

Layla burst outside, sprinted across the grass, and ducked into the shrubs that lined the base of her dorm. She crawled forward, but when the door opened again, she froze and prayed they wouldn't find her.

* * *

Doug sat beside Veronique in the golf cart as they circled past the eighteenth hole to the main parking lot. The tennis courts, the golf course, the stables, the dormitories. Every inch of the school campus exuded wealth right down to Veronique's Jimmy Choos. Unfortunately, without a court order to review the school's financial records, all Doug gained from this particular trip was an enhanced suspicion that something illegal was happening and that the headmaster was likely involved. He needed better access to the school and its financial systems, but the idea of using his daughter to gain it wasn't something he was willing to do.

"Golf, tennis, archery, and horseback riding are the main sporting activities our students enjoy," Veronique said, continuing her description of the amenities the school had to offer. "Many of our students have advanced to play golf professionally."

"That's impressive, although I suspect my daughter would be more interested in riding horses."

Veronique parked between the lot and the main building. "Do you have any questions for me?"

"I'm sure I'll think of a dozen once I speak with my daughter."

"If you would like to arrange for another visit when she can come with you, please don't hesitate to call," Veronique said. "My phone number and email address are in your packet."

Doug held up the folder. "I assume the tuition costs are listed in here as well."

"Yes. The fees are listed for both boarders and day students." She climbed out of the golf cart and waited for Doug to join her on the sidewalk before she continued. "Will your daughter be living on campus?"

"Yes. I'm afraid I still do most of my work in the States."

"We have several students who are from the US. I'm sure your daughter will fit in nicely here."

"Thank you again for your time."

"You're welcome. Again, feel free to call me with any questions."

"Thank you. I will." Doug took a step toward his rental car and clicked the fob to unlock it. A short distance away, a man shouted at the same time Doug opened the car door.

"Look over there."

Doug turned toward the sound. Two men appeared to be searching for something outside one of the dormitories. Or perhaps they were looking for someone.

* * *

Hide. That word kept repeating through Layla's mind. Heart racing, she ducked behind the sedan she had tried to enter a moment ago. Scratches covered her hands and face from when she had been hiding in the bushes, always lying still when the men following her were nearby. Thankfully, they hadn't searched deep enough into the hedges to see her. When they circled the building the last time, she had made it all the way to Madame Martineau's Mercedes, but the door had been locked.

A man's voice carried to her, his words spoken in English. "What's going on over there?"

"I'm sure everything's fine," a woman answered. Was that Madame Martineau?

Layla moved to the next car and tried the door. Locked. She fought against the panic rising inside her. She had tried nearly all the cars in the parking lot. If she tried to leave on foot, she would never escape. Monsieur Auclair would certainly find her long before she made it off school property.

A car door closed. "Maybe we should see if they need some help."

"That won't be necessary," the woman answered.

Layla peeked beneath the car beside her and saw two pairs of feet visible at the edge of the parking lot. The man moved away from her, and the woman followed. Layla waited a moment before she skirted around the back of the car beside her and moved to the next one. Again, she tried to open the door. No luck.

Several seconds passed before the sounds of a moment ago caught up with her. A car door had closed, but the telltale beep of a car locking hadn't sounded. Layla checked under the car again, but this time she couldn't see anyone nearby.

Keeping her body low to avoid being seen, she angled to the next row of cars, where the sound of the car door closing had originated. She tried three before she reached the unfamiliar gray SUV. She tried the door, relief flowing through her when it opened.

She quickly climbed inside, carefully closing the door so as to avoid making any sound. She then crawled over the back seat of the SUV and curled up beside the single suitcase.

Although she didn't know who the SUV belonged to, she needed to stay out of sight, and at the moment, this was her best option.

* * *

Despite Veronique's insistence that he needn't concern himself with the commotion by the dormitory, Doug couldn't help himself. He was halfway to the two men when he identified one as Marcel Auclair. The man's stiff demeanor and his raised voice gave no doubt that something was terribly wrong.

Doug pulled his phone from his pocket as though checking a message. He angled it away from Veronique so she couldn't see the screen, and he snapped a photo of the two men before he crossed the lawn.

"Monsieur Smith, I'm sure Monsieur Auclair has everything under control."

Doug ignored her. "Is everything okay?" he called to the headmaster.

Instantly, the headmaster's scowl disappeared. Like a chameleon blending into his surroundings, Auclair straightened his shoulders and offered a pleasant smile. "Did you enjoy your tour?"

"Very much." Doug looked past the headmaster to the man frozen in place a few yards behind Auclair. Though he was dressed casually in khakis and a polo, the watch on his wrist probably cost the equivalent of Doug's annual salary. "I don't believe we've met."

"Oh, this is one of our instructors at the golf course." Auclair waved at the man. "Please take care of the matter we discussed."

"Yes, sir."

"Do you need any help? It seemed like you were looking for something."

"It's nothing. One of the rabbits from the science lab got loose when the custodian was cleaning. I'm sure it will turn up eventually."

A rabbit? Yeah, right. Doug wasn't buying that story for a minute. It was more likely that one of the kids staying on campus was playing an ill-timed game of hide-and-seek. "I'd be glad to help you look."

"That won't be necessary."

"I really don't mind," Doug offered. "What color is that rabbit?"

"White, but really, we have things under control." Mr. Auclair shook Doug's hand. "It was nice meeting you, Monsieur Smith."

"You as well." So Auclair wasn't going to admit that they'd lost a student. He supposed he couldn't blame the man, especially if he thought Doug was about to fork out thirty thousand dollars a year to his school. "Good luck finding that rabbit."

"*Merci*."

Doug turned to Veronique. "Thank you again for the tour."

He left the two administrators and walked to his car. He didn't care what Auclair said. There was no way that man was telling the truth about who they were looking for, and Doug suspected the rabbit wasn't the only thing he was hiding.

CHAPTER 3

Layla lay still in the back of the SUV, the shouts no longer audible. She debated peeking out the window, but she didn't dare. Would the tinted windows hide her until Monsieur Auclair gave up his search? *Would* he give up?

The car door opened, and she swallowed a scream. Who was the driver? Was it possible he was working with Monsieur Auclair and the other man? For now, she couldn't worry about that. She had to get away from here. She had to escape.

Her mind raced with possibilities. Could she sneak out of the vehicle when it came to a stop? Would the driver discover her as soon as they got where they were going? If she cried for help, would anyone come to her rescue?

If she could make it to the airport, maybe she could find Anna-Lise before her family left for Washington tomorrow. They could help her.

The engine started, and Layla concentrated on breathing quietly. Only a few more minutes until she would be safe. She hoped.

The car backed up and then moved forward. Layla looked up at the canopy of trees lining the main drive. A wave of nostalgia cut through her fear. St. Augustine had been her home for almost six years. She could barely remember life when she still had parents and a home outside of her dorm room. Sure, the first few years at school, her nanny had been her roommate, since Layla technically hadn't been old enough to live on campus, but Madame Sabine had been let go as soon as Layla graduated primary school.

A tear trickled down Layla's cheek. No one she cared about ever stayed in her life for long.

Dappled sunlight filtered through the windows, and Layla angled her body across the cargo section of the SUV to get more comfortable, careful to move slowly and quietly.

The driver spoke, and Layla held her breath.

"Hey. I'm just checking in. I'm leaving the school now."

Layla relaxed. He wasn't talking to her.

"Not much to tell yet. I don't see any way to get the information we need without a court order for the financials."

He paused.

"It looked like something was going on when I left a few minutes ago," he said. "The headmaster was outside with some other guy looking for someone."

Another pause.

"They said they were looking for a rabbit, but I'm not buying it. Marcel Auclair doesn't look like the kind of guy who would be searching for a pet."

A rabbit? Really?

"Sorry I couldn't stay longer to check things out, but I did snap a photo of the headmaster and the guy he was with. I'll forward both to you as soon as I get to the airport. Maybe you can ID the other guy."

Layla's eyebrows drew together. This man didn't sound like a friend of the headmaster. He sounded like a cop—an American cop. What was an American cop doing here? And had she really been lucky enough to climb into a car going to the airport, exactly where she wanted to be?

A wave of relief rushed through her. Whatever this man's reasons for being in France, his timing had probably saved her life.

* * *

Doug navigated his way along the country roads between the boarding school and the airport in Marseille. Excitement swelled inside him, building during the long drive. Today, for the first time, his wife and daughter would step foot in Europe. Jill had jumped through all the necessary hoops to get their passports expedited so they could join him on this business trip. Now, except for some potential follow-up on the money-laundering case, he would be on vacation for the next week.

He had hoped to make it to the airport early, but the tour at St. Augustine had taken longer than he'd anticipated. In keeping with his cover, he had deliberately asked questions about academic programs and campus life, but he would have preferred to have walked in with the proper authorization to view the school's financial records.

His phone rang, and he hit the speaker button.

"Dad, we're here!" Pure joy filled Reagan's voice and brought a smile to Doug's face.

"Welcome to France." Doug glanced at the time on the center console. "Your flight must have landed early."

"Yeah. We're still on the plane."

"My GPS says I'm about a half hour away, but it'll probably take you a bit of time to clear customs."

Jill said something in the background, but Doug couldn't distinguish her words.

"Mom said we can meet you outside the airport."

"Okay. Call me when you walk out so I know which door you're next to."

"I will. Love you."

"Love you too." Doug hung up and changed lanes. Though he was tempted to increase his speed, the last thing he needed was a ticket in a foreign country. Instead, he forced himself to enjoy the scenery: the open fields and clusters of trees, the villages with their charming shops and quaint neighborhoods, the vineyards and their accompanying mansions. He couldn't wait to share it all with Jill and Reagan.

Gray clouds thickened overhead, and fat raindrops splattered on the windshield. Doug flipped on the windshield wipers and continued past some cattle grazing in an open field beside the road.

By the time he reached the airport, it was raining steadily. Not exactly the weather Doug had planned for his family's first day of vacation.

He followed the signs for arrivals and was nearly to the terminal when his phone rang again. Doug hit the speaker button. This time his wife's voice echoed through the car. "We just got to the exit, but it's raining outside. How far away are you?"

"I just pulled up." Doug slowed.

"Okay. We're walking out now," Jill said. "What kind of car are you driving?"

"A gray BMW. It's an SUV." Doug scanned the doors and caught a glimpse of Jill's blonde hair. "I see you."

Doug pulled up to the curb and waved. Before he could climb out to help them with their luggage, Reagan and Jill sprinted through the rain and opened their respective doors on the passenger side.

"Wow. Nice car." Jill handed her bag to Reagan. "Here. Put this in the back next to you."

Reagan settled both suitcases on the seat beside her and shrugged out of her backpack. "I can't believe we're really here."

"Buckle up." Doug checked his mirrors, irritated on principle when the car behind him stopped within a foot of his rear bumper. As soon as Jill and Reagan clicked their seat belts into place, he signaled and started toward the exit.

"Do we get to drive around in this car all week?" Reagan asked.

"You like it?"

Reagan leaned back against the leather seats. "I think I could get used to this."

"Enjoy it while it lasts. I'm not buying a BMW when we get home."

"If you bought a new car, you could let me have yours."

"Nice try. You don't even have your license."

"Only five more months."

"Don't remind me." Eager to change the subject from his daughter's impending driver's license and the fact that she was growing up too fast, he asked, "How was your flight? Did you two get any sleep?"

"A little." Jill slipped her oversized purse off her shoulder and set it on the floor. "We'll probably want a nap once we get to the hotel."

"I know it's hard, but if you can force yourself to stay awake until eight or nine tonight, it'll be a lot easier to get over the jet lag."

"I don't think I could sleep anyway. I want to go out and see things," Reagan said. "There's a really cool cathedral not far from here. We can stop there on our way to the hotel."

"I'd rather settle in first," Jill said. "I don't want to leave our luggage in the car while we're out sightseeing."

"Your mom's right, but as soon as we check into the hotel, we can grab some dinner and find something to do."

"Actually, now that you mention it, I am kind of hungry," Reagan said.

Doug caught a glimpse of movement in his rearview mirror when Reagan lifted her backpack into view. She pushed it over her seat into the trunk to give herself more space.

The backpack dropped out of sight, and a grunt sounded.

"What was that?" Doug checked his rearview mirror again.

Reagan twisted in her seat and looked behind her. "Um, Dad? Why is there a girl in the trunk?"

"What?"

The hotel came into view, and Doug whipped the car into a narrow parking lot wedged between their hotel and another one. As soon as he put the vehicle in park, he jumped out of the SUV and sprinted to the back. The hatch was already open, a young teenager trying to push her way outside into the rain.

"Hold on a minute." Doug grabbed the girl's arm the moment her feet hit the pavement. "Who are you? And what are you doing in my car?"

She looked up at Doug, eyes wide and stricken with terror. She didn't answer, but Doug had a feeling he'd just found Auclair's rabbit.

CHAPTER 4

Caught. Panic streaked through Layla. The dark-haired man might have sounded like a cop while he was on the phone, but that didn't mean he wouldn't send her back. Her instinct to flee kicked in. Layla tried to jerk her arm free of his grasp, but it was firmly caught.

A new wave of terror crashed over her. She had to get away. She had to go somewhere no one could find her.

"I'm not going to hurt you," the man said, his voice calm.

A blonde woman approached, an umbrella lifted to shield her from the steady rain. "Doug, she's terrified." She moved closer and held the umbrella protectively over Layla. Compassion hummed through her words when she added, "I promise, we only want to help."

Did they want to help? Layla longed to believe her, but could she take the risk?

"Do you speak English?" the man—Doug, was it?—asked.

Layla hesitated. If she said no, would they let her go? Or would they find someone to translate?

A girl who wasn't much older than Layla stepped into view. Deciding to take her chances with these tourists, Layla nodded. "Yes, I speak English."

Doug opened his mouth, but before he could say anything, the woman put her hand on his shoulder and said, "Let's get out of the rain. We can talk inside." She wrapped her free arm around Layla's shoulders, and the man released her.

For a brief moment, Layla debated trying her luck at getting away, but she suspected she wouldn't make it very far. Besides, where could she go? She didn't have any money with her, and she didn't know how to call Anna-Lise now that she didn't have her phone.

With gentle pressure against Layla's shoulder, the woman steered her onto the sidewalk and toward the front door of the hotel. "Reagan, help Dad with the luggage."

The woman pulled open the heavy glass door, closed her umbrella, and walked inside. A man wearing a suit stood behind a reception counter, and a bunch of chairs were clustered in the center of the room, a lot like the common area in her dormitory.

"May I help you?" the man behind the counter asked in French.

When none of the Americans responded, Layla said, "He asked if he can help you."

"Do you speak English?" the woman asked the desk clerk.

"*Oui*, madame." He nodded. "Yes."

"We have a reservation."

"Name?"

"Jill and Doug Valdez."

By the time the clerk retrieved their information and passed a key to Jill, Doug and Reagan had followed them inside with their luggage.

"We're all checked in." Jill held up their room keys.

Doug motioned toward a nearby seating area. "Why don't we all sit down and talk."

Uncertainty churned in Layla's stomach and sank like a heavy stone.

Doug guided them to the nearest chairs and waited for everyone to sit before he claimed the seat across from Layla.

"Let's start with the basics," he said. "What's your name?"

"Layla."

Doug introduced himself and his wife and daughter. "Can you tell me why you were hiding in the back of my car?"

"They wanted to kill me." Layla looked from Doug to Reagan to Jill, expecting disbelief or, at the very least, surprise. What she found was shock followed by acceptance.

"Who wanted to kill you?"

"Monsieur Auclair and another man."

"What makes you think that?" Doug asked.

"I overheard them talking. The man I don't know said he didn't care how Monsieur Auclair did it but that he had to make sure I had an accident before spring break ended."

Doug looked around the empty lobby as though making sure they were still alone. "Any idea why they want you dead?"

"I think it has something to do with my family's money."

"We need to call the police," Doug said.

"What if they don't believe me?" The panic returned. "What if they send me back?"

"I'm sure the police can help us contact your family," Jill said gently. "We'll get this sorted out."

The tears came now. "I don't have a family."

Doug put his hand on hers, a gesture of comfort she hadn't experienced from a man since her father passed away. Did this stranger really care what happened to her?

"You're a student at St. Augustine, aren't you?" Doug asked.

Layla nodded.

"Then someone had to be paying your tuition."

"I thought my grandmother was paying it, but Monsieur Auclair said something about my trust fund. He said they would use it all up by the time I graduate."

"Where's your grandmother?"

"She died. That's why I was at the headmaster's office. I wanted to know why no one told me."

"I'm so sorry." Sympathy hung in Jill's voice.

"No one told you she passed away?" Doug asked. "How long ago did she die?"

"Three weeks ago. I found out when my friend lent me her phone and I tried to call Grand-mère."

An odd look crossed Doug's face, a kind of determination mixed with concern.

"Maybe we should go upstairs," Jill suggested.

"You and Reagan can go up. I really need to call the police," Doug said. "It wouldn't look good for me to interfere with a case involving a French citizen."

"I'm not a French citizen," Layla said. "I'm Swiss."

"That isn't much better."

"I'm also American."

* * *

An American? Was the girl telling him the truth, or was she lying as part of a ploy to steer clear of the police? And had she hidden in his car as a way to escape something she had done wrong, or was someone really trying to kill her?

"You don't sound like an American," Reagan said.

Reagan was right. While Layla's English was perfect, she spoke with a European accent Doug couldn't quite pinpoint.

"I haven't lived in the United States since I was seven."

Three couples entered the front door and made their way to the reception desk.

Though his instinct had been to keep Layla out of his family space, the new arrivals and Layla's declaration overrode basic protocols. "Let's take our luggage up to our room. Layla and I need to make some phone calls."

"You're going to call the police." Layla spoke the words with a combination of dread and resignation.

"We'll talk upstairs." Doug stood and asked Jill, "Which way?"

"We're in room 106. It's on the next floor up." Jill headed for the sweeping staircase on the far side of the room.

Doug waited for both girls to follow before bringing up the rear. When he reached the top of the stairs, Jill already had her room key out.

She led the way inside. "Oh, wow."

Slowly, everyone filed inside, luggage in tow. Doug passed the bathroom, where thick cotton robes hung on hooks inside the doorway.

Across the room, light spilled through tall windows and a wrought-iron railing surrounded the private balcony. A living area, complete with a sleek leather couch and two plush chairs, occupied the space beside a curved staircase that led to a loft. In the bedroom to his left, a thick, white comforter covered a king-sized bed.

"We get to stay here?" Reagan put her suitcase down and turned in a circle.

"We get to stay here." Doug set his and Jill's luggage inside the master bedroom. "I think your bedroom is upstairs."

Reagan rushed up the stairs, her backpack hanging off her shoulder.

Layla stood awkwardly beside the living area.

"Go ahead and sit down." Doug waved at the couch and lowered himself into one of the chairs. "You said your name is Layla. What's your full name?"

"Layla Giselle de Felice." Layla sat on the couch. Jill took the spot beside her.

"Do you have any ID?" Doug asked. "A school ID, a passport?"

"No. The headmaster keeps my passports, and I left everything else in my room."

"Any idea when your US passport was issued?"

"I think it was when I started middle school." Layla clasped her hands together. "I never saw my passports, but I remember Madame Martineau taking me to get my passport pictures taken."

"How long ago would that have been?"

"Two summers ago."

Doug pulled out his cell phone and dialed the number for the FBI's legal attaché in Paris, the same person who helped coordinate his investigation here in France. Keith Toblin was also someone he had worked with before, someone he trusted.

Keith answered on the third ring. "I didn't expect to hear from you again so soon. Do you have any new developments?"

"Sort of. I need a favor." Doug's grip tightened on his phone. "Can you run down a passport for me and text me the ID photo?"

"Sure. How soon do you need it?"

"A couple minutes ago."

Curiosity and concern came over the line. "What's this about?"

"I need to confirm the ID of a potential informant."

"An American?"

"That's what I'm trying to determine." Doug gave Layla's full name to Keith. Then he turned to Layla again. "What's your birthday?"

"April 4."

Doug calculated the year and passed that information on as well.

"Your informant is thirteen?"

"That's right," Doug said. "She thinks her passport was issued almost three years ago."

"I'll get on it and have it sent to you."

"Thanks. Can you also find out if the local police have either a missing person report or a suspect report on Layla in their system?" Doug asked. "I'm specifically looking for anything from today."

Layla's expression filled with indignation, but she remained seated, her posture rigid.

"What have you gotten yourself into?" Keith asked.

"I'm not sure yet."

"I'll get back to you with whatever I can find out."

"Thanks." Doug said his goodbyes and hung up.

"You think I did something wrong."

"Did you do anything wrong?" Doug toed off his overpriced shoes.

"No. I didn't do anything except run away," Layla said. "And I wouldn't have done that if I hadn't heard them talking about killing me."

Jill put her hand on Layla's arm. "You poor thing."

Reagan walked downstairs and peeked into the living area. "Is it okay if I come down here?"

"You can join us." Doug nodded at the seat beside him. He retrieved his email on his phone and opened the image Keith sent. On the scanned passport ID page was a younger version of Layla. He retrieved his laptop from his computer bag and opened it. "Now that I've confirmed who you are, start from the beginning. Tell us everything that happened."

Layla explained how the headmaster had previously told her he'd talked to her grandmother last week, then she repeated the conversation she had overheard earlier that day. She described her escape and how she had hidden in the shrubs and sneaked to the parking lot. All the while, Doug took notes on his laptop so he could file a police report.

When Layla finished her story, Reagan leaned forward, her eyes filled with understanding. "If Dad hadn't been at your school, you might not have gotten away."

Layla swallowed hard, and tears glistened in her eyes. Whether his presence had saved her life or not, the girl clearly believed that was the case.

Reagan looked from Layla to Doug. "She's just like me."

"Not exactly." The first time he and Jill met Reagan, she had stumbled upon them while people were literally shooting at her. Reagan's safety had been his first priority. The decision to adopt her had come later. Doug still wasn't sure how much of Layla's story was true. "You said your grandmother passed away three weeks ago, and no one told you?"

Layla nodded. "Her name was Genevieve de Felice."

Doug connected to the internet and typed the name into the search bar. "Here it is." He clicked on the obituary and scrolled to the bottom where Layla was listed as the woman's sole surviving family member.

His phone rang. Keith. "What have you got?"

"No missing person's report. Nothing about Layla de Felice at all."

The possibility of Layla being a runaway moved firmly into the highly unlikely category. He had left the school almost three hours ago, and the headmaster had clearly been aware that she was missing. Surely he would have called the authorities by now.

"Can you do me another favor?"

"I'm starting to feel like your secretary."

"Sorry, but I don't want to take a chance of my call being traced," Doug said. "I want you to call the school and ask to speak with Layla. She's a student there who is supposed to be on campus for spring break."

"Who am I pretending to be?"

"The attorney representing her grandmother's estate." Doug gave Keith a brief overview of Layla's story. "From what Layla told me, it's possible the headmaster and others at the school are already committing fraud with her trust fund."

"And you think they'll try to block any attempt from the attorney to get in touch with her."

"It's worth finding out," Doug said. "I also wanted to see if you can track down the real attorney. If Layla is an heir, that could give us some leads on who might have a special interest in her." Or who might want to get rid of her.

"Okay," Keith said. "I'll make some calls, but you need to file the paperwork to put the girl into protective custody. You also need to file a police report."

"I typed up a report already."

"Send it to me, and I'll file it with the police."

"You realize once we do that, our suspects may destroy any evidence of the money laundering."

"I'll talk to the police chief and try to convince him to get authorization to search their financial systems," Keith said. "If the police will share the information, Layla's claim about her trust fund being overcharged could give us an in we wouldn't have had otherwise."

"That will only work if they do a blanket search that goes beyond Layla's payments."

"We knew we would have to involve the locals eventually if your investigation turned anything up."

"I guess we're to that point," Doug said. "Let me know when you have anything."

"I will," Keith said. "You should also call the state department to see what you need to do to get her a new passport."

"I will. Thanks, Keith." Doug hung up the phone.

Timid brown eyes met his. "What will happen to me now?"

"I need to cut through some red tape, but if you're okay with it, we'll have you stay with us for a few days."

CHAPTER 5

"Stay with you?" Layla repeated the words, certain she must have misunderstood.

Who were these people that they would take in a complete stranger? Doug, with his intense, dark eyes, exuded an air of power and a hint of danger. In contrast, Jill reminded her of a primary school teacher who loved everyone and everything. Hope rose within her, much like when she and Anna-Lise had first asked for Layla to go on vacation with Anna-Lise's family.

"I was supposed to go with my friend to Washington, DC," Layla said. "They fly out tomorrow morning."

Doug shook his head. "You don't have your passport. Besides, until we know exactly what Mr. Auclair is involved with, I don't want you unprotected."

Her confusion deepened.

"I'm a federal agent with the FBI," Doug said. "I'd like to put you into protective custody until we can find out what's really going on at your school."

Curiosity replaced confusion. "If you're an FBI agent, what were you doing at St. Augustine?"

"Investigating."

"Here in France?" Layla asked.

"My investigation involves Americans who attend school at St. Augustine. Or, at least, ones who were supposed to."

Layla still wasn't sure she understood.

"What do you think, Layla?" Jill asked. "Would you mind staying with us? You can sleep upstairs with Reagan."

"You're going to let me crash your vacation?"

"Sure. Why not?" Jill asked.

"Because most people don't want an extra kid around."

"We're not most people," Jill said.

"Mom's a school teacher," Reagan added. "She likes kids."

The teachers she knew couldn't wait to get away from their students. Were these people for real? "I don't have any clothes with me."

"You can borrow some of mine," Reagan offered.

"And I'm sure the front desk has an extra toothbrush for you," Jill added. "We can pick up anything else you need at the store."

The family's casual acceptance of her presence brought with it a blanket of security. Overwhelmed by the unfamiliar sensation, she nodded. "Thank you."

"Now that we have that settled, I'm going to change into something more comfortable." Doug leaned down and picked up his shoes. "It's almost five. Does everyone want to go out for something to eat?"

Reagan pointed at the window. "The rain stopped. We could walk by the water first."

"We can do that."

Layla looked down at the rip in her sleeve and the bloodstain on her jeans from when she had crawled over a particularly sharp rock.

Reagan headed toward the stairs. "Come on, Layla. We'll find something of mine you can wear."

"I have some Band-Aids in my purse if you need them," Jill offered.

"Thanks." Layla followed Reagan up the stairs. At the top, two twin beds occupied the far side of the open space along with a dresser. Reagan's backpack lay on one of the two chairs, her suitcase beside the other.

Reagan tipped her suitcase onto its side and unzipped it. She pushed a few clothes aside before she pulled out a pair of leggings. "You're smaller than me, but these are pretty stretchy. They should work."

Layla took the offering and held them up to her waist. The leggings were a couple inches too long, but they were better than what she was currently wearing.

Reagan dug through several more layers of clothes before she came up with a sweater. "Here. Try this." She pointed to a door opposite the beds. "There's a bathroom right there."

Layla carried the clothes into the bathroom. After she wiped away the dried blood that had smeared across her arm, she changed her clothes. Like the leggings, the sweater was too big, falling halfway down her thighs. She cuffed the sleeves, and rolled up the bottom of the leggings before putting her shoes back on. When she emerged a minute later, Jill was standing by the stairs holding a blue jacket.

She held it out. "You can wear this too."

After Layla put her dirty clothes in the dresser, she slipped the borrowed jacket on over the borrowed clothes.

"Oh, good. It fits." Jill moved closer and helped Reagan cuff Layla's jacket sleeves over the sweater. "Sort of." When Layla's hands were once again visible beneath the jacket, Jill motioned toward the staircase. "Are you ready to go?"

The thought surfaced that Monsieur Auclair or his friend might see her outside.

Jill must have sensed her hesitation. She crossed to Layla and put her hand on her arm. "Don't worry. We won't let anything happen to you."

"My dad is really good at keeping people safe," Reagan added.

An unexpected bond of trust surfaced inside Layla. Forcing herself to move forward, Layla prayed she would figure out what to do next.

* * *

Doug strolled behind Jill and the girls, the scent of salt and the sea wafting on the air. Boats lined the harbor, the clouds overhead still threatening rain. To anyone passing by, they looked like a normal family, but few people would ever experience the trauma both these girls had faced.

Doug scanned the area for anyone familiar. His insistence of running communication through Keith was probably overkill, but after Reagan's stepfather had taken extreme measures to find her a couple years ago, Doug wasn't taking any chances. Though Reagan still bore scars from her childhood, she had thrived since coming into his and Jill's lives. He supposed if anyone could relate to Layla's situation right now, it was Reagan.

An uncomfortable sensation squeezed his heart. What were the odds that he would be the means of escape for two teenage girls in peril? He had started out as Reagan's protector too.

Doug glanced skyward. Had the Lord placed him at Layla's school as a means to facilitate her escape? And if so, what did He expect of Doug now? Had she been a French citizen, she would already be in the custody of France's version of social services. Instead, Doug was faced with the challenge of keeping Layla safe while also protecting his family from any danger that might find her. Doug shook that thought away. Surely Auclair wouldn't think to look for

Layla here. He likely didn't know she'd even made it off campus, at least not in a vehicle.

Jill slipped her hand into his. "Did you get the paperwork sorted out for Layla?"

"Keith is filing it for me, and he's coordinating with social services to grant me temporary custody."

"Isn't it odd that this kind of thing would happen to us twice?" Jill looked up at him, her gorgeous blue eyes reflecting her innate goodness and deep faith.

"I was just thinking that."

"You know what else is about to happen to you again?" A smile played on Jill's lips.

Suspicion surfaced. "What?"

"Shopping."

Doug shook his head. "No. I hate shopping."

"I know, but Layla needs some clothes of her own, and I'm sure Reagan would love to pick up a few things while we're here in France."

"But . . ."

Reagan stopped and turned. "Are we going shopping?"

"I guess so," Doug said, resigned. "Let's eat first, though."

"You're just delaying the inevitable," Jill said.

"He doesn't like shopping?" Layla asked.

"No." Reagan grinned. "He thinks you can buy everything online."

"You can," Doug insisted.

"Not quite." Jill took his hand, and they started forward again.

Across the harbor, a boat motored into a slip and came to a stop between two sailboats.

"Will we be able to go out on the water?" Reagan asked.

"We'll see," Doug said. "I thought we could go see the Notre-Dame Basilica tomorrow."

"You're going to make me learn a bunch of history, aren't you?" Reagan asked.

"It's supposed to be one of the most popular places to visit here in Marseille," Jill said.

"I went there on a field trip a few years ago," Layla said. "It's pretty cool."

Reagan motioned to the water. "I'd rather go out on a boat."

Doug's lips curved. When Reagan had first joined their family, she rarely expressed her wishes. Now, she sounded exactly like any fifteen-year-old should—sure of herself and opinionated.

The scent of freshly baked bread, cooked fish, and spices spilled out of a nearby restaurant.

Reagan stopped when she reached the menu posted outside. "It's in French."

"I can read it for you," Layla offered.

"Do they have seafood?" Jill asked.

"*Oui.*" Layla nodded. "Yes."

"I'm ready to eat," Doug said. "How about all of you?"

Everyone nodded, and Jill led the way inside. White tablecloths covered square tables. The maître d', dressed in what could have passed for a naval dress uniform, stood behind a wooden podium.

The man said something similar to the greeting they had received at the hotel, and Doug braced himself for a potential struggle against the language barrier.

"Table for four." Doug debated which would be less offensive, holding up four fingers to communicate his meaning or assuming the man understood him.

"*Quatre?*" the maître d' asked.

"*Oui, quatre,*" Layla said. She then rattled off something else in French, but the only word Doug recognized was *anglais*.

The maître d' reached behind the wooden podium and retrieved four menus. He led them to a table by the window, with the harbor visible across the street. They all sat, and the host handed them each a menu.

"*Merci,*" Doug said, attempting to use what little French he knew.

The man nodded and said something to Layla before stepping away.

"What did he say?" Reagan asked.

"That our waiter would be here in a minute."

Doug opened his menu and read the first few selections before the words caught up with him. The menu was in English. Nice.

Everyone debated what to order, with Layla describing the various dishes. By the time the waiter arrived, they had already decided. When it quickly became apparent that the waiter didn't speak any more English than Doug did French, Doug ordered by pointing at his selection in the menu.

The waiter asked something else in French.

"He wants to know what you want to drink," Layla said.

"Just water."

"Still or sparkling?" Layla asked.

"What's the difference?" Reagan asked.

"Sparkling has bubbles; still doesn't."

"Still," Doug said.

"Me too," Reagan said.

The waiter finished taking their orders and headed for the kitchen. Doug scanned the restaurant, then let his gaze sweep over the sidewalk outside. When he focused back on his family, Layla was also looking around.

The door opened, and a couple walked in. A glint of fear and uncertainty flashed in Layla's eyes.

Doug assessed the new arrivals before turning back to Layla. "Everything is going to be okay. Really."

"What am I supposed to do now?" she asked, her voice raw with emotion. "I haven't lived anywhere besides St. Augustine since I was seven."

"My friend at the FBI is conducting a search to see if he can find any possible relatives." The words that surfaced next caught in his throat before escaping. "For now, we're your family."

Her eyes sparked with suspicion. "Are you trying to get my money too?"

Saddened that she would assume she was only a means to an end, Doug shook his head. "No. Whatever is yours stays yours."

"We really do only want you to be safe and happy." Jill reached over and put her hand on Layla's arm. "You said your grandmother just passed away. Were you close?"

"I haven't seen her since she dropped me off at school six years ago."

Jill's brow furrowed. "What about at Christmas and summer vacation?"

"I usually stayed on campus," Layla said.

Compassion rose within him, and Doug cleared his throat. "What happened to your family? What happened when you were seven?"

"My parents died in a plane crash."

CHAPTER 6

The bond of trust Layla experienced earlier expanded as she shared the memories of her father teaching her archery and how to play tennis at the villa in Switzerland, and of her mother decorating cookies with her every Christmas. A pang of grief pricked at her heart, a sensation she rarely let herself experience.

"That must have been so hard to lose your parents at such a young age," Jill said.

"Grand-mère let me stay at the villa for a few weeks after the accident."

"She sent you away to school only a few weeks after your parents died?" Jill asked, her voice filled with indignation.

"She hired a nanny to live with me in the dorms until I was old enough to stay there on my own," Layla said. "Primary school is only for day students."

"And your grandmother really didn't come visit you at all?" Reagan asked.

"No." Layla didn't mention that every holiday, every school break, she watched by her window while all the other kids got picked up, always hoping someone would come to take her home.

"Where was home for you before the accident?" Doug asked.

"Papa did most of his work in New York, but we spent the summers and most Christmases at the family villa outside Geneva."

"So you went to school in New York?" Jill asked.

"I had tutors."

"Wait." Reagan's jaw dropped. "You'd never been to school before, and then your grandma just shipped you off right after you lost your parents?" Reagan shook her head with disapproval. "That's cold."

"Grand-mère never did like children."

"Even so, that is quite insensitive," Jill said. "I'm surprised she didn't at least have you go to boarding school in Switzerland so you could have come home easily to visit."

"I think Grand-mère put me in the first school that would take me." Layla fought against the bitterness and the familiar hurt.

Compassion filled Jill's voice. "Everyone has struggles they have to overcome from their past. I'm sorry you girls had to go through so much so young."

Layla replayed her words. Had she said *girls*? Plural? "Both of us?"

Doug and Jill looked at Reagan, a silent communication passing between them.

Reagan drew a deep breath as though gathering her courage. "When I was growing up, my biological mother was heavy into drugs. She died when I was thirteen."

Layla's eyes darted from Reagan to Jill and Doug. "You aren't her parents?"

"We are her parents," Jill corrected, "but we weren't when she was born."

"We adopted Reagan a couple years ago," Doug added.

"I thought . . ." Layla trailed off, her mind trying to wrap around what Reagan told her. Was Reagan really like her? Someone who knew what it was like to feel abandoned and alone?

"How did you get adopted?" Layla asked. "I thought people only wanted babies."

"Many do, but the Lord had other plans for us," Jill said. "We were praying to know whether our family would ever be more than the two of us when the Lord answered and Reagan ran into our lives."

"Literally."

Confused, Layla looked at Reagan. "What do you mean?"

"The day I met my parents, someone was trying to kill me too."

"*Quoi?*" Layla's eyes widened. "What?"

"It's a long story," Doug said, "but when Reagan first came to live with us, she wasn't our daughter. She was a witness."

"Kind of like me," Layla said.

"Yes." Doug swallowed hard as though struggling to speak. "She was like you."

* * *

Doug leaned back on the couch and put his feet up on the coffee table, grateful the shopping trip with Layla was now behind him. Shirts, jeans, leggings, pajamas, socks, underwear. Doug's face heated as he thought of that last item. Thankfully, Jill had ushered Layla through buying the necessities to get her through the next few days while Doug stood guard at the store entrance.

He would have to find a way to stretch his budget a bit to make up for the extra expenses of having Layla join them, but at least their current hotel could accommodate the extra person. Their next stop might not work out quite as well, since their planned room was only large enough to accommodate three guests. If he had the energy, he would start his search for a better alternative, but for now, he needed some time to overcome the mental exhaustion that came from navigating through clothes racks and credit card slips.

Trip planning and work could wait until tomorrow.

Jill padded down the stairs from the loft.

"Are the girls all set?"

"I think so." Jill sat on the couch beside him. "That poor girl."

Doug stretched his arm along the back of the couch and drew her closer. "She'll be okay."

"How can you be so sure?"

"Reagan went through just as much neglect when she was growing up, and look at her." Pride welled inside him. "She's doing great in school; she's playing soccer; she's active in church."

"She's learning to drive."

"You had to bring that up, didn't you?"

"She's growing up so fast."

"I know. I was thinking about that today when I was touring the boarding school." Doug shook his head. "The campus is beautiful, and the educational opportunities are incredible, but I can't imagine dropping our daughter off at school and not seeing her for weeks on end."

"Or years, in Layla's case." Jill straightened. "Have you heard anything from the police yet?"

"No, but I probably won't hear anything until morning." Doug ran his fingers along the back of her neck and kneaded the muscles there. "All of my contact with the locals will go through Keith Toblin. He's the legal attaché now in Paris."

"Why will everything go through him?" Jill turned so he would have better access to her back.

"Protocol." Doug pressed his thumbs along either side of her spine. "I also don't want to take a chance someone might be able to trace our location through my cell phone."

"I'd say you sound paranoid, but we learned the hard way about that in the past." Jill let her head fall forward. "That feels so good."

"You've got to be exhausted."

"I am." She turned and kissed him.

Love swelled inside him. Jill was the most beautiful woman he had ever seen. She was also the best person he had ever known.

He drew her closer and pressed his lips to hers. She melted against him and ran her hands over his shoulders.

When she drew away, her lips curved in a smile. "I can't believe we're really in France."

He brushed a lock of hair from her face. "Tomorrow we'll get out and see more than just the harbor."

"Is it safe for Layla to be out where she can be seen?"

"Her school is over an hour and a half from here, and from what she said, the only people who really know her are her classmates and teachers," Doug said.

"What about when we start driving around the countryside?" Jill asked. "I thought we were only staying here for two nights."

"We can talk to the girls in the morning and adjust our itinerary if we need to," Doug said.

Jill waved a hand to encompass the room. "I have to admit, I'm not sure you'll be able to top this hotel room."

"You're probably right."

Jill stood up and took his hands to pull him to a stand. "Come on. We should go to bed."

"I'll be there in a minute. I want to do a quick check of the hotel first."

"You're worried."

"I just don't want to take any chances." Doug tried to push aside the nagging concern that had plagued him since hearing Layla's story.

"Do you believe those men wanted to kill her?" Jill asked.

"I don't want to believe it, but Layla's story is so extreme. I'm not sure she could have made it up," Doug said. "Every time I check anything about her, it proves to be true."

"You did bring your gun with you, didn't you?"

"Yes. Keith arranged authorization for me to carry it."

Jill gave a nod of approval. "Good."

CHAPTER 7

Layla jolted awake, her heart pounding. She squeezed her eyes closed, afraid to open them as images careened through her mind. Monsieur Auclair, the other man, the American tourists, Grand-mère. It must have all been a dream. Or rather, a nightmare.

A door closed somewhere below. Who was in the dorms during spring break?

Gathering her courage, she opened her eyes. A hotel room, not her dorm. It wasn't a dream.

The pajamas she wore were new, purchased last night at the little boutique they had shopped in after dinner. Shopping bags lined the far wall, some hers, some Reagan's. The way Jill had helped her pick out new clothes reminded her of the few times she'd gone home with Anna-Lise on long weekends to Marseille. Madame Dubois always made time for a trip somewhere to refresh Anna-Lise's wardrobe. In contrast, Layla's clothes were usually ordered by someone on her grandmother's staff and delivered to her at the beginning of each season.

Layla rather liked trying clothes on before buying them. Though technically, she hadn't been the one making the purchases. She'd have to find a way to pay Jill back.

Layla rolled over. Reagan lay on the twin bed across from her, her dark hair fanned out on her pillow. If Layla tried hard enough, she could almost pretend she was back home and it was Anna-Lise in the room with her. Almost.

Yesterday's events surfaced again. Had Monsieur Auclair really been willing to kill her for money? And how crazy was it that a federal agent from the United States just happened to show up right when she needed help? Not that he knew he was helping her at first, but still. Had he not been there, the headmaster would have found her eventually. She might not have survived the day had it not been for Doug.

Layla shuddered, then climbed out of bed. Quietly, she dug through the shopping bags until she found the clothes she wanted to wear today. She went into the bathroom, showered, and changed. Reagan's makeup bag lay on the counter from when Reagan had showered last night. Maybe Reagan would let her borrow some makeup since Layla didn't have any of her own.

She walked back into the bedroom where Reagan still lay in the same position in her bed, sound asleep. Borrowing makeup would have to wait.

Layla debated briefly whether she should stay upstairs and wait for Reagan to wake up or if she should go downstairs and see who was moving around in the living room. A male voice carried to her.

Then the water in the downstairs shower shut off. If Doug was the one on the phone, Jill must have been in the shower.

"That doesn't make any sense," Doug said, his words becoming more understandable as they rose in volume. "Layla's story tracks with what I witnessed yesterday. Auclair and the other guy were looking for someone when I left."

He paused for a moment, probably listening to the person on the phone.

"Did he tell you who?" Doug asked.

Layla peeked over the edge of the loft.

"Hold on." Doug motioned to her. "Layla, who is Anna-Lise Dubois?"

Layla started down the stairs. "She's my roommate."

"Is there any reason the headmaster would think you went on vacation with her and her family?"

"I asked to go with them to Washington, DC, but he said no." Layla paused for a moment. "Or, at least, he told me Grand-mère said no."

"That's what I thought." Doug spoke into his phone again. "Did you hear that?"

Layla reached the living area as Doug started speaking again.

"Did they at least do a search of the headmaster's office?"

He must not have liked what the person on the other end said because his eyes flashed with irritation. "Ask again. Layla doesn't have her passport with her. That means it's at the school. Actually, she probably has two of them. She's a dual citizen."

He paused again. "I'll get the information on the roommate and her family. If we can prove they didn't check her out from school, maybe that will kick the locals into action."

Doug paced across the floor between the closed bedroom door and the living area while he continued his conversation. Or, rather, while he listened. Steering clear of Doug's path, Layla moved to the balcony doors and looked outside. The clouds from yesterday were a mere memory, the blue sky matching the color of the water in the harbor. Directly below their room, tables with umbrellas in their centers lined the wide sidewalk. The umbrellas were still closed after last night's storm, but she suspected they would be open by lunchtime.

A few cars drove by on the street below, most of them boring sedans, one looking just like the next. Even the colors were drab. Black, blue, silver, with only an occasional flash of white.

The bathroom door opened, and Layla turned toward the sound. Jill emerged and carried her clothes into her bedroom. A moment later, she returned and crossed to Layla.

"How are you doing this morning?"

"I keep thinking all of this must be a nightmare, but I don't know how to wake up."

"You experienced a traumatic event yesterday. It takes time to overcome something like that."

"I guess."

When Doug hung up the phone, Jill gave him a questioning look. "You sounded upset. Is everything okay?"

"The local police don't want to go poking around the school without some proof that there's a problem." Doug leaned against the back of a chair. "Keith talked to both the school's CEO and the headmaster."

"He talked to Monsieur Enard?"

"Yes. Why does that surprise you?" Doug asked.

"Because he's hardly ever at the school. Monsieur Auclair is the one who is in charge of everything."

"Well, regardless of who is in charge, no one has reported you missing, and the school gave the police a copy of some log that showed you getting signed out by your roommate's family."

"How do we get the police to take the situation seriously?" Jill asked.

Doug hesitated a moment before he spoke again to Layla. "You said your friends are leaving for the United States today? Any idea what time?"

"It can't be too early because Anna-Lise said her papa could come back and pick me up if Grand-mère changed her mind on letting me go with them."

"Do you know which airline they were flying?"

"Airline?" Layla asked.

"Yes. What company operates the plane they were flying on?"

"Oh, that would be Dubois Chemical."

"It's a private plane?" Doug asked.

"It's her papa's plane."

"I'll have Keith call the airport and see if he can contact the Dubois family before they leave," Doug said. "Once they confirm that Layla isn't with them, the police might move forward with searching the school."

"Then what?" Layla asked.

"It depends on what they find." Doug pointed at her bare feet. "Get your shoes on. As soon as I hand off this task, we're going to the consulate to get you a new passport."

Jill put her hand on the stair railing. "I'll come upstairs with you. Reagan needs to wake up or she'll never adjust to this time zone."

* * *

Doug sat beside Layla in the lobby of the US consulate while they waited for her passport to be processed. His original plan to have Jill and Reagan go to Notre-Dame de la Garde without him took a turn when Reagan begged to have some more time to get ready. How much time did a teenage girl need? He supposed it was just as well. It would have been a shame for him to miss the most visited tourist site in Marseille.

Since the consulate was on the way to the cathedral, Doug had opted to take the metro this morning so Jill and Reagan could pick them up once they were ready.

With any luck, the time they would save by not having to go back to the hotel would allow him time to enjoy their outing together before Keith had any new information for him.

The process of applying for Layla's replacement passport at the consulate had been relatively quick. How long it would take for the state department to create the actual passport was still an unknown.

Doug supposed he shouldn't have used his badge to skip the line, but with what Layla had already been through yesterday, he didn't want her sitting around in a lobby any more than he wanted to waste his vacation cutting through red tape.

Layla fiddled with the ring on her finger, the sapphire in the center catching the overhead light and sending a ray of blue into the air.

"I know this must be overwhelming for you," he said, concerned that she had been so quiet this morning, "but I promise everything will work out."

She pressed her lips together and nodded.

Trying a different approach, he asked, "Where did you get that ring?"

"It was my mother's." She looked up with such sadness in her expression that Doug's heart melted. "I took it right before Grand-mère drove me to school. Is that stealing?"

"If something happened to me and Jill, everything we have would go to Reagan," Doug said. "You were only taking what was yours."

She let out a relieved sigh as though a heavy burden had been removed.

"You've had that since you were seven?"

Layla pulled at the chain from around her neck until a ring appeared from beneath the collar of her sweater. "This one too. It was my papa's." Her shoulders lifted. "Actually it was his grand-père's first, but it was passed down to him."

"Is that a family crest?"

"I think so."

Doug's phone rang. When he saw Keith's name on the screen, he said, "I'm sorry. I have to take this." He pressed the Talk button. "Valdez."

"I wanted to give you an update on the de Felice situation," Keith said. "I spoke with the Dubois family this morning, and they confirmed that they did not check Layla out and that they haven't seen her since they left the school yesterday morning."

"Are the police going to investigate now?"

"I'm about to call them, but I need a favor. Can you take a photo of you with Layla and send it to me? Showing her in your custody will give me the additional proof that she is where we say she is."

"I'll take care of it."

"Great. As soon as you forward that to me, I'll make another call to the local authorities."

"Thanks." Doug hung up as a consulate worker approached.

The woman stopped in front of them. "De Felice?"

"Yes." Doug stood.

"Here you are." She held out a new passport.

Doug flipped it open and confirmed that Layla's name and her new photo were inside. He offered his hand to the worker. "Thank you so much for your help. We really appreciate it."

"I'm glad I could be of assistance."

"Could I ask one more favor?" Doug asked.

"Of course."

Doug held out his cell phone. "Could you take a photo of the two of us?"

She took the phone. As soon as Layla stood, she clicked several photos and handed it back.

"Thanks a lot."

"You're welcome." She nodded to Layla. "Good luck to you."

Doug took a photo of the ID page of Layla's passport, ensuring that the issue date was visible. He then forwarded it along with the photo of him and Layla to Keith. He held it up. "Are you okay with me keeping this for now, at least until we get the police on our side?"

Layla hesitated briefly before she nodded. "What was the picture for?"

Doug slipped the passport into his pocket and explained Keith's request.

Layla huffed out a breath in an unexpected show of frustration. "The police don't want to upset anyone at the school."

"That's my guess," Doug said. "They know that tarnishing the school's reputation will result in a strong backlash from the families who send their children there."

"Image is important," Layla said.

"It can be, but it's never more important than the truth." Doug led the way to the exit. "Are you ready to go to Notre-Dame?"

"*Oui.*"

Doug sent Jill a text. *We're ready. Want to pick us up at the consulate?*

A text came back a moment later. *I can't find the car key.*

Doug slipped his hand into his pocket, and his fingers brushed against the fob. Whoops. *Sorry. I took it with me. We'll meet you back at the hotel.*

"I'm afraid we have to go back to the hotel. I forgot to leave the car key for Jill." Together they walked to the metro station. When they reached the kiosk, Layla helped navigate the screen to buy their tickets. After they passed through the gate, Doug said, "For someone who doesn't get away from school much, how did you get so comfortable with the metro?"

"We go on field trips a few times a year. Paris, Marseille, Lyon. Sometimes they have trips to London or Rome, but my grandmother would never let me go."

They walked down the stairs to the correct platform. A train approached and whooshed to a stop. Layla pressed the button to open the car doors and led the way inside.

"Did your grandmother say she wouldn't let you go on those other field trips, or did Mr. Auclair tell you she said no?" Doug asked as soon as they took their seats.

"Mr. Auclair."

"Interesting."

"What?"

"Well, we know Mr. Auclair lied to keep you from going to the US this week. Maybe this isn't the first time he deliberately made sure you stayed in the country."

"But why would that matter?"

"I don't know, but it's a question worth asking."

* * *

Memories of the past six years rushed through Layla's mind. The two phone calls a year from her grandmother, the way someone always answered Grand-mère's phone on the rare occasions Layla tried calling, and how those calls were never returned.

"Why were you at St. Augustine yesterday?" Layla asked, pushing the hurt aside. "You already thought Monsieur Auclair was doing something wrong, didn't you?"

"I didn't know who was doing what, but I suspected something wasn't right." A kind of wonder came into his expression and softened his features. "If I hadn't been in Paris to question a suspect on another case, I never would have been there. Usually, local agents would have done the legwork for me."

"I'm glad you came when you did."

"Me too."

Their station was announced, and Doug stood. He grabbed the bar overhead as the train rolled to a stop, then led the way to the doors, waiting to make sure Layla was with him before he exited.

They made their way back to the hotel and up to their room. Jill and Reagan sat at the little round table on the balcony, half-eaten sandwiches in front of them.

"Oh, good. You're back." Jill beamed at them. "We picked up some food at a bistro down the block. I thought it would be easier to have an early lunch than to look for something to eat while we're at the cathedral."

"What did you get me?" Doug closed the door behind him.

"We have something called a *jambon-beurre*. I had that. It's surprisingly good." Jill held up a sandwich wrapped in butcher paper. "The other one is some kind of tuna sandwich."

Doug crossed to Reagan and kissed the top of her head. "Hey, sleepyhead. What kind did you get?"

"*Croque monsieur*. It's like a fancy grilled ham and cheese."

"Those all sound good." Doug looked at Layla. "Which kind do you want?"

"The *jambon-beurre*, I guess."

Jill stood and handed it to her. "Do you two want to sit outside? We're almost finished."

"I'm fine in here." Doug took the other sandwich and settled on the couch.

Layla took the seat across from him and unwrapped her food.

"Did you get Layla's passport okay?" Jill asked.

"Yeah. As soon as we eat, I'll pull the car around, and we can get this vacation started."

CHAPTER 8

Doug sat at the desk in the hotel business center and printed out the pdf of the paperwork granting him temporary custody of Layla. Even though Keith was working with the local authorities to investigate yesterday's incident, Doug didn't want to take any chances that they would try to bring Layla in for questioning, especially without him. He folded the printed document and slipped it into his inside jacket pocket where he kept his and Layla's passports, along with his wallet.

With that task complete, Doug walked to the exit. He stepped outside and scanned the area before he headed toward the parking lot. He only made it a few steps before his gaze fell on a black Porsche and the man sitting inside, the same man who had been searching for Layla at St. Augustine.

His heart lurched, and Doug quickly slipped out of sight behind one of the café tables between him and the hotel entrance. How had the man found them? Doug hadn't given Auclair his real name, nor had he given anyone his phone number. His car was a rental . . .

The car. Someone must have written down the license plate. Or they caught it on the surveillance cameras on the property. However they traced him, it didn't matter now. He needed to get Layla out of here, and he needed to ensure his family was safely away from danger.

Doug glanced around. No sign of Auclair. No other parked cars with people in them.

Uncertain if Auclair's friend was alone, Doug turned his back on the man in the Porsche and returned to the hotel. After he walked back inside, he stepped beside the front window to continue his surveillance.

He pulled out his phone and called Jill.

"We're coming," she said when she answered.

"Don't come down."

She must have heard the tenseness in his voice. "What's wrong?"

"One of the men looking for Layla is here."

"What do we do? Should I call the police?"

That would have been Doug's typical response, but something wasn't sitting right. What if Keith had inadvertently given information to the local police and that had led to Layla being found?

Doug's mind whirled with possibilities.

"Doug? What do you want me to do?"

"Stay there. I'm coming to you." Doug checked out the window, then did a double take when a Ferrari approached from the other direction. Auclair. He sat behind the wheel of the sports car, his eyes scanning the sidewalk.

Doug ducked out of view, then rushed up the stairs. He checked the hall to make sure it was empty before he unlocked his hotel room and slipped inside.

Jill emerged from the bathroom, her makeup bag in one hand, his shaving kit in the other.

"What are you doing?"

"Packing." Jill loaded both items into her suitcase. "I assume we won't be able to come back here."

"No, we won't, but we can deal with replacing stuff later," Doug said. "It's more important to get us out of here."

"Whoever these people are, they don't know me or Reagan."

"You're right." Doug flipped the security lock on the door. "What did you tell the girls?"

Jill zipped her suitcase and set it on the floor. "I said you decided we were going to leave Marseille a day early and that they needed to pack."

"Did they buy it?"

"I doubt it, but they're upstairs getting their things." Jill gathered the charging cords for both their phones and stuffed them in her purse. "Have you already called the police?"

"No. I'm worried the police might have helped Auclair find Layla."

"A dirty cop?"

"Or a naive one." Doug fisted his hands. "I can't run the risk of the cops taking her into custody and turning her over to Auclair."

"Then what are we going to do?"

Doug crossed to the balcony doors and looked down the length of the building. The balconies for their entire floor were only separated by waist-high wrought-iron railings. Only two of the umbrellas at the café tables below had been raised; the others were still closed after last night's storm. If Doug climbed over the railing and lowered himself as far as he could while holding on with his hands, the drop would be easy enough for him, but he wasn't so sure Layla would be able to manage it without injury.

How could he get her out of here unseen?

Reagan hurried down the stairs carrying her suitcase and backpack. Layla followed, her belongings consolidated into two shopping bags.

"What's happening?" Reagan asked.

"Do you have that hat I bought you yesterday?" Doug asked.

"You mean my beanie?" Reagan put down her suitcase and fished out the off-white knit cap that had been among her purchases at the boutique.

"Yeah. I need to borrow that."

Reagan handed it over.

"Now I need you to go with Mom." Doug's heart squeezed in his chest at the thought of sending Jill and Reagan outside alone, but they were safer if they weren't seen with him. He motioned to Layla's shopping bags. "Take Layla's stuff with you."

Layla's eyes widened. "They found me."

Doug wanted to reassure her, to protect her from the truth, but he needed her trust. "Yes, they found you, but I'm going to get you out of here."

"How?" Layla asked.

"I'm still working on that." Doug pulled some euros out of his wallet and handed them to Jill. "You and Reagan take the metro to the airport. See if you can rent a car there."

"What about you?"

"As soon as we get clear of these guys, I'll call and tell you where to pick us up."

"Are you sure we shouldn't stay together?"

Doug shook his head. "They're looking for Layla, and they've likely seen me. You two are safe as long as you aren't with us."

Concern reflected in her eyes as Jill leaned forward and kissed him. "Be careful."

"We will." Doug gave Reagan's arm a squeeze and forced confidence into his voice. "You go on. I'll call you soon."

* * *

Layla was going to die.

Jill and Reagan left the hotel room and closed the door behind them. They would go out and live their lives, but today everything would end for her, all because someone wanted her money.

She was too young. She hadn't gotten to do anything yet. This couldn't be happening.

Doug put his hand on her shoulder, and she startled.

"Hey, look at me."

Terror clawed up her throat. She couldn't catch her breath.

"Layla." Doug stepped in front of her and bent his knees so his eyes were level with hers. "We're going to get out of here, but I need you to work with me. Can you do that?"

Layla inhaled sharply and let her breath out in a whoosh.

"That's it. Breathe. In and out."

Layla took another deliberate breath and let her fears spill out. "I'm going to die, aren't I?"

"No. At least not for another seventy years or so."

"How can we get out of here?"

Doug motioned to the balcony. "I'm going to climb over the rail and drop down to the sidewalk. If you see Auclair or his friend, clap your hands to signal me."

Layla grabbed Doug's arm. "Don't leave me!"

"I'm not leaving you. I'm going first," Doug said, his calm voice chipping away at her panic.

"How am I going to get downstairs?"

"See that tall umbrella out there?"

She nodded.

"I'm going to scoot it closer to our balcony, and you're going to climb down it."

Climb down an umbrella? The man was crazy. "I can't."

"Yes, you can. I'll talk you through it, but the sooner we can get past these guys, the better."

"Even if I can climb down, then what?"

Doug handed her the knit cap. "First, put this on. Try to tuck your hair up into it so they can't see it."

Layla put the cap on and then pulled her hair back and tucked it into the hat as best she could.

"Good." Doug peeked out the window. "As soon as we both get down, we're going to walk to the metro and get on the train. Simple as that."

"Unless they see us."

"If they see us, we'll run to the train." Doug looked outside, peering one direction and then the other. "It looks like we're clear. Are you ready?"

Though the word *no* formed in her mind, Layla nodded.

"Stay inside until you see the umbrella next to the balcony. Then come out and climb down."

"Okay."

Doug stepped outside and grabbed the metal railing. He swung one leg over the top, and his jacket hitched up. Was that the handle of a gun in the back of his jeans?

He lifted his other leg over the rail, his toes and hands now the only parts of him still in contact with the balcony. He bent his knees and slid his hands down the metal bars. Then he let one leg drop, followed by the other. For a moment, all Layla could see were his hands gripping the bottom of the metal barrier. Then Doug disappeared completely.

A woman below squeaked in alarm, and Layla leaned forward so she would have a better view of what was happening. Doug grabbed the oversized umbrella and pushed it toward her. The metal base screeched against the cobbled sidewalk.

A waiter emerged from inside the café and spoke with indignation in French. "What are you doing? Stop that."

Doug either didn't understand the man or pretended not to hear him. When the waiter's frustration grew and his language became more colorful, Layla decided it might be best that Doug didn't understand much French.

A knock sounded at the door, and Layla startled. Could Jill and Reagan have come back? Or maybe it was housekeeping.

Doug pushed the umbrella the last few feet so the tip was practically touching the railing.

Another knock on the door.

Layla stepped onto the balcony. Doug waved at her, urging her on. She inched forward and looked down. A new river of panic gushed through her. Had she really thought she could do this? How had Doug climbed down without hurting himself?

She shook her head, unable to climb over the rail. Maybe she could sneak downstairs and exit through the lobby. Maybe Monsieur Auclair wouldn't see her.

Behind her, the lock flipped open, and Layla turned. The door swung wide. Monsieur Auclair!

"There you are." He spoke as though he had caught her sneaking out past curfew. After he looked around the hotel room, he walked inside. "You need to come with me."

Layla shook her head and edged back to keep the distance between them. "I heard you talking. You want to kill me."

"You're mistaken." He took another step forward. "We were talking about a movie."

Layla took another step back. She bumped into the table on the balcony.

"There's no need to make things difficult." Monsieur Auclair's lips curved into a placating smile. "Come back to school with me, and we'll get all of this sorted out. No one wants to hurt you."

His voice was so calm that Layla could almost believe he meant what he said, but everything she had discovered about her grandmother and everything Doug had told her proved Auclair was a liar.

Did she take her chances with Doug, a man she had just met, or did she go with Auclair and hope he wouldn't hurt her? Something flashed in Auclair's eyes, something evil. Layla rounded the table, backing up until the railing was behind her.

Auclair continued forward, and Layla cried out. "No. Stay back!"

"Layla!" Doug shouted. "Come on. You can do it. Trust me."

Trust him. Layla reached behind her, and her hand connected with the heavy fabric of the umbrella. More afraid of her headmaster than of falling, Layla climbed over the railing and wrapped both hands around the top of the umbrella.

"Wait! Stop!" Auclair's footsteps pounded toward her.

Layla took a deep breath, followed by a leap of faith. She stepped off the balcony, and wrapped her legs around the umbrella. Her body slid downward, and her stomach somersaulted. A cry escaped her.

Auclair reached the balcony at the same time Doug's hands grabbed Layla around the waist and her feet hit the ground.

"Stop!" her headmaster yelled.

"Go!" Doug countered. He grabbed her hand and tugged her forward.

Layla cast one last glance behind her. Auclair held his phone to his ear and spoke rapidly. Turning her back on him, she fell into step beside Doug and ran.

CHAPTER 9

Doug led Layla away from the parking lot and matched his pace to hers. If they could reach the metro and get on the subway, they could lose them. Hopefully.

An engine revved behind him, a car increasing speed.

Layla stumbled on the cobbled sidewalk as they skirted past tables outside a bakery. Doug tightened his grip on her hand to keep her upright.

A man in front of him pointed and yelled before darting through the doorway of the bakery.

Doug turned. A black Porsche careened toward them, the wheels on the passenger side driving on the sidewalk.

With nowhere to go, Doug grabbed the nearest table and upended it into the car's path. Brakes squealed.

"In there!" Doug pulled Layla into the bakery as the car impacted the table and sent it flying through the air.

He pushed through the crowd by the counter with Layla right behind him. When he didn't see a rear exit, Doug released Layla's hand and pushed open the door that appeared to lead to the kitchen. He ignored the sign that read *Employés Seulement*. Even in French, the meaning was clear, but at the moment, he didn't care if he was allowed inside or not.

The moment he stepped inside the narrow kitchen, a man wearing a white apron let out a loud string of rapid French.

"Where's the exit?" Doug looked past the ovens lining the wall, two doors visible on the far end of the room.

Layla said something in French, but Doug suspected her words went beyond his simple question.

The chef stopped yelling and pointed.

"*Merci*," Layla mumbled and hurried to the door farthest from them.

Doug put his hand on her shoulder. He stepped in front of Layla and grabbed the door handle. "Ready?"

Layla pressed her lips together, but she nodded.

"Okay. We're sticking with our original plan. We head for the metro."

"What if they follow us?"

"They'll expect us to go for our car." Doug said the words, but doubt crept in. He and Layla had two logical means of escape: their rental car or the metro. Would the two men try to divide and conquer? That's what he would do.

"Wait a minute." Doug stopped, pulled out his phone, and searched for the map of the metro system. He turned the screen toward Layla. "There's another metro station a few streets over. We'll go there in case they're already waiting for us at the closest one."

Layla's eyes met his, fear reflected there, but with it was also a look of trust. The trust surprised him, and a new determination rose within him. He was going to get Layla out of here safely, one way or another.

Sending a silent prayer heavenward, he opened the door slowly and peeked into the narrow alley that separated the bakery from the building behind it. Doug motioned Layla forward and turned in the general direction of the subway station.

Eager to get out of sight, Doug angled to the back door of a business on the parallel street. He tried to open it but found it locked.

"Try the next one," Doug said.

Layla did so. "It's locked too."

Sending up another prayer, Doug moved past her and jogged to the next door. He pulled on the latch, and this time, it opened freely. "Over here."

Layla joined him, and Doug led the way into another kitchen, but instead of a wall of ovens, this one also sported frying vats, steamers, and twice as many prep counters. The scent of raw fish and cooked seafood filled the well-lit space.

A man wearing a chef's hat had his back to them, but one of the three sous chefs pointed.

Doug didn't wait for the protests to start. He rushed toward the door on the other side of the room. Someone called out something Doug didn't understand.

"Come on." Doug burst through the kitchen door into a quaint restaurant. He and Layla weaved through the round tables with exotic floral centerpieces until they reached the front door.

After a quick glance through the front window, Doug led the way outside. Walking quickly, they headed down the street. They were nearly to the corner when a Porsche with a dent in its fender pulled to a stop at the light.

Layla tugged on Doug's arm. "That's him!"

Doug reversed direction, turning back toward the hotel. "Come on. This way."

Together they sprinted down the sidewalk. Doug glanced behind him as their pursuer turned their direction. The driver crossed to the wrong side of the road and jumped the curb.

He clipped a woman carrying a canvas bag filled with groceries. She cried out and dropped to the ground, apples and oranges rolling onto the sidewalk.

Doug drew his weapon and fired. The bullet sparked off the front of the Porsche. The driver slowed briefly, then accelerated again.

Doug fired twice more, first at the engine, then at the center of the windshield. The driver swerved, only to crank the wheel again to avoid oncoming traffic. He nearly made it, but a blue BMW impacted his front bumper.

Headlights shattered. Metal buckled.

One pursuer down, but where was Auclair? Doug and Layla pushed through a line of people standing outside a Starbucks. Doug waited until they passed it before he glanced back. His heart jumped into his throat when the driver of the Porsche pushed out of his car and, ignoring the angry protests of the other driver, raced toward them.

With no clear line of fire, Doug lowered his weapon and kept going. By himself, Doug could likely outrun their pursuer, but Layla wasn't fast enough. Somehow, he had to get her to safety.

* * *

They weren't going to make it. Layla looked behind her again. The man from Auclair's office was closing in on them. Another block or two, and he would catch them. And then her life would be over.

Doug grabbed her hand. "Don't look back."

Layla wanted to ask where they were going, but she couldn't. She struggled to catch her breath, and the muscles in her legs burned.

Sirens wailed in the distance.

Doug rounded the corner as though going back to the hotel, but he turned abruptly when they reached the parking lot.

He let go of her hand, pulled out the car key, and clicked the unlock button. "Get in!"

Layla hurried past him and yanked open the passenger side door. Doug stopped and fired off a shot.

The bullet sparked off a metal table on the sidewalk, and the man chasing them dove for cover.

Doug lowered his gun and scrambled toward the car, jumping into the driver's side.

Monsieur Auclair's Ferrari raced around the corner.

"Look!" Layla pointed.

Doug started the car. "Buckle your seatbelt."

Layla fumbled with her belt. She clicked it into place as Doug fastened his and put the car in gear. Tires squealed when he stomped on the gas and angled toward the exit.

Auclair drove his precious Ferrari into their path.

"Not a good idea." Doug laid on the horn but didn't slow down.

Layla braced for impact, but at the last second, Doug swerved and drove across a patch of grass and the sidewalk. The car lurched when it flew off the curb and onto the street. Doug whipped the wheel hard to the left, and the back of the car fishtailed before straightening.

Layla looked behind her. Auclair's friend jumped into the Ferrari, and the sports car sped after them.

"They're right behind us."

Doug rounded the corner and accelerated past the harbor. He pulled his phone from his pocket and handed it to her. "Call 911. Tell the police what's going on."

"911?" Layla asked.

"Whatever number you call for an emergency."

Layla dialed 112. The operator answered. It took a second for Layla to mentally switch from English to French. "Someone is trying to kill me."

"Where are you?" the woman asked.

"We just passed the harbor." Layla's words tumbled out. "They're chasing us."

"Tell them we're being chased by a black Ferrari," Doug said.

Layla repeated the information.

"I'm dispatching the police," the operator said. "What's the license number?"

She twisted around and recited it to her. For a few seconds, Layla answered the operator's questions. What street were they on? What was the last intersection they passed? Who was after her?

Doug made another quick turn, and Layla's body jerked to the side, held in place by her seatbelt.

She checked for a street sign. When she didn't see one, she relayed what business was on the corner.

"Do they know where we are?" Doug asked.

"Yes."

The light in front of them changed. Doug slammed on the brakes, and the car spun around until it was facing the other way. They jerked to a stop for a split second. Then Doug hit the gas.

The Ferrari screeched to a stop. The man in the passenger seat rose out of the window, a gun in his hand.

"Duck!" Doug pushed Layla's head down.

Shots fired. Doug's window shattered, bits of glass raining down on them. Layla cried out.

The operator's voice came through Doug's phone. "What's happening?"

"They're shooting at us."

"Keep your head down." Doug peered over the dashboard.

The sirens grew louder. Doug turned toward the sound.

Wind whipped into the car and tugged a strand of hair into Layla's eyes.

A police car came into view, lights flashing. Doug turned at the next corner, but this time, he slowed enough to keep the vehicle under control.

The Ferrari followed. So did the police.

CHAPTER 10

Doug straightened enough to glance behind him, little shards of glass raining off him. He couldn't outrun Auclair, but with any luck, the police presence would stop him and his accomplice from shooting.

"Hang up the phone," Doug said.

"Why?" Layla asked.

"I need you to look something up."

Layla complied.

"Pull up the map for the metro."

Layla tapped on the screen. "I've got it, but why are we looking for the metro? The police are behind us."

"Yes, but even though I'm allowed to carry a gun, they'll separate us once they find out I'm armed," Doug said. "I can't take the chance that Auclair will spin this around and make it look like I kidnapped you."

"They were just shooting at us."

"I know, but I shot first." Doug glanced back again. The Ferrari was so close to their rear bumper he could barely see it. Doug hit the brakes. The sports car bumped into the back of them, jolting him and Layla forward. Doug waited a second for the police car to close in before he hit the gas again.

"Where are the closest metro stations?"

"There's one half a kilometer down this street," Layla said. "Another one is down the next street to the right."

"How far?"

"Two tenths of a kilometer."

The light ahead turned red. With nowhere to escape, Doug opted to give the police a hand in catching Auclair.

"Hold on." He slammed on his brakes again, but this time he cranked the wheel and stopped the car so that it blocked the road. Cars on both sides of him skidded to a stop. The Ferrari impacted Doug's door.

"Go out your side." Doug unclipped his seatbelt and climbed the center console to follow her. To gain leverage, he put his hand down on her seat, and glass cut into his hand. Ignoring the pain, he exited the car and pulled Layla down to ensure the SUV kept both of them shielded.

Doug jutted his chin to their right. "That way. Ready?" He peeked through the windows to gauge the threat. Auclair and his friend weren't visible, and the police were nearly upon them. "Now!"

Together Doug and Layla burst out from behind the SUV. They reached the building on the corner safely, and Doug glanced behind him. Auclair's friend was now out of the car and heading their way.

Doug faced forward again, and the sign for the metro came into view. Unfortunately, it was on the opposite side of the street. Doug sidestepped a couple walking arm in arm, who were clearly oblivious to the danger around them.

"Hurry!"

They pushed past the couple, the pedestrians now shielding them from any bullets that might fly their way.

Though Doug's instinct was to draw his weapon, he couldn't risk it. If the police pursued them, they could mistake him as a threat.

They were nearly to the metro when a delivery van double-parked beside a shop.

"Cut in front of that van," Doug puffed out.

Layla pivoted and darted in front of a car and then the van. Doug followed and stepped beside her. He held out an arm to make sure she remained in place until he could check for oncoming traffic.

"Now! Run!"

Layla sprinted toward the subway entrance. Doug followed, a car barely missing him when he darted into the road.

Out of breath, he followed Layla to the open entrance. A gunshot rang out as they raced inside.

"Are you okay?" Doug asked.

Layla nodded.

"Come on." Doug approached the gates separating them from the interior of the station, tall plexiglass barriers denying them entrance. He retrieved his credit card and handed it to Layla. "Get us tickets."

"We can use our tickets from this morning. They still work." She pulled hers from her pocket.

Doug replaced his credit card and dug out the small white ticket. They passed through the ticket machine, but instead of going down the stairs, Doug headed for the exit opposite him.

"The train is that way." Layla pointed.

"Yes, and they'll expect us to be on one of those trains, but we're going to go out on the other side of the station. Then we'll walk away."

"But—"

"Trust me." He led the way out of the station. A handful of people stood beside a sign for a bus stop. "Do these passes work for the bus too?"

"I think so."

Thankfully, a bus rumbled toward them at just that moment.

"In that case, it looks like we found our ride out of here."

* * *

Her legs trembling, Layla crowded behind the few other passengers onto the bus and scanned her transit pass the way she saw everyone else do it. Doug put his hand on her back as though reminding her she wasn't alone.

"How about over there?" Doug motioned to two empty seats a few rows from the back of the bus.

Layla slid into the seat by the window and looked outside for any sign of pursuit. Her body tense and her heart still racing, she braced against the possibilities. What if the police didn't catch Monsieur Auclair and the man with the gun? What if Auclair and his friend found them again? How did they find them in the first place?

Her last question repeated in her mind, and she angled to face Doug. "How did they find me?"

"Best guess is they had surveillance cameras at the school and traced the GPS on my rental car." Apology flashed in his eyes. "I'm so sorry. They won't find you again."

"What about the police? Will they arrest them?"

"I hope so." He looked around again. "Do you still have my phone?"

Layla lifted the cell phone clenched in her grip. She'd forgotten she had it.

"Let me have it." He held out his hand, blood oozing from a cut on his palm.

She passed it to him. "You're bleeding."

"I cut myself on the glass." Gingerly, he typed a text message. Once he sent it, he asked, "Are you okay? Were you injured?"

Layla looked down at her trembling hands. A few minor cuts marred her left hand, but she had otherwise escaped unhurt. "I'm okay."

She looked out the window again. No Ferrari in sight. No man with a gun. No Auclair.

"Where are we going?" Layla asked. "Should we change buses?"

"We'll take this bus until it turns."

"You know where this bus is going?"

"No, but if it turns, it could be circling back to where it started," Doug said. "Once we get off, we'll walk a block or two and have Jill pick us up."

"Then what?"

Doug glanced around the bus before looking at her again. "I have an idea, but we'll talk about it when there aren't so many people around."

He spoke like they were talking about where to eat dinner rather than how to avoid getting killed. How could he be so calm? Layla swallowed that question. If he could sit here and pretend like life was normal, she could too.

The bus rolled to a stop. Passengers exited. Others boarded. The scene repeated every few minutes. A woman hauling groceries from the market, a couple holding hands, a man carrying a toddler. Voices carried around her, French from the locals and English, German, and Italian from the handful of tourists who opted to use public transit.

All the while, Doug sent messages to someone, probably Jill. Each time the bus slowed, he looked up as though making sure there wasn't any danger to either of them. When the bus started moving again, he went back to working on his phone.

When the bus branched off the main road, Doug stood. "Ready?"

Layla nodded. As soon as the bus arrived at the stop, she rose and followed Doug to the sidewalk. Houses lined the streets, and she could no longer smell the ocean. How long had they been driving?

Layla waited until they were away from the other passengers before she asked, "Where are we?"

"I'm not sure." Doug stopped at a small market and searched the name of it on Google Maps. As soon as it popped up on his app, he texted it to Jill. "I don't know how long it will take Jill to pick us up." He reached out and brushed at Layla's sleeve. "You still have some glass on you."

Layla shook her arms, and a few more flecks of glass fell to the ground. "Do you want to get a bandage for your hand?"

"That's a good idea." Doug started to walk into the market.

"You can't buy them in there," Layla said. "We need to go to the pharmacy."

"Okay, then. Lead the way."

* * *

Doug paid cash for the antiseptic wipes, tweezers, and package of Band-Aids. Bag in hand, he lingered by the front window.

While he was on the bus, he had filed a police report with the local authorities. Unfortunately, Doug didn't have access to the status of Auclair and his accomplice.

A sedan slowed as it approached the market. Doug's phone buzzed with an incoming message from Reagan.

We're here.

"I think that's them right there." Doug waited until he identified Reagan in the passenger seat before he led Layla out of the pharmacy. He reached the car as Reagan opened the car door to give him the front seat.

"Stay in the front." Doug opened the rear passenger door for Layla. "Get in and slide over."

Layla did as he asked, and Doug climbed into the car beside her.

"Don't you want the front seat?" Reagan asked.

"Not until we're away from the city."

"I'm so glad you're both okay," Jill said.

"Me too." Doug clicked his seatbelt into place and checked to make sure Layla was buckled.

"Where are we going?" Jill asked.

Doug checked the map on his phone. "For now, just head north, out of the city. I need more information before we decide where to stay tonight."

He twisted around in his seat and watched behind him to make sure no one was following them.

The voice on Reagan's GPS told Jill to turn left. Doug turned back around when he was confident no one followed.

He opened the bag from the pharmacy and dug out the tweezers. Then he activated the flashlight on his phone and handed it to Layla. "Can you shine the light on this for me?"

Layla complied, angling the light onto the wound on his hand. Doug cleaned away the dried blood with an alcohol wipe. He winced when it rubbed across a piece of glass still embedded in his skin.

"What happened, Dad?" Reagan asked. "Are you okay?"

"I just got some glass in my hand."

With Layla holding the light for him, Doug managed to pull the glass out of his skin. He cleaned the wound again and put a Band-Aid on it. He then looked at Layla. "Are you sure you didn't end up with any cuts?"

"Just a couple scrapes, but most of the glass hit you."

"What glass?" Jill asked.

"One of our windows broke when we were driving away."

Jill glanced in her rearview mirror. "Someone isn't telling me everything."

Doug didn't answer. He wasn't in the right frame of mind to walk the tightrope between honesty and protecting his family from information that would worry them.

Doug dialed Keith.

"Don't tell me you need another favor," Keith said in lieu of a greeting. "You're supposed to be on vacation."

"That was my plan until the headmaster of that school showed up at my hotel."

Surprise and concern hummed over the line. "He found you?"

"Best guess is he traced the GPS on the rental. I filed a police report, but can you follow up for me?"

"I can do that. Where are you now?" Keith asked.

"We're leaving the city." Doug debated how much to say in front of his family and Layla. If Auclair had other accomplices and had discovered Doug's real identity, booking another hotel could create a repeat of today. Not to mention, hotels would require him to show ID to check in. "What are the chances the CIA has a safe house we can use?"

"After the bombing in Paris last week, I'm not sure that's going to be feasible," Keith said. "I heard from Genevieve de Felice's attorney a little while ago though. Turns out Layla was her sole heir."

"I suspected as much. Did he give you any information on Layla's legal guardian now that her grandmother passed away?"

"Yeah, but you aren't going to like it," Keith said. "It's Marcel Auclair."

"You can't be serious."

"I'm afraid so. He's also listed as the trustee over Layla's assets," Keith said.

"Is anyone else listed as a trustee?"

"Yes. He's an attorney in New York," Keith said. "From the documents I've turned up, his office only handled the family's corporate interests in the States. In fact, he's not even the attorney of record. He's a junior associate."

"Sounds like he's been trying to play above his pay grade."

"My thought exactly." Concern laced Keith's voice when he added, "You should know his passport scanned in Marseille five days ago."

"Does this guy know about the family's villa?"

"It doesn't appear so. When I spoke with his boss, he said the only address they had on file for the family was their penthouse in Manhattan," Keith said. "I've already had the custody paperwork prepared on your behalf with the courts in Virginia since that's where you live. The papers will be filed on Monday."

"Wait. What?" Doug asked. "Why did you do that? I already have temporary custody."

"Yes, but we need a plausible alternative to Auclair to make sure he doesn't wiggle out of this legal mess and gain permanent custody," Keith said. "Besides, you've already adopted one teenager. The courts won't blink at the request, especially since the circumstances are similar to when you took in Reagan."

Doug couldn't deny the similarities between the two situations, but he hadn't planned on adopting one child. Taking on another who was accustomed to such wealth defied the realm of possibilities. Even as that thought formed, a warmth spread from his chest outward. No child should be alone in the world, rich or poor.

"Don't worry," Keith said, clearly reading the reason for Doug's silence. "We can always file another petition once we find a better alternative, but we need to protect Layla from the people who want her dead."

"I can't disagree with you on that, but any chance you can help me find a place to stay for the night? I don't want to take the chance of using my credit card and being traced, and I need a place that won't scan my passport."

"How about spending a few days in Switzerland?" Keith asked.

"What? Are you talking about the family's villa?"

Beside him, Layla straightened and stared.

"Yes. It will get you out of France and eliminate the possibility that Auclair could gain custody," Keith said. "And all evidence points to Reed Grayson, the attorney at the New York legal office, not having access to any of the family's residential records beyond their place in New York."

"Grayson may not have that information, but I'm sure the school does."

"Not from the looks of the paperwork we pulled," Keith said. "Her enrollment was done through her trust fund, which is handled out of the US, and the only address listed for her was the one in Manhattan."

Still skeptical, Doug asked, "Are you sure?"

"That's what the French authorities told me. Auclair had given them a copy of Layla's registration paperwork when they visited the school," Keith said. "Besides, even if they do know about the villa, they wouldn't expect Layla to be able to cross international borders. They won't know she has a new passport."

"That's true." Somewhat mollified, Doug focused on his next question. "Does the will or trust paperwork say who would inherit Layla's fortune if something were to happen to her?"

"It's an organization I've never heard of called Bergen Foundation."

"Sounds like we need to find out who's running it."

"I'm already ahead of you. The president's name is Lorraine Clermont. I'll send you the photo."

"Thanks." The sooner they identified the people after Layla in addition to Auclair and his partner, the sooner they could catch them. "If we go to the villa, how will we gain access?"

"The caretaker and his wife still live there," Keith said. "According to the family's attorney in Geneva, they've been loyal to the family for a couple generations."

"Any chance we can get access to their bank records and make sure they aren't part of whatever fraud is going on at the school or with the family?" Doug asked. "I have my family with me. I'm not risking them or Layla unless we're sure it's safe."

"I don't blame you. I'll put a request in with the CIA," Keith said.

"Thanks, Keith." Doug hung up and checked the GPS on his phone. "Jill, head for Valence. Reagan, can you plug that into the GPS on your phone for Mom?"

"Sure."

"Is that where we're going to stay tonight?" Jill asked.

"No, but we can stop and pick up something to eat there."

"Where are we staying?" Jill asked.

"I'm waiting on some information, but it looks like we're going to Switzerland."

Layla's gaze met his. "You're taking me home?"

"If all goes as I hope, then yes, I'm taking you home."

CHAPTER 11

Layla was dreaming again. At least, she was pretty sure that was the only explanation for everything that had happened today. Her insides churned with emotions she struggled to name. The lingering adrenaline from her escape from Auclair and his friend had yet to fully subside, her hands still shaking even after almost four hours of driving with the Valdez family. Fear and terror had threatened to take over again when they stopped in Valence for an early dinner, but thankfully, Jill had bought them food at a crepe cart instead of making everyone go in somewhere.

They had played musical chairs when they stopped, Doug taking the spot behind the wheel. Reagan now sat in the back seat with Layla, with Jill in the front seat navigating. Doug had pulled over when he received the phone call he was waiting for. He didn't elaborate on what his friend Keith told him, but whatever it was, Doug had hung up and announced they would be staying at her family's villa tonight.

Excitement or something like it hummed through her as they passed by vineyards and aging châteaus, open fields and wooded hills. Villages sprang up every few kilometers with their charming main streets and little shops.

The trembling in Layla's body increased when they approached the crossing point between France and Switzerland. The sun already hung low in the sky, the blue now streaked with various shades of pink and purple. Layla imagined someone stopping them and pulling her from the car to keep her from leaving France.

Relief flowed through her when they passed through without incident.

She looked back, France now fading into the distance. Was this real? Was she in Switzerland for the first time since she was seven?

She put her hand on her arm and pinched the skin, the accompanying twinge of pain ensuring the truth. She wasn't dreaming.

According to Jill's GPS, they were on the last stretch to her family's villa, but none of it looked familiar. Had everything changed since Layla had been home last, or had she forgotten it all?

"Is the house we're going to the same one you grew up in?" Reagan asked.

"It's one of them. The houses we lived in during the winter were in New York and the Bahamas."

"You had three houses?" Regan asked.

"Two really. The house in the Bahamas was just for vacations." Warm breezes, sandcastles on the beach, her parents playing with her in the waves.

Jill twisted around in her seat. "That must have been quite the change for you, going from traveling with your parents to spending all your time at school."

Layla remembered those first days at school all too well, with her standing at the window waiting for her grandmother's car to come back up the drive, her nanny demanding she do her schoolwork, the other kids in her class getting picked up by their parents or chauffeurs every day.

"According to the information the attorney sent me, we're only another twenty minutes from your villa."

"It's not my villa."

"According to the attorney, technically it is," Doug said. "I haven't seen the paperwork yet, but from what I understand, you inherited the bulk of your grandmother's estate."

"Why would she leave anything to me?" Layla asked. "She didn't even want me around."

"Maybe she just didn't know how to take care of a child," Jill suggested. "Losing family members in that plane crash would have been hard on her too."

"I guess."

"How are we going to get inside?" Reagan asked. "We don't have a key."

"The caretaker is still living there," Doug said.

The image came into Layla's mind of a tall man with gray hair and a pocket filled with her favorite candy. "Monsieur Bachmann."

"That's right," Doug said. "You remember him."

"He was always very nice to me."

"Well, you'll be seeing him again soon."

They passed through the outskirts of Geneva, the city lights blinking on in the growing darkness. Doug continued past the tall buildings clustered together. Within minutes, the city disappeared behind them and the lake came into view, the last of the sun's rays reflecting on the water.

"That must be Lake Geneva," Jill said. "It's beautiful."

"I wish we could have arrived during the daytime," Reagan said. "I bet there's so much to see."

"We'll see plenty tomorrow."

"I can't believe I got to go to both France and Switzerland this week," Reagan said.

Layla studied the girl beside her. Shouldn't she be mad that Layla had messed up her vacation?

They came around a bend in the road, and a sense of familiarity washed over her.

"We should be getting close," Jill said.

Layla caught sight of a brick wall leading to a wrought-iron gate on her left. She sat up straighter. "I think it's the driveway after that one."

Doug slowed as the road climbed higher. It started to dip down again when the familiar stone pillars came into view.

"There." Layla pointed. "Turn in there."

Doug signaled and followed her directions. Tall trees lined the stone drive until they reached the caretaker's cottage.

"Is that the house?" Reagan asked. "I thought it would be bigger."

"The caretaker lives there." Layla leaned forward as Doug continued past the cottage and headed down the little slope through a cluster of trees. Then the main house came into view, the outside lights glowing as if welcoming them.

"That's the main house," Layla said, a rush of emotions bubbling inside her. "This is home."

* * *

"Wow." Doug expected the house to be big, but that didn't diminish the impact of the stone-fronted mansion in front of him. Lights illuminated the house and the path surrounding the circular front lawn. Mature trees flanked the house on either side, and flowers bloomed in the front garden.

Doug parked the car in the spacious driveway and shut off the engine. Though the Bachmanns had clearly received the message they were coming, Doug couldn't shut off his protective instincts. "Wait here while I track down the caretaker."

Doug handed the car key to Jill and climbed out. He walked up the path to the large wooden door. Only a few seconds after he knocked, a tall man answered, his weathered face alight with joy and excitement. Doug studied him for a moment, confirming the man was indeed the person in the ID photo Keith sent him.

"You must be Agent Valdez," he said in English.

"Yes. Mr. Bachmann?"

"Yes, yes." He peered past Doug. "Is Mademoiselle Layla with you?"

"She's waiting in the car," Doug said. "Is anyone else here at the house?"

"Only my wife. She is in the kitchen preparing some dinner for you," he said. "She thought you would be hungry after such a long drive."

"That's very kind of her." Doug stepped back. He needed to do a complete sweep of the property, but he didn't want to leave his family and Layla out in the car while he did so. "I'll go get them."

"May I help you with your luggage?"

Though he normally wouldn't have accepted the offered help, Doug suspected the caretaker was as eager to see Layla as she was to find a safe haven. "I'd appreciate that. Thank you."

"Of course, sir." Bachmann followed him outside and pulled the door closed without letting it latch.

Doug started toward the car. "I understand you've worked for the de Felices for some time."

"Yes, sir. I grew up here. My father was caretaker before me."

"Then you knew Layla's parents."

"Yes. Such a tragedy when we lost them."

They reached the car, and Doug opened the door for Jill and Reagan. "This is my wife, Jill, and our daughter, Reagan."

"Good to meet you both." He bowed slightly. "Please call me Fritz."

Doug circled to the driver's side and opened Layla's door.

She sat inside, the familiar uneasiness reflected on her face.

"I believe there is someone who wants to see you."

When she didn't move, Doug offered his hand. Layla accepted it and climbed out. The moment her gaze landed on Fritz, her face lit up. "Fritz!"

"Oh, Mademoiselle Layla. It's so good to have you home." He closed the distance between them and kissed her on the right cheek, then the left, and then the right again.

Doug popped the trunk and pulled out the first suitcase.

"Are we really staying here tonight?" Reagan asked.

"We are." Doug unloaded a second suitcase and asked Fritz, "That is okay, isn't it?"

"Of course. We already have rooms prepared for you." He released Layla and picked up the two nearest suitcases. "Follow me."

Doug gathered the rest of the luggage, and Jill locked the car.

"This place is amazing." Jill took the shopping bags that contained Reagan's clothes. "I can't wait to see the inside."

"Me too."

CHAPTER 12

Layla walked into the front hall, the chandelier shining brightly overhead. A wide armoire occupied the space to her left and two padded chairs and a wooden bench were pushed against the wall opposite it. It was the same as she remembered, yet it somehow seemed smaller.

"This is huge!" Reagan turned in a circle and looked up the wide staircase that lay beyond the formal entryway.

"May I hang up your coats?" Fritz asked.

Layla shrugged off her new jacket and handed it to him. Fritz opened the armoire and hung it inside, then he repeated the process with Jill and Reagan.

"I'll keep mine with me," Doug said. "I want to check out the property before we settle in for the night."

"I assure you, the villa is quite safe," Fritz said. "Madame de Felice had a security system installed several years ago."

"What about the front gate?" Doug asked.

"I left it open because we were expecting you, but I can close it now." Fritz opened an electronic control panel beside the armoire and hit a button.

Layla continued into the great salon. A wall of windows opened into the darkness that she knew to be a view of the lake. She trailed a finger over the armchair where her mother used to sit and read. So many times, her mom had been there when one of the servants took Layla out to play and was still there when Layla returned.

A door opened somewhere deep in the house, and hurried footsteps approached. Celine Bachmann rushed into the living room. "Oh, you're here."

Layla hugged the older woman, breathing in the familiar scent of fresh bread and spices.

Celine leaned back and studied Layla. "You're so grown up."

"It's been a long time." Layla gestured to Doug when he followed her into the room, along with Jill and Reagan. "These are my friends, Doug, Jill, and Reagan Valdez."

"Thank you for bringing Mademoiselle Layla back to us." She motioned to her husband. "Fritz can show you to your rooms. Supper will be ready in half an hour."

"Thank you," Jill said.

Fritz picked up two suitcases and moved toward the stairs. "This way."

Layla followed after him, trying to pretend she was coming here from New York with her parents instead of arriving with people who were still relative strangers. Even as she had that thought, she readjusted her definition. She had called the Valdezes friends, and that's what they were. Taking her in when she had nothing, buying her new clothes, protecting her.

"Madame and Monsieur Valdez, this is yours." Fritz opened the door to one of the guest rooms. "Mademoiselle Reagan is across the hall. Mademoiselle Layla, I have you in your old room."

While the others sorted out the luggage, Layla continued to her old room. She glanced down the hall to the suite that lay beyond hers, the one that belonged to her parents. Was it the same as it had been when she was last here? For that matter, was her room the same?

Layla pushed open her door and stepped into her past. A pink comforter over a white four-poster bed, her favorite stuffed animal, a teddy bear named Hugo, laying on top. Toys and dolls lined the shelves on the far wall, all the things Grand-mère insisted she wouldn't need while she was away at school.

Layla crossed the room and picked up the bear, clutching it to her chest. Once upon a time, cuddling with Hugo had solved all her problems.

Someone knocked on her open door.

Reagan entered. "Here are your clothes."

"Thanks." Layla took the shopping bags from her and set them on the trunk at the end of her bed.

"Is it weird being back here?"

"Yes." Layla sat on her bed. "Grand-mère didn't let me bring any of my toys with me when I left for school. Sometimes I thought everything here was all a dream I made up in my mind."

"It looks real to me." Reagan looked around the room. "Of course, it also looks like we both just landed in a fairy tale."

"Do you want to see the rest of the house?"

Reagan's eyes lit up. "I'd love that."

"Should we see if your mom and dad want to come with us too?"

"Dad is already checking things out, but I'm sure Mom would love to come."

"Let's go then." Layla pushed off her bed. "We can start with the swimming pool."

"Isn't it too cold in Switzerland to have a swimming pool?"

"Some people have them outside, but they can only use them in the summer." Layla led the way to the door. "Our pool is indoors."

"You have a pool inside your house?" Reagan followed her into the hall. "This may be the best vacation ever." She paused. "Other than the part about people chasing you."

"I'm hoping to forget about that."

"I'll pray you can."

* * *

The moment Doug exited the house, he dialed Keith's number. As soon as his friend answered, Doug asked, "Any updates?"

"The French authorities have Auclair in custody," Keith said.

"What about his accomplice?" Doug headed toward the caretaker's cottage.

"Nothing yet. The car he was driving was reported stolen, but we have a photo of him fleeing the scene. Guess who it was."

"The New York attorney?"

"That's right. Reed Grayson. The police are searching for him now," Keith said. "The police are also conducting a complete search of the school. I already received word that they found both of Layla's passports. Between the lies Auclair told me and with Layla's testimony, his arrest is going to stick."

"Let's hope."

"The local authorities should be forwarding us the financial records sometime tomorrow. I'll grant you access as soon as it comes in."

Doug slowed his steps when the lights from the house faded. "Thanks, Keith."

"No problem," Keith said. "By the way, how's the Swiss villa?"

Doug turned back to study the scene of the massive building with its peaked roof and manicured landscape. "I'd send you a picture, but I don't want to make you jealous."

"Send me a picture anyway."

"Okay, but don't say I didn't warn you." After Doug hung up, he lifted his phone and snapped a photo. Only a minute after he texted it to Keith, a reply popped up on his screen.

Looks like you need some backup.

Doug laughed. *Good luck getting someone to sign off on your travel order.*

Doug turned on his phone's flashlight function and walked to the end of the long driveway. He grabbed the closed iron gate and rattled it. It held firm.

Pointing the flashlight toward the ground, he surveyed the stone fence that separated the villa from the street. Mature trees grew along the perimeter of the property, a mode of access for anyone climbing the wall. Then again, if someone wanted to bypass the gate, it wouldn't be hard with the size of the property.

With that in mind, Doug retreated toward the house. He emerged from the trees and crossed the well-tended lawn. He moved closer to a dark expanse beyond the flood of house lights and stopped when he reached the spot where the yard sloped downward. A sliver of moonlight filtered through a gap in the clouds overhead and shimmered on a body of water below. Lake Geneva.

Lights from the city illuminated the expanse to his right while on his left, the countryside remained mostly dark. Doug discovered a path leading down the hill toward the water. He followed it until he reached a boathouse and a private dock. He tried the door to the boathouse, but it was locked. He peeked in the window. Sure enough, a sleek speedboat was inside.

What a perfect setup. The de Felice villa was just far enough from the city to afford peace and tranquility, but it was accessible by both car and boat. Did Layla's parents and grandparents work in the city? Or did their money come from the work of others?

Doug hiked back up the hill and walked along the side of the house. He reached the back where light spilled out of a bank of windows. Inside, Reagan, Layla, and Jill stood beside a long, narrow swimming pool. Maybe this vacation would turn out okay after all. Reagan laughed at something Jill said, and Doug's heart warmed. His gaze shifted to Layla. The poor kid. What would happen to her now? He really should sit her down and talk to her about the custody petition. At thirteen, she was old enough to express what she wanted her future to look like.

He supposed if she wanted to stay at St. Augustine, assuming her safety could be assured, remaining her guardian wouldn't be that big of a deal. Even as that thought surfaced, a seed of doubt planted deep inside him. What kind of life was that for a kid? Spending every school break and holiday hoping a classmate would invite her home? He couldn't imagine it, and he hated that Layla had already lived that life for so many years.

The Bachmanns were another possibility for guardianship. They had seemed happy enough to see her, but would they be able to provide for Layla's emotional needs? She would have a lot of those in the coming weeks and months. His experience with Reagan had taught him how past traumas could create problems at unexpected moments.

He continued his search of the grounds. A tennis court and a riding ring and then a long white building stretching between the two. The stables?

Something moved inside. Doug's hand went to his gun. With his free hand, he pulled the wooden door open. A horse snorted.

Doug held up his phone and swept his light across the interior of the long building. He found a light switch and flipped it on. Five stalls stood on either side of the wide center pathway. A horse poked his head over the door of his stall.

"You alone in here?" Doug asked.

More equine footsteps sounded until another horse poked his head out. Or maybe it was her head.

"Two of you, huh?" Doug checked the open area by the entrance, which was full of hay and buckets of grain. The storage room across from it held an assortment of saddles and bridles. One by one, he checked the rest of the stalls, but only two were occupied.

At the far end, he located another storage room, but instead of riding gear, it contained tennis and archery equipment.

Doug's phone buzzed with an incoming text, and he checked the screen. It was Jill: *Dinner is ready.*

Coming. Doug left the stables and returned to the house. He tried several doors in the back, but all of them were locked. A good sign. He circled to the front and went in the main entrance.

Fritz stood inside the main hall. "I can take your coat, sir."

Doug shrugged out of it. "Thank you."

"Of course, sir." Fritz hung up the coat and motioned him forward. "The dining hall is this way."

"Is there a place I can wash my hands first?"

Fritz escorted him down a wide hall to a powder room that was decorated like those in the HGTV shows Jill liked to watch.

Knowing his wife, her ideas were already flowing. It was inevitable. He would either be redecorating or buying a new house very soon. But would they still be a family of three when they got to that point, or would they be a family of four?

CHAPTER 13

Layla tried to sleep, but every time she closed her eyes, memories avalanched through her mind. The climb from the hotel balcony, the chase through the city, the sound of gunshots, the car window shattering.

Shadows from the trees played over her room, dappled moonlight filtering through the sheer window curtains.

Layla sat up and clicked on her bedside lamp. The instinct to go into her parents' room surfaced, and a wave of grief washed over her. What she wouldn't give to have her mother wrap her arms around her and hold her close, or for her father to lift her up onto his shoulders and carry her around while walking to the lake's edge.

A tear trickled down her cheek, and she brushed it away. She wasn't seven anymore. She wouldn't ever have people in her life who cared for her that way again. Her stomach clenched, a dull pain starting from her center.

Why couldn't she have a family like everyone else? Was that really too much to ask?

Knuckles rapped softly at her door.

Layla swiped at an errant tear. "Come in."

Jill pushed the door open. "I wanted to check on you before I go to bed." She hesitated a brief moment before entering and crossing to the bed. She sat on the side the way her mother used to. "How are you doing?"

Layla pressed her lips together, and another tear spilled over.

"Hey. Come here." Jill reached out and pulled her close.

The warmth and the naturalness of the gesture brought new tears to the surface. Layla's arms came up and encircled Jill. She clung to her, not ready to let go of the comfort found inside the embrace.

"It's okay." Jill ran her hand over Layla's back, her tone soothing. "Everything is going to be all right. Doug and I are here for you. Reagan too."

Layla's fingers curled into the soft knit of Jill's sweater. She kept expecting Jill to pull away, but she didn't. She simply held her while she cried, murmuring assurances that she would be okay and that everything would work out.

When her tears finally slowed, Layla straightened, and her cheeks heated. "I'm sorry." She sniffled. "I didn't mean to cry all over you."

"I think you deserved a good cry. You've had a tough couple of days." Jill looked around the room. "Are you okay sleeping in here alone? There's an extra bed in Reagan's room."

"She probably wants her own space."

"She'd be happy to let you sleep in her room," Jill insisted. "If anyone can understand what you're going through right now, it's her. She knows what it's like to feel alone and afraid. She's also proof that you can find your happily ever after."

Happily ever after. Layla had stopped believing in fairy tales a long time ago. At the moment, she would settle for finding a safely ever after.

"I think I would like to sleep in Reagan's room."

Jill stood. "Come on. I'll walk you across the hall."

Layla climbed out of bed and grabbed her teddy bear. "Jill?"

"Yes?"

"Thank you."

Jill's face softened, and she put her arm around Layla's shoulders. "Anytime."

* * *

Doug retrieved his portable gun safe from his luggage and set the black metal box on his bedside table. After using the fingerprint scanner on top to unlock it, he secured his sidearm inside.

Jill walked in and closed the door.

"Is everyone all settled?"

"They are now." Jill climbed into bed. "Layla is sleeping in Reagan's room."

"Is she okay?"

"That poor girl. She's so traumatized, and I don't know if being back here is helping any." Jill waited until he climbed into bed beside her before she laid down. "When I went in, she was in tears."

Doug's heart cracked open, and a seed of love planted itself inside. "I talked to Keith while I was out walking the grounds. He filed for custody on our behalf."

Jill pushed up on her elbow. "We have custody of Layla?"

"Yeah. Turns out her grandmother's will named Auclair as her guardian."

"Why would she do that?"

"I have no idea. Maybe she thought that since Layla was living full-time at school anyway, assigning guardianship to the headmaster would ensure she continued her life without interruption."

"Does Layla know about this?"

"No. I wanted to talk to you first," Doug said. "She's already overwhelmed with everything she's been through the past couple days. She has some decisions to make about her future, and that's something she hasn't had a lot of experience with in the past."

"You know the longer she stays with us, the harder it's going to be when she leaves," Jill said.

"Maybe she won't want to leave."

Jill sat up now and stared at him. "Wait. This coming from the man who didn't want to adopt in the first place?"

"You've already proven I was wrong about that." Doug sat up beside her and leaned against the headboard. "When I was driving to St. Augustine, I thought about how hard it would be to let Reagan go away to school. The campus was beautiful; it had all of these amazing programs, but even if I had all the money in the world, I'm too selfish to let her go away."

"That's not selfish. There's nothing wrong with wanting to parent our child ourselves."

Doug waved helplessly toward the hall. "Whether Layla wants to go back to boarding school or not, she needs to know that someone will miss her when she's gone."

Jill's brown eyes warmed. "You want us to be those people who will miss her."

"I sound insane when you put it that way."

"No." Jill leaned in and kissed him. "You sound sweet."

"Not exactly an attribute many would associate with an FBI agent."

"Maybe not, but everyone doesn't know you the way I do." She squeezed his hand. "When do you want to talk to Layla?"

"Personally, I'd like to do it sooner than later, but I think it may be better for her if we give her a day or two to get to know us a bit better."

"That's probably a good idea." Jill laid back down. "We should talk to Reagan too."

"Who do we talk to first?" Doug asked.

"We should talk to Reagan first," Jill said. "She's always wanted a sister."

"Looks like she's about to get her wish."

* * *

Layla awoke from a dreamless sleep, her eyes narrowing against the light streaming through the window. The bedroom door opened, and someone walked in. Layla cracked her eyes open. Reagan stood by the chair in the corner, already dressed, her socks in her hand.

"Morning."

Layla pushed her hair back from her face. "What time is it?"

"Eight." Reagan sat down, an odd smile on her face. "I was thinking about checking out the grounds this morning. Want to come with me?"

A knock sounded at the door before Layla had a chance to answer.

"Everyone decent?" Doug asked.

"Yeah," Reagan said. "Come on in."

Doug and Jill both walked into the room.

"Are you girls ready to go down for breakfast?" Jill put her arm around Reagan and gave her a squeeze. "Madame Bachmann made us some croissants."

The scene was so like a normal family; Layla ached to belong. When she opened her mouth, the question burning inside her tumbled out. "What's going to happen to me?"

Jill and Doug exchanged a look, almost like they were talking without saying anything.

"We found a disturbing development in your grandmother's will," Doug said.

Layla's chest tightened. Did Grand-mère give everything to someone else? Was she alone *and* broke?

Doug continued, his voice breaking into her thoughts. "She named Marcel Auclair as your guardian."

Layla shook her head, the conversation from Monsieur Auclair's office rolling over in her mind. "I don't think that's right."

Doug's eyes sharpened. "Why do you say that?"

"I heard Monsieur Auclair say the new will and trust documents were in place."

Doug's lips pressed together into a hard line, and a dangerous look flashed in his eyes for a brief moment. "My friend and I will look into it. Regardless of whether the legal documents have been tampered with, the courts in the United States have granted me and Jill custody of you."

Hope soared. They wanted her? Then reality crashed. They wanted her money. "Why?"

"For now, it's a way to protect you from Auclair," Doug said.

Jill sat on the edge of Layla's bed. "It also gives you time to decide what you want."

"I get to decide?"

"To a large extent." Doug sat beside his wife. "If you want to go back to school once it's safe, we can arrange that, but you would be able to visit us on breaks if you wanted."

Go back to school where she would always have someone who didn't care about her telling her what to do? "What if I don't want to go back?"

"If there is someone else you want to live with, we can look into that," Doug said. "Otherwise, you can come home with us to the United States."

"I would move in with you?" Layla asked.

Reagan's face lit up. "I'll get a sister?"

Wonder, disbelief, and a dozen emotions Layla couldn't identify flowed through her. "I have lots of money. You could move here and never have to work."

Jill squeezed her hand. "Whatever money your grandmother left you is yours."

"That's right. If you come to live with us, that's something you'd have to get used to," Doug said. "We don't have servants. You'd have to share a room with Reagan until we rearrange some furniture."

Layla looked from Doug to Jill. They were serious. Her eyes darted to Reagan.

Reagan's lips curved. "Pretty cool, huh?"

"What?" Doug asked.

"Getting a real family." Reagan crossed to her parents and motioned to Layla to join them. "Come on. Group hug."

Doug, Jill, and Reagan slipped their arms around each other, Jill and Reagan both holding their arms open in invitation. Layla's heart lifted, and she scrambled off the bed. She rushed into their embrace and, for the first time in years, found home.

CHAPTER 14

Now this was a vacation. Doug leaned back on the chaise lounge on the wide patio in back of the main house while Layla and Jill played tennis and Reagan rode one of the horses in the pasture.

For the past four days, the villa had become their own mini Club Med. The whole family, Layla included, had ventured into Geneva on Sunday, attending church and then walking around the city. Since then, they had remained at the villa enjoying the amenities afforded right here.

Fritz had helped Doug move the boat from the boathouse into the water, both to use during their stay as well as to provide an alternate escape route should one become necessary. Doug prayed their only time spent on the boat would be for pleasure. He had taken the family out on the lake twice already, much to the girls' delight.

Archery had become another favorite activity, Layla's skill outshining them all. The girl rarely missed the bullseye. Doug rarely hit the target. Good thing he was better with a gun. He was also better at investigation.

He had spent a few hours each day on researching the money-laundering operation at St. Augustine. Additional charges had already been brought against Marcel Auclair, and the school's CEO had been arrested. Doug hadn't found evidence that anyone else was involved beyond Grayson, but he still had hours of financial data to sort through.

Doug's phone rang. Keith again.

He hit the Talk button. "Anything new?"

"Nothing on Grayson yet. He's still at large," Keith said, answering Doug's unspoken question. "I finally received a copy of both of Genevieve de Felice's wills and trusts though, the real and the fake."

"Are we sure the will with Auclair on it was a fake?"

"Sure enough to make a case in court. The family attorney's office had a break-in almost two weeks ago. That would time with Layla's story of when Auclair said the new will was put in place."

Opposing emotions tangled inside him, relief that proof had been uncovered and fear that the genuine will would take Layla away from his family. "Who is Layla's guardian in the real will?"

"It was left up to the attorney's discretion."

Relief flowed through him. "So that part was the same."

"Yes, but I found another interesting discrepancy between the two," Keith said. "The executor of the fake will was Lorraine Clermont."

"The president of the organization that would inherit Layla's estate if anything happened to her."

"The very same."

"Email me whatever you've got along with a photo. I'll see if Layla recognizes her."

"Will do. Also, the police arranged for Layla's school records and her passports to be delivered to Geneva by courier today."

Doug sat up. "You gave out this address?"

"No. The police are sending the paperwork to the attorney's office. He said he can arrange for everything to be delivered to you, or he can meet you at his office on Saturday so you can pick it all up on your way to the airport."

Doug relaxed marginally.

"I would have waited to take care of those details until after you left Europe," Keith added, "but the police chief made the arrangements before he consulted me."

"Maybe I'll take the girls into Geneva tomorrow, and I can stop by the attorney's office then."

"Just let me know, and I'll relay the message."

"Thanks, Keith."

"If you really want to thank me, you should put in a request for backup. I could use a few days in the country."

"I'll think about it." Doug grinned and ended the call.

Fritz approached. "Excuse me, sir, but I'm taking my wife to a doctor's appointment. I'm not sure if we'll be back before dinner."

"Take your time. We can manage on our own." Doug stood. "Do I need to close the gate behind you?"

"No. We have a remote." Fritz excused himself and disappeared around the side of the house.

Doug's phone chimed with an incoming email. As expected, it was from Keith. Doug opened the attached photo and sucked in a breath. Except for a few subtle differences, the woman in the photo could have been Veronique Martineau, the woman who had given him the tour at St. Augustine.

Doug dialed Keith.

"That was fast," Keith said.

"I may need that backup after all." Doug headed toward the tennis court. "The woman in the photo looks like she may be related to Veronique Martineau, the admissions director at St. Augustine."

"How sure are you?"

"The resemblance is so strong I'd be shocked if they weren't sisters. They might even be twins." Urgency filled him. "Is it possible the police discussed Layla's location with Veronique?"

"I'm sure they did. Her name was on the paperwork from the school."

"If she knows the passports are being delivered to Geneva, she could already be on her way here. Is there anything that would tie Layla to the villa?" Doug asked.

"I don't think so, but I can't be sure if we received Layla's full file from the school. There's no way of knowing if the villa was listed in the contact information or not."

Doug reached the edge of the court and waved at Jill and Layla to join him. "Does Veronique know that we identified the fake will and trust documents?"

"I doubt it. That information hasn't been shared beyond the bureau and with de Felice's attorney."

"I'm going to pack my family up and get out of here. Better to err on the side of safety," Doug said. "You can set up surveillance in case she shows up."

"I'll contact the local authorities."

Doug hung up and called out to Jill and Layla. "We have to leave."

Alarm lit Layla's face. "What's happening?"

"It looks like Veronique Martineau could be involved with Auclair," Doug said. "We need to move somewhere she can't find us."

"I'll get Reagan." Jill hurried toward the stables.

"The Bachmanns just left." Doug debated his options. Pack everything up now or use their emergency plan? The urgency flowing through him made the decision for him. "I'm going to check the gate. I'll meet you by the dock."

"We're taking the boat?" Jill asked. "What about our things?"

"I'll come back and pack up once I have backup in place."

"Can I come with you?" Layla asked.

"You'd better stay with Jill and Reagan." Doug gave her arm a squeeze. "I'll be back in a minute."

Worry shone in her eyes. "Be careful."

"Stay with Mom and Reagan." He waited until she headed for the stable and then turned back toward the front of the house. Assuming Veronique was working with Grayson, had she managed to access the villa's address and put together the pieces to figure out where Layla was staying? And if so, how long did they have before she sent Grayson to finish the job he had started in Marseille?

* * *

All her life, Layla had followed the rules, always hoping that if she was good, she would someday get to go home. Why she would choose now to disobey, she couldn't explain. After all, she didn't want Doug and Jill to change their minds about keeping her, but something indefinable pushed her to follow Doug into the house, something she couldn't explain.

Doug was nearly to the other side of the room when she entered the great salon. Unlike when she had first arrived at the villa, the room no longer exuded the warmth she expected, despite the light streaming through the windows. Instead, something eerie and cold hung in the air, sort of like when Marie de Mont had left a toad in Layla's bed when she was eleven.

Uneasy, Layla stopped and looked around the room. Doug turned as though sensing her presence. Something moved near the back hall. Make that some*one*.

Her heart jumped into her throat. The man from Marseille! "Doug!"

Doug's gun was in his hand so fast that she wasn't sure if he'd been holding it the whole time.

"Freeze!"

The man didn't freeze. He ducked behind a chair, and an instant later his hand appeared over the top with a pistol gripped in it. He fired a shot in Doug's direction, but Doug had already darted out of the way, using her mother's favorite chair for cover.

"Layla, get down!"

For a second, she couldn't move. This couldn't be happening again. When Doug fired a second time, she dropped to the floor and crawled behind a table.

"Give it up," Doug said. "The police are on their way. You don't want to make this any harder than it has to be."

Her chosen hiding place wasn't nearly good enough. Layla scooted behind a long couch. Another gunshot sounded, and the vase on the table she had just been hiding behind exploded, fragments flying into the air.

Layla squeaked in alarm and covered her head with her hands as bits of pottery rained down on her.

Doug returned fire. At least, she was pretty sure the shot came from his direction.

Wanting to put as much distance between her and the man trying to kill her, Layla crawled along the back side of the couch until she reached the end table. Beyond the table lay another chair, this one her father's favorite. If she made it that far, she would only have a table between her and Doug.

Should she stay where she was, or should she try to move closer to the man who had already saved her life twice?

As though reading her thoughts, Doug leaned back into her line of sight and motioned her forward.

She pressed her lips together and nodded. She could do this. She counted to three and crawled past the table.

Doug fired again. Another shot and another exploding vase. Layla reached her father's chair, her breathing heavy and her heart pounding.

With only a table separating them now, Doug spoke in a whisper. "When I tell you, go behind me and run into the front hall. Hide behind the armoire. Don't go outside. He might not be alone."

Layla drew a deep breath, her brain trying to process his instructions.

"You can do this. I'll be right behind you."

Layla nodded.

"Remember, only go to the armoire." His hand flexed on the handle of his gun. "Ready?"

She squatted so her feet were under her, her hands still on the ground. She nodded again.

"Now." Doug rolled around the far edge of her mom's chair and fired off two shots.

Layla skirted behind him and then sprinted into the hall. She skidded to a stop when she reached the armoire and ducked behind it. Footsteps pounded behind her, and an instant later, Doug was by her side.

He sent another shot into the great salon as though reminding the other man to stay where he was.

"We're going to the door next," Doug whispered, his voice surprisingly calm. "Wait until I tell you before you follow me."

"Okay."

Doug reached out to the alarm control panel and hit a few buttons.

"What are you doing?"

"Setting off the alarm and opening the gate. I want to make sure the police can get in." He dropped his hand. "Ready?"

Even though she didn't think she'd ever be ready, she nodded.

Doug fired another shot, raced to the door, and pulled it open. He took a quick glance outside before aiming his gun back at the great salon.

"Layla, come on."

She forced herself into motion and rushed out the door.

Doug fired again as she passed him. Then he followed her outside and yanked the door closed.

CHAPTER 15

Doug led Layla into the bushes beside the entrance. They worked their way along the edge of the house until they reached a cluster of trees.

After a quick look around to ensure they were alone, he pulled out his phone and dialed Jill.

"Are you okay?" his wife asked, worry carrying over the line. "Were those gunshots?"

"Yes. Are you already at the dock?"

"Yes."

"Good. You and Reagan take the boat. Get as far away from here as you can," Doug said. "And call the police. Let them know we have at least one gunman at the villa."

"What about you and Layla?"

"We'll call you when we get out of here." Anticipating Jill's hesitation to leave them, he added, "I need to know you're safe so I can protect Layla."

"Be careful."

"We will." Doug hung up.

An engine sounded, and a car pulled up the drive. Grayson exited the house, his gun raised, his eyes sweeping the yard.

Doug put his hand on Layla's shoulder to keep her from moving and giving away their hiding place.

The car parked behind Doug's rental, blocking it in. A moment later, two women exited, Lorraine Clermont and Veronique Martineau. Grayson crossed to them, his eyes still scanning. After a hushed conversation, Lorraine opened her trunk and pulled out a hunting rifle. She passed it to Veronique before retrieving a second rifle for herself.

"They're going to hunt us down," Layla whispered, tears in her voice.

"We just have to outsmart them." But how? The police were at least ten to fifteen minutes away.

He had to even the odds or at least raise their odds in his favor.

"I want you to sneak around the corner of the house. As soon as you're out of their sight, run for the stables," Doug said.

"What about you?"

"I'm going to keep them occupied until the police get here." Doug gave her arm a reassuring squeeze. "Take one of the horses and ride to the neighbors'. Stay in the trees as much as you can."

She swallowed hard but nodded.

Lorraine started in their direction while Veronique walked toward the caretaker's house and Grayson headed the opposite way. If he reached the backyard, he would see Layla, but if Doug could distract him, maybe she could make it before anyone realized she wasn't with him.

"Go now."

Layla gulped in a deep breath and quietly moved around the corner and out of sight.

Doug gave her a few seconds' lead before he fired a warning shot at the woman approaching.

"Drop your weapons!"

As Doug hoped, the woman and her partners turned toward him.

Lorraine lifted her rifle.

Doug ducked as she fired, a chunk of wood from the tree above him splintering into the air.

Trying another tactic, Doug shouted, "We know about the fake will! It's all over."

Still crouching down, he moved to his left and aimed his weapon.

The woman fired again, the bullet whizzing over his head.

Doug returned fire, and he didn't miss. Lorraine's rifle fell from her hands, and she dropped onto the ground beside it.

"Lorraine!" Veronique lifted her rifle and fired twice before rushing to the other woman's side.

Both bullets impacted the tree only inches from where Doug stood.

He backed up to the corner of the house and stepped around the side so the wall would protect him. He peered around the edge only to jump back when Grayson aimed his gun at him.

A single shot fired, the bullet striking the wall of stone.

Now what? He couldn't shoot without exposing himself, but he didn't want to lead them to Layla.

He calculated the time it would take her to cross the yard and get to the stables. She should be there by now.

If he moved to the backyard, he could cover her if anyone tried to take a shot at her. And maybe he could get to the stables and ride out of here too.

Without a better option, Doug squatted down, fired one more shot, then turned and ran.

* * *

Disobedience had become the order of the day. The horse was saddled and ready to go, but Layla couldn't bring herself to leave Doug. He was only one man. There were three of them trying to stop him, three of them trying to kill him—and her.

Ignoring Doug's instructions, she hurried to the storage room and retrieved her favorite bow and a quiver of arrows. She entered an empty stall and pulled the top half of the exterior door open. She peeked outside. On the side of the house opposite where Doug had been hiding, the man from Marseille was creeping through the gardens. In the opposite direction, footsteps pounded against the ground. Fear clogged her throat. Did the footsteps belong to Doug or to the other people who wanted her dead?

Layla peeked outside. Doug! He was running toward her, but did he see the man with the gun?

Layla reached back and pulled an arrow from her quiver. She raised her bow and took aim.

The next moment passed by in slow motion.

The man saw Doug. He pointed his gun. Doug stopped and turned.

Layla released the arrow. The arrow speared the man's shoulder as he fired, his gun aiming skyward in the same instant he squeezed the trigger.

Doug dove to the ground, anticipating a bullet that was no longer aimed at him. The man cried out but remained on his feet.

Layla notched another arrow. Could she kill a man if he was trying to kill her?

The debate was still swirling in her head when he lifted his weapon just as Doug rolled over and fired.

This time, the man dropped to the ground with a thud.

Doug scrambled back to his feet and rushed to the stables.

"Layla!"

She backed out of the stall as Doug burst inside.

"I'm sorry . . . I was afraid they would kill you."

Doug enveloped her in a hug. "It's okay."

Layla's arms came around him, and she held on. When Doug stepped back, she said, "You can come with me now. We have two horses."

"We can't risk it. Veronique is still out there, and she has a rifle," Doug said. "I don't want to take the chance she might shoot you while we're trying to make a run for it."

"Then what do we do?"

Doug pulled his cell phone from his pocket and handed it to her. "Call the police. Let them know where we are. Describe Veronique to them and tell them there's an armed US federal agent on site."

Layla leaned her bow against the stall door. "What are you going to do?"

"I'm going to make sure she doesn't get a chance to shoot at us." Doug moved into the stall where she had been a moment ago, and Layla dialed 112. If Doug could believe they were going to get out of this alive, then she would believe it too.

CHAPTER 16

Doug barely reached the window when Veronique came into view. Or rather, Doug caught a glimpse of her hair as some leaves rustled in the trees across the yard. The woman wasn't moving like someone who spent her days behind a desk. She looked more like a hunter who knew how to flush out her prey.

Layla spoke from behind him. "The police are still ten minutes away."

Ten minutes was too long. If they were inside the house, they would have protection from gunfire, but the wooden walls of the stables wouldn't stop the bullets from Veronique's rifle.

As though punctuating his thoughts, a shot fired.

Doug ducked and pulled Layla down with him.

Layla trembled. "She's shooting at us."

"She's trying to flush us out of here."

"What do we do?" Layla asked.

Doug was asking himself the same thing. He needed to get outside where he could get an angle for a shot.

The horse behind him stirred. Another shot fired.

With backup still several minutes away, Doug grasped at an unlikely course of action, one that could get them both killed if it didn't work. Doug sent a silent prayer heavenward and pushed forward. "I have an idea, but I need your help."

"What do you want me to do?"

"First, I want you to crawl over to the stall with the horse in it. When I tell you, let the horse out. I'll send the other one out of here."

"How will that help us?"

"With any luck, I can use the horses as a shield so I can run to the woods. I need to stop her from shooting at you."

"You're leaving me here alone?"

"I won't let her get past me." Doug prayed Veronique wouldn't get past him. He nodded at the stall where Layla had been a moment ago. "When the horses run out, go back to the stall door and shoot an arrow into the trees to our right."

"Then what?"

"Take cover. Stay low to the ground and get back to the middle of the stables."

Doug moved to the horse that was tied up. He looped the bridle over its head and glanced behind him, where Layla squatted by the stall door for the other horse. "Ready?"

She nodded.

"Now."

Layla took the horse's halter and led it out of the stall. Then she swatted it on the rump and sent it running outside. Doug waited until Layla grabbed her bow before he led the other horse to the doors. He sent it outside, running beside it.

An arrow went flying into the trees, the rifle echoed, and Doug sprinted for cover.

* * *

Layla released a second arrow as Doug dove into the trees. Was he hurt? Had he been shot?

Fear pulsed through her, and she hurried out of the stall, keeping her head low like Doug had told her. Another gunshot rang out, and she stumbled. Wood splintered above her. She cried out, and her bow dropped to the ground.

"Layla!" Doug shouted.

He was alive.

"I'm okay!" Layla yelled back.

Another gunshot.

Fury and fear mixed inside her. Finally, she had people in her life who cared about her and who didn't care how much money she had. She had people who made her believe in family again. She wasn't about to let Veronique take that away from her.

Layla snatched up her bow and crawled into the nearest stall. She reached up, unlatched the top part of the stable door, and pulled it open. Then she repeated the process with the next two stalls so Veronique wouldn't know which one she was shooting from.

Choosing the center stall first, Layla notched an arrow. She peeked outside, but she couldn't see Veronique or Doug. Maybe an arrow would get Veronique moving.

Taking aim at a tree in the general direction of where the gunshots had come from, she drew back the arrow and released it. Nothing happened. Layla tried a second time but this time chose her target a few meters closer to the riding ring. When she released her arrow, someone startled and jerked back a step.

The flash of movement rustled in the bushes on the far side of the ring. Then the barrel of a rifle poked through. Layla darted into the center of the stables. Two shots fired almost in tandem, but neither of them appeared to have impacted the building. Creeping to the next stall, Layla peered out again. With a general idea of where Veronique was hiding, she pulled another arrow from her quiver.

Sirens sounded in the distance. The police! Just a few more minutes, and help would be here.

Hope took flight only to be destroyed when Veronique straightened and took cover behind a tree. Her rifle lifted, this time in Doug's direction.

Layla's mind raced, the future she envisioned for herself and her new family evaporating into what-ifs.

Fear for Doug's safety pushed Layla to draw back the arrow. She focused on her target, inhaled, and released.

The arrow shot through the air and hit the barrel of the rifle. Bullseye.

Veronique grunted, and she and the rifle fell to the ground.

Doug rushed out of his hiding place, his pistol aimed at Veronique. "Hold it right there."

Veronique reached for the rifle. Doug fired a warning shot, and she jerked her hand back.

The sirens grew louder.

Doug kept his aim steady. "You don't have to die."

"You killed my sister."

"She tried to kill me."

Veronique reached toward her gun.

Layla sent another arrow through the air, this one landing only inches from Veronique's hand.

Footsteps pounded toward them. Two uniformed police officers rushed into the yard. One aimed at Veronique, and the other aimed at Doug.

"I'm a federal agent with the United States of America," Doug said calmly. "I'll lower my weapon as soon as she is disarmed."

The officers must have understood English because one rushed forward and kicked the rifle farther away from Veronique. Within seconds, he had her on her feet, her hands cuffed behind her back.

Was it over? Finally? Layla dropped her bow and hurried to the main doors. She barely reached them when Doug rushed inside.

"Are you okay?"

Her eyes flooded with tears of relief, but she nodded.

Doug pulled her into a hug and held her tight. "It's over now. You're safe."

She sniffled. "Are you sure?"

"Yes, but I think I'm ready to take you to your new home."

"I'm ready for that too."

CHAPTER 17

Layla descended the stairs into the kitchen of her new home. The tennis rackets from their game last night still leaned against the wall in the living room, and the dog lay beside them, gnawing on one of the tennis balls. They had a dog. She'd always wanted a pet.

Jill looked up from the stove, the scent of blueberry pancakes wafting on the air. "Good morning. Are you hungry?"

"Starving."

"In that case, go get Dad and Reagan. They're in the living room."

Layla's lips curved at the casual way she called Doug "Dad," as though Layla had always been part of this family. She only took one step toward the living room before Reagan passed through the doorway.

"Dad said to tell you he'll be a minute. He had to take a work call."

"In that case, girls, can you set the table please?"

Chores. That was another new development for Layla, but she rather liked the sense of accomplishment that came from doing things to help the rest of the family. She also loved her new school and the fact that she got to come home every night. She missed Anna-Lise, but the Dubois family had already promised to let her come visit this summer.

Layla and Reagan finished setting the table, and Doug walked in.

"Well, I have some very good news."

"What?"

"The team going through the financial records of St. Augustine finished their analysis. They've confirmed that the only people who were receiving funds from the money laundering through the school were the CEO—who has already been arrested—Auclair, Grayson, Veronique, and her sister," Doug said.

"I still don't understand how the whole money-laundering thing was working," Reagan said.

"Basically, some people here in the US were getting money from illegal activities, mostly illegal gambling operations," Doug said. "They deposited cash into accounts set up in the names of children who had died. The money would then be used to pay tuition for kids who weren't really going to school, and then the school donated money to the charity Lorraine Clermont had set up. From there, the charity paid money to a construction company, owned by the people with the gambling operations, for fake projects."

"It sounds so complicated," Jill said. "How did they go from laundering money to trying to kill Layla?"

"The headmaster saw an opportunity when Layla's grandmother passed away. From what we know now, Layla's grandmother suffered from heart problems since before the plane crash."

Jill tilted her head, compassion in her expression. "That might explain why she never came to visit you."

Layla shrugged. She doubted her grandmother wanted to help raise her, but she tried to grasp the little glimmer of brightness Jill offered. "Maybe."

Doug continued. "We also found evidence that Auclair was skimming a good deal of money from your trust fund and logging the expenses as your travel. It looks like your grandmother may have been told you were vacationing during your breaks."

"If she did, she never said anything."

"She was very ill for a very long time," Doug said. "My guess is that Auclair had the fake will and trust documents prepared long before your grandmother actually passed away."

"He was waiting for Layla's grandma to die?" Reagan asked. "That's sick."

"Yes, it is," Doug said. "There's no way to know when Auclair recruited Grayson to switch the real will and trust documents with fake ones, but had they been successful, they would have split nearly two billion dollars between the five of them."

Gratitude swelled within Layla. "If it hadn't been for you, they would have gotten away with it."

"Oh, I don't know. You have pretty good survival instincts." Doug ruffled Layla's hair.

Love took root beside the gratitude.

"Another piece of good news: we were able to recover most of the money that was stolen from your trust fund," Doug said.

"That is good news." Jill set a plate of pancakes on the table.

"Not only that. I spoke with the attorney in Switzerland again. He is going to continue on as the trustee of the de Felice estate, and he has also agreed that the trust will maintain the family home outside Geneva, at least until Layla gets old enough to decide what she wants to do with it."

"Will Fritz and Celine stay there, then?" Layla asked.

"Yes. They'll keep overseeing the maintenance, so it will almost be like having family still there," Doug said.

Jill put a hand on Doug's shoulder. "You know, you do have a lot of vacation time saved up."

Doug's eyebrows rose. "And you have your summers off."

Excitement lit Reagan's eyes. "Are you talking about going back to Europe?"

"It's an idea." Doug turned to Layla. "What do you think, Layla? Would you like to spend a couple weeks in Switzerland this summer?"

"And then we'll come back here?"

"Yes. And then we'll come back home."

Layla's smile bloomed. "Sounds perfect."

SHADOWS OF TRUST

CHAPTER 1

Josh Pierce closed the freezer and snapped the lock into place. The idea to store his supplies in Hillary Adams's basement was the first step in his plan to finally cash in on a real payday—one that would let him get out of the drug business. He was so sick of dealing with addicts.

Quite the irony, he supposed, that to keep his profits coming, he was constantly trying to create new addicts, but once he succeeded, he grew irritated by how needy those people became. Hillary was just one of many. Or she had been until she'd let it slip that the trust fund for her niece and nephew had millions sitting in it, millions Hillary couldn't touch. Well, Josh was going to touch that money, and he knew exactly how to accomplish it.

With his drug supplies safely locked up so Hillary couldn't get into them, Josh left the storage room and walked into a large rec room. The two windows on the far side of the wall were small, too small for him to climb through. He continued into the single bedroom in the back corner of the basement. But it wasn't a bedroom. Rather, it was some sort of craft room, one with a window that wasn't much larger than a couple shoeboxes.

Hillary's voice carried down the stairs. "Aren't you done yet? The kids will be home soon."

Josh returned to the storage room and tugged on the lock to make sure it was secure before he jogged up the steps to where Hillary waited. She was pretty in a worn-out sort of way; her dependence on pain killers had taken its toll on her, aging her a good decade beyond the thirty-two years old he knew her to be.

Josh had no idea if she took the pills to fight the lingering physical pain from the car accident that killed her brother and sister-in-law or if she simply didn't want to face the memories. Either way, he supposed he should feel sorry for her. His sympathies stirred for the briefest moment before he pushed the sensation aside. In his business, he couldn't afford to care about the people he dealt with. He needed to take care of himself and only himself.

"I'll be back on Thursday to restock," Josh said.

"Fine." Hillary stretched her hand out. "I held up my end of the bargain. Now it's your turn."

Josh slipped a bag of pills from his pocket to Hillary's hand.

She immediately pulled two out and walked toward the kitchen.

Josh headed outside, stopping to inspect the security panel on the wall inside the front door. The alarm panel wasn't active, but he couldn't tell if it was turned off or if it had been disconnected entirely. He'd have to find out before he followed through with his plans. It wouldn't do to have an alarm go off at an inopportune time.

Slipping outside, he closed the door behind him and made his way to his car, a black Lexus that helped him look like one of the many well-to-do residents of the Tyson's Corner and McLean areas of northern Virginia. He slid into the driver's seat, rested his hands on the wheel, and watched. Twenty minutes later, Hillary's teenage niece walked down the street alone. She let herself into the house. A half hour later, her seven-year-old brother followed.

Easy targets. The two kids were there for the taking, and so was their money.

* * *

Early morning light streamed through the kitchen window as fourteen-year-old Sophie Adams scraped the bottom of the peanut butter jar and slathered the last bit onto a slice of bread. They'd run out of jelly two days ago.

Her grandmother's large kitchen boasted tall cabinets, an oversized refrigerator, and a walk-in pantry, but it had been months since any of them had been stocked with any regularity. Not since before Grandma had gotten lost again and been put into an assisted-living facility.

A yearning sparked inside Sophie, that need for someone to talk to, someone to care about her, someone to hug her and tell her everything was going to be okay. Sophie let out a sigh. The constant wish that her parents were still alive would never be fulfilled, but she couldn't help hoping Aunt Hillary would let her visit the nursing home. Grandma might not remember much, but surely she would recognize her own granddaughter. Unfortunately, Hillary rarely did much of anything beyond taking pain meds and hanging out with friends. At the rate things were going, Sophie wouldn't see her grandmother again until she was old enough to drive herself. Two years. Grandma really might forget about her by then.

Turning her attention to her current task, Sophie opened her little brother's lunch box and removed the used plastic bags. Carefully, she rinsed them and turned them inside out to dry. She then placed them in the drawer that used to be filled with aluminum foil, plastic wrap, and Ziplocs, trading them for the bags she had washed yesterday.

Leaving the knife sticking out of the empty peanut butter jar, Sophie crossed to the door a short distance down the hall from the kitchen, the one that led to the basement. Her stomach curled at the thought of going down into that dark space, but the chance that there might be more peanut butter tucked away in the room where Grandma kept food storage was motivation enough to move her forward.

She opened the door and flipped on the light, the single overhead fixture illuminating the narrow staircase. Her chest tightened. She could do this.

Slowly, Sophie started down the stairs. The fifth one creaked beneath her weight. Why did the basement creep her out so much? It hadn't bothered her when Grandma had still lived here.

Drawing a deep breath, she kept going. At the bottom, she turned on the two lights illuminating the large space that had once been a rec room. The television that used to hang on the wall was gone, as were the comfy chairs that used to sit opposite it. She missed the days when she, Mason, and Grandma curled up with a bowl of popcorn and a Disney movie.

Those days were over. The mere thought that such moments wouldn't ever repeat themselves brought moisture to Sophie's eyes. She blinked the tears away. Emotions weren't something she could indulge in, not when she had more important things to worry about—like how to come up with lunches for her and her brother.

Sophie opened the door to the storage room, quickly turning on the light. The huge chest freezer stretched along the far wall, a shiny padlock ensuring it remained closed. Sophie suspected Hillary was hiding something in there, but what, Sophie didn't know.

She turned to the bare shelves that had once been lined with the jams and jellies Grandma had canned herself. She checked the shelves where emergency supplies were stored. A tent, cooking supplies, and sleeping bags. No food. The cabinet behind her revealed a handful of unopened spice jars, three jars of relish, and a bottle of ketchup. Not exactly items she could use to make a meal.

After another quick search, Sophie glanced at the padlock. Anything worth having must be inside there. It wasn't fair. All the other kids at her school got to have real lunches and real families. She and Mason were stuck with an aunt who barely knew grocery stores existed.

With a shake of her head, Sophie turned off the lights and hurried back to the kitchen.

Mason's footsteps pounded down the main staircase. A moment later, he walked in, a tattered backpack hanging from his shoulder, his pants an inch too short and one of his mismatched socks poking through the hole in his left sneaker. At seven years old, he didn't care much about whether his clothes matched. But Sophie cared.

If their parents were still alive, Mom would have taken them back-to-school shopping months ago, and they would have received new clothes and toys for Christmas. This year, the extent of their Christmas presents had been a loaf of pumpkin bread from their next-door neighbor and some candy from their school holiday parties.

The familiar ache expanded inside Sophie's chest, but she pushed it away. This was no time for grief and no time for feeling sorry for herself. She might not have any adults in her life who cared about her, but Mason deserved better. And, like it or not, she was all he had.

Her brother climbed onto the barstool opposite her. "Can I have breakfast?"

Not *what* was for breakfast but, rather, *could* he have breakfast. How things had changed.

She unzipped her lunch box. Three oranges and two apples were secured inside, all leftovers from her friends' school lunches, items she had collected when she'd offered to return their trays.

"Do you want an orange or an apple?"

"Can I have toast?" Mason asked hopefully. His expression was the same one he used to have when he asked for pancakes.

"Sorry, bud. We don't have enough bread to last the week if we eat it for breakfast." And she wouldn't have a fresh supply of babysitting money to buy another loaf until Saturday.

Mason's lower lip quivered, but he held out his hand. "An apple."

Hating the disappointed look on his face, she handed one over and put an orange in his lunch box, along with a peanut butter sandwich.

Aunt Hillary sauntered into the kitchen, still wearing her pajamas. "You're still here?"

Sophie closed the two lunch boxes to hide the contents. "Mason's bus doesn't come for another ten minutes."

Hillary circled the counter and grabbed two precious pieces of bread before Sophie could hide that too.

Sophie picked up the knife again and scraped the empty peanut butter jar. Realizing her efforts were futile, she put two pieces of plain bread into a plastic bag and slipped that into her lunch box, carefully keeping the lid low enough so Hillary couldn't see inside. "Can you pick up some peanut butter from the store? We're out again."

"I just bought some for you a few weeks ago."

Sophie tilted the empty jar toward Hillary. "It's all gone."

Hillary rolled her eyes and sighed as though going to the grocery store was a huge inconvenience. "I'll try to pick some up when I go out later."

Hillary-speak for no. Anytime she used the word *try*, the likelihood of her following through was only about ten percent.

"I need something to give Mason for lunches," Sophie pressed. The moment the words were out of her mouth, she regretted them.

Hillary whirled toward her, anger sparking in her eyes. "Look, I'm doing the best I can. If you don't want to live here, you can try foster care, but I seriously doubt you and Mason will end up together."

The sentiment wasn't a new one, but it was enough to light the familiar fear inside Sophie, a fear that was reflected on Mason's face. She forced out an apology. "Sorry."

Hillary's eyes cleared for a moment. "I'm sorry too. I shouldn't have said that. It's just been hard lately keeping up with everything."

Sophie didn't know what Hillary had to keep up with, but she knew better than to ask. She quickly slid her lunch box and the half loaf of bread into her backpack. No telling how much more her aunt might eat if she left the bread in the house. Her appetite was unpredictable at best.

Sliding the straps of her backpack over her shoulders, Sophie headed for the door. "Come on, Mason."

Mason scrambled after her, and they walked outside.

Sophie glanced back at the grand structure with the double columns supporting the second-floor balcony. It was a beautiful house. If only it felt like home.

CHAPTER 2

Doug Valdez sat at the oval table in the Cabinet Room of the White House, still unable to fathom that this was part of his new reality. Secretary of Homeland Security. Six weeks ago, he had still been a special agent with the FBI. Now one of his close personal friends was the president of the United States, and Doug was one of his top advisers.

Two seats down from Doug, the secretary of state briefed the president on her most recent concerns about the North Korean president. The secretary of defense weighed in with his opinions before they moved on to the next item on the agenda. One by one, they discussed the various topics until, finally, the meeting ended.

Doug slid his laptop into his computer bag and pushed back from the table. He only made it as far as the hall before President Whitmore stopped him. "Doug, do you have a minute?"

"Of course, Mr. President." Doug silently congratulated himself for remembering to use Jim's title rather than his name.

Together, they fell into step as they headed toward the Oval Office.

"How are Jill and the kids settling in?" Jim asked.

"They're getting there. Jill's adjusting to her new school, and she likes her class." Doug's lips twitched into a smile. "Of course, if your wife needs to do any stress baking, I'm sure Jill and the girls wouldn't mind some of her cinnamon rolls."

Jim laughed. "Funny you should mention that." He entered the Oval Office and circled behind his desk. "She needed a break from planning the Easter Egg Roll last night."

Doug set his computer bag on the chair closest to him. "Are you telling me there are cinnamon rolls in the residence?"

Jim sat down. "I am, and Katherine has a pan with your name on it waiting in the kitchen."

"Your wife is the best."

"I couldn't agree more." Jim leaned back in his chair. "I'm sure she'll mention it when you pick up the cinnamon rolls, but we wanted to invite you and your family to brunch the morning of the Easter Egg Roll. And of course, you're all welcome to stay for the festivities. We thought your girls would enjoy attending."

"I'm sure the kids would love that."

"I look forward to seeing them," Jim said. "You mentioned Jill likes her new school. What about the girls?"

"So far, so good," Doug said. "Honestly, I'm surprised how good they've been about transferring midyear, especially Layla."

"You were smart to involve them in your decision when you took this position."

Doug smiled. "Seems to me that you were the one to suggest it."

"Positions like ours affect everyone in our families."

"I'm finding that out," Doug said. "And I'm suddenly a lot more open to the idea of allowing telework for some of my top managers."

"As long as the classified work is kept in the office, do what will keep your people happy and productive."

"I'll do my best."

"You're already doing a great job." Jim adjusted his laptop on his desk. "Speaking of which, I had a meeting with the governors yesterday. Several requested assistance for new snow-removal equipment. The paperwork is already at FEMA, but it sounds like it's tangled in red tape."

A severe winter storm combined with a power outage in Kansas City several weeks ago had crippled the region, and Doug doubted they had time to wait, especially with several new storms heading their way. "I'll meet with the director of FEMA and shake those funds loose."

"Thanks, Doug." Jim motioned toward the door. "And don't forget your cinnamon rolls."

"Oh, I won't." Doug picked up his bag. "Thank you. And thanks for giving my kids such great exposure to the White House. Jill and I really appreciate it."

"It's our pleasure."

* * *

Jill hit the button on the garage door opener, overwhelmed by the number of boxes still stacked on her side of the garage. What she really needed right now was a month off and a personal secretary who specialized in cutting through red tape.

Between Doug's appointment as secretary of Homeland Security, moving into a new house, her new job, and settling their two adopted daughters into their new schools, the last thing she and Doug needed was to put something else on their plate. Yet both of them had received promptings that their family wasn't complete. And for her and Doug, that meant another adoption. Unfortunately, the adoption agencies she had looked into had flooded her with paperwork that would last her into the next century.

She gathered the latest set of paperwork from where she'd dropped it on her passenger seat and hurried through the frigid air to the house. The moment she stepped inside, the scent of something baking wafted toward her.

Her heart instantly lifted. Both of her daughters had insisted she teach them how to bake, and now she would reap the benefits, not only in what they produced but in the joy their successes would give them.

"Something smells wonderful." Jill entered the kitchen, where fourteen-year-old Layla stood beside the counter, a rolling pin in her hands as she spread out cookie dough.

Round cookies with a crisscross pattern on them already filled the cooling rack, and the dog lay at her feet, Buster clearly hoping Layla would drop something.

"What are you making?" Jill asked.

"*Sablés*," Layla said with a perfect French accent. She continued in French. "Technically, they're *sablés bretons*, but Americans call them French butter cookies."

Jill took a moment to translate her next comment into French. "Is today a French day?"

"*Oui*." Layla picked up a cookie cutter. Continuing in French once more, she asked, "Do you want to try one?"

"*Oui*." Jill's vocabulary in French was still lacking, but saying yes was one thing she had mastered.

The decision for her, Doug, and Reagan to learn French had been made only a few days after Layla moved in with them. They hadn't wanted Layla to lose the language skills she'd gained after spending most of her childhood at a French boarding school, and the fact that they intended to spend most of their family vacations at the estate in Geneva, which Layla had inherited from her family, made it logical for the rest of them to gain some basic conversational skills.

During Layla's first few months with them, they had spent twenty minutes every night learning together. Once school started, they had forced themselves to develop their language skills even further by designating Mondays, Wednesdays, and Saturdays as days when they would speak only French in their home. Even the dog had learned basic commands in their new language.

Jill bit into one of the cookies, the texture more like shortbread than a typical cookie. "This is good." She took another bite. "What are these for?"

"French class. We're supposed to bring in something to share as part of our presentation on French culture."

"Everyone is making French food?"

"We can do a poster instead, but I thought it would be more fun to make these."

"Let me put my things away, and I'll help you." At least, Jill was pretty sure that's what she said. "Oh, and after dinner, I need to make some cookies of my own. I have a meet-the-teacher night coming up, and I promised to bring treats."

"I don't have much homework tonight. I can help."

Jill had been hoping Layla would say that. She smiled. "*Merci.*"

By the time Jill came back downstairs, both of her daughters were in the kitchen, along with her husband. Doug had already snitched two cookies and was being scolded by Reagan in nearly fluent French.

"*Bonjour.*" Jill crossed to Doug and gave him a kiss.

"*Mon amour.*" Amusement flashed in Doug's dark eyes, and he put his hand on her waist to hold her in place before kissing her again.

"Haven't we already established a rule against kissing in the kitchen?" Reagan asked.

"You've tried." Jill laughed. She pulled back before Doug could embarrass their daughters any further with his show of affection. "What are you doing home so early?"

"My last meeting got cancelled, and I have a lot of personnel files to look over. I thought I could review those here at home." He motioned toward the oven. "And I smelled cookies."

As expected, Reagan and Layla both laughed.

"Since the girls are baking, maybe you can put some hamburgers on the grill for dinner tonight," Jill suggested.

"If you make the hamburger patties up, I'll cook them," Doug said.

"Sounds like a plan," Jill said. "And after that, you can help me fill out some paperwork."

"More?" Doug shook his head. "We just finished writing a book for the last agency."

"Sorry. This whole adoption process is a lot more complicated when you don't stumble into it."

"So we're finding out." Doug eyed the cookies cooling on the counter before he asked Layla, "Are you going to let me steal another one?"

"Only one." Layla held up her spatula. "We're saving the good batches for my class."

Doug lifted his eyebrows. "This isn't a good batch?"

"It could be better."

Doug shook his head. "You sound just like your mother."

Layla beamed at him. "That's a good thing, *non*?"

Doug nodded. "*Oui*."

* * *

Josh leaned against the wall in the lobby of the busy office building, a blue ball cap on his head, his right hand tucked in the pocket of his jeans. To anyone glancing his direction, he would appear to be a well-off client waiting for an appointment, right down to his designer labels. He looked the part, but Josh wouldn't fit in until he had real money of his own. His time was almost here.

A little spurt of adrenaline rushed through him as he pondered his plans to move beyond the drug trade. If his instincts were right—and they usually were—Hillary would show up before the day was out.

Several people entered and exited the lobby before his client arrived and gave the subtle hand signal to indicate he was the one Josh was waiting for. As the man in his twenties approached, Josh withdrew his right hand from his pocket, a small plastic bag tucked between his thumb and his palm. He and his client shook hands and greeted each other as though they were old friends, the drugs passing easily from Josh's hand to his client's.

The man slipped his hand into his jacket pocket, depositing his purchase there and retrieving his payment. After a brief, meaningless conversation, they shook hands again—this time a folded stack of bills passed into Josh's hand.

The client continued into the building and turned down the hall toward a side exit.

Over the next half hour, Josh met with four more clients and received four more payments. Done for the moment, he headed for the door. With a new supply of cash in his pocket, he crossed the parking lot to his car.

A black BMW pulled up a short distance from him, and it took only a moment to identify the blonde woman behind the wheel as Hillary. Josh fought back a smile. Right on time.

Josh diverted from his vehicle and approached her. Keeping his voice low but conversational in tone, he said, "I didn't expect to see you so soon. I don't owe you anything until Thursday."

"But I ran out of pills. I'm good for it. I'll have cash on Monday after I get the grocery money for the kids."

She wasn't good for it, and they both knew it. That was why he'd struck a deal with her to lock the better part of his stash in her basement. Besides granting him access to her house, with the recent crackdowns on the local drug trade, he didn't want to risk a search of his place.

"Tell you what. I'll give you some extra now, but I need a favor." Time to reel her in and put the next piece of his plans in place. He reached into his jacket pocket and retrieved the appropriate amount of product, just enough to give her what she wanted but to also make sure she would be back to see him before the weekend was through. He held the drugs in his hand but didn't pass them to her. "It's too hard for me to wait for you to be home when I need to get my supplies. I need a key and the alarm code to your house."

Her gaze lowered to his hand before she spoke to him, a moment of lucidity in her gaze. "But the kids might be there."

Exactly. Adrenaline rushed through him. "Don't worry about the kids. Get me the key and the code, and I'll give you what you want."

"I can't wait." Desperation hummed through her voice. "I just need you to supply me for a few days, just until Monday."

"Give me the code, and I'll help you out."

"I don't have a code except to the garage. I couldn't afford the bill for the security system."

Excellent. "This will get you through today." He pressed the drugs into her hand. "Get me the key, and I'll give you the rest."

CHAPTER 3

Sophie accepted the offer of an extra chocolate chip cookie to take home to her brother when she finished babysitting Saturday evening, but she turned down the ride home. She needed to stop by the store, and starting from the Corbins' house was closer than walking from her house and back again. Plus, this way, Hillary wouldn't know that she had been earning money instead of going to tutoring like Sophie had claimed.

With twenty dollars in her pocket, she retrieved a basket from the stack by the grocery store entrance, the scent of freshly baked doughnuts and muffins permeating the store. Her mouth watered, but she turned away from the bakery section, the familiar pang of longing cutting through her. She could never afford anything over there. Instead, she turned down the bread aisle and searched for the cheapest option. After typing the price of the store-brand bread into her grandmother's old calculator, she continued to where the peanut butter and jelly were located. Though she preferred strawberry, she chose the grape. It was cheaper.

Ramen noodles came next.

Sophie did the math on the calculator and figured out the taxes. That would leave her another four dollars to buy something for breakfast and still let her save five dollars for new shoes for Mason.

She glanced toward the bakery aisle again but turned away. Her options were limited. Maybe another loaf of bread and some butter so they could have toast. But butter was expensive and not easy to hide from Aunt Hillary. Cereal would cause a similar issue. Even if she had enough for both cereal and milk, Hillary and her boyfriend would wipe out the milk by Monday. No, she needed something that Hillary wouldn't eat.

Sophie continued along the aisles, wishing for the prices to be lower and the money in her pocket to be more. She slowed when she reached the baking section. Pancake mix. A bag of the just-add-water version was on sale, half price for $1.69. Her mood brightened when she spotted a bottle of syrup, also on sale, for $2.29. She added both items to her basket and headed for checkout. As soon as she paid for her purchases, she tucked her change—five dollars and twelve cents—into her shoe. She then loaded the groceries into her backpack, opening the twelve-pack of ramen so she could fit everything in more easily.

Slipping her arms through the straps of her backpack, she walked outside and huddled into her coat. Or rather, her mother's old coat. Hers was too small for her and too pink for Mason.

The wind stung her cheeks and eyes, so she kept her focus on the sidewalk in front of her. The mile walk took the better part of twenty minutes, her face growing numb with each step.

When she reached her house, she walked in to find Hillary pacing in the living room, her latest boyfriend, Duncan, sitting on the couch. Sophie tensed. This boyfriend, like so many of the others, had that dazed look in his eyes, and he looked like he hadn't bothered to comb his overly long hair in a week.

Hillary whirled on Sophie. "Where have you been?"

Sophie took a step back. "I had tutoring, like I do every Saturday."

"Well, we've been waiting to leave for almost an hour. You know we can't leave Mason home alone."

That hadn't stopped Hillary before. Twice in the past month, Sophie had come home to find Mason here by himself, terrified. She suspected the neighbor dropping by and finding Mason home alone last week had left Hillary worried about how it might look if she neglected him again. Or maybe she hadn't had her pain meds yet and was actually thinking clearly for a change.

"I'm sorry, Aunt Hillary," Sophie said, choosing her words carefully. "My teacher offered to tutor me for free. I can't say no since I'm still not doing well in French class."

"I never should have let you take a language class in middle school." Hillary snatched her purse off the couch as her boyfriend stood up. "Make sure you two clean the kitchen and the bathrooms before you go to bed tonight."

"We will." Sophie stayed where she was while Hillary and Duncan headed out the front door. "When will you be home?"

"I don't know, but you'd better be in bed when I get back."

Sophie nodded. She hated being home alone, especially at night, but having Hillary around with her friends was even worse.

As soon as Hillary and Duncan left, Sophie moved to the window. She watched them get into Duncan's truck and waited for them to drive away. Once they did, Sophie locked the door and called out her brother's name.

Mason peeked over the upstairs railing that overlooked the living room. "Are they gone?"

"They're gone, and I have a surprise for you."

"What?"

"Come into the kitchen." She carried her backpack to the kitchen counter and unzipped the front pocket. She pulled out the cookie as Mason walked in.

"A cookie?" He took it. "Thanks!"

"You're welcome."

He bit into it and then held it out. "Do you want some?"

Her heart melted, and Sophie ruffled Mason's unruly hair. She did want one, but she didn't want to be selfish. Mason probably hadn't eaten since she left. "Madam Corbin gave me one before I left her house. That one is all yours."

Mason's eyes lit up, and he took another bite.

"Not only that, I thought we could have one of Mom's favorites for dinner."

"Pork chops?"

"No. Those cost too much." She pulled the pancake mix out of her backpack. "Pancakes. We're having breakfast for dinner."

Mason pumped his fist in victory. "Yes!"

CHAPTER 4

Sophie's backpack was nearly empty when she walked down the school hallway on Wednesday afternoon, the contents consisting only of her lunch box, a plastic grocery bag, and the thin binder she used for all of her classes.

She'd hidden the last of her groceries behind the Lego bin in Mason's closet. Hopefully, Hillary wouldn't think to look there.

The pancake mix had turned out to be an inspired purchase. For the past two days, the school lunches had included fruits and vegetables served in the little plastic dishes that made them impossible to save and take home for later. The constant worry that she and Mason would run out of food hummed through her, but thankfully, Hillary had slept in every day this week and had yet to steal any of their breakfast. At least, she assumed Hillary had slept in. Other than when Hillary had passed out in the living room watching television on Monday night, Sophie hadn't seen her aunt since Hillary had gone out with her boyfriend Sunday night.

Hillary had never been gone that long without checking on them. Come to think of it, Sophie couldn't remember hearing the doorbell ring for her aunt's typical DoorDash delivery for the past few nights. Maybe she should be worried. Or at least feel guilty that she hadn't missed her aunt.

Sophie walked into her French class, immediately distracted by the table on the far side of the room and the food that covered it. Her mouth watered. The food here today could feed her and Mason for weeks. But it wasn't all for them. Sophie prayed for leftovers.

She set her backpack on the floor beside her desk and fished out her assignment, a poster that was little more than a piece of paper from the library printer with some images of crepes and french onion soup pasted onto it.

As expected, when class started, Sophie was called on to go first. With Adams as her last name, she should be used to it, but sometimes she wished she could have a last name that came at the end of the alphabet.

Sophie carried her attempt at the homework assignment up to the front of the class. In her stilted first-year French, she explained how common crepes and french onion soup were in France. At least, that's what the internet said.

After she finished, she handed her paper to her teacher and reclaimed her seat. Every student after her started by collecting a food item off the table and explaining what it was. From the looks of it, the French bakery on Wilson Boulevard had received a lot of business yesterday. Only Layla de Felice presented a homemade version of her selection, some sort of butter cookie that smelled amazing.

Sophie's stomach grumbled through class until, finally, the time came for everyone to sample the food that had been brought in. Despite her hunger, she waited until the rest of her class went, choosing to go last in line.

Excitement filled her when she noted the amount of food still left on the table. Eagerly, she selected one of the fancy slices of cake that had been arranged on a paper wrapping and then loaded up the rest of her plate with cookies that would be easy to slip into her bag to take home.

Sophie ate a bite of the cake, reveling in the contrast of the sweet icing and the spongy middle. She was nearly done with it when the bell rang.

A few people returned to the table to collect their leftovers, but most headed for the door without a backward glance. What would it be like to have so much food that you didn't have to worry about leaving leftovers behind?

Sophie waited until most of her classmates had passed by before she unzipped her backpack and opened the grocery bag she had stashed inside. Her hands trembled, and she glanced around to make sure no one was looking. Then she quickly transferred the cookies into the bag.

Lingering and eyeing the food still on the table, she ate her last bite of cake and threw away the cake wrapper. So much food, and it would give her and Mason something beyond the usual items they could scrounge from others' lunches and her small babysitting wages. Determined to take advantage of the opportunity in front of her, Sophie gathered her courage and carried her plate back to the table, where the teacher and the new girl stood. "Do you think it would be okay if I took some of the leftovers home to my brother?"

"That's a great idea," Madam Corbin said. "I certainly don't want to take it all home with me. Layla, do you want to take some with you too?"

"That would be great, if you don't mind," Layla said with an accent that wasn't quite American. "My mom has a thing tonight. I'm sure she would love to have extra cookies."

"I'll let the two of you decide how you want to divide everything up. I don't need any of it." Madam Corbin eyed an éclair. "Well, maybe just one of these."

As soon as Madam Corbin transferred her éclair onto a plate and set it on her desk, Layla started consolidating cookies onto trays, dividing everything in half. "I think you should take the mille-feuille, the profiteroles, and the éclairs. Those are way too messy for second graders."

Sophie had no idea what second graders Layla was talking about, but her second grader at home was going to think he'd died and gone to heaven when she walked in with all these leftovers. And with the promise of cookies at Mason's meet-the-teacher event tonight, they would be able to save all of this food for later.

Feeling a little guilty that she was taking more than her share, Sophie said, "Maybe you should take more of the cookies then."

"Sounds good." Layla shifted a few cookies from one platter to the other, still leaving Sophie with a third of them.

Curious about the new girl in school, Sophie asked, "Where did you move from?"

"We just moved from Woodbridge, but before that, I lived in France for a few years."

"If you lived in France, why are you in first-year French?" Sophie asked.

"Because this is all they offer in middle school." Layla shrugged. "And I don't want to lose what I already know."

"Living overseas must have been amazing."

"It was interesting." Layla's tone made it seem like her time in France had been far less than amazing.

Madam Corbin returned to the table holding a box of gallon-sized plastic bags. "I'm going to keep one of these croissants for my breakfast tomorrow. You can use these to keep everything fresh."

"*Merci.*" Layla took two bags and divided up the croissants—four for each of them.

"My brother is going to love me forever."

Madam Corbin offered a sympathetic look. "Anything we can do to give him a bright spot in life is a good thing."

Sophie couldn't agree more. Gratitude swelled inside her, and an unexpected bout of tears threatened. She quickly blinked them away. "Thank you." Correcting herself, Sophie added, "*Merci*."

* * *

Jill finished her presentation to the parents and students, ending with the best way to contact her when questions arose. The turnout at tonight's meet-the-teacher event had been higher than she'd expected, nearly every student showing up with at least one family member. The promised cookies had already been well picked over, the students enjoying their treats while the parents asked a few questions.

At the back of the room, Reagan sat at a narrow table, her precalculus book open in front of her. How the girl could concentrate with a roomful of kids and parents, Jill had no idea, but Jill had needed help setting everything up and had enlisted her daughters' assistance. Rather than remain in Jill's classroom during the presentation, Layla had opted to sit in the library down the hall to study for an upcoming science test.

Several kids circled back to the treats as a few parents who had come in late approached and introduced themselves.

Jill spotted Mason and his sister by the refreshment table. The school principal had informed her that the boy had lost his parents in a car accident and was now living with his grandmother. Jill was trying to figure out a polite way to move a particularly overeager parent along so she could talk to Mason when Layla walked in. Her eyes lit with recognition, and she crossed the room to talk to Mason's sister.

Another five minutes passed before Jill was finally able to join them.

"Hi, Mason." Jill gestured to the teenager standing between Mason and Layla. "Is this your sister?"

Mason nodded, his mouth full.

Jill looked around the room before she asked, "Where's your grandma?"

"She couldn't come," Mason's sister said.

"Mom, this is Sophie. She's in my French class at school," Layla said.

"It's nice to meet you, Sophie." Jill shook her hand. "Thanks for bringing Mason."

"He gets excited about cookies."

Jill looked down at the boy's plate. Chunks of pineapple, two miniature egg-salad sandwiches, a cherry tomato, and three ham roll-ups. Not a cookie in sight.

As though sensing Jill's confusion, Sophie put her hand on Mason's shoulder. "Mason, we should go."

He eyed the food on the table. "Do we have to?"

"Yes, but you can bring your plate with you."

Reagan approached. "Do you want to take some of this home with you?" Reagan's gaze met Jill's, an unexpected glimmer of compassion and hope in her eyes. "That's okay, right, Mom?"

"Of course." Jill pointed at her desk. "There should be some disposable containers over there."

"I'll get them." Layla retrieved them as another parent approached with her little girl, a rather shy child who was still trying to find her footing within the school environment.

By the time the last few people left, the refreshment table was bare, and Mason and his sister were gone.

"Thanks for cleaning up, girls." Jill grabbed her purse and took stock of the food that remained. "I thought you two would want to keep some of the ham rolls and banana bread for your lunches.

"I think Sophie and Mason needed them more," Reagan said softly.

"What do you mean they needed them more?" Jill asked. Of the kids in her class, not a single one was on government meal assistance.

"I was watching them," Reagan said, her voice quieting to barely above a whisper. She looked up, her eyes filled with that haunted look she always got when she spoke about her life before coming to live with Jill and Doug. She sniffled before she continued. "I don't think those were snacks for them. With the way they were eating, it looked like that was dinner."

Jill put her hand on Reagan's shoulder. "What makes you think that?"

Reagan blinked against the sudden moisture in her eyes. "They had that air of desperation I remember feeling when I was afraid I would run out of food."

Reagan's statement didn't make sense. The school was in a high-income area, with established neighborhoods. Yet, if anyone would recognize someone who was going without, it was Reagan. She had suffered neglect the first thirteen years of her life. Trying to see beyond the expected, Jill said, "It was odd that Mason didn't have any cookies on his plate."

"That's because they already have a bunch at home," Layla said. "I helped Madam Corbin clean up today. We split the leftovers between the two of us."

"Sounds like I need to pay more attention to what's coming to school in Mason's lunch box."

"My guess is his lunch tomorrow will be leftovers from tonight's refreshments and the cookies from Layla's French party," Reagan said, her tone somber.

The very thought of a child going hungry brought with it a wave of sadness. "I really hope you're wrong."

"So do I."

* * *

Hillary was home, and she wasn't alone. Besides Duncan's truck parked in front of their house, two other cars filled the driveway.

Sophie slowed her bicycle as she approached the house. Mason stopped beside her, a flicker of fear on his face. "She's having a party," Mason whispered.

"Yeah." Was it bad to wish Hillary wasn't home right now? Sophie had hoped to hide some of the food in the fridge before her aunt saw it. Now she wouldn't have a choice but to unload in front of Hillary. Unless Hillary wasn't in the kitchen. Sophie held out hope for that—and that her friends would leave soon.

She climbed off her bicycle and walked to the control panel beside the garage door. "When we go inside, take your backpack up to your room, and hide it in your closet."

Mason nodded.

Sophie punched in the code to open the garage door, and she and Mason stored their bicycles inside next to Grandma's black BMW, the car Hillary used now.

Not sure what to expect when they entered the house, Sophie squared her shoulders, took a deep breath, and led the way into the kitchen. Dishes lay scattered all across the counters, the remnants of various desserts visible on a half dozen plates. Her heart sank. So much for hiding the cheesecake bites, chocolate éclairs, and profiteroles from French class in the crisper drawer.

Sophie closed the garage door and crossed to the refrigerator. Maybe the disaster in the kitchen looked worse than it was. She opened the fridge and stared. Every bit of food was gone. Anything she put in there tonight, she might as well just give to Hillary and her friends.

Quietly, she closed the refrigerator door and ushered Mason forward.

Together they headed for the stairs, but they only made it as far as the living room entrance before Hillary's sharp voice snapped at them. "Where have you two been?"

"At school." Sophie stepped between Hillary and Mason. Her gaze swept over the crowded living room. One guy appeared to be asleep on the couch, his body tilted at an odd angle. Two others played video games on the TV. When she turned her attention back to Hillary's irritated glare, she expanded on her answer. "Mason had a meet-the-teacher night."

"Why didn't you tell me?"

"We only found out about it on Monday." Technically, she'd found out last week, but Hillary hadn't exactly been in a conversational mood the last time she'd seen her.

Duncan, Hillary's boyfriend, got up from the couch and swaggered across the room until he reached Hillary's side. "You should have at least called or texted Hillary to let her know where you were."

"I would have, if I had a phone." Or if she still had a phone. Hers had disappeared from her room only a few days after Grandma had been put in the nursing home. Sophie suspected Hillary had taken it, just like she had taken the money from Mason's piggy bank and the cash from Sophie's wallet.

A little flash of surprise appeared on Duncan's face, but he pressed on. "You could have left a note."

Sophie's gaze swept past him and landed on the nearly empty bottle of wine—or maybe it was champagne. Sophie could never tell the difference. Regardless, if Hillary had been drinking, Sophie needed to get Mason out of here. Hillary was not a nice drunk.

She turned to her brother. "Mason, go on upstairs. I'll be up in a minute."

Mason gave her his wide-eyed look, the one that showed he was afraid.

"It's okay. I'll be right up."

Mason nodded and scampered up the stairs.

Sophie turned back to face Hillary and forced out an apology. "Sorry. I didn't mean to worry you."

"You should be sorry. You're just like your dad, always doing whatever he wanted while I was stuck at home." Hillary leaned in, the smell of alcohol on her breath. "Don't forget; if it wasn't for me, you'd be out on the streets. You and Mason."

Sophie's palms dampened, and panic shot through her. The chill from her ride home hadn't yet faded from her hands and face. What would she do if she and Mason didn't have a place to live? "I'm sorry." She gulped. "It won't happen again."

She stepped back, instinctively trying to keep her backpack out of view. It didn't work. Hillary focused on it. "What did you bring back with you?"

"Nothing."

Hillary reached out and snatched the backpack from Sophie's hand. The moment she unzipped it and saw the contents, her lips curved upward. "Hey, everyone. My niece brought us food." Hillary pulled out the ham rolls and passed them to Duncan.

"Nice." Duncan took the offering and headed back to the couch.

"What else do we have in here?" One by one, Hillary pulled out the plastic bags filled with leftovers: mini-sandwiches, pineapple chunks, broccoli and cauliflower pieces, and the rest of the cookies from French class.

"Can I at least give Mason some of the veggies?" Sophie asked. He'd like the pineapple better, but that wouldn't pack as well in lunches.

"You already had some at your party tonight." Hillary dropped Sophie's backpack to the floor and turned back to her friends, taking the food with her.

Sophie snatched it up and quickly moved to the stairs. She needed to hide everything Mason had brought home in his backpack before Hillary came looking for more food.

Laughter carried from downstairs, and an uneasiness flowed through Sophie. Maybe she should have Mason sleep in her room tonight.

CHAPTER 5

Josh had everything in place, if only Hillary would show up with the blasted key. He didn't know who had been supplying her for the past few days, but someone was cutting in on his business, and it was time he found out who.

He handled several deals throughout the morning and lunchtime, a local deli serving as his chosen site for today. When he didn't receive any messages from Hillary, he climbed into his car and headed for McLean. It was time for a little house call.

The woman still owed him enough money to warrant a visit—especially since the people above him expected their cut. And he needed that key. Breaking and entering wasn't really his thing, especially in a neighborhood filled with video doorbells and security systems.

When he reached Hillary's house, he parked beside a mature oak tree that obscured his car from the house beside Hillary's to avoid making it obvious that he was visiting her. He strode to the front door and used his knuckle to ring the bell.

A minute passed. He rang the bell again.

This time, shuffled footsteps sounded on the other side of the door.

Hillary pulled it open, her eyes glazed over. Yep, someone was definitely cutting into his business.

"What are you doing here?" she asked, her confusion obvious.

Josh pushed his way into the house and closed the door behind him. Two empty cartons from a Chinese food restaurant lay on the end table in the living room, a fork sticking out of one of them. An empty padded envelope lay on the couch, an open prescription bottle beside it.

Josh picked up the bottle, noting that the name wasn't for Hillary. Apparently, she'd managed to steal her mom's meds again, and she'd been binging on more than just Chinese food.

"I expected to hear from you a few days ago."

Her confusion intensified.

"You were supposed to bring me a key. Remember?"

"A key?" Hillary asked. "For what?"

"For this house." Taking a more direct approach, Josh asked, "Where's your spare key?"

"On the hook in the kitchen."

That was easier than he'd expected. Josh continued deeper into the house. Sure enough, a set of keys hung from a designer rack on the wall. Josh snatched the entire keyring and pocketed it. When he spotted a spare garage door opener, he grabbed that too. The garage door opener might prove even more useful than the house key.

With a satisfied smirk, he took stock of the layout of the kitchen, including the door leading to the garage. Then he headed for the basement. Might as well restock while he was here.

* * *

For the past two days, Jill had made a point of walking past her class's lunch table after they had all settled down to eat. Half the kids opted to buy lunch from the school cafeteria. The other half dined on a variety of meals ranging from sandwiches, chips, and store-bought desserts to fancy wraps and bakery treats.

Yesterday, Mason's battered lunch box had contained leftover cookies from Sophie and Layla's French class along with a croissant. No fruits or vegetables. No drink of any kind. From what she could tell, there wasn't any sort of protein either. He had cookies again today, but the croissant had been traded out for a simple peanut butter sandwich.

Alarm bells sounded in Jill's head as her suspicions matched Reagan's. Something wasn't right here.

"Hey, Mason." Jill knelt down beside the young boy with dark hair in need of a trim. "Did you make your own lunch today?"

He shook his head. "My sister made it."

"Sophie, right?"

He nodded.

"Does she always make your lunch?" Jill asked. That might explain the lack of balance inside his lunch box.

He nodded again. "And she made me pancakes."

The absolute joy in his voice and his obvious adoration for his sister gave Jill some comfort. Clearly, he felt loved.

"That's sweet of her." Fishing for information, she asked, "Does your grandma make pancakes for you too?"

His expression clouded. "She doesn't live with us anymore."

"Why not?"

"She had to go to a nursing home."

"Who takes care of you and Sophie now?"

He shrugged but didn't answer.

Surely these two children weren't living on their own. "Who do you live with?"

"Aunt Hillary."

Jill didn't recall any information about an aunt in Mason's file. She straightened. "You enjoy the rest of your lunch."

Mason took a bite of his sandwich as Jill continued out of the cafeteria.

Was the evidence of the past few days enough to warrant getting involved in Mason's home life? Jill thought so, but she had no idea how her principal would take her suggestion that the school administration intervene. And Jill risked the very real possibility of being tagged as a troublemaker or, worse, being let go for overstepping. Technically, she was still in her trial period and would remain so for the next three years.

Jill shook those thoughts away. She couldn't sit back and do nothing.

Rather than return to her classroom to eat her own lunch, she diverted to the front office. After offering a quick greeting to the receptionist, she continued to the principal's office and knocked on the open door.

"Karen, do you have a minute?"

The principal looked up and waved her inside. "What's up?"

Jill entered and closed the door behind her. "I'm concerned about Mason Adams."

"How so?" She gestured for Jill to sit.

Jill described what she and her daughters had witnessed at the meet-the-teacher night as well as her observations of Mason's lunches for the past two days and Mason's comments about his grandmother and aunt.

Karen tapped on her keyboard. "I don't see any record of an aunt listed on his contact or guardian information."

"It may have been a simple oversight when the grandmother moved into a nursing home, but from what Mason said, it sounds like his sister is preparing his meals." Jill's concerns simmered, bubbling into an increased fear for the young boy's well-being. "I'm probably overreacting, and I know this likely isn't common at this school, but I really think a home study is in order."

Karen fell silent for a long moment, clearly pondering the implications of calling attention to the concern that one of their students wasn't being properly cared for. Finally, she said, "Let me poke around and see who Mason is living with. If I sense anything isn't right, we'll consider moving forward with a home study."

Jill recognized the runaround and suspected Karen would do little more than make a phone call and update the school's records. Despite her frustration, Jill stood. "Thank you."

Karen swiveled in her chair, angling away from her computer and toward Jill. "In the meantime, let me know if you see anything else. And make sure you document your conversation with Mason today as well as your observations."

"I will." Though Jill doubted Karen would follow through. Irritated that Karen was either unwilling or afraid to act, Jill left the principal's office and headed back to her classroom. Nine more minutes until she needed to pick up her students from the cafeteria. Mason might not be the only person subsisting on cookies for lunch today.

* * *

Sophie sat at her normal spot in the cafeteria, her lunch box in hand. As she had feared, the leftovers Mrs. Valdez had sent home with her and Mason hadn't lasted through the night. With several of Hillary's friends still passed out in the living room yesterday morning, Sophie hadn't dared try to make breakfast in the kitchen, so she and Mason had been forced to make do with leftover carrot sticks and croissants for breakfast. Thankfully, there were enough croissants for her to use those for their lunches too.

Today had been a little better. Hillary's friends had all left at some point yesterday, and this morning her aunt hadn't been around. Mason had been thrilled to have pancakes for breakfast. She hadn't had the heart to tell him that she'd used the last of the pancake mix this morning and that they'd be going without tomorrow.

Layla approached with her lunch box in hand and, for the second day in a row, sat beside her. Sophie still couldn't believe Layla's mom was her brother's second-grade teacher. Thank goodness Mrs. Valdez was nice. Poor Mason had really struggled with the constant stream of substitutes over the past few months, before Mrs. Valdez had been hired.

Emily and Angela, two of Sophie's usual lunchtime crowd, sat down across from her, pizza on both of their trays. Sophie's mouth watered. She couldn't remember the last time she'd had a slice of pizza.

"What are you all doing this weekend?" Emily asked.

"I'm babysitting," Sophie said.

"You're always babysitting," Emily complained. "You should come with me and Angela to DC. We're going to see Riverdance."

Sophie wasn't sure what Riverdance was, but maybe that was a good thing. She didn't like thinking about the experiences her friends got to have without her. "Sorry. I can't."

"What about you, Layla?" Angela asked. "I bet my mom can get you a ticket."

"Thanks, but I already have plans too," Layla said. "Maybe next time."

"You two are missing out," Emily said.

Sophie didn't need her friend to state the obvious. A cloud fell over her as the conversation shifted from Angela and Emily's weekend plans to the new iPhone Angela wanted.

When their lunch period ended, Layla stood and motioned to Sophie's lunch box, which now only held her used sandwich bags. "Do you want me to throw away your trash?"

"No, that's okay. I can do it." Or not. Sophie needed to save the plastic bags. Another one had ripped when she washed it out this morning.

Layla threw her trash away and returned to Sophie's side. As soon as Emily and Angela left to return their trays, Layla said, "I don't mean to be nosy, but do you mind me asking what happened to your parents?"

The familiar ache surfaced. "They died in a car accident."

"I'm so sorry. It's hard to lose your parents so unexpectedly." Something flashed in Layla's expression, as though she was experiencing a similar grief. "How old were you?"

"Ten."

"I was seven," Layla said, a wistfulness in her tone. "I lost my parents in a plane crash."

"You're an orphan?" Sophie narrowed her eyes. "But I thought Mrs. Valdez was your mom."

"She is now. I moved in with her and Dad almost a year ago."

A piece of the anchor weighing down Sophie's heart chipped away. Finally, someone who understood. "Do you still miss them?"

"Every day, but I know they'd want me to be happy." Layla started toward the door. "I'm sure your parents would want the same thing for you."

Sophie sighed. "That might be what they would want, but that doesn't mean it's going to happen."

"Why not?"

Part of her wanted to tell Layla what life was really like right now, but if she did, what would happen? Would her aunt follow through on her threats and turn her and Mason over to foster care or, worse, throw them out onto the street? Would they be separated or freeze to death? Afraid to take the risk, Sophie said simply, "It just isn't."

* * *

Jill's chat with Mason at lunch kept circling through her head, a heaviness pressing in on her that she couldn't explain. She'd stayed late after school to review the boy's assessment scores and past work. Mason demonstrated a high level of intelligence, but the work he turned in was sloppy or missing with an occasional assignment looking far too neat, suggesting someone else had done it for him.

The inconsistency suggested a less-than-stable home environment, but whether that instability warranted outside interference remained to be seen. If the churning in her stomach was any indication, it did. If only Karen agreed that Jill's concerns warranted a real investigation.

With snow in the forecast, Jill packed up some extra work to take home with her for the weekend, including the notes the school social worker had provided on Mason. When she arrived at her house, she opened the garage door, expecting to see the usual cluster of boxes preventing her from pulling into what would eventually become her parking spot. To her surprise, the space was empty except for a few boxes, which had been stacked along one wall.

Jill pulled into the garage for the first time since moving in, not sure who to thank for the privilege. Since Doug's spot was empty, her girls must have been the culprits.

Gathering her things, she closed the garage door and walked into the mudroom. The scent of tomato sauce hung in the air. A clean garage and dinner waiting for her? What had she done to deserve this good fortune? Usually, when she came home, she had to scramble to get dinner on the table. One of these days, she was going to get more organized and actually plan out their meals.

She toed off her shoes and left them on the rack by the door. When she stepped into the kitchen, Layla sat at the table, a book open in front of her and Buster at her feet. Reagan lay on the love seat in the living room, her legs dangling over the edge, her phone lifted so she could see the screen.

"Something smells good." She inhaled and spotted the takeout boxes on the kitchen counter. "You ordered out?"

Reagan held up her phone. "Dad said we could."

"After a long week, I'm thrilled to eat anything I didn't have to cook." Jill set her bag on the kitchen chair beside Layla. "Did you two clean out the garage?"

"A few people from church stopped by." Reagan rolled off the love seat and joined them in the kitchen. "Dad said we had to help."

Layla looked up from her book and glanced at her sister. "You hardly helped at all until the missionaries showed up."

Jill bit back a smile. "The missionaries were cute, huh?"

"Oh yeah." Reagan grinned. "I guess the elders quorum president asked Dad if we needed anything before the storm hits."

"He actually said yes?" Jill lifted her eyebrows. "It's a miracle."

"I think this new job is good for him," Reagan said.

"You're probably right." Jill couldn't deny that since Doug had started working with President James Whitmore—Jim to his friends—Doug's time had been consumed with ensuring the safety and well-being of others. That often left him little time to worry about what was going on at home. "Any idea when Dad's supposed to be home?"

Layla looked at the clock on the wall. "About ten minutes."

"I'm going to change. I'll be right back." Jill started toward the stairs.

"Oh, Madam Corbin wants you to call her." Layla dug through her notebook and produced a scrap of paper with a phone number on it.

"Any idea what she wants?"

"She wanted to know if I can help her tutor on Saturday."

This was unexpected. "Do you want to help her tutor?" Jill asked.

Layla nodded, an eagerness shining in her eyes. "It would only be for about three hours on Saturday afternoons. Madam Corbin said she does three tutoring sessions back to back, and they're small groups—only eight students per hour."

"I'll give her a call." Jill headed upstairs and changed into her favorite jeans and one of Doug's old FBI T-shirts. Though she wasn't sure how she felt about her fourteen-year-old taking on a job, she dialed Madam Corbin's number.

After exchanging greetings, Madam Corbin described the tutoring services she provided for middle and high school students.

"With Layla's fluency in the language, she would be a great help," Madam Corbin continued.

Jill had no doubt Layla would do a fabulous job, but Jill's protectiveness pushed to the forefront. "I'm sure she would be wonderful, but I'm not sure we'd feel comfortable with her working one-on-one with students."

"We actually work in groups of four," Madam Corbin said. "Everything is at my house, so I would have her in the living room while I'm in the dining room. There's a large opening between the two, so I'll be able to see her the whole time."

That alleviated some worry, but not all. Jill was all too aware of how kids could sense when a teacher's attention was diverted elsewhere and take advantage of the situation.

Clearly sensing Jill's internal dilemma, Madam Corbin continued. "How would you feel about letting her come tomorrow to try it out? You're welcome to observe so you can get a sense of how the tutoring sessions work."

Though Jill still wasn't sure she wanted Layla working while she was still adjusting to a new home and a new school, she hadn't missed the excitement in her daughter's expression. "I suppose we can give it a try."

"Wonderful. We run three one-hour-long sessions starting at one. If she could come over about fifteen minutes earlier, that would be great."

"We'll see you then."

CHAPTER 6

Sophie bundled her coat tighter around her as she walked to Madam Corbin's house. She wished she could be one of the students being tutored by her French teacher, but instead of studying, she would be making money by babysitting Madam Corbin's two children.

The wind stung her face, her nose and cheeks already numb. Sophie quickened her step. The mile-and-a-half walk usually wasn't that bad, but today she wished she could stay home with Mason, curl up in front of the television, and watch a movie.

Mason was hopefully still doing exactly that. Hillary hadn't been up when Sophie left, so she'd set Mason up with two of his favorite DVDs, a peanut butter sandwich, and the last of the leftover cookies from the meet-the-teacher night.

If it hadn't been so cold, she might have tried to bring Mason with her today, but she couldn't imagine him walking so far, especially since she'd need to walk back home with their groceries. Not to mention, she still didn't have quite enough money for a new pair of shoes for him.

A gust of wind stole her breath, and Sophie gasped. Only two more blocks. Ignoring the sharp pain in her lungs, she quickened her step. She'd be inside soon.

Another gust of arctic air rushed past her, a reminder of the clouds hanging low in the sky. The smell was familiar, that crisp scent that hinted of snow. She didn't need snow right now.

A car pulled up in front of Madam Corbin's house as Sophie reached it, and Layla emerged from the passenger side. "Hey, Sophie."

Sophie nodded a greeting, not sure she could form words without her teeth chattering.

Mrs. Valdez climbed out of the driver's side and circled the car until she reached Layla and Sophie. "Sophie, it's good to see you again. Are you here for tutoring?"

Sophie shook her head and continued to the front porch. She needed to get out of this cold.

Layla and Mrs. Valdez followed.

Sophie pressed the doorbell, and a moment later, the door opened, a rush of warm air flowing over her.

"Oh, you're all here." Madam Corbin ushered them inside, waiting until she closed the door before focusing on Layla's mom. "You must be Mrs. Valdez."

"Please, call me Jill." Mrs. Valdez shook Madam Corbin's extended hand.

"And I'm Tasha." Madam Corbin turned to Sophie. "Gabriel and Mikaela are downstairs in the playroom. I told them they could watch one movie, but they need to clean up down there first."

Sophie nodded and continued down the hall to the basement stairs. The scent of freshly baked brownies carried on the air, bringing with it memories of her early childhood. Grief swept over her, a longing to once again experience her mother's embrace, to hear her father's laughter, to be a real family with a real home.

Her chest tightened, and she grabbed the railing with her frozen fingers. That wasn't her life anymore. Somehow, she had to survive until she was old enough to access her inheritance. Once she had money, she could be the one to take care of Mason. She would learn how to make brownies and chocolate chip cookies and pork chops. And she and Mason would have movie nights every weekend—without Hillary and her pain meds.

* * *

A kidnapping in broad daylight. It was bold, but if he timed this right, Josh would be in and out without anyone knowing he was there.

He waited in a borrowed black BMW down the street from Hillary's house, his lips curving when Hillary drove by in her mom's car, a car identical to his current ride. That was too easy. An offer of a hotel room for a few days in Virginia Beach, along with a bit of extra product to get her through the week, and she'd left right on time. Josh had handed off her drugs to an associate. He'd also indicated that Hillary only had until four o'clock to pick them up.

Based on his observations over the past few weeks, Hillary's niece wouldn't get home until at least four thirty. That meant he would have time to drug the boy and settle him in the trunk of his car before dealing with the girl. Since the girl always entered using the code in the garage, all he had to do was wait behind the door leading to the kitchen. She would walk in; he'd drug her from behind. Nice and simple.

Theoretically, he could take just the one kid, but if he took both and waited a couple days to make his demands, the cops would be hard pressed to figure out when the kidnapping had occurred, much less try to track him down using traffic cameras. He watched enough TV to know how those things worked. And then there would be the ransom of five million dollars—high enough to leave Josh set for life and low enough for the kids' trust fund to cover the cost.

Confident in his plan, Josh waited five minutes to ensure Hillary was really gone before he drove down the street and pulled into the driveway, hitting the garage door opener as he went. He pulled inside and took Hillary's spot in the garage. Then he hit the garage door opener again to close himself inside before exiting the vehicle.

He approached the door leading to the kitchen. Voices carried from the living room, and Josh froze. It only took a moment to determine the sound came from the TV. Perfect.

Moving forward slowly, he crossed the kitchen and entryway. The chairs angled toward the television were both empty, and he couldn't see anyone sitting on the couch. Then again, the kid might not be tall enough for Josh to see him from this distance.

Josh pulled a syringe from his pocket, checking to make sure he had the one with the child-sized dose of the fast-acting sedative. It wouldn't do for the boy to die, at least not yet.

Three more steps were all it took for Josh to close the distance between him and the couch. Sure enough, the boy sat in the center, his head leaning back against the cushions. Without hesitation, Josh gripped the boy's shoulder and slid the needle into his arm.

The boy yelped with surprise. Then he tried to pull away. Only a few seconds passed before his struggles ceased, and his little body went limp.

* * *

For three hours, Jill worked on her lesson plans, watched her youngest daughter speaking in French with a group of high school students, and worried about Sophie.

The girl's red nose and cheeks when she arrived at Tasha's home suggested she had walked some distance in the cold, which begged the question, why?

Across the room, a boy who appeared to be around seventeen stumbled over a response, but rather than break into English, he rephrased his answer to use his existing vocabulary. Apparently, Madam Corbin's ruse of telling everyone Layla was a new student from France had pressured the teenagers into trying to speak French, unaware that Layla was fluent in English as well.

Madam Corbin finished up with her group of students and sent them into the kitchen for snacks. She joined Layla's group briefly before nudging them into the kitchen as well, Layla included.

"Well, what do you think?" Tasha asked Jill.

"I have to admit, I was a little nervous about Layla working with kids older than her, but she did great."

"I agree. She far exceeded my expectations," Tasha said. "And it's so great for the students to speak with people their age."

Jill lowered her voice. "How long are you going to let them think Layla doesn't speak English?"

Tasha tilted her head toward the back of the house, clearly listening to the conversation going on in the kitchen, a conversation that was primarily in French. "As long as I can get away with it."

Jill laughed. "I don't blame you."

Layla walked into the living room and asked in French, "What do you think, *Maman*? Can I keep helping?"

"You had fun?" Jill asked, also speaking in French.

"Very much."

"Well, Saturdays are French days. If you want to continue, I'm sure we can make it work."

Layla's face lit up. "*Merci!*" She gave Jill a hug.

"Can you do me a favor?" Tasha asked Layla, her voice low. "Can you go tell Sophie she can bring the kids up to have a snack? And let her know that we aren't telling my students you speak English."

Layla nodded, her smile still in place. "Where is she?"

"In the basement. The stairs are down the hall to the left."

Layla left the room, heading in the direction of the basement stairs.

"Does Sophie babysit for you every week?"

"She does." Tasha moved deeper into the living room, away from the students. "I don't know what's going on in her home, but I get the feeling that she needs the money for basics rather than for fun."

"How far away does she live?"

"About a mile and a half, but I only know that because I looked it up in her file," Tasha said. "She never lets me pick her up or take her home, but she's here on time every week."

"Maybe I can convince her to let me drop her off," Jill suggested. "It might be easier for me since Layla is her age, and I'm not one of her teachers."

"That would be great if you can get her to say yes. It's too cold out there for her to walk."

"Agreed."

Several of the students headed out the front door, calling out their goodbyes in French. The rest followed, Layla and Sophie bringing up the rear. As soon as the door closed behind the last of the students, Tasha pulled a twenty-dollar bill from her pocket and handed it to Sophie. "Sophie, thanks so much for your help today."

"You're welcome."

Jill looked down at the money, trying to see the situation through Reagan's eyes. What would Sophie use the money for? From the looks of the frayed hem of her jeans and the hole in Mason's shoe, neither of the children were buying new clothes.

Determined to find out more about her daughter's new friend, Jill said, "We should get going. Sophie, why don't you let us give you a ride."

"It's okay. I don't mind walking."

"I can't let you walk home, not in this weather." As though the Lord was giving her an extra excuse to take Sophie home, snowflakes flurried outside the window. "It's already starting to snow."

"I—" Sophie started.

Jill cut her off. "Come on, girls. I need to stop by the store on my way home, and we don't want to let too much snow accumulate on the roads."

Tasha led the way to the door and rested her hand on the knob. "Enjoy the rest of your weekend."

Jill stepped outside, the snow now falling steadily. She unlocked the door to her car, grateful that Sophie climbed in without complaint. As soon as everyone was inside, she swiveled in her seat so she could see Sophie. "Are you okay if we stop at the store? I thought you might need to pick up a few things too."

Relief shone on Sophie's face. "Actually, I do have some shopping I need to do."

"Great," Jill said. "As soon as we get to the store, we'll divide and conquer."

* * *

Mrs. Valdez wasn't kidding when she said they were going to divide and conquer. As soon as the three of them walked into the store, they each grabbed a cart, and Sophie was left alone to do her shopping without an audience. Layla had been sent to the baking and cereal aisles, while Mrs. Valdez headed toward the produce section.

Sophie hurried through her typical purchases—bread, peanut butter, and ramen—before checking the price on the pancake mix. Unfortunately, the sale had ended, and the price was once again out of her range. Though she should probably buy another loaf of bread, Sophie didn't want Mrs. Valdez or Layla to see exactly what she was buying, and she had no idea how long it would take for them to do their shopping.

Using the self-checkout lane, Sophie paid for her purchases. She then moved to a bench at the front of the store and sat down, quickly loading everything into her backpack. Within five minutes, Layla and her mom moved through one of the regular checkout lines, their carts full. They reached the bench where Sophie waited.

Mrs. Valdez scanned the empty bench beside her. "Did you already finish your shopping?"

Sophie nodded. "I put everything in my backpack."

"In that case, let's get you home before the snow gets any worse." Mrs. Valdez led the way out to the car. A light dusting of snow already covered the windshield. They quickly loaded the groceries into the trunk and climbed inside.

A few minutes later, Mrs. Valdez pulled into the driveway behind where Hillary parked her car.

Sophie unbuckled her seatbelt. "Thanks for the ride."

"You're welcome." Mrs. Valdez turned off the car and popped the trunk. "I hope your aunt doesn't mind, but we bought a few things for your family too."

Sophie blinked several times. "You what?"

"I wanted to make sure you wouldn't have to go out again until after the storm passes." Mrs. Valdez climbed out of the car. So did Layla.

Still stunned that someone would buy her and Mason groceries, Sophie took a moment before she, too, opened her car door. The wind whipped over her, the falling snow coming down at an angle and swirling around them.

Mrs. Valdez held out two grocery bags to Sophie. "Can you take these?"

Numbly, Sophie nodded. Not sure what to think about Mrs. Valdez's generosity, she said simply, "Thank you."

She moved to the garage and punched in the security code to open it. When she turned back to wave goodbye, Layla stood behind her, a gallon of milk in one hand and two more grocery bags hanging from the fingers of her other hand. Mrs. Valdez was right behind her, carrying several more bags.

"All of that is for us?" Sophie asked.

Mrs. Valdez nodded. "It's supposed to be a big storm."

Stunned beyond words, Sophie stepped inside the garage. If she had to guess, Layla and her mom were only keeping half of what they'd bought.

Her mind was still spinning as she moved past Hillary's car. Not sure what her aunt would do if she walked in with someone unannounced, Sophie stopped beside the door leading to the kitchen. "You can just set that down there. I can bring it all in."

"We don't mind helping you," Mrs. Valdez said.

Sophie was still trying to come up with an excuse to prevent a possible confrontation with her aunt when her gaze landed on the black car beside them, a car that didn't have a scratch along the driver's side door. Narrowing her eyes, she set the groceries down and took a step toward the car.

"Is something wrong?" Mrs. Valdez asked.

Sophie peered through the driver's side window. No trash on the floor, no garage door opener clipped to the passenger side visor, no extra clothes strewn across the back seat. Sophie's chest tightened. "This isn't our car."

CHAPTER 7

A SUDDEN CHILL THAT HAD nothing to do with the weather rushed through Jill. She shifted all the grocery bags into her left hand and put her right on Sophie's shoulder to keep her from entering the house. "Sophie, can you call your aunt? Maybe she can tell us why there's a different car here."

"I don't have a phone."

"You can use mine."

Sophie shook her head. "I don't know Aunt Hillary's number."

Another wave of unease rushed through Jill. Though it didn't make any sense, the mere possibility of anyone walking into the house sent a streak of panic through her. "Girls, go back out to the car."

"But Mason's in there." Sophie tried to pull away.

Sophie's sense of fear rippled through Jill and caused her to tighten her grip on Sophie's arm. "Sophie, trust me. I'm going to call my husband. We'll have him come over and make sure everything is okay inside."

"Come on, Sophie." Layla reached for the bags in Jill's hand. "Let's put all of this back in the trunk until my dad gets here."

Jill let Layla take the extra groceries, and she shifted so she was between Sophie and the door leading into the house. She pulled her cell phone from her coat pocket and dialed Doug, walking to the rear of the black BMW.

"Hey," Doug greeted her. "When are you going to be home? I don't want you out on these roads."

"I need you to come check out a student's house," Jill said, her voice low. "There's a car in the garage that isn't theirs, and I have a really bad feeling."

Doug's voice instantly changed into cop mode. "Text me the address. I'll be right there."

Jill ended the call and texted the address to Doug. She then took a photo of the license plate. She texted the image to Doug and returned to the car where Sophie stood next to the rear passenger door, Layla right beside her.

Snow continued to fall steadily, both of the girls now with a light dusting on their hair.

"Come on." Jill opened her car door and focused on Sophie. "We'll wait in the car until my husband gets here."

"Can't we just go inside and check on Mason really quick?" Sophie asked.

Jill shook her head. "It will only be a few minutes." She hoped. They only lived about a mile away, but the weather could very well slow Doug down.

Layla opened her door and got into the car. Reluctantly, Sophie followed suit, and Jill joined them. She glanced at her watch and prayed Doug would get here soon.

* * *

A full-size SUV pulled into the driveway next to them, and a man climbed out. Sophie guessed the man with broad shoulders and short, dark hair was Layla's dad. What she didn't expect was the vest beneath his jacket that sported the bright-yellow letters *FBI*.

Keeping his focus on the house, the man motioned with his hand for Mrs. Valdez to roll down the window. Mr. Valdez whispered something to Mrs. Valdez. Then he looked at Sophie and Layla. "I need all of you to stay down and out of sight. I'll be back in a minute."

Sophie's heart raced as she tried to comprehend what was happening. Why did they need to hide? And from whom? Surely Mason was okay. The car in the garage might be one of Hillary's friends. Maybe Hillary had broken down, and someone else had brought her home. But it was weird that it was the exact same kind of car and the same color.

A sense of urgency rushed through her. "I should go in with him," Sophie said. "Mason is going to freak out if some random guy walks in."

"My husband will take care of him," Mrs. Valdez assured her.

Sophie peeked between the two front seats, terrified of what would happen when Mason saw Mr. Valdez rush inside. "He's holding a gun."

"That's just a precaution until he's sure everyone inside is okay." Mrs. Valdez turned to face Sophie. "I'm sure everything is fine, but it's better to be safe than sorry."

The Valdez family took that phrase to a level that might as well be in the stratosphere.

Mr. Valdez had a gun. Mason was inside. And she was just sitting here. She needed to do something. But what? Her body trembled, fear crippling her.

The sound of police sirens carried to them, and Sophie peeked out the window. She wasn't the only one. Mrs. Valdez sat up and put the car in gear, pulling out onto the street. A police car took their place in the driveway.

Mrs. Valdez parked in front of the house next door. "Girls, you can sit up now."

Sophie lifted her head higher and swiveled in her seat as two police officers knocked on her front door. A moment later, the door opened, but it wasn't Hillary or Mason who answered. It was Mr. Valdez.

Though Sophie expected the two policemen to walk inside, they separated instead, each of them circling the house from opposite directions.

Sophie's stomach turned queasy as a new question pushed to the forefront of her mind. Why had she told Mrs. Valdez about the car? Now the police were here, and if they found out Hillary wasn't taking care of them, they might separate her and Mason. The very thought brought tears to her eyes. Mason was the only real family she had left. Sophie squeezed her eyes closed.

A cell phone rang, and Mrs. Valdez answered it, lifting the phone to her ear rather than letting the call come through the speakers in the car. "Is everything okay?" she asked.

For a moment, she didn't say anything. Then she said, "Be careful, and call me as soon as you can." She paused again before adding, "I love you."

Mrs. Valdez put the car in gear and started down the street.

Panic set in, and Sophie grabbed the back of Layla's seat. "Where are we going? Mason is still back there."

"My husband will call us in a little while so Mason can talk to you on the phone," Mrs. Valdez said. "Then we'll decide what to do."

"There isn't anything to do," Sophie insisted. A tremor worked through her as fear joined her sense of panic. "I need to be home with Mason."

"I know this is scary," Mrs. Valdez said gently, "but right now, you need to trust me."

A lump formed in her throat. Sophie turned around to look through the rear window, her house disappearing from view.

CHAPTER 8

Doug turned away from the front door and headed for the stairs. The police would follow the footsteps leading away from the back deck, but he had a more important task: finding Jill's student.

He'd already checked the entire main level. The TV was still on, but so far, he hadn't seen any sign of the boy or whatever adult was caring for him.

Heading for the stairs, Doug called out again. "FBI! Is anyone home?" Technically, he wasn't FBI anymore, but since the Bureau was under his jurisdiction, he doubted anyone would question his authority. Plus, he couldn't deny that he shared his wife's uneasiness that something wasn't right here.

Gun still in hand, he climbed the stairs. The master bedroom and bath were both empty and didn't look like they had been used in some time. The next bedroom was a disaster, clothes strewn across the floor and the bed. More on the chair in the corner. An empty pill bottle lay on the floor beside an empty wine bottle.

Doug checked under the bed and in the closet. He continued into the next room, one that appeared to belong to a younger child. Legos in the closet, a dirty pair of socks under the bed, both with holes in them. Still no sign of Mason.

"Mason? Are you here?" Doug called out.

He finished checking the other two bedrooms upstairs without any sign of the boy. The basement came next. A storage room, a rec room, a workout room, and a craft room. Nothing.

The doorbell rang again as he reached the main level, the door opening before he could cross to it. One of the police officers walked in.

"We have a cruiser circling the neighborhood, but so far, no sign of anyone out there," the officer said. "Without a description of who we're looking for, there's not much we can do. For all we know, it could have been the boy and his aunt going out to play in the snow."

"The footprints were for one person, and the shoe size definitely looked like they belong to a man." Doug pulled out his cell, pulled up the image of the license plate of the car in the garage, and passed the phone to the officer. "Do me a favor. Run this plate."

The officer gave a curt nod and headed outside to his cruiser.

Doug took another look around the main level, stopping when he reached the living room. The television still playing, a cup of water on the end table, along with an empty plate. It was possible the aunt had taken the boy out somewhere, but with the snow coming down, it didn't make sense that they would have left without a good reason.

The policeman returned and held up Doug's phone. "The car in the garage was stolen two days ago from Tysons Corner."

Doug's unease multiplied. "Let's check it out." He led the way into the garage, the chill cutting through him despite the shelter the garage provided. "Do you have an extra pair of gloves?"

The officer pulled out a pair of crime-scene gloves and passed them to Doug.

Doug quickly tugged them on and opened the car door. "Get a forensics team down here to dust for prints."

"Will do." The policeman radioed in his request while Doug searched the glove compartment. Nothing beyond the basics: registration, a tire gauge, a travel pack of tissues, and a pair of scissors. All was clear under the seats except for a water bottle, which had been wedged beneath the passenger seat.

He hit the button to pop the trunk and circled to the back of the car. Inside the trunk lay a young boy, his skin pale. Doug pressed his fingers against the boy's neck, where a pulse throbbed at a rate that was far too slow. Doug shouted to the policeman, "Call an ambulance!" Then he scooped the boy into his arms and rushed into the house.

* * *

Sophie stood beside the living room window in the Valdez home, a dozen fears repeating on a loop through her head. Why hadn't Mr. Valdez called yet? At least a half hour had passed since they'd left her house. Surely it hadn't taken Mr. Valdez long to find Mason. Even if Mason got scared and hid, he was only seven. A federal agent would certainly be able to find him.

The thought of a strange man rushing into their house, of Mason freaking out without her nearby, made her heart ache.

Snow continued to fall, the white powder now deep enough to cover the ground and the road, only a few tire tracks breaking up the otherwise pristine view. But right now, Sophie didn't care about the winter beauty before her. She needed to talk to her brother.

The scent of home wafted toward her in the form of hot chocolate. Memories of her childhood pressed to the forefront of her mind, the times when her mom would let her and Mason go outside and play in the snow, hot chocolate and marshmallows always waiting for them when they came back in. Hillary had been different too back then, before the accident that had claimed Sophie's parents' lives and left Hillary in the hospital for several weeks.

Footsteps approached behind her. "Sophie?" Mrs. Valdez moved to her side and held out a cup of hot chocolate. "Here. I thought you might want this." She waved toward the kitchen. "We have marshmallows and whipped cream if you want."

"Marshmallows?"

"I'll get some for you." Mrs. Valdez disappeared into the kitchen, the hot chocolate still in her hand. When she returned a moment later, she passed the mug to Sophie.

"Why hasn't Mr. Valdez called?"

"I don't know." The worry in Mrs. Valdez's voice mirrored her own.

"Can you call him?"

"I tried a few minutes ago." Mrs. Valdez moved to the couch and gestured for Sophie to sit.

Sophie lowered into the chair by the window, her legs trembling as she did so. Maybe she was hungry again. The only thing she'd eaten today was a brownie and a cookie from Madam Corbin's house. Or maybe the shaky feeling in her legs was from being cold, not hungry. She sipped the hot chocolate, the warmth seeping through her.

The Valdezes' fluffy, black dog approached and put his paws on the edge of Sophie's chair.

"Buster, get down."

The dog complied, but Sophie couldn't resist running her fingers over the dog's soft fur.

"Does your aunt usually leave Mason home alone?" Mrs. Valdez asked.

Even though it had happened more than once, Sophie shook her head. She couldn't risk ending up in foster care.

"What does she do for a living?"

"I don't think she has a job right now."

"So she didn't have a reason to leave the house today," Jill said, almost as though talking to herself instead of Sophie.

Layla's older sister, Reagan, walked into the living room. To Sophie's surprise, she spoke in French. It took a moment for Sophie to translate the simple question. "Mom, do you want me to start on dinner?"

Mrs. Valdez didn't answer her daughter but, rather, directed her next question to Sophie. Thankfully, she spoke in English. "Do you like chili?"

Sophie nodded. Did the question mean that she planned to let Sophie eat with her family?

Mrs. Valdez nodded and continued in English. "Reagan, why don't you fix some chili and see if Layla will make cornbread."

"*Oui, Maman.*" Reagan headed back to the kitchen and rattled off something else in French. Buster abandoned Sophie's side and trotted after Reagan.

Curious and momentarily distracted, Sophie asked, "Is your family from France?"

"No, but some of Layla's family used to live in Switzerland. We decided when Layla joined our family that we should all learn French for when we visit there."

"So you speak French at home?"

"Three days a week," she said. "But don't worry. We can speak in English while you're here."

Sophie kind of liked the idea of having to speak a different language. "It doesn't matter." She took another sip of her hot chocolate and looked out the window. No cars on the road, the snow thickening, the fat snowflakes making it hard to see beyond the front yard.

A cell phone rang, and Sophie straightened as Mrs. Valdez glanced at the screen and quickly answered the call.

"Is everyone all right?" Mrs. Valdez asked.

Sophie leaned forward, straining to hear the voice on the other end. A mumbled male voice was all she could make out.

Mrs. Valdez's face paled, and Sophie sucked in a quick breath, fear rushing through her.

Mrs. Valdez took a deep breath of her own and let it out in whoosh. "Thank goodness."

Did her words mean Mason was okay? Sophie gripped her hot chocolate mug with both hands, waiting impatiently for Mrs. Valdez to finish her call.

Finally, she said, "Let me know when you head home." She said her goodbyes and hung up, angling her body toward Sophie. "He's okay."

"Can I talk to him?"

"He's sleeping right now."

Sleeping? It couldn't be later than five or six o'clock. Mason never went to bed before eight.

"My husband will call as soon as Mason is awake."

"What aren't you telling me?"

"I don't know the details, but when my husband found Mason, he was unconscious. We think he may have been drugged."

"Drugged?" Sophie shot to her feet. "But how?" Even as the words passed her lips, her suspicions bloomed. Hillary wouldn't drug Mason to keep him out of her way, would she?

"I don't know what happened, but as a precaution, my husband took Mason to the hospital to get checked out."

"The hospital?" A new wave of panic washed over her.

"He's going to be just fine and well taken care of. I'm sure my husband will fill us in when he gets here," Jill said. "In the meantime, make yourself at home. Dinner should be ready in about thirty minutes."

Hot chocolate *and* dinner? Sophie could hardly remember the last time she'd had both on the same day.

* * *

Doug sat in the hospital room, the curly-haired boy sleeping in the center of the hospital bed, the rails lifted to protect him from falling in case he woke up disoriented. Doug had already put in a call to social services to place Mason and Sophie into his and Jill's custody until the aunt could be found and an investigation could be conducted.

The police had only had to canvas half the block before they found a neighbor who expressed concerns that the little boy had been left alone a couple weeks earlier. The reason for a possible kidnapping remained unknown, but judging from the size of the house, Doug suspected the family had money. How the aunt played into today's events remained to be seen.

Mason's hand twitched, and he stirred slightly. Doug stayed seated. The boy would be scared enough to wake up in unfamiliar surroundings. The last thing he needed was to have a grown man hovering over him.

A knock sounded at the door, and the doctor walked in. "Has he woken up at all?"

"He moved a minute ago, but that's about it."

"Based on the lab work, the sedatives in his system should be wearing off any time now." The doctor moved to Mason's side and pressed his fingers to the boy's wrist. "His pulse is steady, and his body temperature is back to normal. He's very lucky you found him when you did. Another ten to fifteen minutes, and the hypothermia may have been too much for him."

"I think we have to chalk this one up to divine intervention." How else could he explain Jill's prompting to keep Sophie from going into the house? The presence of a strange car alone could have been explained away, but his wife had always been one to sense when something wasn't quite right. And the current living situation for Mason and Sophie Adams was clearly very wrong.

The boy stirred again, and this time, his eyes opened slowly. Confusion colored his expression for several seconds, and fear quickly replaced it.

"It's okay," the doctor assured him. "You're at the hospital."

The fear in the boy's eyes didn't lessen. Rather, it intensified.

"Do you want to talk to Sophie?" Doug asked, forcing himself to remain seated.

Mason didn't answer, his breathing coming in rapid gasps.

Doug pulled his phone out of his pocket and FaceTimed Jill. As soon as she answered, he said, "Hey, can you put Sophie on? I think Mason would feel better if she talked to him."

"Just a minute." The image shifted from the kitchen to the living room, and Jill spoke to Sophie. "Mason is on the phone for you."

Sophie's image came on the screen, her concern obvious. "Is he okay?"

"He's just fine." Doug turned the phone toward Mason. "Here you go, bud. There's your sister for you."

Mason scooted backward on the bed, but the moment he saw his sister, his eyes brightened. "Sophie!"

"Hi, Mason. Are you okay?" Sophie's concern carried in her voice, but with it was the soothing tone he had heard Jill use when dealing with a frightened child. "What happened?"

"I don't know. Why am I here?"

"You fell asleep, and we were worried about you," Doug said.

"Can I go home now?" Mason asked, his tone pleading.

"I don't know," Sophie said.

Doug looked up at the doctor. "What do you say, Doc? Can I take Mason to see his sister?"

"Under the circumstances, I think I can be persuaded to send him home, provided he's adequately supervised."

"Does that mean yes?" Sophie asked.

The doctor nodded, now focusing on Mason. "That means yes."

CHAPTER 9

Sophie had barely hung up with her brother when Jill's phone rang again. Jill glanced down at the screen. Doug. Clearly, he wanted to speak with her without the kids being privy to the conversation.

"Hey there," Jill said, greeting her husband. "Hold on a sec." Jill lowered her phone and spoke to Sophie. "I need to take this call, but you can hang out in here or go see if the girls need any help in the kitchen."

Sophie nodded but made no move to leave the chair she currently occupied in the living room.

Jill headed upstairs, waiting until she reached her bedroom before she said, "Okay, I'm alone now. What's going on?"

"I wanted to make sure you're okay with what I just did."

"What did you do?" Jill sat on the edge of her bed.

"After what happened, I had to report the incident to social services."

The thought of Sophie and Mason being placed in foster care, even temporarily, gave her pause. What if they couldn't keep the two of them together? "What's going to happen to them?"

"That depends on you. As of now, we're their foster parents."

Jill's relief was instant. "Should we put them in the guest room together, or do you think it would be better to have Sophie stay in Layla's room?"

"I really love you."

"I love you too, but you didn't answer my question."

Doug chuckled. "For tonight, let's ask Sophie what she suggests. Tomorrow, we can all work on cleaning out the other spare room so they can have their own."

"How long are they staying with us?" Jill asked.

"At this point, I don't know, but I don't want them returning home until we have a better understanding of what's going on with their aunt."

"Any word on that yet?" Jill asked.

"No, but I'll check with the police again as soon as we get home," Doug said. "At this point, there's no way to be sure if she was working with the person who drugged Mason, if she's a victim of a crime, or if she's simply not home."

"I hope she's okay."

"Me too."

Not wanting to dwell on the what-ifs that she couldn't control, Jill changed the subject. "Should we hold dinner for you?"

"Go ahead and start without us. I don't know how long it will take for the hospital to release Mason."

"Okay. Drive safe."

"I will."

Jill hung up the phone and headed into the guest room. A queen-sized bed occupied the spot beside the two windows, and a twin bed had been tucked along the near wall. She made sure the beds had clean sheets and blankets before continuing downstairs.

The living room was empty when she passed through, and voices carried from the kitchen. To Jill's surprise, the words were spoken in French. She walked in to find the girls setting the table for six.

"Sophie, I spoke to my husband," Jill began in English. "We'd like you and Mason to stay here until we know where your aunt is and we have the chance to make sure everything is okay at your house."

"*Maman, en français*," Layla said.

Jill switched to French. "I don't know that Sophie will want to speak in French."

"*C'est bon*," Sophie said, indicating that she was okay with their current language choice.

Though Jill wasn't sure Sophie would understand everything, they could always replay the conversation in English if needed. Jill continued in French. "One of our upstairs bedrooms isn't set up yet, so you have a choice of sleeping in the same room as your brother, or we can put Mason in the guest room and let you sleep in the spare bed in Layla's room."

Sophie stared at her as though she hadn't understood. Jill was about to repeat her words in English when Sophie asked, "We're spending the night?"

"Yes, you'll be staying here, at least for now."

A combination of relief and reservation flashed in her expression. "I want to be with Mason."

Jill nodded her approval. "That may make him more comfortable staying here."

"How long until Dad and Mason get here?" Reagan asked.

"I'm not sure, but Dad said to start dinner without him."

Reagan motioned to the pot of chili on the stove. "In that case, *bon appétit.*"

* * *

Doug took one look at Mason's state of dress and came to an uncomfortable conclusion. Despite the steadily falling snow and as much as he wanted to get home, a trip to the store needed to come first.

He settled Mason in the back seat, ensuring the seatbelt was properly fastened. "How about we stop and pick up some new shoes for you on our way to my house?"

The look on the boy's face suggested this wasn't a common question. When Mason didn't answer, Doug closed his car door and took his place behind the wheel. Hoping to put Mason at ease, Doug asked, "What kind of toys do you like to play with?"

"Legos."

"Do you have a lot of Legos?"

"I have the big kind."

"Maybe we can find you some Legos while we're at the store too." Doug carefully pulled out of the parking garage and debated whether he should head toward Walmart or take advantage of the covered parking at Tysons Corner. The thought of dealing with trekking through the mall made the decision for him. If they were quick at Walmart, he shouldn't have too much trouble clearing the snow off the windshield.

They traveled in silence for a few minutes. When Doug pulled up to a light, he glanced back at Mason. "Do you remember what happened today before you fell asleep?"

He shook his head.

"Were you awake when your aunt left?"

This time he nodded. "She drove away."

"Was she by herself?"

He shrugged.

"Does she leave you alone a lot?"

Mason shrugged again.

Suspecting Jill's concern about neglect was valid, Doug fell silent once more. The boy would be far more forthcoming if he got to know Doug first.

Doug suspected the same would be true of the older sister. With no sign of forced entry and no sign of foul play, beyond Mason's presence in the trunk, Doug was starting to think the aunt had left before the intruder had arrived.

He continued to Walmart. The parking lot was far less crowded than normal, likely due to the weather, and Doug chose a relatively close parking spot so Mason wouldn't have to walk far with that hole in his shoe.

"Okay, bud. The faster we get this shopping done, the faster we can go home and get some dinner." Doug ushered Mason inside and grabbed a cart. "Let's start with some shoes."

Shoes, shirts, pants, socks, underwear, pajamas, a sweatshirt, a winter coat, a car seat, and two new Lego sets. The shopping for Mason was completed within fifteen minutes. Then they moved to the juniors' section. Doug couldn't believe he was attempting to shop for a teenage girl by himself. But he wasn't by himself. He looked down at Mason.

"Want to help me pick out some clothes for your sister?"

Mason nodded enthusiastically.

"Great." Doug sent a quick text to Jill to get a guess on Sophie's sizes. By the time they reached a rack of long-sleeve shirts, Jill had replied with a full list of suggestions. With Mason's help, they chose a variety of clothes, opting to buy some of the essentials in multiple sizes. By the time they finished, Doug was physically and mentally exhausted.

They paid for their purchases and then stopped by the restroom so Mason could change into some of his new clothes—no need to let the kid freeze while they crossed the parking lot. The decision turned out to be a wise one. Another half inch of snow had fallen during their forty-five-minute shopping spree.

Doug settled Mason into his new booster seat and stowed the rest of their purchases in the trunk. Then he used the ice scraper to clear off the windshield and slid behind the wheel. Time to go home.

* * *

Sophie's stomach was full, and she had managed to follow most of the conversation at the dinner table, even though it was all in French. She'd never realized how much she'd learned, both in French class and at Madam Corbin's house while babysitting. She was debating whether there was a way to stash a piece of cornbread for later when the garage door rumbled open.

A minute later, Mason walked in, a look of apprehension on his face.

Relieved beyond words to see him, Sophie scrambled out of her chair. The moment he spotted her, Mason's face lit up. He rushed across the room and wrapped his arms around her waist.

Sophie pulled him close. He really was okay. And they were together.

Mason looked up at Mrs. Valdez. "Is this your house?"

"It is." Mrs. Valdez smiled. "And I'm so glad you can stay with us."

Sophie stepped back and released her brother. The shirt Mason wore wasn't one she'd seen before. Her gaze swept down. New sweatpants that fell all the way past his ankles and bright white sneakers that didn't have any holes in them.

She was still processing her brother's new clothes when Mr. Valdez set several bags down on the edge of the kitchen counter.

Mr. Valdez crossed to his wife and kissed her cheek. "Sorry we took so long. I wanted to make sure Mason and Sophie had a few things to last them through the weekend," he said in English.

"Wait." Reagan held up her hand, also speaking in English. "You went shopping? On purpose?"

"I know." Mr. Valdez leaned down and petted the dog. "It's proof that miracles really do happen."

Sophie struggled to keep her jaw from dropping. "You bought Mason new clothes?"

"I picked up a few things for you too." He waved at the bags on the counter. "If they don't fit, I'm sure one of our girls can lend you something to wear until the weather clears and we can exchange them."

"You bought me clothes?" Who were these people?

Mr. Valdez simply nodded. "Mason, meet Buster." He motioned Mason forward, giving Mason a minute to decide if he wanted to pet the dog or not.

Mason must have decided to try it because he reached out his hand and ran it along the dog's head. An instant later, Mason looked up, his expression alight with wonder.

Mr. Valdez sat at one of the empty seats at the table. "Come on, Mason. Let's have some dinner."

Those words brought Mason to life. He sat beside Mr. Valdez, his eyes widening when Mrs. Valdez ladled chili into a bowl for him *and* gave him a piece of cornbread. Sophie understood his thoughts exactly. They almost never had enough food to be able to eat two different things at the same meal.

"Mason, after you eat, we'll show you up to your room." Mrs. Valdez carried her chili bowl to the sink.

"Mom, do you want me and Layla to show Sophie the guest room?" Reagan asked.

"Actually, that would be great, if you don't mind." Mrs. Valdez nodded at the bags her husband had set on the counter. "Why don't you take all of that upstairs too so Sophie can make sure she has something to sleep in tonight and fresh clothes for tomorrow."

Layla set her bowl in the sink. "Does that mean you're doing the dishes?"

"You girls cooked. It's only fair."

"Thanks, Mom." Layla picked up two of the bags. "Come on, Sophie. It's this way."

Sophie cast a glance at Mason to make sure he knew he was safe. He dipped his spoon into his bowl of chili and ate another bite.

"Don't worry. We'll keep an eye on him," Mr. Valdez said.

"Thanks." Sophie picked up a few of the bags, Reagan collecting the last of them.

Together, they walked upstairs.

"My room is over there, and Layla's is the next one down," Reagan said. "We share a bathroom, so you and Mason can use the one down the hall."

Layla led the way into the bedroom across from Reagan's. "This is where you'll be staying."

Sophie followed her into the large bedroom. Two beds, both with thick comforters and fluffy pillows on them, were pushed against opposite walls. Layla set the bags she carried on the larger of the two beds, and Reagan did the same.

"Should we see what my dad bought for you?" Reagan asked.

Someone had bought Sophie new clothes. She still couldn't quite believe it. She set her bags down and nodded. She opened the first plastic bag and pulled out a pair of sweatpants that looked like they would fit Mason, and then another and another. Three pairs of sweatpants, plus the one he was already wearing. These would double his wardrobe. More importantly, he would finally have clothes that fit.

Reagan held up a pair of jeans. "You should try these on." She motioned to the door across the room. "The walk-in closet is huge. You can change in there."

"Oh, and try this sweater too." Layla handed her a cream-colored sweater that looked like it would fall all the way to her hips.

Sophie found the light switch in the closet and stepped inside the space that had boxes on one side. She changed into the new clothes, surprised that the jeans fit. The sweater was a little baggy, but in a good way. She opened the closet door and stepped out into the bedroom.

"Oh, I like that," Reagan said.

"Me too." Layla nodded her approval. "Who knew Dad could shop?"

"You know," Reagan said, "the only times he ever shops for clothes is when he ends up taking in a new kid."

"Does he let people stay with him a lot?" Sophie asked, a little unsettled by the thought that she and Mason were among a stream of many kids who had stayed with the Valdez family.

"He's only done this twice before," Reagan said. "Three years ago, when they adopted me, and last year, when Layla came to live with us."

Sophie stared at the two girls in front of her, two girls who looked like they were part of a normal family in every way. "You're both adopted?"

"Yep." Reagan waved toward the stairs. "Mom and Dad are pretty amazing."

Sophie looked down at the clothes stacked on her bed. "Yeah. They really are."

CHAPTER 10

Jill fought the urge to ask for details from Doug on what had happened at Sophie and Mason's house after she left with the girls. That conversation would have to wait until after the kids were all settled in bed.

After Doug and Mason finished eating dinner, Doug had taken Mason upstairs in search of Sophie. Once the dishes were in the dishwasher, Jill went to check on them. Her smile was instant when she found Mason bouncing on the bed in the guest room while Sophie modeled her clothes for Layla and Reagan.

Her current ensemble included a pair of black yoga pants and a bright-pink T-shirt.

"Looks like Dad did okay," Jill said.

"He really did." Layla nodded. "I'm kind of surprised."

"Honey, he surprises me every day." Jill glanced at her watch and turned to Mason. "It's only seven. What do you say we all play a family game?"

Reagan didn't give Mason a chance to answer. "I say we play Uno."

"Do you both know how to play?" Jill asked.

Sophie nodded. Mason shook his head.

"Mason, you can be on my team," Jill offered.

The lights flickered once, and the fire detector beeped at the same time. Then they flickered again before the house went dark.

Mason whimpered.

"It's okay." Jill reached out until her hand connected with Mason's shoulder. Within seconds, Reagan turned on her phone's flashlight.

Doug entered a moment later, his phone flashlight also shining. "Are you all okay?"

"Yes." Jill kept her hand on Mason's shoulder to assure him that he wasn't alone. "We were just talking about playing Uno. Any chance you know where the lantern is?"

"As a matter of fact, I do," Doug said. "I'll get it; you find the Uno cards. We'll meet in the living room."

Five minutes later, the six of them sat on the floor in the living room, a lantern shining beside the draw pile, a fire blazing in the fireplace, and Buster's chin resting on Sophie's leg.

They played one game with Jill teaching Mason as they did so. Within minutes, Mason seemed to have a good idea of what he was doing, and Jill encouraged him to make the choice of which card to play. Laughter, complaints, several shouts of Uno that didn't turn into victories. The game lasted a half hour, and Layla ultimately won.

"I want a rematch," Jill said.

"You always want a rematch," Reagan said.

"Yes, because I never win at this game." Jill collected all the cards and started shuffling. "Mason, do you want to play on your own this time?"

He looked up at her, a little flash of panic on his face.

Hoping to put him at ease, Jill motioned to the cards. "Tell you what. We'll play together again, but I'm just going to be here to help you. Sound good?"

He pressed his lips together, but only a second passed before he nodded.

"Great."

Cards were shuffled and dealt. Jill helped organize Mason's hand so he could hold the cards without any of them falling. They played through the first few turns, and she adjusted the cards again, fanning them out for Mason.

At one point, he played a wild card and chose blue, even though he had far more yellow cards in his hand. Though Jill would have made a different choice, she didn't say anything. The game continued until Mason had only two cards left in his hand, while everyone else had at least five.

When Mason was about to play, Jill leaned forward and whispered, "Don't forget to say 'Uno.'"

He quickly played his chosen card and shouted, "Uno!"

When Reagan played a wild card a moment later, a discussion ensued about what color she should choose.

"Mason picked blue last time he had a wild," Layla said.

"That's right. He did," Doug agreed.

"Let's do yellow then," Reagan said.

Mason's face lit with victory, and he played his final card.

A combination of groans and congratulations followed.

"Now I know," Jill said. "The only way I can win is if I'm on Mason's team and I don't do anything."

Reagan laughed. "Sounds about right."

Doug's phone chimed with an incoming text, and he read it. "Looks like the power is going to be out for a while, and we can't run the generator during the storm."

"Should we pull out the sleeping bags and have everyone camp here in the living room tonight?" Jill asked. "The bedrooms may get too cold."

"What do you kids think?" Doug asked.

"Layla, you get the sleeping bags," Reagan said. "I'll get the stuff for s'mores."

"I can't carry them all by myself," Layla said.

In true big-sister form, Reagan said, "Have Sophie help you."

Doug picked up the lantern and stood. "Come on, girls. I'll help too." He led the way into the garage, where the camping gear was stored. The dog trotted along behind them.

In the light of the fire, Mason looked up at Jill. "Are we really going to sleep in the living room?"

"We are." Jill shifted to her left so she could see Mason's face more clearly. "Is that okay with you?"

Before he could answer, Reagan returned to the living room with a box of graham crackers tucked under her arm, a bag of marshmallows in one hand, and a package of chocolate bars in the other. "I had to raid the emergency kit for the chocolate. I hope that's all right."

"I think a power outage qualifies as an emergency," Jill said. She turned her attention back to Mason. "What do you think, kiddo? Are you up for a campout in the living room?"

Mason eyed the food in Reagan's hands. Then he nodded.

* * *

Doug waited until the kids had all fallen asleep before he crept out of the living room, donned his boots, coat, and sidearm, and headed into the storm. Five inches of snow had already accumulated, and he suspected there would be double that by morning.

The white blanket covering his yard remained undisturbed, save the remnants of his tire tracks when he'd returned home with Mason and the few tracks Buster had made when he went out to go to the bathroom. Doug still couldn't quite get a handle on Mason and Sophie's living situation. The house was expansive, larger than his and Jill's, and the furnishings appeared to be pricey as well, although a little worn. But the aunt they lived with was a complete mystery.

He'd taken the time to call in a few favors based on what Mason, Sophie, and Jill had told him. From what he could find, their aunt Hillary hadn't worked a job or filed taxes since her late twenties. Assuming he had the right person, she was now thirty-two. Three years was a long time to go without employment. It also begged the question: how was she surviving without an income? Doug's suspicions left only two possibilities. Either someone was supporting her, or she was doing something illegal. He hoped it was the former.

With snow pelting his face and the wind cutting through his clothes, Doug circled the house, his pistol in his shoulder holster and his flashlight aimed at the ground. Thankfully, the snow made it impossible for anyone to approach the house without leaving tracks. After he ensured no one was hiding in the bushes, Doug returned to the house. Not surprisingly, Jill waited for him inside, two cups of hot chocolate in her hands.

"Everything okay out there?" she whispered.

"Yeah." Doug toed off his boots and left them by the door. After he shed his coat, he led the way into the office off the main entrance.

Jill followed, waiting for him to close the door before she handed him a mug. "What can you tell me?"

Doug leaned against the front of his desk and sipped his hot chocolate, the warm liquid fighting away the worst of the chill that had seeped into him. "We found Mason in the trunk of the car in the garage."

"What?" Jill set her cup down on his desk. "That poor kid. Who would do that?"

"I don't know. The police were only able to track the intruder a couple streets over. It's possible he had an accomplice waiting for him."

Jill shuddered and dropped into one of the two chairs that sat opposite his desk. "That's so scary."

"I know. We did find out that the aunt has left Mason home alone before. A neighbor came over two weeks ago, and he was there by himself," Doug said. "The aunt told the neighbor that she thought Sophie was at home, but apparently, Sophie was babysitting for someone else. It's possible it was a miscommunication."

"But you don't think so." Jill picked up her cup again. "And neither do I. Sophie babysits at the same time every Saturday. Her aunt should know that."

"The kids' wardrobes don't fit with the neighborhood they live in either." Doug sipped his hot chocolate. "I left a note for the aunt, letting her know the kids are okay and telling her to call social services when she gets back."

"I really thought we would have heard from her by now."

"The fact that we haven't suggests neglect is a real possibility, but that doesn't explain why someone would try to kidnap Mason."

"Why would anyone do that to a child?" Jill asked.

"Motivations for a kidnapping can fall into a lot of categories. Since it looks like the intruder may have been trying to grab both kids, my guess is either a family member wanted to take them away from here or someone was hoping to exploit the family for money."

"From what I've gathered from Sophie, I think their aunt is the only family they have left."

Doug set his empty mug aside. "Then someone is out to get money, but why did they target these two kids, and if there is money to get, how do they know about it?"

"I have no idea, but I trust you're going to find out."

"Yes." Doug didn't know how, but he couldn't let those kids go back home without making sure they'd be safe. "Yes, I am."

* * *

Josh's heart was still racing when he reached his condo overlooking Tyson's Corner. He'd barely managed to slip into an open garage when the cops made their way down the street looking for him. If it hadn't been for the teenagers playing football in the snow, Josh's footprints would have given away his location. As it was, he'd hidden behind an ATV in the far bay of the open three-car garage while the occupants of the house had been talking to some neighbors down the road.

The cops had stopped to talk to the teenagers and the few parents who were outside, but if anyone had spotted Josh, they hadn't seen where he went.

More than an hour had passed before darkness settled over the quiet neighborhood and Josh finally dared to sneak out of the garage and make his way to the main street. A favor from a regular client had taken him out of McLean and back to the mall at Tyson's. From there, he'd walked home.

Now, with the streets below relatively quiet except for the occasional snowplow, he analyzed his next move. Hillary would be home on Wednesday, but he had no idea where the kids would be kept until then.

He shook his head. There was no way around it. He would have to wait until Hillary got back and the children were returned to her. And once that happened, he would be ready. No more elaborate plans. Josh would simply let Hillary have enough of her favorite drugs, wait for her to fall asleep, and then slip in and take the kids while no one was watching.

CHAPTER 11

Church at home. Sophie had never heard of such a thing. Then again, she'd never camped out in the living room before either. The power had been restored at some point during the night, and now instead of sleeping bags all over the floor, a plate of bread and a tray with small cups were set on the coffee table, cloth napkins covering them up as Doug knelt to bless them.

Sophie remembered going to church with her parents and then with her grandmother until Grandma started forgetting things, but she didn't remember church being anything like this. Layla had said a prayer at the beginning of their little meeting, followed by Doug blessing the sacrament. Sophie and Mason both followed Layla and Reagan's lead, first eating a piece of bread when Mr. Valdez offered it to them, then drinking the little cup of water.

After the sacrament, they read scriptures and talked about them. Like, really talked. It wasn't like when a preacher told them what the scriptures meant. This was more like trying to figure everything out together.

Jill read the story from the Bible of the Samaritan woman at the well. When she finished, she asked, "Can you imagine what it would be like to live in a time when people had to walk, sometimes miles, to draw their water out of a well?" she asked.

Sophie suspected it wouldn't be much different than carrying her groceries home every week.

"I find it interesting that the prejudices between the Jews and the Samaritans are so similar to the ones that still happen in many parts of the world today," Doug said.

The conversation continued, morphing as they spoke about the struggles of people in today's world—struggles like illness, not having enough food, how to recognize truth in a confusing world. The range of topics varied greatly, but somehow, the way the Valdezes talked, it all seemed to make sense and relate to some greater whole.

When the meeting concluded, the whole family converged on the kitchen for lunch, Buster included. Despite the food in his bowl, the dog seemed much more interested in everyone else's food. Large sandwich rolls, ham, turkey, cheese, lettuce, and cucumbers. They even had three different kinds of mustard. Sophie couldn't remember the last time she had the chance to make her own lunch with so many ingredients at her fingertips.

She set out two plates, one for herself and one for Mason. "Mason, what do you want on yours?"

Mason shrugged, the way he always did when he was feeling overwhelmed.

"You can have some of everything if you want," Mrs. Valdez said.

He perked up a bit, and Sophie suspected he was afraid to ask for too much.

Sophie watched Layla fix her sandwich and matched the amount of meat and cheese as she made her lunch and Mason's. When she finished, she led Mason to the table to sit with everyone else.

"I'm surprised we haven't heard from your aunt yet," Mrs. Valdez said as she took her seat.

"Maybe she couldn't get home in the storm," Layla said.

"Maybe," Mr. Valdez said, but suspicion hummed through his voice.

"The roads aren't looking great out there." Mrs. Valdez cut her sandwich in half. "I have a feeling we won't have school tomorrow."

"There's more snow rolling in tonight," Mr. Valdez said. "The schools aren't going to open until Wednesday at the earliest." He turned his attention to Sophie and Mason. "I hope you two don't mind staying here for a while longer."

"Can we sleep in the living room again tonight?" Mason asked hopefully.

Mr. Valdez laughed. "I think we should try sleeping in beds, but maybe we can play another family game after dinner."

Family games. Dinner that wasn't ramen. A dog to cuddle with. People to talk to who weren't taking bad pills all the time. Sophie picked up her sandwich and hoped this weekend would never end.

* * *

No school. Jill couldn't deny that the news of the cancellation due to weather had brightened her mood. Now she could spend time with the kids and hopefully learn more about the life Sophie and Mason lived when they were at home. But first, she was going to indulge by making a breakfast that didn't include cold cereal or breakfast bars.

Jill lined up ingredients on the counter to make french toast and bacon. She had just put the bacon into the oven when Doug walked in from outside. She didn't need to ask to know that he'd gone out to make sure their home was secure. His easy demeanor answered that question in the affirmative.

"I'm about to make french toast," Jill said. "Do you have time to eat before you go to work?"

Doug took off his gloves and stuffed them into his coat pocket. "The government is shut down because of the storm, so I'm going to work from home." He glanced in the direction of the living room. "Just to be safe."

Jill crossed to him and leaned in for a kiss. "I kind of like the idea of you being here today."

"Me too." He drew her closer and kissed her again.

Footsteps sounded on the stairs. Reagan's voice interrupted the private moment. "Really? Kissing in the kitchen again? We have rules about that."

Jill drew back and glanced toward the family room where Reagan stood with Layla, Sophie, and Mason.

Doug kissed Jill's cheek before he released her. "I think it's more accurate to say you keep trying to make rules about that, and we keep ignoring you."

Reagan lifted both eyebrows. "Clearly."

"Is breakfast almost ready?" Layla asked.

"It will be in about fifteen minutes."

"Can we play a game or something?" Layla asked. "We're bored."

Doug's grin was instant. "Oh, really? You know what we haven't done in a while?" He circled the counter and headed for the living room. "Self-defense practice."

Layla shook her head. "Oh no. That's not what I meant."

"Come on." Doug motioned the kids forward. "Sophie and Mason, you come too."

Sophie furrowed her brow. "You practice self-defense in your living room?"

"Dad has this thing about making sure we know how to protect ourselves." Reagan leaned closer to Mason. "I think he just likes us to prove that we're stronger than him."

Mason's lips twitched into a smile.

Jill turned on her electric griddle, appreciating the way Doug gently instructed Mason and Sophie on how to defend themselves without talking about what might happen if Mason's attacker came back. She hated the very thought that these two children might have to use self-defense skills to protect themselves in the future.

The class continued in the living room. Reagan and Layla helped demonstrate the different moves, from how to carry car or house keys so they could be used as a weapon to how to use their feet and elbows to strike someone who attacked from behind.

The french toast and bacon were nearly done when Sophie caught Doug in the ribs with her elbow a little harder than expected. Doug stepped back and gave her a nod of approval. "That was good." He rubbed his side. "But you can take it easy on me when it's just us practicing."

"That's Dad-speak for saying you're stronger than him," Reagan said.

Doug laughed, and Jill didn't miss the glow of accomplishment on Sophie's face.

"Come on, kids. Time to set the table." Jill pulled the bacon from the oven. "You can beat up on Dad again after breakfast."

CHAPTER 12

Doug drove down the freshly plowed road and turned into Sophie and Mason's neighborhood. Even though the schools had been closed for the past two days, he'd made the trek to their house each day in search of answers. So far, he hadn't found any. The aunt had yet to return from wherever she'd disappeared to, and the authorities hadn't reported any sightings of the car she was supposed to be driving.

As he continued down the road, he scanned the houses on either side. All the driveways had been cleared with one exception: Sophie and Mason's house. No sign of tire tracks leading into the garage, and the only footprints leading to the front porch were his. Doug parked along the curb and followed the tracks he'd made yesterday, his boots crunching the layer of ice that had formed beneath the snow.

Though he didn't expect an answer, Doug rang the doorbell. A minute passed with no indication of life within the house. He rang the bell a second time with the same results.

When he returned to his car, a woman standing on the front porch of the house next door carefully descended the stairs and approached him. She appeared to be in her mid-fifties, a thick parka covering her legs down to the knees.

"Is everything okay with Sophie and Mason?" she asked.

"They're fine." Doug offered his hand. "I'm Doug Valdez, with the FBI. What can you tell me about their aunt?"

"Is she in some sort of trouble?"

"We're just trying to locate her."

"I saw her leave on Saturday. Then a car that looked just like hers drove by a few minutes later."

The woman's phrasing suggested she was well aware that the car found in the garage wasn't really Hillary's. Pushing for more information, Doug asked, "When did you see her leave?"

"About an hour before Sophie got home. So probably around three thirty or four."

"And you're sure she's the one who was driving away?" Doug asked.

"Yes. I remember being annoyed that she was leaving again before Sophie got home," the woman said.

Doug noted the woman's address and pulled a business card out of his wallet. "If you see anyone go into the house, can you please give me a call?"

She took the card and read his name. She must have read his title too because she looked up at him, her eyes widening. "What's the secretary of Homeland Security doing investigating a case?"

"Let's just say this one sort of fell into my lap."

She held up his card. "I'll be sure to call if I see anyone show up."

"I appreciate it." Doug climbed into his car and waved to the neighbor. As he headed home, questions continued to circle. Where was Sophie and Mason's aunt? Why had she deliberately left the children alone? And was someone or something preventing her from returning to them?

* * *

As far as Sophie was concerned, she hoped Aunt Hillary never came back. A little twinge of guilt pricked at her, but after three days staying with the Valdez family, she couldn't help but yearn for life to continue just like this.

Sophie patted the huge snowball that would soon become a snowman's head before rolling it toward the base that Reagan and Layla had helped Mason create in the middle of the backyard. Buster had decided to watch from the safety of the deck a short distance away. Sophie made it to within five yards of their masterpiece when she called out to her brother. "Hey, Mason. Help me put this on top."

With a grin, Mason raced toward her and helped her roll the head to the half-built snowman.

"Let me help you." Reagan leaned down and joined their efforts in lifting the oversized snowball up onto the base.

As soon as the head was in place, Layla held out the buttons Mrs. Valdez had given them. "Mason, do you want to do the eyes?"

"Yes!" He took them from her, but he couldn't quite reach the top of the head.

Sophie lifted him, holding him up until he pressed the buttons into place. The buttons weren't quite level, but Sophie didn't care. Her brother was smiling and laughing, and he didn't have holes in his shoes. This was the life.

Together, Sophie, Mason, Layla, and Reagan finished making the face using a carrot for the nose and more buttons for the mouth.

Reagan stepped back after placing the last button and gave a nod of approval. "That is one good-looking snowman."

The back door opened, and Mrs. Valdez stepped outside. "Kids, time to come in."

"Do we have to?" Mason asked.

Mrs. Valdez simply smiled. "I have hot chocolate with whipped cream and marshmallows."

Those were the magic words. Mason rushed up the stairs onto the deck, startling the dog as he did so.

Layla followed and turned back to Sophie. "I think Mason's a little excited about the hot chocolate."

"And marshmallows," Sophie said. She already dreaded when she and Mason had to go back to her budget for groceries and Mason could no longer have such treats.

They walked into the house, all of them taking off their shoes as they entered and leaving them on a towel that Mrs. Valdez had left beside the door. Four mugs of hot chocolate already waited for them on the kitchen counter, an open bag of marshmallows and a tub of Cool Whip sitting beside them.

Sophie tugged off the gloves she'd borrowed from Layla and took one of the cups. She turned to ask Mason what he wanted in his, but Mrs. Valdez beat her to it.

"Mom, can we have some cookies too?" Layla asked.

"They're in the cookie jar."

Within minutes, they were all sitting around the table, sipping hot chocolate, eating cookies, and debating whether school would open again tomorrow or whether they would get another day off because of the snow.

"Whether we have school tomorrow or not, I want all of you to go upstairs and clean your rooms," Mrs. Valdez said. "And, Sophie and Mason, let's get your laundry done to make sure you have something to wear to school tomorrow in case it isn't cancelled."

Laundry. Sophie was well versed in that particular chore. With the number of pants and shirts Mason had that had still fit him, she didn't have a choice but to do the wash every few days.

Layla finished her hot chocolate first and carried her cup to the sink. The door opened, and Mr. Valdez walked in from the garage. He leaned in and kissed his wife's cheek before focusing on Sophie. His serious expression made her insides tense. It was the sort of look the policeman had when he came to her house and told the babysitter that Sophie's parents had been killed in a car accident.

Mr. Valdez spoke to his daughters. "Reagan, Layla, can you take Mason upstairs for a few minutes?"

A look passed between Reagan and her dad, as though she knew something wasn't quite right. She stood. "Come on, Mason. Let's go play with your new Legos."

Mason glanced at Sophie as though asking permission.

"It's okay," Sophie assured him.

"We'll be upstairs," Reagan said and led Mason and Layla out of the room.

As soon as they left, Sophie asked, "Is something wrong?"

"I'm not sure." Mr. Valdez sat in one of the chairs across from her. "I stopped by your house to see if your aunt was home yet, but there's still no sign of her."

"I don't know where she is."

"Has she disappeared like this before?" Mr. Valdez asked.

Sophie started to shake her head, but she made the mistake of looking Mr. Valdez in the eye. Something in the way he was staring at her stopped her. But even though she didn't manage to say no, she also couldn't bring herself to say yes. What if she and Mason were put into foster care forever? What if someone took Mason away?

As though sensing her internal dilemma, Mrs. Valdez sat beside Sophie. "I know all of this must be unsettling for you, but you can trust us. We only want what's best for you and Mason."

"I'm what's best for Mason," Sophie blurted out. "He needs to stay with me."

Mr. and Mrs. Valdez exchanged a look before Mr. Valdez spoke again. "The two of you should stay together. You're family. But we need to find out what happened to your aunt. And in order to do that, we need to know more about her normal routine."

"I don't know what her normal routine is," Sophie said.

"What about your normal routine?" Mrs. Valdez asked. "Are you the one who gets up and fixes Mason's lunch every day?"

Slowly, Sophie nodded. "Aunt Hillary isn't always up when we leave for school."

"Do you see her when you get home from school?" Mr. Valdez asked.

"Sometimes."

"Are there ever times when you don't see her for more than a day or two?" Mr. Valdez asked.

Sophie shrugged. "I guess."

"That helps a lot." Mr. Valdez stood. "And I agree with what my wife said. We really do want what's best for you and Mason."

An odd warmth filled Sophie. "Thanks."

CHAPTER 13

Getting ready for school with four kids. Jill never expected to have that opportunity, and she loved every minute of it.

Doug hadn't wanted to take Mason and Sophie back to their house, not while their aunt's and the intruder's locations were still unknown. Instead, Jill had raided her and Doug's closet for old backpacks so they would have one Mason could use. Thankfully, Doug had insisted they keep the daypacks they typically used when they went hiking.

One look at the contents of Sophie's backpack had prompted Jill to dig into the excess school supplies she always stored in Doug's office. It hadn't taken long to outfit both of their guests with everything they would need over the next few days.

Now all four kids sat at the table eating cereal, their backpacks lined up beside the door leading to the mudroom.

"Are you all okay with buying lunch today?" Jill asked.

Sophie looked up, a look of panic on her face. "Buy?"

It didn't take a genius to identify the source of her concern. "Do you and Mason have money on your school accounts?"

Slowly, Sophie shook her head.

"We'll take care of that this morning then."

Doug walked in through the back door, his gaze meeting Jill's. His nod was subtle, but it gave her the assurance that everything outside was as it should be. She seriously doubted anyone would be able to find Mason and Sophie here, but past incidents with Reagan and Layla were enough to keep them cautious.

"Doug, would you mind making sure the girls all have money on their lunch accounts when you drop them off this morning?"

"Why is Dad taking us to school?" Reagan asked.

Doug answered. "Because the roads still aren't as clear as I'd like, and you're a teenage driver."

Reagan lifted both eyebrows. "You're being overprotective again."

Doug just grinned. "Yeah. Don't you love it?"

Reagan shook her head and looked down at her cereal, but not before Jill spotted the smile forming on her lips. Reagan might play the independent teenager when it suited her, but she loved having parents who cared.

Doug crossed to Jill and kissed her cheek. "And yes, I'll put money on their accounts."

"Thanks."

Sophie glanced at Mason, concern still evident on her face.

"Don't worry, Sophie," Jill said. "I'll make sure Mason has money on his account too."

"I get to buy lunch?" Mason asked.

"You do. You can look at the menu when we get to school." Jill glanced at the time again. "Speaking of which, Mason, are you about ready? We need to go."

Mason nodded.

Sophie stood and cleared both her dish and Mason's. "Mason, go get your shoes on, and don't forget your coat."

Sophie's tone could have been that of a parent.

Compassion swelled inside Jill. No fourteen-year-old should ever have to take on the responsibility of a parent, at least not to the extent that Sophie had demonstrated over the past few days.

Doug must have had the same thought because he reached out both hands. "I'll take care of the dishes. You girls get ready too. We're leaving in ten minutes."

Sophie surrendered the empty cereal bowls, and Doug rinsed them before putting them in the dishwasher.

As soon as all the kids left to retrieve their shoes and coats, Doug put his hands on Jill's arms. "I've already arranged to have a school resource officer at the elementary school all day today, but you let me know if you see anything that feels off."

"What do I do if Mason's aunt shows up after school to pick him up?"

"You refer her to his caseworker," Doug said. "Technically, they're in the system, and we're their foster parents."

"Am I crazy to think that they aren't safe if they go back home?" Jill asked.

Doug shook his head. "You aren't crazy."

* * *

Josh waited in the four-wheel-drive SUV in the parking garage at the mall, scanning each approaching vehicle for Hillary's brassy blonde hair. As he'd suspected, she had messaged looking for product within minutes of checking out of her hotel in Virginia Beach. He bet she didn't even know that the kids were in foster care. At least, that's where he assumed they were. They certainly didn't have any friends or family who were likely to take them in.

For the past four days, Josh had met with several of his clients, clients who were outwardly upstanding citizens above reproach. An attorney with a taste for oxy had already agreed to file the needed paperwork to get the kids back for Hillary. Another woman, one who had spent the weekend in the hospital after a car accident, would pose as the would-be babysitter for Hillary while she was in Virginia Beach. That woman would give Hillary the alibi needed to show she was fit to be a guardian. The pretend babysitter would be paid in heroin. Now all he needed was Hillary.

Knowing her, she wouldn't even go home before coming to see him.

His lips twitched slightly when the familiar BMW pulled in. She parked two spots away before climbing out and crossing to him.

"We have a situation," Josh began without preamble. "The cops came and found your kids home alone."

"They aren't my kids," she said, clearly too focused on her next dose to comprehend the seriousness of the situation.

Josh leaned in and lowered his voice. "No, but they are your source of income."

That got her. A flash of panic cut through the euphoria of her high. "Where are they?"

"I'm not sure," Josh said, "but I'm going to help you get them back."

"How?"

"First, you need to take it easy on the pills for a few days."

"But—"

"I'll make sure you have enough to take the edge off," Josh assured her. "Now, this is what I need you to do."

Josh explained his plan for getting the kids back, pleased at how quickly Hillary fell in line. He smiled slowly. If she was this easy to manipulate, maybe he wouldn't just use the kids to gain access to the family's wealth; he would also blame the whole thing on their aunt while he was at it. She would make the ransom demand. She would pick up the ransom money while he watched from a close distance. And she would be the person he would frame when the two kids didn't survive their ordeal.

* * *

"What do you mean they have to go back home?" *They are home.* Doug managed to keep those last three words from passing through his lips as he paced his office, his grip tightening on his cell phone. He and Jill hadn't said the words aloud, but he suspected his wife felt the same way he did. They had planned to adopt another child. Now that they'd met Sophie and Mason, he hoped to adopt two.

The caseworker for Sophie and Mason spoke in a sympathetic but determined voice. "I'm sorry, but the aunt filed a motion for custody with the courts this morning, and the judge granted it."

"Why wasn't I informed?" Doug asked. "Did the judge even hold a hearing?"

"The hearing was this morning," the social worker said. "And you weren't informed because, technically, you're just the temporary foster parents."

"What do I need to do to file for permanent custody?"

The social worker's surprise carried through her voice. "You're not serious."

"I am serious." And he might be in serious trouble if his wife knew he was making such a decision without talking to her first. Surely, Jill wouldn't want Sophie and Mason in an unsafe environment any more than he did. And they had already been through this twice before. Each time they'd been in a similar situation, she'd been the first to support keeping the kids with them.

"We have a home study this afternoon. If I have any concerns after that, I can file a motion on your behalf."

"You need to speak with the kids without their aunt present," Doug said. "The only clothes they have that fit them are what I bought them, and the pantry was completely empty when I did the search for Mason."

"I'll note that in my report."

Her report. That sounded like red tape rather than a resolution. "You do realize that the man who tried to kidnap the kids is still at large, right?"

"I am aware of that, and so is the judge."

"Is the judge also aware that Mason was home alone when he was nearly abducted and that he'd been drugged and left in the trunk of a car?"

"I did bring that up."

The social worker's businesslike tone chilled his blood. "And?"

"The aunt claims she had a babysitter lined up to watch the kids when she left. Apparently, the woman thought Sophie was already home when she ran out to get some groceries and was in a car accident."

"You've got to be kidding me." Doug blew out a frustrated breath. "I doubt that's true. Mason never mentioned any babysitter coming over when his aunt left."

The sympathy was back. "I understand your concerns, Secretary Valdez. Quite frankly, I share them, but that doesn't negate the fact that Hillary Adams has a court order that demands her niece and nephew be returned to her custody."

"How soon?" Doug glanced at the clock. It was already one thirty.

"I'll be picking the kids up from school today to return them to their home," she said. "I'll speak with your wife when I stop by the elementary school."

Though everything in Doug demanded he intervene, he couldn't deny that, as a former law enforcement officer and the current secretary of Homeland Security, his hands were tied. He had to uphold the law, even when he didn't agree with it.

"I want a filing with the court as soon as you finish your home study," Doug said, using his most authoritative voice. "Those kids shouldn't be in that house any longer than absolutely necessary."

"I'll keep you informed."

Doug ended the call and checked his schedule. He then secured his computer, grabbed his coat, and headed for the door. He reached his secretary's desk. "Alexa, can you reschedule my meeting with Thomas for tomorrow? I have some errands to run."

Alexa glanced at him as he shrugged into his coat. "Will you be back for your four o'clock?"

"No. I should be able to call in for it, but I'll talk to Mitch about running the meeting. Give me a call on my cell if anything critical comes up." Doug continued out the door. An hour later, he pulled up in front of the high school, a clear bag from the local Best Buy lying in the passenger seat, a new cell phone inside.

A quick glance at his watch revealed he had only twenty minutes until school ended for the day. After going through the basic security check at the front door, Doug entered the front office. When he informed the secretary that he wanted to see Sophie, he was redirected to the counseling office. Not surprisingly, the social worker already waited inside.

She spotted him and stood. "Secretary Valdez. I didn't expect to see you here."

Before he could explain the reasons for his presence, Sophie walked into the counseling office.

She glanced briefly at the social worker before she focused on Doug. "Is something wrong?"

"Sophie? I'm Mrs. Castillo, with child protective services." She motioned toward the small conference room behind her. "Let's have a chat in here."

A flash of panic sparked in Sophie's eyes.

Unwilling to let her receive the unnerving news alone, Doug didn't give the social worker the chance to uninvite him from the intended meeting. Instead, he moved to the conference room door and waited for Sophie and Mrs. Castillo to enter before following them inside.

CHAPTER 14

Sophie sat at the table where Mrs. Castillo indicated and clasped her hands together. If she was being called out of class to meet with a social worker, something must be very wrong.

Instinctively, she focused on Mr. Valdez. He'd made her feel safe before. She hoped his presence would give her that sensation again, but the grim look on his face only increased her apprehension.

"Sophie, I'm here to take you back home," Mrs. Castillo said.

Sophie's panic multiplied, and she focused on Doug again. "But I thought—" She cut herself off. Maybe the Valdez family didn't want her. Maybe they didn't want Mason. Hurt, anger, disappointment, fear. Every negative emotion flooded through her.

Another terrifying thought surfaced. Maybe they only wanted Mason, and she really would be separated from him.

"Your aunt is back home, and she filed a motion with the court to regain custody of you and your brother."

Her aunt filed with the court? Sophie didn't know a lot about that sort of thing, but the idea that her aunt would even talk to a lawyer, much less care about whether she and Mason were home, sent alarm bells ringing in her head. "You're sure it was my aunt?"

Mrs. Castillo nodded. "I'll be driving you and Mason home today. We'll pick him up next."

Sophie tried to focus on the positive. She and Mason would still be together, but the idea of someone trying to take Mason from her was still too fresh in her mind. Tears formed in her eyes, and she blinked against them. "Why can't we stay with Mr. and Mrs. Valdez?"

"We're going to ask for you to come back to live with us," Doug said. "That is, if it's okay with you."

She pressed her lips together and nodded. He might just be saying that to make her feel better, but she didn't think so. Maybe he really would let her and Mason go back to stay with them. Maybe they could even live with them permanently, like what had happened for Layla and Reagan.

Mr. Valdez held up a clear plastic bag. "I got this for you. I already programmed my phone number into it along with my wife's, my daughters', and Mrs. Castillo's."

She focused on the contents of the bag. A small rectangular box rested inside, the image of a cell phone displayed on the outside. "You bought me a phone?"

Mr. Valdez nodded. "If at any time you need something or don't feel safe, you call me."

The worst of her swirling emotions settled. "Thank you."

Mr. Valdez handed her the phone, bag and all. Sophie took the phone out of the box and put it into her jacket pocket to make sure Hillary wouldn't see it. Then she put the box into her backpack.

Mrs. Castillo motioned to the door. "Sophie, are you ready to go?"

She wasn't, but she nodded anyway.

Mrs. Castillo led her to the door before turning back to Mr. Valdez. "We'll be in touch."

Mr. Valdez gave a single nod before focusing on Sophie again. "Call us anytime."

Sophie wanted to say thank you again, but she couldn't push the words past the lump in her throat. Instead, she blinked against the tears still trying to fall, followed Mrs. Castillo out the door, and prepared to live her old life again, a life that would be so much harsher now that she had been reminded of what a family really could be.

* * *

Jill's heart broke as she watched the social worker pull out of the elementary school parking lot, Mason's tear-streaked face peering at her through the car window.

School wouldn't end for a few more minutes, but the principal had been kind enough to take her class so Jill could walk Mason out to the parking lot.

The car turned, and Sophie, too, looked back through the rear window, a look of such sadness on her face.

Jill's eyes watered, stinging with unwanted emotions. The Adams kids had only been with her family for a long weekend, but their presence had filled a hole in her heart. These were the children she wanted to add to her family, the children she wanted as her own.

Jill pulled out her phone and called Doug. He answered on the first ring. "The social worker just took Mason and Sophie. We can't let them go back home."

"I already asked Mrs. Castillo to file a request with the courts for us to gain permanent custody." He paused, apology now carrying through his voice. "I'm sorry. I know I should have talked to you first, but I panicked."

Her husband panicked? That was a first.

She also couldn't deny that she would have agreed had they spoken first. Permanent custody. Warmth spread through her. Their family could be expanding again. She hoped.

The school bell rang. "What do we do now?"

"For now, we wait and we pray."

"Will that be enough?"

"I hope so," Doug said. "Also, I'm texting you and the girls a new contact. I bought Sophie a cell phone so she'll have a way to contact us."

Jill's lips tugged into the beginnings of a smile. "Of course you did."

"Are you okay with it if I bring in a lawyer to work on our case?" Doug asked. "I think Mrs. Castillo agrees that the kids will be better off with us, but she also works for the state. It would be best if we had someone representing us and the kids' best interest—who doesn't have someone else to report to."

"You know the legal system better than I do. If that's what we need to do, go ahead and make it happen."

"I'll make the call and see you at home," Doug said. "We need to talk to the girls before this goes any further."

Another wash of warmth rushed through her. "I really love you right now."

"I really love you right back."

* * *

Sophie trudged up the front walk behind Mrs. Castillo and Mason. Maybe when they walked inside and Mrs. Castillo saw what their house looked like, she'd let them go back to stay with the Valdez family. Or maybe Mr. and Mrs. Valdez really didn't want to take on two more kids. But Mr. Valdez had given her a cell phone. That wasn't something people did for just anyone.

Mason's steps slowed as they approached the house, and Sophie put her hand on his shoulder as much to provide comfort as to receive it.

Mrs. Castillo rang the doorbell, and only a few seconds passed before Hillary answered.

"You must be Mrs. Castillo. Thank you so much for bringing the kids home." Hillary moved past the social worker and hugged Mason. "Thank goodness you're both okay."

Hillary hugged Sophie in turn, and Sophie wasn't sure what to do. Her aunt hadn't hugged her since she was a kid, since before the accident.

"May I come in?" Mrs. Castillo asked.

"Yeah." Hillary stepped aside.

Sophie took Mason's hand and walked in, Hillary in front of them and Mrs. Castillo bringing up the rear. The scent of pine hung in the air rather than the usual stench of body odor from Hillary and her friends when they hadn't bothered to shower.

"Sophie, why don't you and Mason get a snack in the kitchen while I talk to Mrs. Castillo," Hillary said.

"Actually, I'd like to see the kitchen too," Mrs. Castillo said. "That's part of the home inspection."

"Oh yeah. Go ahead," Hillary said as if she didn't have any worries about the empty fridge and pantry.

Sophie and Mason led the way into the kitchen, Sophie's eyes widening when they walked inside. A plate of chocolate chip cookies lay on the counter beside a fruit basket that contained both apples and bananas.

"Cookies?" Mason widened his eyes, and he looked up at Sophie. "Can I have one?"

Sophie nodded, not able to form words. She picked up the plate and held it down at Mason's level so it would be easier for Mason to take one. Then she put it back on the counter and took a cookie for herself.

Mrs. Castillo walked to the refrigerator and opened it. Sophie looked inside, and her jaw dropped. Milk, juice, cheese, lunch meat, lettuce, baby carrots, mayonnaise. Even the open box of baking soda Grandma had left in the back had been cleaned out.

The pantry came next, and again, Sophie couldn't believe her eyes. Two kinds of cereal occupied the top shelf. A box of spaghetti noodles lay beside a jar of spaghetti sauce. Then there were crackers, bread, and peanut butter, along with cans of chili, soup, and green beans.

Sophie wasn't a fan of green beans, but anything that she didn't have to buy herself was a huge bonus. Usually when Hillary went to the store, she didn't get much beyond some frozen dinners and snacks with an occasional loaf of bread or a jar of peanut butter thrown in.

"Sorry there's not much in here," Hillary said. "I only had time to pick up a few things at the store on my way home."

"Sophie, Mason, can you show me your rooms?"

"I can show you," Hillary offered.

"That's okay," Mrs. Castillo said. "I'm sure the kids can show me themselves."

Something in Mrs. Castillo's expression suggested she wasn't fooled by the scene before her. Maybe she wanted to talk to Sophie and Mason without Hillary around. Maybe she wanted to take them back to the Valdezes' house.

With hope blooming inside her, Sophie headed for the stairs. "Our rooms are this way."

They reached Mason's room first. Sophie opened the door to a tidy space, the bed neatly made, a new teddy bear on top.

Mason rushed inside and picked it up. "Hey, Sophie. Look." He clutched it to his chest. "Can I keep it?"

Sophie wanted to say yes, but she had no idea if Hillary would take it away once the social worker left. "Maybe. We'll see."

"I gather that's new?" Mrs. Castillo said.

Sophie nodded.

Mrs. Castillo opened the door to Mason's closet. His old pair of shoes were missing, a brand-new pair of sneakers positioned neatly in their place.

Mrs. Castillo picked up the right shoe and motioned to the bed. "Hey, Mason. Can you put this on for me?"

Mason took off the shoes Mr. Valdez had bought him and tried to put on the one Mrs. Castillo gave him. Sophie knew before he tried that it was going to be too small.

Mason turned his foot from side to side to try to put the shoe on, but as suspected, it didn't fit.

Mrs. Castillo took it from him. "Thanks for trying." She then turned to Sophie. "Do you know what size shoe Mason wears?"

"His old ones were a two, but they were too small. A three maybe?" That was the size she had planned to buy for him before Mr. Valdez had taken care of that need for her.

Mrs. Castillo checked the size on the shoe Mason had been wearing. "Yep. It's a three." She handed the shoe to Mason. "Where did you get the ones you're wearing?"

"Mr. Valdez bought them." He grabbed the front of his shirt and held it out. "This too. I like green."

"I like green too," Mrs. Castillo said with a smile that didn't quite reach her eyes.

They went to Sophie's room next. A new pair of jeans hung beside the ones she'd been wearing since last year, but beyond that, her room looked the same.

Mrs. Castillo motioned for her and Mason to sit on Sophie's bed before she sat in the wooden chair beside Sophie's desk. "I need to ask you a few questions. Is that okay?"

Sophie and Mason both nodded.

"Does your aunt buy you new clothes and toys very often?" she asked.

Mason shook his head, and Sophie forced herself to do the same.

"When was the last time she bought you new clothes?" She waved at Sophie's closet. "Before today."

Never. The word burned on Sophie's tongue, but she couldn't quite force it out. Fear pushed to the front of her mind, fear of the social worker taking them and sending them to different houses.

"Mason, do you remember your aunt Hillary buying you stuff before?"

Slowly, he shook his head.

"What about meals? Who usually cooks for you?"

"Sophie made me pancakes." Mason grinned now. "For dinner."

"I see." Mrs. Castillo made a note in her file. "One more question. If you had the choice between living here and living with the Valdez family, which would you choose?"

"Would we be together?" Sophie asked.

"Yes, you would be together."

Sophie looked down at Mason, hope shining in his eyes. Though it was a risk, she let the truth spill out. "We'd want to live with the Valdezes."

"Thank you for being honest with me." Mrs. Castillo stood.

"Can we go back there now?" Mason asked.

"I need to talk to the judge first, but I'll see what I can do," Mrs. Castillo said. "In the meantime, call me if you need anything."

Mrs. Castillo was leaving them alone. With Hillary. And with that man who tried to take Mason still out there somewhere. Tears filled Sophie's eyes, but she managed to nod.

"Just hang in there a little longer," Mrs. Castillo said. "It'll all work out. I promise."

CHAPTER 15

Josh waited until well after dark before he pulled up in front of Hillary's house. He'd "borrowed" her boyfriend's truck after Duncan had settled into his apartment for the night, a nice little supply of pick-me-ups now in Duncan's possession.

Josh had hoped to wait until Friday night to make his next move, but when Hillary had told him about the conversation she'd overheard between the social worker and the kids, he'd been left with no choice. The courts were going to take the kids away from Hillary, and he had to act now. And with Hillary's recent instability, he was no longer willing to take chances with her being any part of his kidnapping plans.

Josh took a moment to ensure none of the cars parked along the street were occupied before he finally climbed out and headed up the front walk.

Hillary opened the door before he had the chance to knock. "Where have you been? I've been waiting for hours."

"I needed to take care of a few things."

"I've been hurting all day."

Hurting, as in fighting the addiction. Josh had been counting on that.

He followed her inside and closed the door behind him before reaching into his pocket. "I have a little something that will help take off the edge."

"I need a bit more than that."

He'd been counting on that too. The fentanyl he'd mixed with Hillary's usual drugs would not only eliminate Hillary as a potential obstacle to taking the kids out of the house, but it would also ensure she wouldn't live to tell anyone he'd been here. It really was too bad he couldn't have simply framed her for the kidnapping, but she was the only witness against him, and he wasn't taking any unnecessary chances.

Keeping his gloves on, he passed her the small plastic bag containing what looked like her usual purchase. "I'll put it on your tab."

"What am I going to do about that social worker?" Hillary asked. "If the kids get taken away from me, I won't have any access to their money."

"You leave that little problem to me," Josh said.

* * *

Sophie couldn't sleep. Thoughts kept circling through her mind, questions about whether she and Mason would have to stay with Hillary, along with the fear that the man who had tried to take Mason would return.

She still had no idea why someone would try to kidnap him, but the very thought of what he'd already been through kept her eyes open despite the late hour.

A thud sounded downstairs. Sophie shot up in bed, her heart racing.

It was probably just Hillary dropping something again. Sophie tried to tell herself that, but fear propelled her across the room. As an afterthought, she grabbed her cell phone before she crept down the hall and peered down the stairs.

Hillary lay on the floor a short distance from the bottom step. She'd fallen asleep in lots of weird positions in the past, but this was odd even for her.

A man stepped into view, a man Sophie had never seen before.

Everything in her froze, even the scream that tried to rise inside her. Was he the one who had tried to take Mason?

The man leaned down as though to pick something up, but Sophie didn't wait to see what it was. She hurried down the hall, pausing briefly when she reached her room. She started to go inside, but instead, she quietly closed the door and then rushed into Mason's room. This time when she closed the door, she also flipped the lock.

Her breathing coming in gasps, she pulled up the contacts in her phone and pressed the button for Doug Valdez.

He answered on the first ring. "Are you okay?"

"There's a man here," she said, her words tumbling over one another. "I think he did something to Aunt Hillary."

"Where are you?" Mr. Valdez asked, his voice brisk.

"In Mason's room."

"I'm on my way, but you need to hide, somewhere away from your bedrooms. Lock Mason's door behind you so the man thinks that's where you are."

She should have done that with her door.

"I'll be there as soon as I can," Mr. Valdez said before the call disconnected.

Sophie drew a deep breath and leaned down to jostle Mason's shoulder. His eyes opened, his expression groggy and dazed.

"Mason, wake up." She held one finger over her lips. Though she needed him to understand the seriousness of their situation, she also couldn't afford for him to cry out. A thought popped into her head, and she rolled with it. "We need to play a game of hide-and-seek from Aunt Hillary and her friends."

Fear shone on Mason's face, but he nodded.

Sophie started to lead Mason to the door, but she stepped on the oversized teddy bear and stumbled. She managed to keep herself upright, but her ankle twisted as she fought for her footing. Pain shot through her, and she clenched her jaw to keep from crying out.

Instinctively, she leaned down and picked up the offending obstacle. Why Hillary had decided Mason now needed a stuffed animal that was nearly as big as he was, Sophie had no idea.

She set it on Mason's bed; as an afterthought, she pulled the covers over it so it would look like Mason was still there.

Limping, she led the way to Mason's door.

Footsteps sounded in the hall, and Sophie pulled Mason to her side so they would both be behind the door if the man managed to open it despite it being locked.

But no one jiggled the doorknob. Instead, the footsteps faded toward her room.

Though terrified to do so, Sophie flipped the lock on Mason's door. "As soon as I open the door, run to Grandma's room and hide. You have to be quiet though."

Mason nodded. Sophie opened the door. Mason ran, his little feet barely making a sound as he raced down the hall. Sophie locked his bedroom door again, slipped into the hall, and pulled the door closed behind her.

She made it as far as Hillary's room before she sensed someone coming. Still limping, she darted into Hillary's room, tucking herself behind the open door to stay out of sight. She could only pray Mason had hid himself well and that the man wouldn't find them before Mr. Valdez got here.

CHAPTER 16

Doug pulled out of the garage, his tires squealing as he put the car in gear. He'd barely grabbed shoes and socks on his way out the door, his sidearm tucked into the center console of his SUV, belt holster and all. Of course, the holster wouldn't do him any good since he wasn't wearing a belt. Maybe he should have changed out of his pajamas, but he hadn't been willing to waste that much time.

He turned onto the main road that connected his neighborhood to Sophie and Mason's. His chest tightened as what-ifs ran through his head. Those kids had to be okay. They just had to.

He knew he shouldn't have let them go back home, but he had followed his training and honored the court order—a court order that never should have been granted.

Why hadn't he thought to spend the night outside their house to make sure they stayed safe? Okay, so maybe he had thought of it, but he also hadn't expected the kidnapper to make another move so quickly.

Doug gripped the wheel tighter and turned into Sophie and Mason's neighborhood. Just another minute and he'd be there.

* * *

Josh tried to turn the knob of the closed door. Locked. He shook his head. Did these kids really think they could hide from him?

He ran his hand along the top of the doorjamb in search of a key. When he didn't find one, he checked the doorjamb across the hall. Again, no luck. The bathroom door came next. His fingers grazed the small metallic object, and he gripped it.

When he pulled it into view, he smiled. Time to get these kids and get out of here.

He slid the universal key into place, and the lock popped open. Josh stepped into the room, a swath of moonlight spilling across the bed. The lump beneath the covers suggested the little boy had chosen to hide there. But where was the girl? Since her room was empty, he had expected her to be here too.

Josh checked the closet first, then under the bed. Nothing. Maybe she'd taken refuge in another room, leaving her little brother to fend for himself. Typical teenager.

He retrieved a syringe filled with fast-acting sedative from his pocket, quickly checked the dose, and pulled back the covers. But it wasn't the boy hiding beneath the blankets. It was an oversized teddy bear.

Frustration bubbled inside him. He shouldn't even be here right now. If the girl had come inside like she should have last Saturday, he would have already cashed in on the kids' trust funds and would be sitting happily on a private beach somewhere.

Stuffing the syringe back into his jacket pocket, he looked quickly around the room again. Then he headed back into the hall. The kids had to be here somewhere. And it was only a matter of time before he found them. This time, there would be no escape.

* * *

Sophie had waited until the man went into Mason's room before she raced after Mason to their grandma's room. Unfortunately, hiding places were limited to under the bed and in the closet. Sophie chose the closet. Once inside, she had only needed a second to choose the best hiding place for her brother. The shelf on the right of their grandmother's walk-in closet had been nearly empty until she boosted Mason onto it. She passed him a blanket to hide under and then set two oversize hats on top of him. "Stay there until I come back for you."

Mason must have nodded because one of the hats tumbled down onto her.

Sophie quickly pushed it back into place. "Stay still, and be quiet."

Sophie started to limp back out into her grandma's bedroom, but when the doorknob rattled, she jumped back into the closet. Taking the only hiding place available to her, she tucked herself behind the hanging evening gowns her grandmother had worn over the years, each of them encased in plastic.

The door opened, and the unfamiliar scent of the intruder competed with the musty smell of clothes that hadn't been worn in far too long and the bowls of potpourri that had been left on her grandma's dressers.

Sophie pressed her body back against the closet wall, behind the full-length dresses, her eyes trained on the tiny crack between a poofy red gown and a sleek blue one.

Only a few seconds passed before the man entered the room. In the dim light, she couldn't make out much beyond his jacket, which fell past his waist, and his hand fisted like he was holding something.

He ran his hand along the clothes on the opposite side of the closet, leaning down as though trying to determine whether any of the shoes on the floor had feet in them. Sophie fought the urge to step back even farther, although she doubted that was possible.

She held her breath, afraid the mere act of inhaling and exhaling might give her away. Then the man turned and ran his hand along the gowns hanging in front of her. His fingers nearly missed her, but one grazed her shoulder.

She gasped.

The man shoved the dresses aside, leaving Sophie exposed. Her heart pounded, and she squeaked in alarm, ducking when he reached for her. Somehow, she managed to avoid his grasp and dart past him.

Praying Mason would stay hidden and silent, Sophie raced down the hall, her ankle throbbing with each step. If the man followed, maybe she could get him to go outside. Maybe Mr. Valdez would get here before it was too late.

* * *

Josh chased after the girl, his focus on his objective nearly blocking out the sound of a car engine outside. Probably a neighbor. He already knew the kids didn't have access to a phone.

The girl was halfway down the stairs when he reached her. With a syringe gripped in one hand—the same drug he'd used on her brother last weekend—he grabbed her arm with his other hand.

She gasped.

He tightened his grip.

She twisted, trying to break free.

He lifted the needle.

She batted his hand away, but his grip didn't falter, not on the girl's arm or on the syringe that would render her unconscious, assuming he had the dosage right. Worst case, he'd leave a second victim in the house and use the boy to get a hefty ransom. After the fiasco last weekend, he would make do with only one kid if he had to.

Josh shoved the girl's sleeve up and lifted the needle again.

She jerked back again, this time using her weight to pull him with her as she took another step down the staircase.

"Don't make this harder than it has to be," Josh warned. He lifted the needle again, but this time instead of trying to bat his hand away, she grabbed it and sank her teeth into his flesh.

He cried out, instinctively releasing the syringe and dropping it onto the carpeted steps.

Fury rushed through him, and he struck out. She ducked to avoid the backhand slap, but he still caught her on the side of the face.

She screamed and tried to pull away once more.

Josh tightened his grip. When he leaned down to retrieve the needle, she jerked her weight forward and screamed again.

CHAPTER 17

Doug was nearly to the door when he heard the scream. Sophie!

Even though the police should arrive any minute, Doug couldn't wait. His pistol in hand, he rushed to the front door and pushed it open.

Weapon raised, he peeked inside. A woman lay on the floor a short distance away, and Sophie was halfway up the stairs, a man in his late twenties holding her in place.

The man yanked Sophie in front of him, holding her as a shield. He held up a syringe and pressed it to the side of her neck. "Don't come any closer. I'll kill her."

Sophie whimpered, and tears filled her eyes.

Doug tried to think of Sophie as just another victim who needed saving. Tried and failed.

Thankfully, his training was ingrained enough to override his emotional attachment. He lifted his weapon, aiming at the part of the man's head that was visible beyond Sophie. He could make the shot, but he'd try for a less traumatic resolution first.

"You don't want to hurt her," Doug said, his voice steady despite the fear running through him. "You hurt her, you die." Doug paused, tilting his head as though pondering a deep philosophical topic. "You don't look like you want to die today."

"Back up, and let me out of here."

"What do you want with her?" Doug asked. The police should be here any minute, but he didn't know if their presence would make things better or worse. "Let the girl go, and you can walk right out of here."

"Do you really think I'm that stupid?"

Doug had hoped so.

Rapid footsteps pounded in the upstairs hall. For a brief second, Doug considered that this man might have a partner. Then the sound registered more fully. Not adult footsteps. A child's.

Mason appeared at the open section of the hall upstairs. "Let go of my sister!"

"Mason, stay back!" Doug shouted.

"He's going to hurt Sophie." Rather than retreat, Mason took another step forward.

Doug couldn't shoot this man with both kids watching, but he couldn't let him hurt Sophie either.

Doug kept his gun trained on the man's head, but he dropped his gaze to Sophie. The fear was still there, but the moment her gaze connected with his, a spark of determination illuminated her eyes.

Sirens blared in the distance. It was now or never.

* * *

Though no words were spoken, Sophie knew what she had to do. Mr. Valdez had taught her basic self-defense, and he needed her to use it now. If she didn't, she might die.

"Let go of her!" Mason shouted again.

Mr. Valdez dipped his chin in a subtle nod. He needed her to act now. And she needed to avoid the needle currently pressed to her neck.

Steeling her nerves, she closed her eyes for a brief moment, visualizing what needed to happen next. Then she tilted her head away from the needle and thrust her elbow into the man's stomach.

He grunted, and his hand holding the needle lowered, but his grip around her throat tightened instead of loosening.

She tried to gasp for air but couldn't.

Panicked, she plowed her elbow back again. Then suddenly, she was free. She fought for balance for a split second before the man shoved her from behind. Her body pitched forward, and she tripped down the stairs.

Mr. Valdez rushed toward her, and she stumbled three steps before her body slammed into his. He lifted his free hand to steady her, and at the same time, he yelled, "Mason, run!"

Sophie turned as Mason raced back toward the bedrooms, and the man with the needle sprinted after him.

* * *

Doug steadied Sophie and rushed up the stairs, calling over his shoulder. "Stay there."

A door slammed, and Doug could easily visualize Mason trying to hide in his room. The rattle of something spilling followed. Legos?

A shoulder thudded against the door, the sound repeating as Doug rushed forward. Doug was nearly to the intruder when the man thrust his shoulder against the door a third time. The doorjamb splintered, and the door flew open.

The man only took two steps inside before he stumbled and let out an obscenity.

Doug reached the now-open doorway. Mason stood on his bed, his little body pressed as far into the corner of the room as he could manage. In front of Mason, toys covered the floor, everything from toy cars to Duplo blocks.

Doug lifted his weapon and aimed at the intruder. "Stop right there."

The man froze, but Doug suspected his lack of action was due more to indecision than defeat.

"You take one more step toward that boy, and I will shoot you," Doug said, his voice even and stern.

The man's body leaned slightly toward Mason, and Doug suspected he was debating whether he could grab the boy and use him as a shield before Doug could shoot him.

"Don't try it," Doug warned. "When I shoot, I don't miss."

The man's posture changed, a sort of defeat in the way his shoulders dropped. He slowly held his hands up and turned toward Doug.

The sirens outside grew louder and then suddenly stopped. The cops were here.

"Now, on your knees." Doug kept his weapon aimed at the man's head as he first kicked several blocks out of his way and then lowered himself to his knees. "Lace your fingers behind your head."

Footsteps pounded toward him, and Doug caught sight of a policeman out of the corner of his eye. "Doug Valdez, secretary of Homeland Security," Doug said, identifying himself. "Do me a favor and cuff this guy."

The policeman retrieved his handcuffs from his belt. "Yes, sir."

The moment the policeman had the man in custody, Doug lowered his weapon and crossed to Mason. Instantly, Mason flew into Doug's embrace.

"Hey, buddy. It's okay. Everything's going to be fine now."

Mason clung to Doug, and the dampness on Doug's shirt clued him in to the tears the boy shed.

Sophie rushed into the room, and Doug lifted one hand from Mason's back to wave her forward. Instantly, she was enveloped in a group hug.

Several seconds passed before Mason pulled back and sniffled. "Can we go to your house now?"

Doug released the two children and eased back. "How about we make it your house too?"

For a second, Mason didn't seem to understand, but the tears in Sophie's eyes suggested she understood his meaning.

Mason widened his eyes and looked at Sophie, then back at Doug. "We can live with you?"

"You can." Doug put one hand on his shoulder and the other on Sophie's. "But only if that's what you want."

Mason nodded quickly.

"That's one yes." Doug focused on Sophie. "What do you think, Sophie? Would you be okay if my wife and I took care of you?"

"You'd be our new mom and dad?" Sophie asked, her hope carrying in her voice.

"Jill and I would like that very much."

Sophie's face lit up, and she nodded. Then, without warning, she launched herself into his arms.

CHAPTER 18

Six weeks later

They were going to the White House, and they were going to meet the president. Sophie still couldn't quite believe it. Then again, the Easter basket on her new dresser and the dog snoozing on her bed proved that she and Mason were now living in an alternate reality.

Hillary had been released from the hospital after recovering from the drugs that man had given to her, but instead of going home, she had been put into some sort of rehab center to help her get better.

At first, Sophie had worried that she and Mason would have to go back to live with her once she got out, but Mr. Valdez had taken care of that. Apparently, that locked freezer had contained all sorts of drugs in it, which was enough to convince the judge that Sophie and Mason weren't safe living with Hillary whether she recovered or not. Whether Hillary would end up going to jail for her involvement with the man who tried to kidnap them remained to be seen.

The only decision Sophie had really cared about had come a few days ago when Mr. and Mrs. Valdez—or, rather, Mom and Dad—had been granted permanent custody. Not only that, the Valdezes had taken her and Mason to visit Grandma every week since they'd moved in. And Grandma even remembered them. Most of the time, anyway.

Still feeling like she had landed in a fairy tale, Sophie grabbed her shoes and sat on the edge of her bed in her new room.

Mason rushed inside and spoke quickly. "Hurry up. *Maman* said it's time to go."

"I'm coming," Sophie said in French. Mason might have only learned to speak a few words in French, but his understanding of basic phrases was already quite impressive.

It was hard to believe that Sophie used to think speaking this language was so hard. Since moving in with the Valdezes, French had become her favorite class in school.

"Come on." Mason waved toward the front door.

Sophie tugged her shoes on and followed Mason into the hall. When they reached the bottom of the stairs, the rest of the family already waited for them.

Mom—she could call Mrs. Valdez that now—held a basket in her hands, and Reagan was debating with their dad over whose turn it was to drive.

"I'm bigger and scarier looking." Dad plucked his keys out of Reagan's hand. "That makes it my turn."

"Let's go!" Mason headed for the garage as though he had lived in this house his whole life.

"I think he's a little excited." Mom laughed.

"Are we really going to meet the president?" Sophie asked.

"Yes." Mom nodded. "President and Mrs. Whitmore have been our dear friends for many years. They're looking forward to meeting you and Mason."

"They're looking forward to meeting us?" Sophie couldn't imagine the president and first lady even knowing she and her brother existed.

"They are." Mom put her arm around her shoulder as they followed Reagan and Layla to the garage. "They want to meet the rest of our family."

Family. Warmth spread through Sophie, and she couldn't help but smile. She and Mason were together, and they finally had a family who wanted them, a family they could call their own.

ABOUT THE AUTHOR

Traci Hunter Abramson, a former Central Intelligence Agency officer, was born in Arizona, where she lived until moving to Venezuela for a study-abroad program. After graduating from Brigham Young University, she worked for the CIA for six years until she resigned to raise her family. She credits the agency with giving her a wealth of ideas and the skills needed to survive her children's teenage years.

Traci is a popular writing instructor and keynote speaker and enjoys sharing her knowledge with aspiring writers. She recently retired after spending twenty-six years coaching her local high school swim team and now spends a lot of time traveling, which she loves.

She has written more than forty best-selling novels and is a 2022 and 2023 Silver Falchion Award Mystery/Suspense finalist, 2022 Rone Award finalist, and eight-time Whitney Award winner, including Best Novel of the Year in both 2017 and 2019. She received the 2021 Swoony Award for Best Mystery/Suspense Romance.

She also loves hearing from her readers. If you would like to contact her, she can be reached through the following:

Website: www.traciabramson.com
Facebook page: facebook.com/tracihabramson
Facebook group: Traci's Friends
Bookbub: bookbub.com/authors/traci-hunter-abramson
X: @traciabramson
Instagram: instagram.com/traciabramson